Praise for the Devil's Isle Novels

"Neill is truly a master storyteller!"   —RT Book Reviews

"Neill's sequel to *The Veil* continues to prove her adept at world building and nonstop action. Claire's honesty and straightforward attitude make her a great character for a harrowing time."

—*Library Journal*

"[Neill's] postapocalyptic New Orleans is so rich and full of detail that I felt immersed in the characters' struggle[s] right alongside them."

—A Book Obsession

"An action-packed, intense story in a dark urban fantasy world."

—The Reading Cafe

"Chloe Neill continues to expand the arc with a compelling narrative, unique characters, and nuanced story lines."   —Smexy Books

"The world building was fabulous; the characters were likable; the plot and tension provided a great 'what's going to happen next?' feeling that kept me engaged."   —Paranormal Haven

W9-BWZ-148

OTHER NOVELS BY CHLOE NEILL

THE
BEYOND

A DEVIL'S ISLE NOVEL

CHLOE NEILL

BERKLEY
NEW YORK

BERKLEY
An imprint of Penguin Random House LLC
1745 Broadway, New York, NY 10019

Copyright © 2019 by Chloe Neill
Excerpt from *Wild Hunger* copyright © 2018 by Chloe Neill
Penguin Random House supports copyright. Copyright fuels creativity, encourages diverse
voices, promotes free speech, and creates a vibrant culture. Thank you for buying an authorized
edition of this book and for complying with copyright laws by not reproducing, scanning, or
distributing any part of it in any form without permission. You are supporting writers and
allowing Penguin Random House to continue to publish books for every reader.

BERKLEY and the BERKLEY & B colophon are registered trademarks of
Penguin Random House LLC.

Library of Congress Cataloging-in-Publication Data

Names: Neill, Chloe, author.
Title: The beyond / Chloe Neill.
Description: First Edition. | New York : Berkley, 2019. | Series: A devil's isle novel
Identifiers: LCCN 2018055809| ISBN 9780440001119 (pbk.) | ISBN 9780440001126 (ebook)
Subjects: LCSH: Paranormal fiction. | GSAFD: Fantasy fiction. | Occult fiction.
Classification: LCC PS3614.E4432 B49 2019 | DDC 813/.6--dc23
LC record available at https://lccn.loc.gov/2018055809

First Edition: June 2019

Printed in the United States of America
1   3   5   7   9   10   8   6   4   2

Cover art by Blake Morrow/Shannon Associates
Cover design by Adam Auerbach

This is a work of fiction. Names, characters, places, and incidents either are the product of the
author's imagination or are used fictitiously, and any resemblance to actual persons, living or
dead, business establishments, events, or locales is entirely coincidental.

Come away, come away, death,
And in sad cypress let me be laid;
Fly away, fly away, breath:
I am slain by a fair cruel maid.

—William Shakespeare, Twelfth Night

THE BEYOND

Magic was thick as humidity in the southern Louisiana air. And it felt glorious.

Today, there was no hiding. No pretending. We were humans, but not just humans. We were Sensitives, and we were doing magic in public.

My students stood in a line on a plot of green, facing downriver and staring intently at the small objects on the grass in front of them. A wooden box, a ceramic vase, a knitted cube, an old FM radio, and an agate bookend.

"Get those shoulders back!"

I turned my gaze to the man who stood beside me. He was nearly four feet of attitude, stubby black horns, and more magic than my body could safely hold. Moses was a Paranormal, one of the good guys, and one of my favorite people.

He also had a sass mouth, as Earlene, the oldest of my Sensitives, liked to say. It was one of the things I loved most about him.

"You look like trolls." Moses hunched his shoulders. "Stand up straight, for crap's sake."

"We talked about positive reinforcement," I murmured, hands on my hips, as the sun bore down on us, hard as a punch.

He held up a fist. "I'll show them positive reinforcement if they don't get this right."

"And Moses will be playing bad cop today," I said to the group. A few managed weak chuckles, but the rest were fixated on their foci, the objects they'd attempt to fill with their excess magic.

They were tall, short. Dark, pale. Big, small. Old, young. Magic was the thing they had in common—their unique sensitivities to the power that had crept into our world from the Beyond, the world of Paras. One could freeze matter, one could call animals, and one could communicate telepathically.

Their powers were new, and they were untrained. I was here not to teach them how to use their magic, to make them better at freezing or calling, but to help them stay sane.

Once upon a time, the Veil—a ribbon of magic that separated the Beyond from the human world—had kept the magic on their side. Nearly eight years ago, the Paras tore it open, ravaging the southern U.S., including New Orleans. Sensitives had helped magically sew it shut again, even if a little power had seeped through the stitches. But humans, being humans, had made a very bad mistake, and it had been ripped apart again. This time, it left a mile-long gap, and magic and Paras had been streaming into our world ever since.

A few "lucky" humans could sense that power, use it. About seven percent of the population, as far as Containment could tell. But human bodies weren't built for the burden of otherworldly energy. Too much magic warped bone and broke down muscle, turning Sensitives into skeletal wraiths whose only desire was the very magic that degraded them, even if they had to kill to get it. And there was no coming back from wraithdom.

I was teaching these Sensitives to find balance, to keep the right amount of magic spooled in their bodies. Enough to use if necessary, but not so much that it overwhelmed and broke them. This was the fourth group I'd trained since the Veil had been breached. Forty people who were willing to admit to their condition and get help for it. Probably not everyone affected. But I couldn't make anyone face their demons. Even if that meant they'd face them as wraiths later.

We stood in the pulsing heat on a greenway in Devil's Isle, the neighborhood-turned-prison-turned–neighborhood for Paranormals. It had been the Fabourg Marigny, had become a prison for all Paranormals, and now served as a prison for some and a refuge for others, because humans had acknowledged not all magic—and not all Paranormals—were evil. It was only after the Veil had been opened again that the former Paranormal Combatant Command, and its Containment unit that operated Devil's Isle, had finally admitted there were two groups of Paranormals, and only one group was our enemy. The Court of Dawn led the war; they'd magically conscripted their enemies, the Consularis, to fight.

Containment had allowed the Consularis to leave Devil's Isle if they'd wanted to, but kept the Court imprisoned. And as Court members slithered into our world again through the breach in the Veil, many of the freed Consularis Paras had stayed to fight. The PCC had become the Unified Combat Command, humans and Consularis Paras bound together to fight the Court of Dawn.

And fight we had. It was good that they were still outside the perimeter Containment had been able to establish around New Orleans. But that had been a matter of will as much as of strength. *Crack*s of magic and *pop*s of ammunition rolled like thunder across the city, which was down to military personnel and the thousand or so hardy humans who'd refused to leave their homes. But we'd stay as long as we could. As long as we could hold New Orleans.

"Focus on your foci," I said, realizing how corny that sounded only when the words were out of my mouth. I walked down the line, feeling out the magic that quivered around them. "And go step by step, just like we've talked about."

"Find it. Grasp it. Cast it. Bind it," they repeated together.

The rhyme had been my idea, a mnemonic device to give them something familiar to hold on to as they dropped their minds into the magic and tried to wring it out again.

"I still think mine was better," Moses muttered, scratching the edge of one dark and gleaming horn.

"Yours was filthy," I said, giving him a flat look.

His grin was as devilish as the horns. "That's what made it perfect."

Biting back a smile, I turned back to the Sensitives. "Find it," I repeated, and they closed their eyes, began to feel out the threads of magic that permeated their bodies.

"Grasp it." Their faces were studies in concentration as they pulled the magic together—winding or braiding or balling it up—in preparation for dragging it out. Sweaty, narrow eyed, and red cheeked from working in the oppressive heat. But it had to be done. They had to learn control under even bad conditions. Because in the real world, they might not have a choice.

"Cast it," I said, and waves of power began to shimmer in the air like heat rising from asphalt. The foci began to vibrate as magic was stuffed into them, as energy fought mass.

A little movement was fine; magic was a powerful thing. So I didn't notice the wooden box hopping off the ground until Moses started shouting.

"Incoming!" he said, and wrapped his short arms around his head.

"Everybody watch out!" I yelled, and Sensitives darted for cover.

The box exploded, sending a gust of magic and needle-sharp splinters into the air.

Every hair lifted in the tingling air, I opened an eye and looked around. Moses sat up, legs extended, rubbing his eyes.

"You okay?" I asked.

He looked at me, blinked. "There two of you, or just one?" He squinted. "Or maybe just two of your hair. You look like an orange cloud."

"You keep complimenting me, and Liam's going to get jealous," I said, offering a hand to help him to his feet.

He took it, snorted. "I don't date orange clouds."

"My heart breaks," I said dryly.

Around us were torn jeans, ripped T-shirts, and blown-back hair. The air smelled faintly of burned things, and mine wasn't the only puffy hair.

"*Lo siento,*" said Mariah, the owner of the box, or what remained of it. She had light brown skin and long dark hair she'd pulled into a knot. Tendrils had blown out of the bun and surrounded her face like a Renaissance halo. "The magic got away from me."

A former Containment soldier named Dave, with tan skin and military-short blond hair, stamped out the smoldering remains with his boot-clad foot.

"Well," I said, "all things considered, I still think that went better than last time. Anybody lose a finger?"

"No," they all called out.

"Definitely better than last time," Moses said with a nod.

"Happens to the best of us," I said. "And I mean that literally. I exploded a cypress stump once upon a time."

There were relieved murmurs down the line.

"You'll get better," I said to Mariah. Not just supportive words, but the absolute truth. Mariah had a literal spark—in her fingertips she could manifest power, tiny threads of electricity that were very handy in a place where the grid was inconsistent.

"You've shown today that you can gather up the magic," I said. "Next step is to get it bound without an explosion."

I'd intended to give them instructions, to remind them of our next scheduled practice. But before I could say anything else, at the back of my neck was a flutter, delicate as a caress but touched with magic.

I glanced back, found golden eyes staring back at me.

Liam was home.

It had been six days since I'd seen him. Too long, especially now that he stood at the edge of the park, tall and muscled, a gleam of desire in his expression.

Thick brows topped his blue eyes, his nose a straight wedge, his eyelashes thick and dark, like his hair. He wore jeans, muddy at the knees, and a V-neck T-shirt streaked with more dirt. A camouflage backpack was slung over one shoulder, and magic, invisible but tangible, hovered in the air around him.

Liam wasn't a Sensitive; like his grandmother Eleanor, he'd gotten his magic in battle via a strike from someone with power. That power had somehow transferred, giving him the ability to mirror another person's magic.

He was still dealing with that, with the fact that he now stood on the other side of the line he'd walked since Paras had first set foot in our world.

His brother, Gavin, stood behind him with an identical backpack, but rolling his eyes. They were a couple of years apart but looked unmistakably fraternal. Same tall and muscular build, same dark hair, same sculpted cheekbones. Gavin was a little leaner than Liam, his features a little sharper, as if the second edition had been honed a little more than the first. I, of course, preferred the original.

Liam and I walked toward each other, gazes locked.

"Ms. Connolly."

"Mr. Quinn."

He tugged a lock of my red hair, his blue eyes piercing mine. Then he slid that gaze to the shrapnel spread across the ground. "Mos," he said questioningly. "I thought you were going to keep her out of trouble."

"What am I, a freaking wizard? And not her fault, anyway. These damn kids," he said with a shake of his head, even though I'd have bet some of those kids were older than he was.

"Whom you're supposed to be teaching," Liam said with a grin that pulled the dimples in his cheeks. God, I loved those dimples.

Moses waved a hand like he was swatting away the idea. "They've done all they're going to do today. Practice tonight," he told the group.

Liam took my hand, linked his fingers with mine, and, when we reached the edge of the green, pulled me behind an oak tree with branches that gracefully arced over our heads before skimming the grass.

"I've been waiting on this for a week," he said, then fastened his lips to mine.

Since I was sticky and hot, I decided his mud didn't make much difference. I wrapped my arms around his neck and drew him closer. "Same here."

"You taste like summer."

"I taste like New Orleans. Sticky."

I could feel his smile. "You taste like Claire."

"It would be awkward if I didn't," I said. "I missed you."

"I missed you, too."

He leaned back. "Did you spend the week binge-watching old movies?"

"God, I wish. I don't suppose you happened to bring back some reliable Internet access?"

He felt his jeans pockets, front, then back. "Damn. I forgot again. So I guess no binge-watching."

"Unless you mean watching Sensitives destroy their foci. But no lost fingers."

His lips curled. Just seeing him smile—seeing happiness on his face—was enough to lift my mood.

"That makes this a red-letter week," he said. "Did you see the goats while I was gone?"

"Not a single one." Supposedly, Containment had imported three herds of goats to keep shrubs and plant growth in New Orleans—at least in the areas not already scorched by magic—at manageable levels. "I'm starting to wonder if it's an urban myth. Or a post-urban myth."

"I saw one," Gavin called out.

Liam shook his head, rolled his eyes. "That was a deer."

"They're both ungulates."

We both looked back at him, and he lifted a shoulder. "I found a book of crosswords. Been working on my vocab."

"Suspicious," I murmured, and looked back at Liam, searched his eyes. "What did you actually see?"

Liam was a bounty hunter, had worked after the war to track Paranormals who hadn't been captured by Containment and bring them into Devil's Isle. But he knew the truth about Court and Consularis, and he'd been very particular about his bounties—and helping Consularis Paras stay hidden. Now he was using his skills to scout New Orleans and its surroundings, watch for Court movements into the area.

"There's a new encampment," he said. "North side of Lake Pontchartrain. About forty of them. All Seelies."

My stomach sank. Although they seemed pale and delicate, Seelies were among the fiercest of Court fighters. They'd been part of the first guard unit that had fought us when the Veil was ripped open—with their furious eyes and golden weapons—and we'd barely survived the attack. One of us hadn't. Erida, a Consularis Para and, I later learned, my father's secret paramour, had taken a fatal wound for me.

We hadn't seen any Seelies since that battle; that they were amassing outside New Orleans didn't bode well.

"Forty Seelies," I said, trying to imagine the havoc they could wreak. "How did a group that large get past Containment?" The Veil's gap at Belle Chasse—while plenty wide to cause trouble—was the only existing void, and Containment had an outpost right there. And we'd have heard about a battle against forty Seelies. Gunnar, one of my best friends and a Containment higher-up, would have had many thoughts.

"Probably a few at a time," Liam said. "I'm going to talk to Gunnar."

"They're preparing for something?"

"I don't know. It's certainly possible, but they also don't like to mingle with other Paras. Royalty among peasants."

I put a hand on his cheek. "I'm glad you made it back."

"I made it back, too," Gavin called out.

"I'm not talking to you," I said.

"I said I was sorry."

"You did say that. But it doesn't excuse what you did."

"I didn't put the possum in the truck."

"You left the windows open. In a wildlife refuge. Overnight."

He didn't have a response to that.

Liam's lips were at my ear. "Please try not to kill my brother. We've just returned to our homeland, and that's a little too Greek tragedy for me."

"I'll do what I can," I said, but narrowed my gaze at Gavin.

He almost managed not to smile.

"Come on, *frère*," Liam said. "We have a debrief to get to. You two can snipe at each other later."

Gavin muttered something in Cajun, and Liam flipped him off. That was their chemistry.

"I'll see you tonight," I said, and tugged Liam down for one last kiss. "And don't forget about the party."

"What party?" Gavin asked. "And will there be sexy ladies?"

"Tadji's birthday party."

"Oh, right. I forgot about that." He ran a hand through his hair, which he was letting grow out. It nearly reached his shoulders now. "Do I need a present? And does she like hot sauce?"

"Stop scavenging for that mess," Liam said. "It's at least eight years old."

"Like diamonds, pepper sauce is forever," Gavin said with a grin.

There wasn't a praline to be found in the entire city of New Orleans, but not even war had decimated our supply of souvenir hot sauce.

"Does Tadji know about the surprise guest?" Liam asked.

"She does not," I said. And I hoped that didn't come back to bite me. Neither of us was big on surprises; we'd seen plenty of drama in our lives. I was making one very large exception tonight.

"It's going to be spectacular," I said. And hoped I was right.

CHAPTER TWO

Liam, Gavin, Moses, and I stood in the makeshift community hall, the empty shell of the former Marigny Market, where food and souvenirs had once been sold, and the place where we'd prepared for an attack on Devil's Isle by an antimagic cult.

It now held long folding tables and a few dozen humans and Paras, and someone had stuffed an old zydeco cassette into an even older tape player. The bright sounds of accordion, drums, and horns moved through the hall like a musical second line, and we'd pieced together a HAPPY BIRTHDAY banner from old magazine pages.

My closest friends came in together. Gunnar was tall and tan, his dark hair swooped over his forehead, the sides trimmed short. He was handsome in a best-friend kind of way, with big hazel eyes and a killer smile.

He was the second-in-command of Devil's Isle, the Commandant's lead strategist, and he wore the dark Containment fatigues that officers preferred, with sleeves rolled up and patches on the arms and chest.

Tadji was only a little shorter, with brown skin and an abundance of dark curls around a lovely face marked by gorgeous cheekbones. She paired shorts with a floaty sleeveless top and sling-style sandals, and she wore her key to the front door of Royal Mercantile—my family's store, which she now managed—on a chain around her neck.

"Happy birthday!" I said as I gave her a hug.

"Thanks." She pulled back, gave Liam an appraising look beneath arched brows. "You appear to be in one piece."

"We made it through."

"Where's your feckless brother?"

"I'm not feckless, *cher*," Gavin said, stepping around her. "I just like to conserve my energy."

"He just went along for the ride," Liam said.

"I kept your ass from getting nailed by Seelies when you climbed out of that canal." He pulled a silver flask from his pocket, unscrewed the top, took a swig, then offered it to me.

I waved the drink away, since Gavin's taste in liquor ran to "anything available." But the possibility of Liam in danger made my heart thump hard against my chest. "You nearly got nailed by Seelies?"

"He's exaggerating," Liam said, sniffing at the flask and screwing up his features in distaste. "What the hell is this?"

"Homemade," Gavin said with a grin, taking it back and shoving it into a pocket.

Liam rolled his eyes, glanced at me. "Swimming's the only way to get up by Bayou St. John. The line's thin over there," he added, with a glance at Gunnar.

"We're working on it," he said. "President and Congress are fighting about military spending again."

"Abandon hope, all ye who enter New Orleans," Gavin said.

"Seelies?" I prompted.

"They weren't near us," Liam said, running a hand down my arm, which managed to excite and soothe at the same time. "He was hurrying me to get out of the canal because he found a blackberry bramble. And then we found evidence of a scout about a quarter mile down the road."

"How were the blackberries?" Tadji asked with a smile.

"Luscious."

She rolled her eyes and looked at me. "And how was practice?"

"Pretty good, actually."

"In that nobody is a wraith."

My smile was wry. "Sometimes, you have to look on the bright side."

"You do what you can," Tadji said, squeezing my arm. "The rest is up to them. Now," she said, narrowing her gaze, "would someone like to tell me why I had to arrive at precisely six thirty when it looks like everyone else has been milling around this place for a while?"

"We actually have a surprise for you," I said.

Tadji's eyes narrowed. "I don't like surprises."

"Well aware," Gunnar said, holding up a hand. "And I did not approve of this little venture, but I was outvoted. So blame Claire."

"Coward," I muttered.

"Oh, absolutely."

Understandable, given that the look Tadji aimed at me was not exactly comforting. Or even a little bit friendly.

"I love you," I said lightly, and her eyes narrowed even more.

"*Claire.*"

I opened my mouth to respond, to say something appropriate, something that would mark the moment. But I was saved the trouble.

There was a soft *thud* behind us, the sound of full canvas against tile. Of someone's duffel bag hitting the ground, packed with clothes and gear he'd taken with him to DC . . . and brought back to New Orleans.

"Tadji." Burke was tall, with dark skin and eyes, generous eyes.

And there was no denying the affection in his deep, warm voice when he said her name.

Tadji hadn't yet turned around, but there was a change in her posture. Shoulders lifting, as if her heart had swelled. Fingers suddenly fidgeting with the thin gold rings she wore on her right hand.

She turned so slowly she might have been moving through honey. And I wasn't sure if she was afraid—or wanted to prolong the moment. Or whether she'd want to slap me when all was said and done.

But then I saw it in her eyes. The recognition, the excitement, the relief. And I knew her wrath would be worth it. Even if Containment called him away again, she'd have this memory to return to.

"Burke."

"Hey, Tadj," he said, and strode toward her and wrapped her into his arms so that she nearly disappeared in the muscular mountain of his body. And it didn't look like she minded at all.

I gave myself a mental fist bump. God, I loved reunions. And two in one night? That was pretty spectacular.

The room erupted into applause. They knew a good thing when they saw it; they knew happiness when they saw it.

Liam reached out and squeezed my hand, and I gave myself a moment to enjoy it, to bask in love and happiness and excitement. Because we were still in the middle of a war.

"This is why you wanted the surprise," Gavin said, sidling beside us. "You wanted to witness this."

"We take our joy where we can find it," I said, and leaned into Liam.

Moses knew where to find his joy. "Let's eat!" he said, and clapped his hands together. People started moving toward the tables, and I skimmed past Tadji.

"You better take tomorrow off," I murmured, and gave her a wink.

Moments later, I was staring down at the slimy mass of boiled pods some creative soul had paired with orange gelatin.

Creative adventures in okra.

Food scarcity was an issue. The city's population had dropped, but getting food into the Zone, the southern part of the U.S. touched by war, wasn't easy. We'd planted three more community gardens in New Orleans and started tending a dozen abandoned pecan and fruit trees. We gathered, hunted, and fished what we could. Late summer was a time of plenty in New Orleans, and there were lots more shrimp in the water without humans for nearly eight years.

But this particular travesty wasn't about necessity. This was about Moses and his very weird sense of taste.

"Whaddya think?" he asked, nodding in approval at the dish.

"I mean—that is something." Something that I would avoid. I'd seen what Moses ate—very old crawfish and canned food bursting with botulism.

Thankfully, the table held plenty of more traditionally NOLA fare, at least what we could pull off with the food available. There was corn, shrimp gumbo, fried squash, bread pudding, pickled mirliton, slices of Creole tomatoes, blackberries that looked ready to burst.

"I'm not sure how I feel about a joint human-Para potluck," Liam said, sidling beside me as he added slices of tomato to his plate and sprinkled them with the waiting salt.

"Good about the diplomacy," I said. "Bad about the food."

"You just don't get it," Moses muttered, and scooped wiggly okra-in-gelatin onto his plate.

"I'm okay not getting that," Liam said, and offered him a scoop of bread pudding.

Moses wrinkled his nose. "I'm not eating that wet bread garbage."

"Of course you aren't," Liam said, and added the food to his own plate. "Because it doesn't smell like week-old roadkill."

We took our seats, watched Sensitives, soldiers, and Paras shuffle plates of food to their seats. People still clumped together in the groups they recognized and felt part of, with Sensitives serving as a kind of bridge between the two worlds.

Some of the attendees were old friends, some new.

Mariah talked to Darby Craig, who loved retro clothes and had the perfect pinup figure for them, and was a fellow member of Delta, the formerly rogue group that had secretly defied Containment's unilateral ban on magic. Darby had run her own underground lab until the war had begun again, when Containment had finally wised up and given back her official status. Now she spent her time researching ways to repair the Zone.

Solomon, Moses's cousin and the former leader of the Devil's Isle Para underground, talked with Malachi, an angel with blond curls that framed his chiseled face and golden eyes. His body was equally chiseled, and we haven't even gotten to the enormous ivory wings. His figure was an interesting foil to Solomon's small and stocky build.

Lizzie, a nurse at the Devil's Isle clinic and a powerful fire Para in her own right, sat with Dave. They were using their fingers to trace movements on the tabletop, and I guessed it was soccer related. Both played in Containment's recreational soccer league.

A year ago, this wouldn't have been possible. Paras were imprisoned, Sensitives were illegal, and humans didn't cross the treacherous line between mundane and magical. I wouldn't have wished for tragedy to bring us together, but bring us together it did.

I looked over at Tadji and Burke. She still appeared to be in shock—thrilled to see Burke and utterly surprised that he was there. Proving that love could be nourished and grown, could outlast time and outpace distance. And allow us to be who we were without disguise or camouflage.

I glanced over at Liam, who sat in a folding chair beside Moses, his hand on Moses's shoulder as they talked earnestly. I felt better just seeing him at the other end of the table. Knowing that he was safe, at least for now, and that I wouldn't stand alone against an incursion.

And still . . . fear was a hard and bitter seed. I knew I couldn't take anything for granted in the Zone, but something felt different. The air itself was tense, as if the molecules were poised and waiting. Something was coming. Maybe the Seelies, maybe some other monsters. But it felt like New Orleans was moving toward the inevitable . . .

Gavin sat down beside me, a dill pickle spear sticking out of his mouth like a cigar.

"Good spread," he said, and crunched a bit before adding the remainder of the spear to a plate loaded with meat.

"It is," I said, and glanced at him, wondering if he was prepared for a serious talk. Given he'd taken a seat that put his back against the wall—and gave him a view of all the doors and angles, and he was scanning those angles while he shoveled in food with a plastic fork—I figured he was prepared enough.

"How's Liam?" I asked.

Gavin loved to tease, to comment, to snark. But he was also a loyal brother. That it took him a moment to answer tightened something in my belly.

"He's okay," he said, wiping his mouth with a paper napkin, which he balled in his fist. "Dealing. Didn't talk about his magic, but not talking is the Quinn way."

"Did he use it?"

"No." He scooped some dirty rice, chewed. "He got closest, I think, when we found the Seelies. There were a lot of them, and they were powerful. I could tell that he was feeling it. That their magic had an appeal. He had a look in his eyes."

"Lust," I said, and didn't mean it lightly. And Gavin's expression said he knew what I'd meant.

"Yeah. But he didn't say anything about it."

I nodded, pushed food around my plate, my appetite suddenly gone.

"He's happier now that he's back with you." Gavin turned his head to look at me, and there was something appreciative in his eyes. "You center him. Remind him the magic can be a feature, not a bug. You're good for him, Red."

I narrowed my gaze. "Did you just compliment me?"

"Don't get used to it," he said with a grin. "Reunions make me sappy."

"Same," I said.

I put down my plastic fork, crossed my arms. When Liam had first gotten his magic, he'd been so unnerved by the anger and hate he'd felt—derived from the magic of a very twisted Sensitive—that he'd left New Orleans and disappeared into the bayou for five weeks. He'd been afraid he was going to hurt me.

"He's not going to leave you again."

Not on purpose, I thought. Not because he'd want to. But maybe because of where we lived, how we lived, Tadji and Burke were proof enough that love could flourish and bloom; but that didn't mean it couldn't also be torn apart by war and magic.

"Maybe he won't have a choice," I said.

"Optimism," Gavin said. "We're going to hope for the best. He loves you, Claire. Believe me on that. He talked about you nonstop."

"He . . . what?" My cheeks flushed even as I felt almost stupidly proud.

Gavin grinned again, chewed more pickle. "He loves you," he said with a shrug. "And he's proud of you. You survived the war. You stuck it out here. That impresses the hell out of him. And maybe most importantly, he trusts you. Magic is uncomfortable to him, and you understand magic, the cost of having it, more than most humans. So keep on doing what you're doing."

Then, because he was Gavin, he stole my corn bread, putting a crescent-shaped bite in the clean edge before dropping it to my plate.

"Now we're even for the possum."

"You are really bad at this," I said, but he was already walking away.

CHAPTER THREE

I slept better than I had in a week, heavy as a log and equally as unaware of the world.

"Let's have a lazy day."

I blinked at Liam through a curtain of red hair. He lay beside me in the bed that was just barely large enough for the two of us, wearing boxers patterned with Tabasco bottles, one hand behind his head, gaze on the tin ceiling.

With Tadji manning Royal Mercantile, I'd moved from the store's third-floor apartment into the modified gas station that held my father's collection of supernatural objects, where I could keep an eye on them. While I'd donated most of the weapons to Malachi, our winged Consularis friend, we'd moved the rest of the objects from the display tables my father had created to the building's fortified basement—with Malachi's blessing. Now the gas station was less museum and more urban loft. A postapocalyptic apartment.

The building had been renovated by someone with a taste for chrome, leather, and primary colors. We'd filled the living area with furniture we'd found in the neighborhood—mostly leather and wood, since they had held up in the heat better than fabric. Gavin, Tadji, and Malachi had helped us redecorate. But only Malachi knew about the building's purpose as a magical archive, or that my father had assembled the collection. That kept the rest of the artifacts safer, or so we hoped.

Liam spent most nights here with me in the small bedroom loft—at least when he wasn't on patrol with Gavin. I worked late on nights like that, helping Tadji at the store, Gunnar with some Containment task, or Lizzie at the clinic in Devil's Isle. If I stayed busy, I worried less about the danger Liam faced.

He hadn't officially moved in. We were exclusive, but despite Gavin's plea for optimism, I wasn't ready to build expectations about forever and happy ever after. Not when those hopes could be dashed apart so easily.

But I was smart enough to take joy and happiness when I could find them.

"A lazy day?" I asked, pushed my hair aside, then glanced at the clock. Not quite seven in the morning. Too early to be awake, although it was the latest I'd slept in a while.

"Chicory coffee," Liam said. "Beignets and the paper, watching the tourists. Then a nap, some crawfish étouffée, maybe an afternoon on a balcony with a breeze and a Sazerac. And when the sun goes down, a brass band and machine full of frozen strawberry daiquiris."

"There's a daiquiri machine in your fantasy New Orleans?"

"I'm being historically accurate." He turned his head to look at me. "Isn't there in yours?"

"I haven't really thought about it. Mostly I imagine finding an enormous cache of Empire-style furniture and meeting the interior designer who wants to buy the entire lot from me at once."

The thought gave me warm fuzzies.

"You're a capitalist to the bone."

"Especially during lean times." I sat up, stretched. "I don't have chicory coffee, beignets, a paper, crawfish, Sazeracs, a jazz band, or a daiquiri machine." I considered our inventory. "But I can get you some instant coffee, year-old Pop-Tarts, Gavin's very bad moonshine, and Dr. John on vinyl."

"And the daiquiri machine?" he asked.

I paused. "Gavin can fan you while you drink his moonshine?"

He laughed deeply, then rolled and captured me beneath him. "Let's just try this and worry about the extras later."

"Oh, I forgot," I said, slipping out of his arms. "We might actually have some extras!" I pulled on a robe and belted the waist.

Liam sat up, muscles bunching from the movement. "Have I been gone so long that you've forgotten how this works? We at least need to be in the same room."

"A box came from Eleanor!" I called out, already moving down the narrow spiral staircase to the first floor. Eleanor's spirit was strong, but her hidden magic had put her at risk, and the Quinn boys had moved her out of New Orleans. She was now in Charleston, outside the Zone.

I heard Liam coming down the stairs behind me, metal treads creaking with use, as I grabbed the box I'd put on the table that had formerly held my father's banned magical-artifact collection. The box had been carefully wrapped in brown paper, the address neatly written in old-fashioned cursive.

"Presents," I said, offering it to him.

He pulled a folded knife from the pocket of jeans he hadn't yet managed to button. "Presents indeed. I wondered when this was going to get here."

He slit a seam and put the knife away, each move careful and precise. I had to bite back a growl of impatience. She was his grandmother, and it was his box to open, but she always included a treat for me.

"I can feel you vibrating."

"Anticipation," I said, drawing the word out.

He opened the flaps, the contents hidden by a sheet of white tissue paper, and just looked at me.

"You're cruel."

Liam lifted an eyebrow. "You left me naked and wanting for the mere possibility of candy."

"It's more than a mere possibility," I said with a grin. Not the strongest defense, but an honest one.

He rolled his eyes, folded the white paper away, and began pulling out the gifts.

"For you," he said, and offered me the bar of chocolate snugged between two chilly gel packs.

"*Yes,*" I hissed, and took the bundle to the kitchen. The gel packs went into the freezer to be used again, the chocolate into the fridge.

By the time I walked back, Liam had pulled out a box of fleur de sel, as sea salt had healing powers for Paras, and three boxes of shelf-stable chocolate milk. That was for Gavin.

He'd also pulled out an envelope in pale pink, an "E" in delicate gilding on the flap. He opened it, pulled out a letter on matching letterhead.

"'Liam and Claire,'" he read, leaning back against the table. "'I hope this finds you safe and sound. Life in Charleston is lovely, but hot. Foster loves going for walks and playing in the neighborhood sprinklers.'"

Foster was Eleanor's Labrador retriever. He'd accompanied her out of the Zone.

"'I've hired a lovely young woman to walk him, and they are the best of friends. I think it's true love. I am also enjoying the food. Low Country and Creole have common elements, but they are very different.

"'Please tell Gavin to be good and clean his apartment, and that I look forward to hearing he has settled down with a nice young woman.'" Liam looked up. "I am absolutely not going to tell him that."

"Not it," I said, raising a hand. "He's your brother."

"That's exactly why you should tell him. He won't still be related to you."

I just gave him a look.

He frowned, but looked down at the letter. "Where was I?"

"Settling down."

"Right. 'As you asked, I do believe the magic is fading. The thing-amajigs don't have quite the same intensity that they did before I left. Their colors aren't as vibrant, but I'm not certain if that's because of my magic fading or theirs. And I'm still deciding how I feel about that. If that's what life brings, so be it.'"

Liam paused. "'I suppose I should wrap this up. All my love, Eleanor.'"

"Thingumajigs?" I asked.

"A couple of old remote controls," Liam said with a smile. "Moses had them in his collection for years, and they became instilled with magic over that time. She could see their colors."

I watched him for a minute, folding the letter carefully before tucking it into its envelope again.

"You wondered what would happen if you left New Orleans."

He looked at me quietly for a moment, then put the letter back in the box. "I'm not ready to give up. But, yeah, I wanted to know what might happen. If we left."

I was worried by the fact that he'd thought about leaving. And worried and comforted by the fact that he'd thought about our leaving together. Was that what he expected? That I'd walk away from New Orleans?

I'd lived here my entire life. I ran the store my great-grandfather had started, had buried my father here when war had taken him away. My memories of him were rooted in this place. Sometimes I could smell his cologne, hear his voice, feel his hugs. And even when war came again, I took the chaos and want and fear because as long as I stayed here, some part of him stayed with me.

Could I leave all that behind?

"My ties to the city aren't as strong as yours are," Liam said. Ironic, since his families—the Quinns and Arsenaults—had been in southern Louisiana for generations. "To the land, yeah. But not to the city. I'm comfortable carrying those memories with me."

He crossed his arms and looked away, frowning as he stared into space, as if he was working something out. "And magic isn't as comfortable for me as it is for you. For Eleanor. For Burke. So I wondered what would happen. If magic was something we'd have to leave behind, too."

"It looks like you wouldn't have a choice," I said. "I mean, if Eleanor's experience is typical, you lose the power, or the sensitivity to it, when you're gone."

And I wasn't sure how I felt about that, either. Relieved that I wouldn't have to carry the burden? Or sad that I'd no longer be a girl with a gift? I'd once hidden my magic, believing it was inherently bad. Then I'd used it in hiding because while my attitude had changed, it was still banned. Now it was part of who I was—the good and the bad. Who would I be without it?

"It's complicated," I said, and he put an arm around my shoulder, drew me in.

"Complicated," he agreed, then tipped up my chin with a fingertip, blue gaze drilling into mine, flecks of gold at the edges of his irises like glimmers of a hidden jewel.

"Sometimes the answers are easier than the questions. Sometimes we have exactly as much as we need."

He kissed me, and I wanted to stay in that place—in that moment—forever.

Since Tadji had the day off, we made our way to the Quarter to open Royal Mercantile.

Scarlet provided the transportation. We'd found her, a red and curvy Ford from the 1940s that someone had mostly rehabbed, before Belle Chasse, and she'd been serving us well since then. A streak of inky black now curved along the back passenger-side wheel well, a scar from a fire sprite. But she ran like a top, and I considered the scar a badge of honor.

It was still early morning, but the heat and humidity had already settled in. The city was hazy and quiet, the French Quarter equally so. Puddles lined the edges of the street where rain had fallen overnight. Two Containment officers patrolling on horses, hooves clip-clopping against brick and asphalt, waved as we passed.

Like many of the remaining buildings in the French Quarter, Royal Mercantile was a three-floor town house, with iron-railed balconies along the second and third floors in front of tall, narrow windows that reached from floor to ceiling. A purple flag marked with gold fleurs-de-lis, the standard of postwar New Orleans, hung limply from the second balcony.

My father had once sold fancy antiques to tourists and locals alike. There'd been German clocks, French secretaries, and English silver. Velvet and linen and gold and mahogany. Now we sold MREs and duct tape, bottled water and filtration kits, offered vegetables and herbs from the community gardens. The lending library had been Tadji's idea, as had the Friday night open mic. Soldiers and citizens alike shared poetry, played guitar, and otherwise worked to stay sane in a city that rarely was.

I unlocked the door, we walked inside, and I flipped the CLOSED sign to OPEN.

The floors were hardwood, the walls hung with the cuckoo clocks my father had collected. A creaking staircase tucked against the right wall led up to the second floor, where I'd stored excess inventory, and to the third floor, where I'd lived before moving into the garage. Since Tadji had declined my offer to move her in—she'd wanted to keep work and personal space separate—it now stored the antiques we'd moved out of the first floor to make room for the new meeting space. My telekinesis had come in very handy that day.

I walked straight to the air conditioner and flipped it on, then stood in front of the vent, eyes closed. It was my daily meditation on the joys of electricity.

"Quit hogging the bought air," Liam said, sidling beside me.

"You could just ask me nicely to share," I said, eyes closed as chilly air blew my hair back.

He put an arm around my waist, nipped my neck. "What would be the fun in that?"

"Rewards for good behavior."

"You have a point."

"I usually do." As if in reward, he trailed kisses across my neck. "We have to open the store," I reminded him, even as my toes curled inside my boots.

Figuring we had at least a couple of minutes, I tilted my neck, happened to shift my gaze back to the windows. And when I couldn't see Royal Street through the glass, momentarily wondered if Liam had actually managed to fog it up.

But it wasn't condensation on the glass; it was something in the air outside. Like fog, but fog wasn't the color of sulfur, and it didn't put a buzz of magic in the air that tingled like pins and needles across my fingertips.

"Liam. Outside."

He must have heard something in my voice, because he went still, turned his gaze to the windows. "You feel the magic?" he asked.

"Yeah."

It hadn't set off the Containment magic alarms, because Containment had disabled the magic sensors months ago; they weren't worth the resources, not when the good guys could use magic legally.

"What is it?" I asked. "Some type of gas? Poison?"

"I doubt it. If you have enough power to do whatever that is, it doesn't seem you'd need to bother with poison. You could take people out with magic alone. So maybe this is a side effect of some bigger magic?"

"Or a literal smoke screen," I said. We were well within the Containment line around New Orleans. Maybe this was the Seelies' way to get inside.

"Maybe," Liam said. And he sounded grimly confident that I'd guessed correctly.

We walked back to the front of the store, watched the substance roll through the street in wisps and puffs tall enough that I couldn't see the shell of the buildings across from the store. But I could still see the buildings upriver, which meant the fog hadn't gotten there yet. It was coming from somewhere downriver.

Somewhere in the direction of Devil's Isle. A good thing I hadn't had time to cast off yesterday; I was probably going to need that magic.

"So much for beignets and the paper," I said.

"We may have to settle for companionable ass kicking." He rolled his neck, then looked down at me, anticipation in his eyes. And not much trepidation.

I'd long ago given up the hope that he'd take cover, that there was any possibility I could keep him locked away and safe in the middle of a war. He'd run toward the sound of battle. And he'd given me the courage to do the same. Fighting together was much better than worrying alone.

We opened the door, stepped onto the sidewalk together. The door closed behind us, the bell ringing its good-bye as I linked my fingers with his.

The fog enrobed us both. I couldn't see beyond my hand.

"It's going to be hard to make it a mile without seeing," he said.

"We'll walk against the curb," I said. "We take Royal and go slowly, just in case."

We stepped into the street, and I heard scuffing as he traced his foot against the granite blocks that edged it. One foot at a time, we began to move.

It was like walking through a yellow-tinged cloud—if clouds tingled with power and smelled oily and sharp. And it was unnerving to walk through a neighborhood I'd long ago memorized, buildings and ruins I could name forward and backward like cards in a deck. Now there was no up or down, no horizon to give me bearings. Everything felt unfamiliar. Alien and unwelcome. And it didn't help that the fog was growing thicker—the magic growing stronger— with each step we took toward Devil's Isle.

We walked in eerie silence to the edge of the French Quarter, when something clacked against asphalt, and I pulled Liam to a stop, strained my ears over the wild beating of my heart to hear what might be coming for us.

Clack. Clack. Clack. Clack.

The sound was hard and tinny, and bounced around the fog so much I couldn't tell where it was coming from.

The monster snorted, and I nearly jumped. Until I recognized the sound.

I reached out and up, fingers brushing against the slick coat. "It's a Containment horse," I said, feeling my way from saddled belly to neck. "It's lost its rider." The horse snuffled me, as if comforted by finding something familiar—a human—in the soup of magic.

"We need to tie her up," I said, feeling for the leather reins. "At least until this clears."

"Balcony railing," Liam said, and guided us until we reached one. I pulled the reins through, made a knot that I hoped would stay snug.

"I'm not a good knotter," I told Liam, giving the horse's neck a final soothing rub before we started walking again.

"Fortunately, that's not on my top ten list."

"Redhead better be number one on that list."

"Sass is number one. Redhead is number two. So you're solid." He took my hand again, squeezed it.

"I feel much relief."

"I bet."

The wall around Devil's Isle, dozens of feet of concrete and steel topped by the generator-powered electrical grid that kept incarcerated Paras from simply flying away, seemed to materialize from the mist. It was tall and imposing and, at the moment, comfortingly solid.

Hands on the wall, we made our way toward the guardhouse—and saw the gate standing wide-open. We walked inside, sounds cutting through the silence. Alarms, shouts, footsteps. But they bounced and echoed through the fog, and it was impossible to tell where they originated.

"The source is definitely in here," I said. The fog had gotten thicker, the scent stronger, as we walked north, father into the neighborhood.

"If you wanted a diversion," I said, "you couldn't do better than this."

"The gate was open," Liam said. "That may not be a coincidence. We have to get rid of it. But I don't know how we can make magic just disappear."

I waved my fingers through the mist. I couldn't feel anything, but I could see the shadows, the shifting dark and light.

"Maybe not," I said. "But I bet we can move it."

"Move it," he said quietly. "Could we do that? This much?"

A gunshot pinged somewhere to our left, probably fired by an agent who couldn't see two feet in front of him. Liam's fingers tightened around mine.

"So, we try to move it toward the river?"

I smiled. "I'm glad you've warmed up to the idea. I'll grab it, direct it. You follow my lead."

"Every time," Liam said.

We turned back toward the south, and I took a deep breath, centered myself. Then I closed my eyes, opened my mind to the glimmering filaments of magic that permeated the air, the fog, and, because I hadn't cast off the magic, my body. Normally I'd braid them together into a kind of magical cord I could use to lasso the object I wanted to move. But this fog was a different animal. It didn't have boundaries, or at least not that we could see, and that was going to be a challenge.

I lifted my free hand as I stared toward the river on the other side of the levee, which was on the other side of the southern Devil's Isle wall. Like the Veil, the Mississippi was an artery through New Orleans. I didn't need to see it in order to steer something toward it.

I imagined the combined space of our bodies was a net, a broom, that could push the fog forward.

"Now," I quietly said, and his fingers tightened as we began to walk forward, and to exert our own magic.

The mist reacted immediately, tingling up and down my arms as we shoved it toward the river. But shafts of light began to spear down through the gray where the fog had begun to thin. This was working.

"Keep going," I said, the tingling getting stronger—now pins and needles against my skin—as we shuffled along, one slow step at a time, and swept the magic out of the way.

"Stop," Liam said, and I did.

She stood twenty feet away, tendrils of fog swirling around her feet. Short and curvy, with pale skin and cropped white hair. And the telltale streak of crimson down the center of her forehead, nose, and lips, and the tips of her fingers.

Seelie.

She wore a sleeveless white tunic beneath a golden chest plate, and leather sandals that laced nearly to the knee. Her hair was short and blond; her eyes were piercingly blue. She was staring straight ahead, face tight with concentration. Her hands were at her sides, palms up, her lips moving slightly as she tried to keep control of her magic.

She was the source of the fog. If one Seelie was involved, could the others Liam had seen be close behind?

"Liam."

"Yeah."

And she saw us, and loathing flared in her eyes. Not just distaste or an absence of approval, but full-blown animosity. She hated us. And I'd never seen her before.

"Not fog," he said. "It's Seelie magic. They're air spirits."

"That explains the flying," I said, and made myself look at her, look past the loathing. "They can control, what, weather?"

"I don't know," he admitted. "They usually just go for the hand-to-hand."

"Present company excluded," I said, and braced as the woman drew her hands and fingers together, index fingers pointed as if aiming the barrel of a red-tipped gun at us. Magic began to flow from her hands like waves of heat above pavement, rippling through the air as it moved toward us. The pins and needles became stabbing pain as she channeled her hatred into magic.

"I could use her," Liam said, and my gaze snapped to his, even as I worked to concentrate against pain that tried to shatter my thoughts and my focus.

It was the first time I'd seen his face since the fog had descended. It was still gorgeous. But hatred blazed gold in his eyes now, hot as a new star. It put a chill through me.

"That emotion isn't yours," I told him. "It's hers. You're feeling her emotions through her magic. You have to ignore it, Liam. You have to ignore her and focus."

"She hates us. Would kill us if she could. But that is not the plan. That is not the need."

Okay, maybe we could use this. If I could keep him from killing someone. "What plan, Liam? What do they need?"

"To prepare. To be ready."

"For whom? For what?"

"For their plans. For their . . . reunion?" His face was clenched, forehead beading with effort. He shook his head. "I don't know. I'm losing it, Claire. She's gaining ground."

"Then we'll stop her," I said, and looked at her again, gathered up every glimmer of magic I could find. "Push it back," I murmured, a demand to myself, the words gritted as I spooled in more magic and shoved it against the volley she returned.

She was strong, and her magic was inherent. Ours was foreign and accidental. But together—my magic and Liam's twined and twisted—we were stronger. It was like combustion, his magic a catalyst for mine, and it glimmered through the air, dissolving the fog even as it leached the magic from my body.

The fog was now a carpet at our feet, wisps covering the ground and curling at our ankles—and no longer obscuring our vision.

Containment guards, who'd been waiting to finally see the battlefield, ran toward the Seelie. They grabbed her, breaking her magical focus, her concentration. She reached out, struck one, and he wrapped a hand around her arm, twisted. She flailed as they took her, kicking and screaming in an unintelligible language, puncturing skin with nails and teeth.

She managed to wrench away, to run, and made it ten feet before a soldier pulled out a stunner and sent a stream in her direction.

I jerked as her body did. She collapsed to the ground with a thud, and the magic melted away, fog evaporating in the rising sun.

I hit the ground on my knees, breath heaving in and out as the magic rushed back in, filling the vacuum it had left behind. My chest was tight, as if my lungs had been pushed aside by the magic. I had to get rid of it. I'd already cut it too close.

But there was no time.

Air raid sirens began to wail.

saw a flash and looked up, found nothing but enormous white clouds in a tropical blue sky. And then, as if someone had tossed jewels into the sky, a diamond-like glint, then another. And then there were two dozen gleaming diamonds.

No, not gemstones, I realized when my brain had caught up, understood what it was seeing. Gleaming golden spears and bows held by two dozen Seelies. They were all female, or appeared to be, with golden chest plates and shin guards over white tunics. Some were pale, some dark, but all had the same streak of crimson across their faces, across the fingers curled around their spears.

The fog had absolutely been a diversion.

I squeezed my eyes shut, prayed for the strength to push the magic down into a hot little ball in the center of my belly, where it could wait until I had time to deal with it.

When I opened them again, Paras, drawn by the fog's dissipation, stood in front of their cottages, wondering at the alarm and the commotion in the streets. They hadn't yet seen the weapons.

"Liam!" I said, and pointed to the houses. "Get them inside!"

"Claire," he said, expression drawn with concern, but I shook my head, waved him off. My legs were too wobbly.

"Don't wait for me. Just go."

I could see the frustration in his eyes, but he nodded back, ran toward the cottages, calling out warnings. "Get inside! Close your doors and get inside." There was screaming and frantic movement as parents scooped up children, slammed doors, let curtains obscure windows.

It took another five seconds for me to stand, ten to reach the nearest building and flatten myself against the wall beneath an overhanging balcony. Liam stood across the street in nearly the same position as we waited for the barrage.

But nothing hit the ground. We weren't the target. Or weren't yet.

Sparks filled the air as the Seelie weapons slammed into the high transformers that fueled the overhead security grid. Booms rattled the neighborhood as one transformer after another burst into flames.

The green glow of the security grid—visible even in daylight—flickered, then faded. Devil's Isle was open to the sky.

For a moment, there was only silence, and then the background buzz of the grid replaced by the chirp of birds and the silence of stunned humans and Paras. And then the air came alive.

Wind barreled through the street with the force of a marauding army, throwing dust and dirt into the air, and was nearly strong enough to shove us backward. And it smelled sickeningly of cloves. The scent of Seelie magic.

I turned toward the wall, leaned against it, fingernails digging in, to stay upright, and squinted to keep the grit out of my eyes. The wind slapped hard as a hand, and left an angry buzz of magic in its wake. Branches cracked and snapped, and shingles flew like Frisbees, and a plastic chair somersaulted down the middle of the street like a gymnast.

And the Seelies hadn't even gotten started.

The wind shifted, and spears began to fall like hail, whistling through the air and puncturing asphalt, concrete, grass, shingles, without discrimination. They were beautiful in their way, slender and glinting in the sunlight, still vibrating with energy and magic.

There was a guttural scream as a Containment agent shoved a Para child out of the street and was struck by a spear. My heart nearly stopped when Gunnar ran forward, scooped up the child, deposited him into his mother's waiting arms, then ran back into the street and began to drag the agent to safety, the spear rising defiantly from his abdomen as Gunnar hustled him beneath the awning of a town house.

In a matter of seconds, the street was empty.

I had only a moment to wonder what they wanted, what they'd planned, when a woman emerged from a passageway between two houses, a slim figure in dingy white cotton.

She was a Seelie, pale but for the crimson streak that lined her face and stained her long and slender fingers. Her neck was long, her cheekbones high, her eyes and mouth were open wide, and she had a slight underbite that made her look even more fey. Her hair was platinum blond and twined into a complicated braid.

I'd seen her before, standing behind a fence in Devil's Isle. There'd been hatred in her eyes then, cold and seething, and it didn't look like her attitude had improved.

She was completely untouched by the wind as she moved through the street, not even her pale hair shifting in the current.

Containment agents shouted out instructions and converged on her position, heads down and hands fisted as they tried to barrel through the wall of air. But the Seelies just increased the wind's force and pushed them back.

Now in a ring-shaped formation, they reached out their hands to her, faces shining with—not joy exactly, but fulfillment. Satisfaction.

She smiled at them before turning her gaze on the humans and Paras who watched, braced against the wind and squinting to see.

"Judgment," she said, the word traveling on the wind, powerful as a crack of thunder. And then she raised her hand toward her sisters-in-arms, and rose into the air.

She joined their circle, and something snapped into place, the sound ricocheting through the air.

A blink, and they were gone. And the wind simply dropped away.

Containment agents ran forward, weapons pointed up. But the Paras were already gone, leaving behind the wounded, the dust and debris of the storm they'd created, and the flames that dripped ominously from transformers.

Liam ran across the street, cupped my face in his hands, looked me over. "Are you all right?"

"I'm fine. Magically spent, but fine. You okay?"

"Just scratches," he said, and wrapped his arms around me.

I closed my eyes, let myself lean into him. Let myself feel safe. "This is why they were camped near the lake. Because they were coming to get her."

"Yeah," Liam said. "Containment will send troops to the camp. But if any remained behind, they won't be there now. They'll be looking for a new location."

We both looked up warily at the sudden concussion of moving air.

Malachi, ivory wings open and gleaming in the sun, lowered toward the street. He'd been a commander in the Consularis army, brought into our world under magical duress. Now he worked to protect the rest of the Consularis, and occasionally us, from Containment, war, and the Court.

When he touched down, his wings closed and disappeared. Apparently seeing his presence as a beacon of safety, Paras began to emerge from their houses again, watching him carefully to figure out what they should do next.

"You saw the fight?" Liam asked when he'd reached us.

"I heard the explosion," Malachi said. "What happened?"

"Seelies," I said, and sketched the basics. "They came for the Seelie who lived in Devil's Isle. Busted the power grid and literally flew away."

The concern etched in Malachi's face wasn't reassuring. "Her name is Aeryth—the apparently former Devil's Isle Seelie."

"She wanted judgment," I said. "Or was going to deliver it. Or maybe both. It's what she said when she lifted up."

Malachi considered that quietly, which didn't make me feel any better.

"What would they have planned?" Liam asked.

Was this the finale, he meant, or just the first act?

"I don't know," Malachi said. "If they have a plan, it will likely be something intended to cause pain to us."

"'Us' meaning humans, or Consularis?" Liam asked.

"Yes" was Malachi's grim response.

Gunnar came toward us with the stride of a man in charge. And since he looked damage-free, I relaxed a little.

"Y'all okay?" he asked.

"We're fine. Containment?"

"Still assessing. Right now, two agents dead, along with the Seelie who made the fog. At current count, more than a dozen wounded, mostly Paras and agents who were struck by flying objects."

That was fewer injuries than I'd have expected from a Seelie attack.

"It wasn't an attack," Malachi said, clearly thinking along the same lines. "It sounds like an extraction."

"She's the only one missing, at least as far as we're aware," Gunnar said.

"And there are other Court Paras in Devil's Isle," Malachi said.

"She would not have wanted to hurt them. Or perhaps risk Containment taking out their anger on those who remain here."

I lifted my gaze to the high walls, fluffy clouds moving briskly above them. "But outside the walls . . . ," I began, and Malachi nodded.

"Outside the walls is a different matter altogether."

"How did Aeryth get out of the cage?" Liam asked.

I stared at Gunnar. "You had her in a cage?"

"Metaphorical," Gunnar said. "She was held in a town house, but there were cold iron stakes around the perimeter. They kept her from using magic."

"And none of the other Paras removed them?"

"Other Paras don't much like Seelies," he said. "And we had a few allies who ensured the stakes stayed in place."

"So how did she get out?" I asked, but knew the answer as soon as I'd finished. "The fog. That's why they needed the diversion."

"Yeah," Gunnar said. "We're just starting the investigation, but it looks like a human guard removed the stakes while we were dealing with this."

"A human," Malachi said, brows lifted.

"He's infatuated with her," Gunnar said flatly. "We aren't sure how much of that is Aeryth, and how much is him. He said she asked him to remove them today, and told him when. There wasn't any fog in that part of Devil's Isle."

"All the better for him to see," Liam said, echoing the fairy tale.

"So she knew they were coming," I said. "Knew there would be a diversion?"

"It's early," Gunnar said. "But it seems that way."

"She likely learned from the other Seelies," Malachi said. "They are able to silently share thoughts. It's one of the reasons they're so effective in battle."

"We have to find her," Gunnar said. "Them." He rubbed the back of his neck. "We'll take a look at her rooms, see if there's anything that would tell us what might be planned. But it's unlikely she left anything incriminating behind."

He blew out a breath, then settled his gaze on Malachi. "We'll hold a briefing later today, and I think the Commandant would appreciate any particular expertise you can offer."

Malachi nodded.

"What can we do in the meantime?" I asked.

"We're shorthanded as it is, and we're going to be focused on the grid. You can help canvass the neighborhood. Talk to residents, ask if they've heard anything about her plans. Politely," he added.

"Good thing I left my brass knuckles at the store," Liam said dryly.

"You're hilarious as always," Gunnar said, but squeezed his arm warmly. "I'm going back to the insanity."

When he was gone, I looked back at Malachi. "You want to go with us? They might be more willing to talk if you are."

"I don't think that's necessarily true. But regardless, no. I want to look."

I presumed he meant by air, flying above New Orleans for some sign of the Seelies.

"Good flying," Liam said.

But instead of lifting into the air, Malachi glanced at me, concern etched in his face. "You're nearly at the edge."

I didn't need to ask what he meant. Not when my head was still spinning. "I know. I can feel it. I haven't had a chance to cast it off yet."

"Find the time," Malachi said. He strode away in the direction of the cottages and of the Paras beginning to emerge to look around, check the status of their neighborhood.

"I didn't see it."

I looked back at Liam, found glimmering heat in his eyes. "See what?"

"The magic. You're swimming in it."

"I'm fine," I said. "Or I will be when I cast off. I can deal."

"I didn't see it," he said again, and this time the words were edged with frustration. When he strode away from me, it took a moment for me to gather my wits enough to follow him.

"Hey," I said, and, trotting until I'd reached him, grabbed his hand. "What's going on?"

"The end of the fucking world, and I'm not competent enough with magic so that I can actually see you're hurting."

There was an edge to his voice—anger and frustration and irritation warring together.

"I'm fine."

"Malachi knows you aren't fine."

I didn't think this was about jealousy or balancing magic, or anything other than the fight we'd just witnessed. I moved in front of him, put my hands on his cheeks. "Look at me," I said, and waited until he did.

"I'm in charge of my body and my magic, not you, not Malachi, not anyone else. That's my burden and I'm dealing with it. It's not a thing you can control—or need to. And I'm fine."

"He saw it."

"Yeah, and I told him the same thing."

This wasn't like Liam—either the sniping jealousy or the insecurity. Liam was no less confident than Malachi was. So what was really going on here? What had put that unfamiliar grimness in his eyes?

I searched his face, as if I could find the answers there, laid bare. But I couldn't read the cause. "What's wrong?"

"I should be taking care of you."

I lifted my brows. "As you're well aware, I don't need taking care of. But since you're a guy with plenty of alpha in him and I understand your urge to protect, I'll remind you that we fought together. So try again."

"We live in a war zone."

"Also not new information. Try again."

He growled, put his hands behind his head, showing a tantalizing strip of hard muscle between shirt hem and jeans as he paced like a caged tiger. And when I looked at him—really looked at him—I realized there wasn't just anger in his eyes, but worry. Fear.

The magic.

Stupid, I thought. Stupid that I hadn't seen that until now, that I hadn't realized he was still grappling with his own battles. He was fighting his own war with magic, and had worried—or assumed—that I was, too.

"You held your own."

He stopped short, looked at me for a long time. "Did I?" There was a rawness, a vulnerability, in his eyes that was so unlike him, and it made my heart ache to see it. Liam was a man with a plan, with strategies, with solutions. A man who'd lived through war and come out the other side. He wasn't accustomed to being uncomfortable.

"It was like she was made of power and hatred. I could feel that, all of it, running through me. I'm glad you don't have to face that."

"So am I. And I'm glad it chose you, because I know you're strong enough to deal with it."

He looked back at me, doubt in his eyes.

"You didn't give in to it," I said, "even when you wanted to. Even when it was calling to you, and reaching inside you. You said no and you fought with me against it."

I closed the distance he'd put between us, put a hand on his cheek, and turned his face to mine. "Magic is a burden for us. That's just a fact of life. But you're handling it. You're thinking through it, and not giving in. And when you felt it fighting back, you asked for help."

He put a hand over mine, squeezed. "You are amazing."

"Yeah, sometimes I am." I grinned at him. "And if you suggest one more time that it's your job to protect me, I'll punch you in the mouth. And throw out all the pad thai MREs."

His eyes narrowed, glinted dangerously. "You wouldn't dare. They're the best ones."

"Then you better shape up."

His mouth curled, and he turned his head, pressed his lips to my palm, and had my toes curling. But then he frowned.

"Hey," he said, turning my arm. "You're bleeding."

I craned my head to look, found a bright red slash just below my elbow. "I guess I am. It's okay."

"I got it," he said, and pulled a handkerchief from his pocket. It was linen and embroidered with birds of paradise, and bore a fancy "E" in one corner.

"Your grandmother's?" I asked as he folded it into a triangle, then rolled it up to form a long strip, which he tied around my elbow.

"It is. I found a few things she left behind."

I winced as he tugged the bandage tight. "Anything you want to get rid of?"

He looked down at me, smiled. "Always looking for a good deal."

"I try." And it made him smile, which had been the point.

Liam finished the make-do bandage, pressed a kiss to my forehead. He lingered, as if taking a moment to reassure himself that I was there. "That'll do for now. And thank you for centering me."

"You're welcome. Thank you for bandaging me. Now, let's go see how we can help."

It had been a long time since I'd strolled up and down the streets of any neighborhood in New Orleans and simply stopped to talk to the people I passed.

The wedge of the Marigny had been a lively neighborhood, famous for the jazz clubs on Frenchmen Street, which had once overflowed with tourists and locals. To the east had been colorful Creole cottages, shotgun houses, and town houses that characterized New Orleans architecture. There'd also been a handful of warehouses and industrial buildings.

The neighborhood was considerably thinner now. The war had destroyed dozens of houses and buildings that hadn't been rebuilt, and Containment had taken down others to provide a better line of sight to the occupants, or to make room for Devil's Isle facilities. Still, even with the gap-teeth of empty lots and blocks, the Marigny was still New Orleans. It still reflected the city's history—the influence of the Spanish and French—even as it housed people who were new not just to New Orleans, but to our world.

A few of those stood on their narrow stoops or in the street, children close, as they looked around, watched us, or simply stared at the sky. This might have been the first time the children born in Devil's Isle had seen the sky without the green haze of the security grid. The first time they'd seen the blue. Some began to weep, to smile. And some looked rueful, as if angry they'd missed out on the color for so long.

Liam and I talked with two dozen people as we walked, and all the responses were nearly identical. They didn't like Seelies, they didn't know how information about the Seelies' attack could have been passed to Aeryth, and they didn't know anything about the Seelies' plans. If the Seelies had allies in Devil's Isle, we didn't meet them.

When we'd walked for two hours—and my hands were beginning to shake from excess magic—I knew I was running out of time.

"Let's go back to the store," I said. "I could use food, and we both need a break."

He wiped his brow, looked guilty. "We shouldn't have to take a break."

"In an ideal world, no. But I need to cast off, and I feel weird doing that here." Notwithstanding that I'd taught Sensitives how to do it, my casting off in Devil's Isle still felt like cheating. Unfair to be a human who could deal with her magic without penalty in a place where Paras had been imprisoned for it.

"You know how war works. It's hard on everyone—mentally, physically, emotionally. If you can take a few minutes away, a little time to clear your head, that's what you do. And don't discount the magic," I said. "It screws with your mind, Liam. It's no friend to humans, and yet we use and manipulate it because it's the best tool we've got. Sometimes it's the only tool we've got."

He looked at me for a long moment, and I watched the fight finally go out of his eyes.

"Break," he said.

"Break. They're going to want help searching, and that's right inside your wheelhouse. But Containment will have to get organized first. We'll find Gunnar, tell him we're going back to the store and he can find us there when he's ready for civilian help."

Liam's eyes warmed. He leaned down, kissed my forehead. "You're a marvel."

"Remember that next time you come up with 'I have to protect you' nonsense. I've had magic a lot longer than you."

When Liam snorted, I knew we were okay.

We found Gunnar near the gate, hands on his hips and squinting toward the sky at the workers who futzed with the transformer.

"They making any progress?" Liam asked.

"Hell if I know." He dropped his gaze to us. "You leaving?"

"Going back to the store," I said. "We need a rest."

"Be careful," Gunnar said, squeezing my hand. "The search is on for the Seelies, but this is a very big city, and it's going to take a hell of a lot of luck to find them. I'll be in touch once I've talked to the Commandant."

"You be careful, too," I said, and pressed a kiss to his sweaty cheek. They were all probably roasting in their black fatigues. Whoever had come up with that design idea, I thought, had probably never been to New Orleans in summer.

We walked out of Devil's Isle—and out of the Marigny—and the city became immediately quieter, more still. There weren't many people left in the city, and fewer still in the French Quarter, and we saw no one as we neared Jackson Square, the small park of grass and palm trees and overgrown shrubs, and the statue of Andrew Jackson that had bullheadedly survived the war. I stopped, watched a swaying tree, and felt calmer for it.

"I'm going to cast off here."

Liam looked at me, worked hard not to argue. But still looked around. "The Seelies could still be close."

"You know they aren't. They'll have wanted to get away from the Quarter, put space between them and Containment, and regroup."

He sighed, nodded. "You're right."

"It's my favorite thing to be. Besides, even if something happened, Containment HQ is literally right there." I pointed at the Cabildo, on the other side of the plaza.

Liam breathed out, and I could tell he was forcing himself to relax. "Be careful."

"Always." I stood on tiptoes, kissed him lightly. "Find me something to eat at the store. I'm going to need it."

And I left him standing on the stone slabs where psychics and artists had once hawked their services, and walked into the park.

He let me be, but I knew he wasn't done, that he wasn't over his imagined shortcomings.

I couldn't worry about that now. Not when my hands trembled and my legs felt like they'd barely carry me through the wrought-iron gate. I'd worry about him when I was in control of myself.

I grabbed a fence post to calm myself, jerked back after sensing the searing heat that had settled into the dark iron. I guess my brain wasn't working any better than the rest of my body.

Was this how the wraiths began to go? The body becoming numb and the mind following, until there was nothing but a base and primal thirst for magic? Until need replaced logic?

I walked to a curved oak, went down to my knees in a move that wasn't exactly controlled or elegant. And there, on my knees in the shade, I closed my eyes and gripped handfuls of grass until I could feel myself center.

I took several breaths, rolled my shoulders until the tension loosened. I'd done this dozens of times, but that didn't make it easier. It was still a small war—a battle between human and power that didn't like to be controlled. There was more than there should have been, and it had to be expelled carefully, deliberately—an exhalation of magic. And so it didn't sneak its way inside again, it had to be bound somewhere else.

But I hadn't brought anything to cast the magic into. I considered the detritus in my pockets—store keys, pocketknife—but they weren't big or solid enough. I looked around, and my gaze settled on Andrew Jackson, his statue still standing proudly in the middle of the park. He was on horseback, and he and the horse were positioned atop a large pedestal proclaiming the Union had to be preserved.

Jackson might have been an asshole, but the words still applied.

The stone and metal were plenty sturdy. And if I destroyed them, I'd blame the Seelies.

I looked at the plinth, focused my gaze on the sculpture until the rest of the world faded away, my peripheral vision blanked, and my attention narrowed to myself, the magic, and the make-do focus.

"Far from me," I murmured. "Cast away and bound, out of my hands, secured and safe."

I'd started using a mantra after war had begun again; it was harder to concentrate when guns were firing, or silence might be interrupted by air raid sirens. That's how I'd come up with the mnemonic for the students—because the mantra had worked for me.

I closed my eyes, but let myself reach out, feel the magic in the air. And while it might have been deadly, it was beautiful. Shimmering strands of power that sparkled in the air, particularly this close to Devil's Isle and its Paranormals. I could feel them inside me as well, the slight vibration of the threads that spooled inside my body, always grasping, always seeking more of itself, like drawn to like.

I visualized gathering the strands, pulling them together into a kind of sheaf. And slowly and carefully, I imagined drawing them from my body, the sensation cold and jittery, and leaving a hollow ache in my chest. But that was usual—and preferable to the magic overtaking me until there was nothing left.

I stayed very still, slowly batted my eyes open, and kept my gaze on the pedestal. On my target.

With the power cast in my magical grasp, I lifted my hand to the sculpture, imagined its size increasing until it was larger than me, a doorway, a closet. A place of storage. A place of confinement.

A kind of battery, if someone could figure out a way to pull the magic out again.

And then I shoved the magic into the metal and stone. The welds creaked as the magic filled and settled. The metal seemed to breathe as it absorbed the magic, molecules stretching to incorporate the power.

I waited for a moment, arm now shaking with effort, gaze trained on the sculpture, for the signal that my work was done. Or the explosion that would mean I'd failed.

One more wobble, and Jackson went still, accepting the offering.

The weight of magic lifted from my body, from my fingers, from my chest. I closed my eyes, raised my face to the sky, and breathed deeply, air filling the space where magic had been. For now, that was enough.

CHAPTER FIVE

I saw no one, Seelie or otherwise, on the walk back to the store.

The AC wasn't running, and the store was dark but for the light that slanted through the windows. The power was out again, probably because of the busted transformer or the magic that had literally fogged the Quarter. Magic and electricity weren't friends, and power outages were frequent.

I found a glass of tea and a bowl of red beans and rice waiting for me on the counter. While I appreciated the gesture, we made them on Sunday, as was the New Orleans tradition, and ate them through the week, supplemented by vegetables from the garden, unless something better came along. This week, like many other weeks, it hadn't—with the exception of Tadji's party. If I never had to eat red beans again, I'd be fine with that.

Liam came downstairs, naked but for jeans, a T-shirt in his hand. He must have taken a shower, had probably wanted to rinse away the grit of magic.

He paused when he saw me, hand on the banister. "You all right?"

"I'm okay. You?"

He nodded, came toward me. "I'm managing."

"Good. Because this is probably going to get worse before it gets better."

He kissed my forehead. "You are ever the optimist."

"Realist," I corrected. "Pragmatist. Better to see things the way they are than pretend otherwise."

He put a hand on my cheek, stroked a thumb along my jaw. "Some things don't need pretending."

"No," I agreed, closing my eyes and letting myself focus on the sensation of his hand, the soft and soothing touch. "Some things don't."

We opened the store and kept ourselves busy, offered bottled water to the few Paras and Containment agents who came in, sat down at the community table, and talked through what had happened. We'd left a pile of scavenged fans on the counter—card-stock ads attached to pieces of wood shaped like Popsicle sticks. They fanned themselves as they talked, wiped cold bottled water—kept in an old-fashioned metal cooler with a literal block of ice—across their brows.

It seemed friendly, communal. But there was something beneath it. A tension that hadn't been there at Tadji's birthday party or my practice with the Sensitives. A new kind of fear. A new kind of waiting.

The anticipation of terrible things to come.

Burke had been called into the Cabildo, interrupting his and Tadji's reunion, so she came to the store for the update. Tadji was normally stoic, but even she looked frazzled today.

"There's something in the air," Tadji said as we stood together behind the counter. A united front against . . . something.

"I know," I said. "I feel it, too."

"What do you think they're going to do?" she asked, wiping away water that had settled on the counter.

"I don't know. But I don't think 'judgment' means anything good."

"Yeah," she said, and tucked a curl behind her ear. "That's what I was afraid of."

An agent in fatigues came in, but from the strong stride it was obvious he wasn't there for refreshments or conversation. Tadji, Liam, and I watched him move toward us with a summons from the Commandant, delivered via a pretty card with gilded edges, a gold wax seal, and a flourished "G."

"He always had a thing for good paper," Tadji said, smiling at the card. "At least some things never change."

"At least," I said, and prepared for the beckoning.

The Cabildo had been the seat of New Orleans's government, the seat of the Louisiana Supreme Court, a museum. Now it was Containment's New Orleans headquarters. The interior was old—hardwood and columns and glass and chandeliers. There'd once been weddings in this space, brides and grooms making promises about love and lifetimes.

War had broken so many of the promises we'd made to one another.

I'd been to the Cabildo before Belle Chasse, had found Gunnar among the dozens of soldiers, analysts, assistants, and clerks who worked to keep Devil's Isle running and secure. The mood had been subdued and bureaucratic, and I'd been nervous about the visit, because magic had still been banned, which made my existence illegal. But I wasn't the enemy anymore, and there was a different energy in the building now, a focus that hadn't been here before. The difference between soldiers in peace and soldiers in wartime.

The windows were open to let in the minimal cross breeze, with people fanning themselves as they worked.

Gunnar came striding toward us, offered bottles of water beading with condensation. Gavin walked behind him, his own bottle nearly half-empty.

"Sorry for the note," Gunnar said. "I couldn't get away." He scooped a hand through his hair. He'd probably done that so many times to-day I was half-surprised he hadn't tunneled grooves through it.

"No problem," I said.

"You need food?" Liam asked. "We've got red beans and rice at the store."

"I'm all right. Mariah brought by some tamales."

"My Mariah?" I asked, glad he'd gotten food and jealous I hadn't been the recipient. Mariah was a hell of a cook when she could get the ingredients.

"Your Mariah. Pork, masa, spices. Exquisite."

"Jealous," I admitted. "Although it's gonna be hard for you to go back to MREs after that." Week-old red beans and rice were less of a stretch, unless Gavin flattened and fried them into the cakes he took on scouting trips. Nutritious, but mouth-puckeringly dry.

Liam looked at his brother. "How'd you end up here?"

"I was in Algiers," he said. "Enjoying a fine beverage at a little club I know."

"There's a club in Algiers?" Gunnar asked, brow lifted.

"It's the bed of an abandoned pickup truck and a fifth of Wild Turkey," Gavin said with a grin. "But it does the job. Couple of agents took a break from patrol. And drank only water," he added primly, glancing at Gunnar. "Found out from them, so I came down here."

We were all quiet for a moment.

"Did you bring the Wild Turkey?" Liam asked. War had done a number on even New Orleans's supply of booze.

"Wasn't mine to bring," Gavin said, lifting a shoulder. "But it went down smooth."

"Lest we should be late because we're talking about booze," Gunnar said, "let's go to the Commandant's office."

We followed him down the sunny corridor and through a door at the end. It was quieter here, with a few well-worn rugs muffling the sounds of footsteps on hardwood. Only a single desk in this room, where a tall and slender woman, cheeks flushed in the heat and hair pulled into a bun, clacked fingertips against the keys of an old typewriter.

"He's ready," she said, without looking up, and Gunnar walked to the door, knocked.

"*In.*" The Commandant's bass voice boomed through the door.

We walked inside, found an office that wouldn't have been out of place in a prewar law firm. There were two chairs in front of the desk, and two more in a corner seating area. The desk's wooden surface gleamed; it was a lovely antique. The art was good quality and gilt framed. A long table sat on the far side with a mix of chairs around it.

The Commandant smiled, came around his desk. He was a tall man with dark skin, shorn gray hair, and the build of a soldier. Still muscled beneath his fatigues, even though he'd been behind the desk for several years.

"I can see the appraisal in your eyes, Ms. Connolly. Antiques are one of your specialties, are they not?"

"It's genetic," I said.

"Everything in the building was salvaged or saved," the Commandant explained as I moved toward the desk. "Materiel wanted to fill the building with furniture from outside the Zone, have it all shipped in. Inefficient, to my mind, and it ignores the opportunity we have."

"Opportunity?" Liam asked.

"This is one of the most secure buildings in the city. I thought we should take advantage, bring in and save what we could." He gestured to the ceiling. "Two rooms upstairs are filled with tables, sideboards, silver sets, Baccarat."

I may have squeaked.

"Perhaps, if we make it through this particular fight, I'll be able to give you a tour."

"That would be fantastic."

Gunnar cleared his throat. "Very interesting girlfriend you have there, Liam."

"She's a unique treasure," Liam said.

"Not unlike the desk," I said with a smile.

Malachi walked in, looking generally uncomfortable. I bet he'd been in the Cabildo before, but he certainly didn't look eager to repeat the experience now.

"Malachi," the Commandant said, and they shook. "Now that we're nearly all here, let's move down to the briefing room."

"Nearly all?" I asked quietly, as we followed the Commandant into the hallway. "Who else are we waiting for?"

"No idea," Liam said, squeezing my hand. "Political leaders? Paranormal debutantes? Vampire butlers?"

I glanced at him. "Right off the top of your head?"

"I'm a clever man, Claire."

I couldn't argue with that.

It was my first time in an official briefing, and I wasn't disappointed to find the briefing room looked a lot like those I'd seen in cop shows growing up. Lines of tables in a rectangular room with a podium at the front. Except the tables and chairs were a mix of cheap office plastic and scavenged Empire-style antiques.

Liam must have seen the desire in my eyes. "Keep a handle on it. You can antique the roadshow later."

"Quit talking dirty to me in public," I said, and at Gunnar's nod, we took empty seats in the first row, acknowledging the other agents who sat around us.

A woman walked to the door, looked inside. Rachel Lewis, Containment's operations director. She was a gorgeous woman, with pale skin, blue-green eyes, and a generous mouth. She also wore fatigues, her long, dark hair pulled into an immaculate bun at the back of her neck—not a single hair out of place.

"You'll remember Captain Lewis," the Commandant said, gesturing to the woman. "She's been coordinating the search for the Seelies."

Rachel nodded efficiently. "My apologies for the delay, Commandant. We've just returned to the Quarter."

"Understood, Agent. Take a seat."

She walked toward the tables, her gaze slipping from person to person, and all but jolting to a halt when she saw Malachi.

There was history between them, something that had happened during the first war, probably while they'd worked together to close the Veil. Something I didn't know nearly enough about.

She took a seat at the table across the aisle, gave her attention to the Commandant, who stepped to the podium, rested his joined hands atop it.

"We're here to discuss the Seelies, their likely targets, and the manner in which we will bring them all to Devil's Isle. Because we will bring them all to Devil's Isle."

There was no doubt in his tone, just absolute confidence in his people. No wonder Gunnar was so loyal.

"Gunnar," he said, gesturing. "If you'd start us off."

"Sir," Gunnar said. He'd stood a few feet from the podium, replaced the Commandant there when he moved.

"We're in the early stages of the investigation of the breach this morning," Gunnar said, and gave a brief summary of the escape and the attack, an update on the injuries and fatalities.

"We've searched Aeryth's quarters, found nothing. There was no destruction, no personal effects left behind. There are no other Seelies in Devil's Isle, and if she had Paranormal allies, we haven't found them. She seems to have been generally loathed."

An agent in the back of the room raised a hand—a petite woman with tan skin and straight dark hair pulled into a tight bun.

"Jefferson," Gunnar said, pointing at her.

"Were there Seelies in Devil's Isle previously?" Jefferson asked.

"Only two," Gunnar said. "Both were captured just after the war began, but they didn't last long in Devil's Isle. Ritual suicides," he added grimly.

"Seelies are proud, arrogant," Malachi offered from his position near the door. "They wouldn't be interested in being prisoners of war."

"And yet Aeryth didn't go that route," Jefferson said.

"And now appears to be interested in passing judgment," the Commandant said, without moving back to the podium. He looked at Rachel. "Captain. The status of your search to date?"

Rachel rose, hands behind her, shoulders back. "Sir. Based on the information provided by the Quinns, we searched the camp on the north side of the lake." She shifted her gaze to Liam. "They were gone by the time we arrived, no sign of the camp."

"They weren't all at Devil's Isle today," Liam said. "The camp was bigger."

Rachel nodded. "If the remainder has established a new camp, we haven't yet located it." She looked back at the Commandant, promise in her eyes. "But we will. Sir, we need more volunteers."

"We'll get to that," the Commandant said. "Before we discuss next steps and assignments, it's crucial that we understand who and what we're dealing with. Know thine enemy," he said, and shifted his gaze to Malachi. "And, fortunately, we have an expert in the house. Commander, if you could provide some background for the benefit of those who aren't familiar with this particular Para?"

Malachi looked around the room. His expression was unreadable, and I wondered if he was relieved to see a dedicated team of human allies, or if he'd have preferred a team of Paras like him, who could face the Seelies with magic.

Either way, there was no denying he looked perfectly comfortable preparing to brief a bunch of humans. He was a commander of soldiers, whatever their biology.

"There was war, once," he began. "Separate societies of beings who fought, killed, pillaged. The angels, the Seelies, the Valkyries, among many others. After much death and destruction, the Consularis—those who supported the creation of a unified council to rule our world—came to power. The world became more peaceful. Cleaner. Safer. Healthier. But . . . the same."

"In what respect?" a second agent asked, an older man with pale skin, a bulky build, and the closely cropped hair and short mustache that male cops and soldiers seemed to prefer.

"This is Agent Baumeister," Gunnar said to Malachi, who nodded.

"The Consularis believed the things that separated us should be minimized. That we would be unified only if we gave up our differences and found solidarity. Similarity, at least within the tiers of Consularis society."

"You mean the other cultures were wiped out," Baumeister said, his voice matter-of-fact.

"Not the beings, but the customs, yes. The language, the song, the dress, the mythology. All were exchanged for a new, unified tradition. A regimented tradition."

Malachi kept his feelings closely guarded, and rarely allowed emotion to peek through. Maybe that was the cost of having lived in rebellion. I watched him now, trying to figure out how he really felt about the conflict, the Consularis. But he didn't show it.

"There had always been those who did not support unification, the Consularis, the notion of the council. But they had also seen war and death, so they learned to live with their concerns. But as generations passed, and memories of the chaos faded, more and more decided they wanted something different."

"And so the Court of Dawn was born," Gunnar said.

"Yes," Malachi said. "Seelies abhorred unification, at least with outsiders. Internally, they are tight-knit. They held to their customs, their belief in their inherent superiority, even as the world around them rejected that idea. Joining the rebellion came naturally."

"And how did Aeryth end up in Devil's Isle?" Jefferson asked.

Gunnar looked at Liam, and concern narrowed his eyes.

My heart thudded in response as I realized what he was going to say.

"Gavin and I brought her in," Liam said. There was no fear in his voice, which made me feel a little better. He was smart enough to know whether he ought to be worried.

"We were on Grand Isle," Liam said, glancing at Gavin. "It was about two years after the war. We hadn't been looking for her particularly. We'd been in Breaux Bridge, had heard rumors about a band of Paras who were stealing supplies, food near the coast."

"It wasn't an unusual rumor," Gavin said. "Humans did plenty of stealing after the war. Some for need, some for profit. But we decided to check it out."

Liam picked up the story. "We made our way down to Grand Isle and heard the same rumors, including talk about a flying ghost who didn't have wings."

"A Seelie," Gunnar said, and he nodded.

"We found her by accident. Decided to stop for the night in an abandoned fishing camp—a small house on stilts," Gavin explained, "and we found her inside. She'd been dead asleep, was shocked to see us."

"Surprise was probably the only reason we were able to bring her in peacefully," Liam said.

"And our impressive physical prowess," Gavin put in, and the agents chuckled.

"I'm certain that was the case," the Commandant said with a mild smile. "Continue."

"She's thin," Liam said, "and she was even thinner then. Withered away, maybe because she hadn't been eating enough, because she was in hiding, because she didn't have access to the Beyond's magic." He looked at Malachi for confirmation.

"Likely a combination of all three," Malachi said.

Liam nodded. "We used cold iron cuffs, borrowed a jeep for the drive back to the city, had to camp out overnight when the power failed. We didn't trust her, and trusted her less on foot than in the vehicle. Eventually we made it back here, turned her over to Containment."

"I doubt she even remembers us," Gavin said, meeting my gaze. "As you've seen, she's not generally impressed with humans."

I nodded, grateful that he was trying to offer comfort, to relieve the concern that was probably obvious on my face.

Judgment, she'd said. But against who?

"Why was she so far south?" Rachel asked.

"We didn't get much out of her. She said she was looking for her sister, but we didn't have any intel about family relationships, so we weren't sure if that was true or not." He looked at Gunnar. "Did she ever discuss that inside? Her family?"

"Not that I'm aware of," Gunnar said, and glanced around the room, settled his gaze on someone in the back. "Flores is the supervisor for our problem children like Aeryth. Miguel?"

"Nothing," said the man behind us. "She rarely talked. And if she did, she asked questions."

"About what?" Malachi asked.

"Humans. New Orleans. The government. She liked information, and we'd bargain for it sometimes. Nothing confidential or classified, of course. Textbook stuff. Basics. She was smart, curious. I had the sense that knowing information made her feel, I suppose, a little more in control of her circumstances."

Malachi nodded, seemed impressed by the analysis.

"If Aeryth's been here for years," Rachel said, "why didn't they try to break her out before?"

"Because there weren't enough of them," Malachi said. "Seelies' magic is inherent, part of who they are, but they are what you might call collective creatures. The strength of their magic depends on their being together. Individually, they have potent but limited magic. But in an assembly, their power expands."

"Their magic snapped together." I hadn't meant to speak aloud, and all eyes turned to me, including Malachi's.

"What's that?" Gunnar asked, puzzlement in his face.

"When Aeryth joined them in the air," I said. "When they were together. I felt something click. Maybe like their magic had—I don't know—coalesced?"

"I am surprised a human could feel that," Malachi said, "and I suspect you are right."

"Sensitives are cooler than AC," Gavin said, giving me a supportive nod.

Rachel drummed a yellow pencil on the table. "So it actually benefited Containment that she was the only one captured."

"Containment would not have been able to successfully hold the entire group," Malachi said.

Gavin sighed. "So maybe she wasn't so much intimidated by us as just not at full capacity. That's a shot to the ego."

"You can handle it," Liam said dryly, earning chuckles behind us.

"What exactly are their powers?" asked an agent to our right. "They can fly; they can fight. Fog, wind. What about rain? Lightning?"

"They are spirits of air," Malachi said. "They cannot manifest rain, lightning. But they can strengthen it, control it, just as they controlled the wind today. And their own magic—the fog."

"Will she go back to the Beyond?" the Commandant asked. "Her desire for 'judgment' may apply to the Consularis if she has unfinished business."

"I doubt it," Malachi said. "She has more to gain, and less to lose, in your world. It was the Court's original plan, after all. To come here, to see, to conquer."

"So what's the judgment?" Gavin asked. "Punish Containment for imprisoning her? The other Paras for not helping her?"

"If she wanted to punish the Paras," Gunnar said, "she could have done that today. She was right there."

"True," Gavin said.

"She now has history in New Orleans," Malachi said. "In Devil's Isle. And I suspect she would not have mentioned her coming 'judgment' to an audience who'd never see it."

"You think she'll target New Orleans," Liam said.

"I think it's the most likely scenario."

"I don't imagine it will take her long to show us how she intends to issue her sentence," the Commandant said. He glanced at Gunnar, then at Rachel. "Finding them is now your number one priority. And as I have a satellite call with Washington—at least as long as electricity continues to function—I'll leave you to arrange it."

The agents stood as the Commandant exited, and then they looked at Gunnar and Rachel.

"The city has been broken into grids," she said, "and we'll continue to search each uniformly. We'll put drones in the air, but they'll only work when the power allows. We'll take as many human volunteers as we can get."

I looked at Liam. "I presume you're interested in hunting this particular bounty?"

"Bet your ass, *cher*," he murmured, and draped his arm over the back of my chair.

Rachel looked at Malachi. "You'll have a better view than most if you can canvass by air."

"I've been searching," Malachi said, and let no emotion show on his face. "And I will continue to do so."

I wasn't sure if he was rejecting her implicit request, or just stating a fact. Whichever it was, she didn't look fazed by it. Not being intimidated by the gorgeous angel was probably a requirement for dating him. He wouldn't have liked the wilting-orchid type.

Gavin clapped Liam on the shoulder. "We taking a ride to find some Seelies?"

"We are," he said, and looked at me. "But with an addition."

Gavin smiled at me. "Welcome to the club."

Bummer he hadn't brought the Wild Turkey. I had a feeling I was going to need it.

CHAPTER SIX

We were assigned a chunk of the city north of the Quarter that included Tremé and the Seventh Ward, and given flares to signal the rest of the teams if we found anything. Our job was to recon, to locate, and not to engage unless absolutely necessary.

The power was on again by the time we made it back to the store, and we luxuriated in the AC for a solid minute before heading out into swampy air again.

I kept a bag behind the counter with bottles of water, protein bars, first-aid supplies, and an icon of wrought iron that had once hung on the Ursuline Convent. The icon wouldn't have any effect on Paras, but cold iron worked as well as the fairy tales suggested. Liam's .44 could also do plenty of damage. They were as susceptible to gunshots as we were.

Tadji would stay at the store, which would serve as the rendezvous point while Containment worked on Devil's Isle. "I want more ice," she told Gunnar, who'd walked back with us to the store, with a pointed finger. "Our block is nearly gone. I know you've got it, and it's going to be miserable out there this afternoon. People need to stay hydrated. I want three bags, in the cooler, within the hour."

"Who's giving who orders?" Gunnar asked.

"You want sweetened peach tea?"

His eyes went big. "Yeah, I want."

She patted his cheek. "Then get me the ice, soldier boy."

Gunnar obviously wanted to argue, but his shoulders drooped and he headed for the door.

"That was effective." I was one of the few who preferred my tea without cups of added sugar. You could hardly taste the tea that way.

"I mashed a few of those fallen peaches you brought in, reduced it. I've been adding the syrup to every pitcher. It is addictive, which promotes good behavior."

"And serves as a really good bribe."

"Damn right," she said with a wink.

I narrowed my eyes when she offered Liam an old, plaid thermos probably filled with tea and ice.

"Where's my thermos?" I asked both of them.

She just grinned. "That's his reward for moving that heavy-ass bureau downstairs."

I glanced at Liam, my brows lifted.

"It was heavy-ass," he agreed, then gave me a wink. "I'll share my tea with you anytime, *cher*."

I bet he would.

We met outside at the truck, Gavin wearing an enormous straw sun hat with a strap that dangled under his chin, a long-sleeved white T-shirt, and a pair of wraparound shades.

Liam stopped, just looked at him.

"It's hot," Gavin said.

"And you think that's going to make you cooler?"

"Well, it will help." Then he held up a second thermos, smiled at me. "So will the tea."

I rolled my eyes, hitched a thumb toward the back of the truck. "Get in."

"I've got my own ride today, thanks." He gestured at a Containment jeep parked down the block. "I borrowed a vehicle." He looked at Malachi. "You want to ride or fly?"

"Air," he said. "I'll stay above you, drop down if we need to talk or if I see something."

"Works for me."

I stowed my bag on the bench seat between us, then climbed into the cab. Liam climbed into the passenger side, closed the door.

"Sometimes I think Gavin does these things just for the comic effect."

"You think?" I started the truck. "You're the hot one. He's the funny one. That's his thing."

Liam slid his gaze to me. "Excuse me?"

"Are you angry about the 'hot' thing, or the 'funny' thing?"

"I think I'm insulted by both."

"You're funny, too. But he's the class clown. Someday he'll settle down, get serious. But not today."

"Not with that hat," Liam said, glancing at his side mirror. "Probably has 'Fuck you, Seelies' painted on the top."

"You've just invented a new line of anti-Paranormal gear. You're the creative one, too."

"Well," Liam said after a moment, "that's something."

We drove through the Quarter, then past Congo Square and Louis Armstrong Park and into the heart of Tremé. We'd start there first, then work our way northeast into the Seventh Ward. And in the meantime, I had something on my mind.

"Do you think she'll target you?"

"Who?" Liam asked, but I could tell he was playing it off, pretending it wasn't a big deal.

"You know who, and you know why."

He sighed. The windows were down, his arm on the door, fingers tapping against the truck's exterior. "I can't imagine that she would. I think Gavin was right—we aren't individually interesting enough to matter to her. She could have easily hit me or you in Devil's Isle, and she didn't."

I wasn't sure considering the vulnerability made me feel any better.

He reached out a hand, covered mine. "Don't worry about it, Claire. She won't get to you, or me, or anyone else we love."

I nodded, blew out a breath to center myself. There wasn't any point in worrying about it; that was a waste of energy. We were all vulnerable here, and we knew it. And we'd stayed in New Orleans anyway.

"I'm sure we can find something else to worry about," I said with a smile.

And then I turned the corner . . . and the entire world slammed against the truck.

We flew forward, then back again, my head slamming against the back of the bench seat. And then we were spinning, and I could feel the world disappear below us as Tremé spun around us.

Something hit the windshield with a *crack* that echoed like a gunshot, and we touched the earth again, metal groaning as it battled concrete. We were slammed sideways again until wheels hit the curb and we bounced to rest.

For a moment the world was gray, spinning, and I stared through a fractured world. And realized a moment later that the world hadn't shattered. There was a spiderweb crack across Scarlet's front window.

A hand touched my face. "Claire."

I looked to my left, found him standing at the door, his face irresistibly beautiful, his eyes golden and shimmering. *Mine* was my first gut response. And it took me a moment to realize—to remember—who he was.

"Liam."

He smiled, just a little. And blood dripped from a gash at the corner of his jaw.

"You're hurt," I said, and couldn't stop the tears from welling.

"I'm fine. Are you okay?"

"I don't—" I touched my forehead, found blood on my fingers. "Cut, I think. But I'm okay. And my head is spinning. What happened?"

"Look at me," he said, and tilted my chin up, squinted as he looked at my eyes, and seemed relieved by whatever he saw there.

"What happened?" I asked again, and could feel the rising edge of panic.

"That," he said, and turned his gaze back to the windshield.

I followed his gaze, my movement slower than his—the world was still shaking—to poor Scarlet's glass. And then my eyes focused past the spiderweb to the neighborhood beyond it.

"Oh, my God." The words fell away as I pushed past him to climb out of the truck, had to grab his arm again when my knees wobbled. Gavin already stood, looking down the street, outside the Containment jeep, which hadn't sustained any damage.

The neighborhood had been annihilated.

The asphalt was beaten into chunks that speared up from the road. Trees were denuded, their bark stripped away. Houses were broken into splinters, into piles of wood scattered like tossed matches over what remained of the road. Vehicles were on their roofs, rusted bellies toward the sky, still wobbling.

And in the distance, debris spiraled in the air in a two-hundred-foot-tall column.

"Tornado?" I said, trying to process what I was seeing. "Did we run into a tornado?"

But that didn't make sense. There'd been no clouds, no rain, no wind before we'd turned that corner. There'd been warmth and humidity and smiles—and then the shattering.

"An artificial one," Liam said grimly. "A Seelie tornado."

And then we heard the scream.

"Help! Anyone? Someone! Help, please!"

"Shit," Liam said. "Light the flare," he yelled at Gavin. Without waiting for a response, we ran down the street and vaulted obstacles: a broken wooden swing set, the yellow swings limp on the ground; a bureau on its side, silk flowing like water from an open drawer; and candy-colored hurricane shutters torn from their moorings.

"Here!" the woman shouted. "Over here!"

"We're coming!" Liam said, and we kept running until we found a woman on her stomach on the ground, her pale hand extended to another that reached out from beneath a pile of wood and cabinetry. Maybe part of a kitchen wall?

It was Darby, our Delta colleague. She looked up, blue eyes wide against pale skin tracked with dirt and tears. A red bandanna covered her hair, and she wore dark capri leggings, a tank top, and sneakers. She looked back at the sound of our approach, and the fear in her eyes changed to relief.

"Thank God," she said. "A woman's trapped under here. I think she's broken her leg."

"What are you doing here?" Liam asked, going to his belly beside her to take a look. His fearlessness was occasionally terrifying. "You don't live in Tremé, right?"

Darby shook her head. "I was running. Then all hell broke loose, and I heard her crying. I can't move the bookcases or cabinets or whatever the hell this is."

There was an ominous creak as the entire pile shifted, settled again. Liam froze, hands in the air.

Sobs echoed from beneath it.

"It's all right," Darby said, fingers gripped around the woman's hand.

"It's going to be fine," Liam assured, looking through the gap at the woman beyond. He gave her a charming smile. "Just give us a few minutes for the rescue, yeah?"

Then he climbed back to his feet, wiped his hands on his jeans. "Too much for us to move quickly. I think this is one for you, Claire."

The words rang through me like a church bell. Something I could do. A way I could help.

I nodded at Liam, while feeling out the magic. An easy task, since the Seelies had left so much of it behind. And then I looked over the mountain that had once been someone's house. I needed time to assess it, to plan, to figure out how to move it without crushing the woman beneath. But there wasn't time. Not when it was already unstable, and a woman lay bleeding.

"What's her name?" Liam asked as I gathered filaments.

"Joanne," Darby said.

"Tell her to get ready, and to curl into a little ball as much as she can. Claire's going to move the pile. It might shift, so we want her to stay in that little ball until it's clear. And then we're going to help her out. Okay?"

"Okay," Darby said, and turned back to the woman. The sobbing grew louder; the woman was probably terrified. But I couldn't think about that. I couldn't worry about her and help her at the same time. I had to focus.

"Everybody out of the way," I said quietly, not even wanting to raise my voice and waste what little energy that would take.

"Everybody back!" Liam said, and began directing them back into the street.

It was going to require a lot of magic to lift it, to move it, to set it down again—and to keep it together and stable while it was airborne. But too much magic and I'd lose control completely. Or become overwhelmed by the power.

I pushed myself, pulling in magic right up to the knife-sharp edge of my control, until my fingers were shaking with it. I wrapped the magic around the pile, circling it again and again until it was wrapped like a rubber band ball.

"Get ready," I said, and felt Liam tense.

And I began to raise my hand, to guide it upward. Gravity fought back, gripping the slivers of what had once been a house like a lover refusing to let go.

I fought harder, heard a crack as wood shifted, but ignored it, and worked until sweat dripped down my face and there was a sliver of light between earth and debris.

Joanne let out a cry and I jolted, the material shuddering along with me, and Liam looked back.

"She's fine, Claire. Just startled. Keep going! You're nearly there."

That became my mantra. *Nearly there,* I told myself, and made myself push despite the heat, the overwhelming magic, the trembling arms.

"Now!" Liam said. I kept my focus on the pile, but caught their movement in my peripheral vision as they scrambled forward. Seconds later, Liam was carrying the crying woman, covered in dirt and grime and holding her right arm at an awkward angle, out and away.

"Clear!" he shouted back.

I dropped the magic.

The pile hit the ground with an earthshaking thud, and sent a cloud of dust and dirt and plaster into the air.

My vision dimmed at the edges, and I leaned over, hands on my knees, willing myself not to pass out.

"Claire," Liam said, rushing back over.

"Postconcussion magic maybe not a good idea," I said, pain beating my head like a hammer, eyes closed as I focused on not vomiting from the pain. "Very, very bad idea."

"All right," he said. "Just breathe. Can I get a bottle of water over here?"

I heard shuffling, and then cold plastic was pressed against my hand. I took it, stood up, pressed it to my forehead.

The chill seemed to push back the worst of it. After a minute, I opened my eyes again.

"Hi," Liam said. "Bummer we weren't dating when I moved into the town house. You could have hauled Eleanor's couch upstairs."

"I'm not available for rent," I said weakly, but appreciated the stab at humor.

"Damn right you aren't," he said, then put a hand at the back of my neck, pressed his forehead to mine. "You did good."

"Joanne?"

"Darby's checking on her, and Containment's on the way. You can probably hear the sirens."

I couldn't hear much of anything over the roaring in my ears, but didn't tell him that. It would only have made him worry, and I was pretty sure the effect would fade.

I breathed through pursed lips, and after a few seconds felt better enough to take a drink of water.

"I think she'll hold," Darby said, when Gavin had taken over for her. "You saved her," she said to me. "I'd give you a Good Samaritan badge if I had one."

"We should get badges or patches or something," I said. "For honorable civilian work during an asshole of a war."

"Gavin gets one in flirting," Darby said, glancing back at him. "Joanne's at least thirty years older than him."

Liam snorted. "Gavin's like the post office. Snow's not going to keep them from delivering the mail, and a little thing like age isn't going to keep him from checking out women. He's an equal-opportunity flirt."

Darby smiled. I might have still been addled from the whiplash, but I thought I saw something sweet in that smile. And . . . interested.

"You said you were running when you found her?" Liam asked.

She nodded. "It's the only thing that keeps me sane these days. Or as close as I'm likely to get. Then they came."

"You saw the Seelies?"

She nodded again. "I was running, and I've said that twice now." She shook her head, as if clearing it. "Sorry. I'm a little off my game. I heard this whirring, turned around, and they were there." She looked up, pointed at the sky. "In a circle, and the wind picked up. It felt cyclonic, but I couldn't actually see a tornado. Of course, there was no rain or debris field yet, and that's generally the visible portion of the—" She cut herself off with a raised hand. "Off my game and rambling. I ducked into an outbuilding," she said, gesturing to the mostly still-standing remains of a shed across the street. "Figured it would keep me hidden and safe from debris, and if the whole thing fell down, it wouldn't pin me. Joanne wasn't so lucky."

She looked back at the street, the houses mostly leveled, the street mostly impassable. "They'll destroy us if they can."

I looked at her, found nothing angry or sad in her expression. Just a kind of dark understanding.

"Yeah," I said. "They'll tear the city apart one block at a time." I looked back at Liam. "Containment has to stop this. They have to."

"We'll talk to Gunnar," Liam said. Because what else could we do?

Wings fluttered above us and Malachi touched down. The look on his face—anger tinged with sadness—said enough.

"How bad?" Liam asked.

"Nearly a square mile," Malachi said. "So much destruction."

"Why?" Darby asked. "Why are they doing this? Are they so angry at us? At Containment? At humans?"

"They already told us," Gavin said, putting a supportive hand at her back. "Judgment."

I caught a glimpse of something red, and thought at first a Seelie had stayed behind, either to cause more trouble or to watch us take all this in. But it wasn't a person. It was paint.

I stepped carefully across broken paneling and drywall that crumbled beneath my feet to the only standing wall of a former Creole cottage. It was salmon pink, the color deep and saturated.

A long stripe of deep crimson had been painted down the middle, the same color that stained the Seelies' faces. And beside the mark was a message: CALLYTH was written in large letters in the same wine-dark stain.

"They left a calling card," I yelled, and waited while they picked their way over detritus and joined me to stare at the wall. Silence fell as we looked at the mark. At the threat. At, maybe, a reason for the judgment the Seelies wanted to pass.

Anger was a wave that flashed over me, hot as the sun-drenched asphalt. We'd worked for years to keep New Orleans running. To survive the first war, the aftermath, the second. We weren't the aggressors; they were.

"Who or what is 'Callyth'?" Gavin asked.

Liam shook his head, glanced at Malachi. "Mean anything to you?"

There was a crease between Malachi's brows as he stared at the wall, tried to puzzle out its meaning. "No."

"I guess we'd better find out," Liam said.

A man came toward us, skin dark, patch across his left eye, dressed in jeans and a Saints T-shirt.

Tony Mercier was a New Orleans legend. He was Big Chief of the Vanguard, his crew of Mardi Gras Indians. He'd lost his eye in the Second Battle of New Orleans.

"Chief," Liam said. "You all right?"

Tony nodded, ran a hand over his dark, cropped hair, which was flecked with bits of drywall or insulation, as he looked at the wall.

"My house is two blocks upriver," he said. "Went to school, met my wife, raised four children in this neighborhood."

Past-tense verbs, because his wife, Clarice, had been killed during the war, along with his oldest son. His other three children had left the Zone.

"Heard the noise, came over." He scanned the horizon. "Not many left in Tremé. I'd counted that as a loss until today. Today, maybe something to be grateful for. Most of these houses were empty, but I don't imagine that was the point." He paused. "They're trying to erase us."

He shook his head ruefully at the wall, then moved back to the street, slammed the tip of his cane against the ground.

"We will not walk away!" he yelled, voice echoing through the silence. "We will not cede this ground to you who would take it from us. We will *not*."

Some didn't have the choice to walk away. Tony had found one more injured human, and two who hadn't survived the attack.

Containment arrived with Burke, but without Gunnar, who the agents told us was at the Cabildo, coordinating the citywide search for the Seelies.

"Did you engage them?" Burke asked as other agents worked to treat Joanne and began searching the other houses for survivors. Or those who literally hadn't made it out alive.

"Unfortunately not," I said, and was disappointed, because I'd had enough of Seelie arrogance, and was eager for a little violence of my own.

"We hit the edge of it," Liam said. "Turned the corner and drove right into it. Wind pushed the truck around, and then it was moving downriver. Darby saw them."

"I'll talk to her," he said, and glanced back at me. "Y'all might want to talk to the medics. Looks like you got roughed up a little."

"We'll hold," I said, and looked back at Joanne. "They should focus on her."

"I'm going to do that, too," Burke said. "You know anything about Callyth?"

"We don't," Liam said. "But that seems to be the key to this. Or at least one of them."

"In addition to the general sociopathy," Burke added.

"In addition," Liam agreed.

"Take care," Burke said. "I'm going to check on everyone else."

"My turn to say let's go," Liam said, and rubbed the back of my neck. "Some AC and water will do you good. You look disgusting." His face was marked with dirt and dripping with sweat. I assumed I looked about the same.

"I feel disgusting," I said, and used the underside hem of my T-shirt to wipe the sweat from my face. "I need a weeklong shower."

"Earmuffs," Gavin said, turning for his borrowed jeep. "I don't need to hear about your sex games."

Liam thumped him on the ear. "Keep your mind out of the gutter, *mon frère*."

"We live in the Zone," Gavin said, looking back at the street. "Life is much more fun with my head in the gutter."

We gave Scarlet a once-over, found no flat tires or leaking fluids. The windshield was cracked mostly on the passenger side, so she was still drivable, and we made it back to the Quarter without incident.

"I'm going to take a look at her," Liam said, when we reached the store and I climbed out. "Just in case."

I handed him the keys. "I'm going to take a shower." I didn't want to be grimy anymore or wait until we were back at the garage.

"I'm going back to the thing we're calling a bar," Gavin said from the jeep. "In case there's still Wild Turkey. Although I don't think there's enough booze in the Zone right now to make me feel better."

"Be careful," Liam said.

Gavin grumbled, but didn't argue. While Liam checked out the truck, I went inside, found a scattering of Containment agents in the store and Tadji at the counter. She walked around it to me.

"Thank God," she said. "I was worried. We heard the noise, the sirens. Knew they'd taken out part of Tremé, but we didn't get any details about who was involved."

Guilt piled onto exhaustion and irritation.

"We're fine."

"You're bleeding." She frowned at my forehead. "Go sit down in the back, and I'll get you a towel, a bandage."

I didn't want a towel or a bandage. I did want to sit down, to be quiet, so I went into the back of the store, sat down at the table.

Tadji was back in a moment with a damp towel and a first-aid kit.

She put the kit on the table, reached out with the damp towel toward my forehead.

"Stop," I said, and moved back out of reach. "I don't need to be babied. I just need some time to breathe."

Slowly, Tadji drew back her hand, but I could feel her eyes boring into me. And she didn't need to say a thing.

"I'm sorry," I said. "I'm so pissed off. So fucking angry, and it's not at you. I'm just—you're here." I put my elbows on the table, my head in my hands, tried to rub the headache out of my skull. And gave myself three breaths before I looked up at her again.

I expected to see the same irritation I'd given her. But she looked worried, not angry.

"I'm sorry," I said again. "It was bad, Tadji. It was . . . so bad."

She put the cloth on the table, pulled out a chair, and sat down beside me. "Yeah?"

"Yeah. A chunk of Tremé, completely wiped out. We managed to get a woman out who was pinned, but her house is gone. Tony was helping, and he's wiped out. We're all just wiped out. And when we have the energy, really, really pissed off."

"Being here," she said, lifting her gaze to the agents who talked in small clusters in other parts of the store, "living in war, can make you hard. I figure that's good and necessary in some ways. You need it to get through the day, to keep moving, to take care of yourself if you end up cornered." She looked back at me. "But being resilient isn't far from being callous, from becoming cruel. That's the part we have to learn to balance. That's the thing we have to protect against. Because, after all this, if we survive and the Paras are gone, but we've destroyed ourselves? Maybe the cost was too high."

She'd put it into words, this nameless dread I'd been feeling—or at least the part that wasn't just reflecting the Seelies' magic. It was the questions we'd asked ourselves a thousand times before, and would probably keep asking: When had we given too much to this city? At what point had we become sacrifices to what we were trying to save?

"We're doing the right thing," she said, lifting the cloth again. "So buck up, put on your big-girl panties, and let me clean that wound."

I could hardly argue with that.

I took a shower and balanced my magic, then came down again for water and a protein bar—and to let Tadji bandage my head.

As the day progressed, we waited for news from Containment about the Seelies, additional attacks, additional wounded.

And we weren't the only ones on edge. Rain fell, hours passed, and the conversations in the store grew louder—fueled by fear, loathing, and caffeine. And it didn't take long for the already-short fuse to reach the point of detonation.

A wooden chair hit the floor, and all eyes turned to two soldiers who stood at opposite sides of the table.

"The fuck do you know, Claude?" A soldier threw a hand of cards on the table. "You sit in an office all goddamn day."

The soldier across from him, who I assumed was Claude, pointed a finger, his body nearly vibrating with anger. "You think that makes me less than you? That I contribute less? You wouldn't have ammunition if it wasn't for me. You wouldn't have gas in that jeep you drive around town, and let's not pretend you've ever even fired on a Para, you asshole."

"Fuck you," the other one said. "This is all Containment's fault. All of it. Because paper pushers need a war to justify their existence."

They began inching around the table toward each other.

"Hey," Liam said, striding toward them. "Take a breath and calm down, or take this shit outside. No fighting in here."

"Come at me, asshole," Claude said, ignoring him.

"You think you could take me? You think sitting at a desk all day makes you strong?"

They were nearly in chest-bumping range when Liam reached them, put hands on their chests, and pushed them back. "You think this shit helps? You think infighting is going to serve us during war?"

The first guy turned his furious gaze on Liam. "You think we're going to win this fucking war? That there's a chance we save this city? There's no chance. There's no fucking point."

"So you want to just turn over your city to them?" Liam looked at each of them. "You're going to just give up? Is that what Containment taught you? Is that what war taught you? That humans should just be cowards and let Seelies roll over us?"

The first guy muttered something under his breath and looked away.

"Yeah, look away," Liam said. "Look away and pretend you don't know what they did, or what they're doing." He looked over the crowd in the store.

"Never forget," he said. "War is a bitch. But we aren't fighting because it's fun. If you wanted peace, you shouldn't have joined Containment." He took a step closer. "Now, either soldier up, sit down, and drink your goddamned coffee, or get the hell out of this store. Claire and Tadji don't have time for the bullshit."

The soldier's mouth worked angrily, but he didn't speak. He sat down, put his hands around his coffee mug, and brooded into it.

"That guy is so hot," came the whisper from somewhere behind me.

I didn't correct her, since I didn't disagree. "That was a powerful speech," I said, when I'd followed Liam into the kitchen.

"They come into the Zone thinking they're going to have an adventure." He lifted his water glass. "Welcome to adventure. Everything's hot but the coffee, and Paras constantly want to kill you."

"Hey, I made that coffee, and it was plenty warm. Until the power went off."

"Until the power went off," he said with a smile.

"Sorry to interrupt," Tadji said, stepping into the doorway, "but this just arrived." She handed over a white card.

"We are getting a lot of correspondence lately," I said, and opened it, scanned it. "Darby wants us to meet her at eight tomorrow at the museum. She said she may have found something. Something that could help bring down the Seelies."

"Then I know where we'll be at eight a.m.," Liam said.

Another thing I didn't disagree with.

Liam and I let Tadji and Burke close up the store and headed back to the gas station, raided the cache of chocolate Eleanor had sent, and climbed onto the building's roof with a half bottle of wine and a military-surplus sleeping bag.

Steam rose from the roof as we flipped rainwater off the tarp, spread out the sleeping bag, and sat down.

While Liam pulled the cork on the wine, I slid a finger beneath the chocolate's foil wrapper and was transported to my childhood, when the act of slipping chocolate from its prison was a reverent act of anticipation. Of the nearly-there. And then the bar, with its perfect squares and imprinted letters, was ready for devouring.

Liam hadn't bothered with glasses; that was just more to carry. I broke off a piece of chocolate, offered it to him. He took a drink of wine from the bottle, and then looked at me.

"You probably shouldn't drink if you have a concussion."

"Not a concussion," I said, and pointed to the bandage on my forehead, then rubbed the back of my neck. "Just a cut and some whiplash. Give me the wine or I will take it from you."

His eyes widened with interest. "Will you?"

"With magic," I said dryly. "No touching required."

"Disappointing," he said, and passed over the bottle. "The wine tastes like . . ." He smacked his lips, trying to decide. "What does it taste like?"

I took a sip, grimaced. "Like someone who'd never tasted a strawberry tried to imagine the flavor."

"And added eau de red plastic."

"With hints of gasoline," I said, and took a bite of the chocolate to get rid of the aftertaste.

The chocolate was a little waxy, and marked with white crystals that meant it had gotten too warm or cold during its journey to New Orleans. But it was delicious, and the simple reminder of life before the war nearly brought tears to my eyes.

"We take pleasure in what we can," Liam said. "In the little things. Like this." He lay back, crossed his ankles, and pointed upward. "Like that."

I looked up.

The sky was dark and clear, the stars bright. One of the planets—maybe Venus?—was a gleaming dot close enough to the crescent moon that it seemed to be nestled within the shadow.

"Come here," Liam said, and opened his arm. I put the chocolate and wine aside, and stretched out beside him, watched the stars spin overhead.

New Orleans was never entirely silent, even at night. Night birds cawed; animals rustled through grass and leaves. But there were no guns or blasts, at least for the moment.

In the quiet, Liam began to sing. His voice was soft, the words in

Cajun French, a lullaby Eleanor had sung to him and Gavin as children. He broke it out occasionally in times like this, when it was easy to imagine he was home again on the bayou, with glassy black water and soaring pelicans.

"Fais do do," he sang quietly, and in the darkness, I began to drift to sleep.

CHAPTER SEVEN

I wouldn't say I was feeling more optimistic as we drove to the French Quarter the next morning, but a good night's sleep and a reliable partner didn't hurt. Yes, we were in a crisis, but we'd handled crises before and lived through them. We'd figure out a way to live through this one.

Not that we had another choice.

We rode in silence, and our destination wasn't the store but the brand-new—at least by New Orleans standards—headquarters of Delta. Me, Burke, Liam, Malachi, Darby, and Gavin were members.

Darby had picked the New Orleans Pharmacy Museum, a salmon pink three-story building that had once housed a nineteenth-century apothecary shop. She'd left the slightly creepy interior—wood and stone and thousands of glass bottles containing powders and concoctions—intact, and did her work at the former soda fountain and mixing table.

It had rained overnight, and the Quarter's streets were wet and dotted with puddles. The thick and unmistakable smell of post-rain New Orleans hung heavily in the damp air.

The museum was on Chartres and only a couple of blocks from the store. We pulled up in front, found Malachi in the middle of the street, wings extended. As we hopped out of the truck, he lifted them and, with a rush of air, pushed them down again. The force blew back our hair and sent a fine spray of water in our direction.

"Um," Liam said, wiping a hand across his face.

Malachi looked back, and his expression went unusually sheepish. "I'm sorry," he said, wings folding and disappearing again. "I didn't know you were there."

"I'm sure there's a joke in here somewhere," I said, and wiped a hand across my face, "but I'll leave it to Gavin to make it."

There was chuckling behind us. We glanced back, found Gavin leaning against the hood of the truck. "How did you not know he was going to do that?"

"Because Consularis grooming techniques aren't our area of expertise?" I said.

"More's the pity," he said, and walked to the museum, pulled open the door. "Let's go see what our friendly scientist is up to today."

"Do me a favor," Liam said to Malachi, hands on his hips and gaze narrowed as Gavin walked inside.

"What's that?"

Liam slid his gaze to Gavin. "Next time, aim for him."

I'd been to the museum only a couple of times. Darby had been working directly with Containment, and I'd been teaching, working on the garden, and helping Tadji in the store (and that was role reversal enough).

Added to that, the place was just creepy. It had been a functioning apothecary shop and it still looked it. As if the pharmacist had simply up and walked away from his job. There were plenty of houses in New Orleans in the same condition—everything left behind when humans evacuated. I found them equally unsettling, maybe because they reminded me of how isolated we'd become.

The inventory, on the other hand, I was into. The antique jars, the marble soda fountain, the wooden display cases, would have brought a pretty penny in a place with an actual market for antiques, which New Orleans wasn't anymore.

Darby wasn't in sight, so I knocked against one of the countertops that still held a display of concoctions and scales. "Knock, knock. Anybody home?"

The floor began to shake, and I first thought we were under a Seelie attack.

But the man who stepped into the room was no Seelie. He was enormous. At least six and a half feet, with the build of a man who spent a lot of time lifting weights. His bulging arms strained the seams of a yellow T-shirt bearing a purple triangle, and the shirt ended just above the hem of a dun Utilikilt. His skin was golden tan, his head bald, and his features were broad.

And in the middle of his forehead was a single, blinking eye, the iris a swirl of glimmering gold.

I wasn't sure if he identified as a Cyclops, but that was the best word I had to describe him.

"Who's asking?" the man said, his voice like boots on gravel.

"Claire and company," I said, not entirely sure where I was supposed to look. At the eye? Definitely not at the eye? He worked the fingers of his meaty hands, pulling each one in turn to stretch or pop knuckles. I didn't want to trigger him to use them on me.

He squinted suspiciously as he looked us over. "What do you want?"

"Darby asked us to come."

"I'm Lowes."

"Hi, Lowes," I said. "It's nice to meet you."

"It's *Lowes*."

He said the name more slowly, obviously trying to correct me, but I had no idea what he was saying differently, or what I'd missed.

"Lowes?" I offered hesitantly, and noticed that Liam, Gavin, and Malachi had gone suspiciously silent behind me.

"*Lowes,*" he said again, loudly enough that glass jars rattled around us. Since I was obviously still missing something, and half-afraid the next bellow would shatter every bit of glass in the place like a sour note, I glanced back at Liam.

"Fix this."

He bit back a smile, stepped forward. "I'm Liam," he said. "You're Lowes?"

The man nodded. "Lowes."

I'd have sworn on a stack of antique family Bibles that Liam had said the exact same thing I had, but no matter.

"I'm her new assistant," Lowes said. "I help with the science."

"I'm glad to hear she's gotten some help," Liam said. "Could you tell her Delta is here?"

That was apparently the pass code, as Lowes immediately straightened. "I'll find her. Tell her."

"That would be great. We'll just wait in the courtyard," I said.

The wooden floors creaked angrily as we moved toward the door. Liam held it open, smiled as I walked through.

"What?" I asked suspiciously.

"You have to be sure to pronounce the 'L.'"

"It's the first letter of his name, so I was obviously pronouncing it."

He grinned at me. "I'm sure you'll get it with practice."

I just managed not to growl at him.

—————

I liked the courtyard a lot more than the building's interior. Courtyards were to the French Quarter what backyards were to Metairie. Pretty much everybody had one. They were usually behind the buildings, or nestled between facing buildings, with lots of brick and plenty of greenery. There were probably fountains and wrought-iron bistro tables or benches, and with the shade and water, they were usually the coolest places on the block.

This one was a long and narrow rectangle with troughs of plants along the sides, including angel's trumpet that had grown large enough to buckle the brick and tower over the space, and an oval fountain at the far end. There was a trellis of bougainvillea and a long and well-worn table in the middle, surrounded by mismatched chairs.

Burke already sat at one of them, hands folded in his lap as he leaned over to study a notebook. He looked up, expression grim. "Darby thinks she's found something?"

"That's what she said," Liam said with a nod, and we sat down to wait in the shade.

"Sorry," Darby said, squeezing through the door a minute later, wearing a lab coat over flats, leggings, and a flowy red shirt. Her dark hair was shiny, her eyes framed by red glasses.

"I hear you met Lowes," she said.

"You're pronouncing it wrong," Liam said.

"Oh, I know." Darby grinned. "He tells me constantly."

"I still don't hear it," I said.

"You have to really hit the 'L.'" This time, Liam and Burke said it together.

I just ignored them.

"Moses recommended him," Darby said. "Apparently they were close in DI." She glanced at me. "How's your head? Gunnar said you were banged up?"

"Much better." I pointed to the bandage. "Just this at the moment."

"And Liam has one to match," she said, noting the bandage at his jaw.

"You said you had an idea," Liam said. "Something to help us with the Seelies."

She looked at me, frowning with concern, and I knew I wasn't going to like it.

"I do," she said. "But it's from Laura Blackwell's notes."

The woman who'd used her brains, tools, and power to try to destroy Paranormals—Court or Consularis. The woman we'd stopped seconds before she'd injected poison into the Veil. The human currently in prison in Devil's Isle.

My mother.

This week just kept getting better.

Emotion thrummed through my body like a plucked string. I wasn't sure if it was anger or sadness or betrayal that Darby was bringing Blackwell into play again, making her part of this. I didn't want her to be part of anything.

I'd spent enough time in the last few months worrying about how much of her I carried. Was she the reason I loved to fix things? Because she was a scientist? Was she the reason I'd been alone for so long? Because, like her, I'd pushed others away.

Talking about her—learning more about her—meant the possibility I'd also find out we had similarities. I didn't want to be like her any more than I wanted to think about the fact that she'd left me and my father because she hadn't cared enough to stay.

"I got the notes, her research, all the documents collected when she was arrested," Darby was saying. "A lot of it's useless. Ego-filled pap, theories about humans and Paras that edge a little too close to eugenics for my comfort. Numbers that don't mean anything."

She looked at me. "I didn't want to tell you that I had them, or that I was looking at them, until I knew if the search was going to lead to something. Her being your mom is bad enough. I didn't want to bring her up unless I had to."

My irritation at her faded away. "I appreciate the consideration. You think you found something?"

"I did. A device intended to nullify magic." Darby moved around some of the notebooks, pulled up a black one, opened it to a ribbon-marked page.

There was a pencil sketch across the page, the lines of some kind of sculpture or other object, thin and crisp. There were three pieces: a carved piece in the shape of a doughnut; a round jewel that sat in the "hole" of the doughnut and was cracked down the middle; and a crescent-shaped holder.

"Cake or glazed?" Gavin asked.

"Not a doughnut," Darby said. "Although I had the same thought. A weapon."

"It's called the Devil's Snare," Malachi said.

I looked back at him, found his gaze on the paper. And I couldn't read his expression. His tone was flat, his words measured and careful. Whatever he was feeling he was carefully holding back.

"You recognize it," I said quietly, and he nodded.

"What is it?" Liam asked.

It took another moment for Malachi to speak, and the silence stretched uncomfortably. "There were some who wanted the rebellion to be over sooner rather than later. The Devil's Snare was the weapon the Consularis designed for that purpose."

"What does it do?" I asked.

"As Darby said, it was intended to nullify someone's abilities. It was intended to strip the Court's magic, and thus their power, in order to bring them into line."

"That doesn't sound especially democratic," I said.

"The Beyond is not a democracy," Malachi said. "And the Consularis desired peace over chaos. Unity over uniqueness." He looked at me. "It would work like casting off magic. Except there isn't a choice, and it was intended to make no distinction between the purpose of the magic, the use of magic, Court or Consularis. It would be . . . devastatingly effective."

Gavin whistled. "A vacuum for magic would be a very effective weapon in a war against the Court. Whether in the Beyond or here."

"It would be an effective weapon against any creatures of magic," Malachi said, jaw tight. "But the weapon was only designed. Never created, never used. Who would have the moral and ethical right to wield it?"

"Who would have the ethical and moral right to ignore it?" Gavin asked. "When they make war against us through no fault of our own, don't they invite the possibility?"

Anger flashed in Malachi's eyes. "Of destroying who they are?"

"All due respect, man, they have destroyed lives, families, property. All because they didn't think they'd gotten enough respect in their own world."

"War is cruel," Malachi said. "As is the weapon." He looked down at the paper again. "I do not know how the idea found its way into human hands."

"Did the Court know about the weapon?" Liam asked. "Or the concept?"

"I don't know. The design was created shortly before the Veil was breached. It may have leaked, and the Consularis may have become nervous. The elements of the weapon exist." He pointed at the doughnut. "The Abethyl." He pointed at the center circle. "The Inclusion Stone. As far as I'm aware, they were never joined together to create the weapon."

"And then the Court learned about it and came into our world," Liam said. "And became someone else's problem."

"We could try to make one."

The courtyard went silent at Darby's words.

"I do not know if this weapon would work," Malachi said after a moment. "And more importantly, I do not know if its effects could be targeted—limited—so it doesn't strip away the magic of all of those within its reach. That could be deadly. The Devil's Snare is intended to eliminate part of who they are."

"The Consularis wouldn't have developed a weapon that would take away their magic," I said. "Surely they'd thought about that, factored it in."

"They may have," Malachi said, then gestured to the notes. "But these are sketches, ideas. They are not blueprints. There is nothing specific here about construction, about controls, about use. However far the Consularis got in conceptualizing this weapon, that detail is not here."

Quiet fell again, so the only sound was the trickling of water in the fountain, the chirping of birds.

"I'm sorry," Darby said, pulling back the notebook, rearranging the page marker, closing it again. "I thought this was something that would work. And now I've gotten everyone's hopes up."

"You haven't," Liam said. "You presented us with a concept the Consularis created. We don't have the elements, but we now have the idea. Maybe there's something in that we could work from." He looked at Malachi. "Something we could adapt and use—and control—here."

"I'll keep looking," she said.

"Not fast enough," Gavin said, and shifted his gaze to Darby. "Even if you came up with some way to harness this idea—and I'm sure you could—it would take time. Then we'd have to figure out a way to build it. To test it. What do we do in the meantime?"

"That's why we have Containment," Liam said. "To handle Para issues when they crop up."

"They have certainly cropped," Gavin murmured. "Patrols and drones aren't going to be enough for this."

"It's been twenty-four hours," Liam said. "War isn't won in a day."

"Too many days," Darby said, "and there won't be anything left here to win."

Liam looked at Malachi. "Then maybe we consider our other options."

Before Malachi could respond, the sky flashed red. Once, then twice.

My heart thumped against my chest, already anticipating the next battle. We were up in an instant and running back through the pharmacy and to the windows. But the street was clear.

Liam was the first one out the door, and I was right behind him.

We stepped into the street, looked around, and saw nothing until we turned lakeside and could see in the sky the pair of crimson flares, like double comets, harbingers of something wicked.

Something had happened.

We'd have only a few minutes to find them before the flares faded. I pulled Scarlet's keys from my pocket. "Let's go."

We left Darby at the museum to keep looking for ideas. Gavin in the bed, me and Liam in the cab, and Malachi overhead, we took Canal to Elysian Fields north toward the lake, following the flares like magi looking for a star. We went as far as Hayne, and followed two Containment trucks into a small parking lot near the railroad tracks.

I came to a stop a little fast and felt something roll in the bed, and realized with a wince it was probably Gavin.

Malachi touched down as Liam and I jumped out of the truck and agents spilled from the Containment trucks.

"What is this?" Malachi asked, wings folding behind him.

"It's Seabrook," Liam said. "One of the floodgates."

"I'm fine—thanks for asking!" Gavin said, climbing out and stretching out the kinks.

I ran across the gravel, where steel beams had been left to bake and rust in the sun, to the edge of the canal and stared down into the water.

New Orleans was a bowl. The north and south edges—the bank of Lake Pontchartrain to the north, and the bank of the Mississippi River to the south—were the city's highest points, and they were still below sea level. Everything in between was even farther down. Dangerous features for a tropical city of swamps and canals, including canals that led directly to the Gulf of Mexico.

New Orleans depended on a complicated system of pumps, canals, levees, walls, and gates that worked to keep the city dry. Without them, there'd be no New Orleans. Just a big and soggy puddle between the lake, the river, and the Gulf.

Seabrook was one of those protections. It had been constructed after Katrina. Tons of steel and concrete. There were supposed to be two wedge-shaped gates that spun around and two huge sluice doors that could slide down, both intended to keep rising waters in Lake Pontchartrain from flooding the city.

Supposed to be.

But the Seelies had destroyed them.

The concrete had been broken and crushed, the steel barriers twisted like corkscrews. Ropes of floats and buoys were twisted through the mangled mess like streamers.

The detritus of the gates now rose out of lake water that could inundate the city at will.

Destroy the city at will.

A waterspout danced gracefully offshore, a backdrop to the crimson mark splashed across the railroad bridge. And across the canal, agents stood over two motionless bodies.

Two more fatalities today. And that didn't include the deaths that destroying the gates could bring.

"Fuck these people," Gavin said beside us. "Fuck them completely."

"Yeah," Liam said.

A Containment jeep stormed into the parking lot, dust in its wake. When it reached us, Gunnar climbed out of the passenger seat, and he looked absolutely grim.

He was a problem solver and a smart-ass. But there was no humor in his face now, not as he walked to the shoreline and looked over the wreckage.

"They targeted Seabrook," Gunnar said after a moment, "because Tropical Storm Frieda has formed over the Bahamas. The current path sends it over southern Florida and into the Gulf. And then into New Orleans."

I swore under my breath.

"How strong?" Liam asked.

"The Atlantic and Gulf are unseasonably warm this year, so there's a potential for big." He looked back at us. "As big as the Storm."

The Storm was Katrina. The biggest and baddest of them all. Katrina's storm surge had nearly destroyed the city, and some areas had never recovered.

"How long do we have?" I asked.

"Three days, maybe four. Depends on how fast it makes landfall, how much it strengthens in the Gulf. Containment's going to send out some supplies, just in case."

"They knew," I said, looking back at the twisted metal. "They did this on purpose."

"Judgment," Liam said. "They destroy what we need to survive, our community, and they can watch us suffer—emotionally and physically—in the meantime."

"And they swoop in after they've cleared out the human roaches," Gavin added through gritted teeth.

"They won't stop with New Orleans."

We looked at Malachi. His wings were still folded behind him, as if he hadn't yet thought to let them disappear. Sunlight made them glitter like diamonds, which was a sad contrast to the grim expression on his face.

"They didn't stop in the Beyond," he said, "even with concessions made by the Consularis. I had hoped Aeryth's extraction, the neighborhood damage, might be enough for them. I fear I was wrong."

Silence fell as a trio of pelicans swooped low across the water.

"We'll see if the storm intensifies," Gunnar said, "and where it goes. In the meantime, prepare. Cover the windows; sandbag the doors; move what you can to the second floor. Stock water and candles. You know the drill."

I did know the drill, as did everyone else in New Orleans. We knew it was only a matter of time before another big one soaked the city. We just hadn't planned on dealing with Seelies, too.

"Anything on Callyth?" I asked Gunnar.

"Nothing yet. I've got as many people on it as I can spare." He glanced at Malachi. "If they're as insular as we believe, it's likely Callyth is a Seelie. Who else would they care about?"

"That's logical," he agreed.

"But it's not enough," Gunnar said. "We need to know who or what it is and why the Seelies are using it to exact judgment now if there's any chance of negotiation. Or using Callyth as bait."

I didn't like the sound of that, but we didn't have much choice. On the other hand . . . "If he or she was still alive, wouldn't Aeryth have asked for their release? Or help in finding them?"

Gunnar blinked. "Good point. Probably safest to assume she—and let's go with 'she' for ease of argument—is dead."

"So you check fatality records for Seelies," Liam said.

"Yeah, we do." Gunnar took a tiny notepad from his pocket, scribbled a note to himself.

"Callyth may be a reason," Malachi said. "Or Aeryth may have convinced herself that she is. But she would not be the main reason. Seelies attack because they desire to. They rarely need motivation. I would suggest you do not waste resources on that issue."

"Fair point. But hard to ignore when checking our records is one of the few things we can actually control." Gunnar looked back over the complex. "And so much else is out of our hands."

It felt like it was slipping away. That after fighting for so long, after battles and blackouts and MREs, this was the beginning of the end of New Orleans. The place where I'd grown up, where I'd lost two parents and found friends and love. Where my memories were stored. New Orleans was the city of my heart. I couldn't just let it go.

Liam put an arm around me, drew me close, rested his chin atop my head.

"We'll figure something out," he said quietly as I gripped his T-shirt in white-knuckled hands.

I nearly said that we already had, reminded him of the weapon design we'd found. But Malachi got there before I did.

"I think we may have to consider the Devil's Snare."

CHAPTER EIGHT

"That's the weapon sketch Darby found," Gunnar said, frowning as he looked at Malachi. "She sent me a note this morning. But the pieces are probably in the Beyond, right? And we don't even know if it would work?"

Malachi paused. "A portion of it is in the Beyond. But I believe another portion . . . is here." He looked at me, his gaze expectant.

"Here," I said.

"In one of your father's storage areas."

"In one of—" I felt dumb that it was taking me so long to grok what he'd meant—in the garage, in my father's collection of magical artifacts. But I didn't remember seeing any piece of the Devil's Snare among that stuff, and I'd lived with it for some time.

"Are you sure?"

"Sure enough," Malachi said.

"Were you going to mention that?" Gunnar asked, his voice taking on a testy edge.

"No," Malachi said, unfazed. "Not least because it's only one piece of the weapon. But humans did not create this problem. You have done what you could to protect your people as you deemed fit, even if I did not always agree with your methods. It's time to consider something different."

"But the other half is still in the Beyond," Gavin said.

"It is," Malachi said. "Stored in the Citadel—a temple in the capital city. For now."

"For now," Gunnar repeated. "As in, until you retrieve it?"

"No," he said. "Until *we* retrieve it. Me, Gavin, Liam, and Claire."

Gunnar's eyes went huge, and I could feel Liam tense beside me.

"Are you out of your fucking mind?" Liam asked.

"Not that I'm aware of."

"Exactly what a person out of his mind would say," Gavin muttered.

"How badly do you want to save your homes?" Malachi asked. "I think it's probably time for a bit of insanity."

I could admit I was intrigued by the possibility of going into the Beyond, of seeing the place that had caused so many problems for us. But it was still the Beyond, an unfamiliar land of unfamiliar magic. And we were still enemies of at least some of its residents.

"Why us particularly?" Liam asked. "We're humans, none of us are active military, and Containment's going to want to know your reasons."

Malachi smiled. "We are friends, are we not?"

"Sure," Gavin said carefully. "But friends don't let friends cross boundaries into enemy worlds, do they?"

Malachi just looked at him.

"And that joke did not land," Gavin said. "I'm giving the mic back to you."

Malachi looked down at Gavin's empty and outstretched hand, then shook his head and turned his gaze to Liam. "Because you're humans, and none of you are active military. Soldiers would be a threat. Regular humans, less so. Gavin and Liam are trained scouts; you know how to move over rough terrain. Claire and Liam have powers that might be useful, and both of you have been affected profoundly by magic. If we are to have a chance at bringing back the

Abethyl, we will need to show them, to demonstrate, how their inaction has affected you."

"So we're the examples," I said.

"In a sense," Malachi agreed.

"Have humans been in the Beyond before?" I asked.

"I don't know of any reliable reports of humans crossing the border," Gunnar said, glancing at Malachi. "You?"

Malachi shook his head. "No. But other than the magic, our worlds are similar chemically, so your humanity should not present a biological problem."

"But the magic's the problem, isn't it?" Gavin asked. "Can Liam and Claire even survive a trip through the Veil?"

"Way to finesse that, brother o' mine," Liam said.

"No point in beating around the vetiver."

"Bush."

"Whatever. Malachi?"

"To be honest," he said, looking at me, "I'm not entirely certain how your bodies will react to the magic. I assume absorption will be an issue."

"Going through the Veil was hard," I said. "I mean, I haven't been into the Beyond per se, but when the Veil moved over me, it was intense. You can't immediately become a wraith, right?"

"We will check your levels before you enter the Veil, and keep an eye on them while you're there."

"And if we don't?" Liam asked. "What's the risk?"

"Death, I imagine."

"Oh, good," Gavin said. "What about Liam?"

"There may be no effect, at least immediately, since his body is not absorbent in the same way as Claire's."

"Because Claire's a magic mop," Gavin said, and Liam slugged him in the arm without bothering to look.

"In a sense," Malachi said kindly. "But the temptation for Liam to draw on another's power will likely be greater, because their power will be greater."

Gavin frowned. "Consularis are more powerful than Court, you mean?"

"No, but power in the Beyond is greater than power outside it. The root of magic is in the Beyond, not here. Distance to that root, access to it, matters. You'll want it more. And it will be more powerful if you use it."

There was grim determination in the set of Liam's jaw as he fought his own inner war. He took a drink of water, then leaned against the truck and looked out over the lake.

"I don't see that we have a choice," Gavin said. "We try this— hard as it may be—or we let them win. We let them destroy New Orleans and wash our hands of it."

"We have to try," I agreed. "We don't have a better idea, and we can't just walk away. It wouldn't be right."

Liam looked back at me for a moment—pride and concern dueling in his face—then at Malachi. "We'd have to go through the line to get to the Veil," he said. "Then go into the Beyond, make it to this Citadel."

"I could get you to the Citadel," Malachi said. "It's approximately twenty miles from the Veil to the city, another mile to the building. And then convince them to provide the Abethyl."

"And the ethical issues?" I asked quietly.

Malachi looked over twisted steel and broken concrete. "As I said, you are at war, not by your doing, but because our world interjected its issues into yours. It would hardly be fair of me to prohibit you from using a weapon we designed, when it might make a difference. Darby has impressive skills, and she might be able to create safeguards. And even if not . . . I was among those who brought war into your world. Not willingly, but still. If I take no risks in order to stop it, am I any better than the Seelies?"

Gunnar's expression softened.

"If the tropical storm is one of the reasons we're going," I said, "could we get into the Beyond, get the Abethyl, and get back in time to actually do any good?"

"One day to the Citadel," Malachi said. "We discuss, we get the Abethyl, we return. If all goes well, it's a two-day trip."

If all goes well. Four words loaded with hope and danger and assumptions. And if all this risk was going to be worthwhile, I knew there was one more box we'd have to check. "We have to talk to her first. To Blackwell."

I hated that I had to say it. Hated that I had to suggest anything that would put me in the same room with her. But that was the reality of our situation.

I looked at Malachi. "You said the drawing was only a concept, not a blueprint. Blackwell might have information that isn't in these notes. And if we're going to try to make this work, we're going to need more details. We don't have time for Darby to start from scratch."

"She might lie," Liam said. "She might not tell us, any of us, the truth. And she might not talk at all."

"I think she has enough ego to talk," I said. "But you're right about the truth. We can try to verify what she tells us, but I think we have to ask."

An agent called Gunnar's name.

"I'll be right there," he said, without shifting his gaze from me. "I don't have time to discuss this right now, and I think even the suggestion is insane." His voice was low and angry, words tight as he worked to maintain control. But then he looked back at Seabrook, at the body bags Containment was moving into transport vehicles as Gavin made a cross over his chest with his fingertips.

"But talking to Blackwell is easy." He looked at me. "I mean politically, if not emotionally. We can arrange that, see what we find out. And depending on how that goes, we can talk about the rest. But I'm not making any promises."

With that, shoulders still tense, he walked away.

"Containment's going to want the weapon," Gavin said, watching as soldiers with very large weapons patrolled the site. Then he shifted his gaze to Malachi. "They'll want to use it as a weapon against Paras here, or at least a deterrent for anyone who might think of coming through the Veil later."

Did we trust Containment with that kind of power? God knew I loved Gunnar, liked Burke, and respected the Commandant. But they were pieces of a very big puzzle.

One that had included my mother.

"Leave that to me," Malachi said.

Gavin stayed behind to help Containment, and I drove Scarlet back to the garage.

I led Liam and Malachi into the basement, where we'd packed the rest of the magical objects into the army-surplus trunks my father had kept downstairs.

"Everything I haven't already given you is here." I gestured to the trunks. "So I guess we better start unloading."

We'd spent ten minutes unlocking and opening them when Malachi drew out a long, thin object wrapped in newspaper. He unwrapped it, revealing a heavy gold staff with a circular glass case on top. The case was surrounded by a waving frame of the same gold, and an arcing halo of gold stars across the top.

He opened the glass, tipped the contents into his palm. And there sat a circular stone in gleaming red, with a white crack running through its interior. "This is the Inclusion Stone. The element that sits in the center of the Devil's Snare."

"In the doughnut," I said.

Malachi blinked, and I waved him off. "Never mind. What about the staff?"

"No," he said. "The vessel isn't ours."

"It's Catholic," Liam said. "Called a monstrance. It's used to carry the Host in processions. Here," he said, and held out his hand to Malachi, who handed back the now-empty staff. Because I'd trained him well, Liam wrapped it thoroughly again.

"I wonder how the Inclusion Stone ended up in this thing." He glanced at me. "Did you happen to see your father bring this in? Or talk to him about it?"

I shook my head. "First time I saw it was in the gas station. It wasn't unusual for him to buy religious items, but they didn't pop up very often. I don't know where he got this one." I looked at Malachi. "Do you?"

He shook his head. "I'd seen the staff—the monstrance—when it was upstairs with the other items. And I'd seen the glint of red, but hadn't put together exactly what it was until we saw the sketch. I don't know how it ended up in this world, or in your father's possession."

"What was the stone for?" I asked. "In the Beyond, I mean?"

"In the common history of the Beyond, it was a relic of a great battle." Malachi turned it over in his hand. "When the world was created, the two great gods—darkness and light—fought for control of the land, for the hills and rivers, the trees and stones, the riches and jewels.

"In particular, they both wanted a garnet from the Great Hill that shone bright as a beacon. Darkness wanted to take it because he believed the darkness should be complete. Light wanted to take it because he wanted no competition. In their fight, they damaged the stone, causing it to crack and creating the inclusion."

"How did the battle end?" I asked.

"In a draw," he said with a smile, "which is why we have night and day. Some say their battle continued in the sky, which is why days and nights grow longer and shorter."

Liam frowned. "So, what does it do? Why is it so important for the Devil's Snare?"

"On its own, very little. It has no innate power. But that's not to say it does not have value. Let's go upstairs."

When we had, he put the stone on the kitchen counter, glanced at me. "Use your magic to lift it."

I knew there was a trick—he didn't need me to pick up a stone he'd just held—but I wasn't sure what it was. So I followed the instruction I'd been given.

I closed my eyes, reached out a hand, and found plenty of magic inside the station from the accumulation of magical objects. I grabbed threads, silver and glimmering, and pulled them taut around the stone—and felt them snap into place, lock around the stone like the stone itself was pulling them back.

"Oh, wow."

I opened my eyes at the sound of Liam's voice . . . and stared.

The stone glowed a brilliant red—and sent shafts of glimmering gold through the air to the far wall, where they made a delicate pattern of shimmering and lace.

"Wow" was the only thing I could think to say, too. I dropped my "grip" on the magic and walked across the room beside the beam. It looked like someone had tossed delicate glass glitter into the air—and then frozen time to hold it in place.

"It's a prism," I said. "Not of light, but of magic."

"Exactly," Malachi said. "The effect will fade as the magic fades. It would require a continuous supply of magic to keep the effect going."

"It's beautiful," Liam said, staring at it a few feet away.

"Can I touch it?" I asked, looking back at Malachi.

"It's your magic," he said. And even Malachi, who was generally hard to impress, smiled contentedly as he stared up at the beams.

I extended my hand toward the light, and nearly shivered at the strange sensation. The magic was warmer than the surrounding air, and seemed to thicken it, if that was possible. Not unlike the sensation of the fog the Seelie had created, probably because both were physical manifestations of magic.

"It's amazing," I said, and nodded at Liam so he'd try it, too. He lifted his hand, skimmed fingers along the edge of the beam, and smiled brilliantly.

"It's . . . like good wine. Complex. Dark and light. Sunshine and shadow."

"That's Claire," Malachi said, a corner of his mouth lifted. "Not the stone. You're feeling her."

Liam's grin widened, and he winged up his eyebrows in what would have been a perfect imitation of Gavin. "Am I?"

I rolled my eyes, and turned my gaze back to the beam, watching until it faded, the glitter drifting away into the air. The stone itself grew darker, the shine fading, until the garage was normal again.

"Powerful," Liam said.

Malachi nodded. "It need not have magic to have a profound effect." He picked up the stone, slid it into his pocket. "That is half our mission."

Liam nodded. "Then I guess we better see about the other half."

By the time we got back to the store, Gunnar and Darby were already waiting.

"You find it?"

"We did," Malachi said.

"Good. We've got approval to talk to Blackwell." He looked at me. "Right now. I'll drive us over."

I guess I wasn't going to freshen up before seeing her. Not that I cared what she thought of me, but an estranged daughter liked to make a good impression.

"Okay," I said. "Let's go see her."

A T-shirt would have to do.

She was being held in Devil's Isle, and the irony didn't escape me. A prison for Paranormals, now also a home for refugee Paras and a prison for a human who'd tried to eradicate them.

Gunnar drove us to a low building, and not very large. Three squat windows, and a door right in the middle. The rusting tin roof was pitched high toward the back, and the exterior had been a shade of dusky green, at least based on the peeling strips of color that remained. DIXIE BEER had been painted in enormous white letters across the front. A steal at forty-five cents a glass.

"We've used it for solitary confinement," Gunnar said. "Mostly for humans who need to be kept apart from the Paranormal population."

He pressed his hand to a plate beside the door. Locks opened with a click, and he pushed inside.

Containment had left the original exterior, probably to disguise the building's purpose, but remodeled the inside. The front room was small and Spartan but well lit, with an old desk and a few chairs. A Containment officer at the desk rose to attention when Gunnar entered.

"Sir. I received the memo that you'd be visiting." He glanced at us and made a quick visual inspection, and his eyes widened when he reached me.

We looked alike, Laura Blackwell and I. I guessed he'd noticed that.

"Problem, Officer?" Gunnar asked mildly, stepping just enough to put his body in front of mine—and break the soldier's line of sight.

"No, sir," he said, quickly looking back at Gunnar. "No problem. You'll find the detainee down the main hall and to the right."

"Thank you. Does she know we're here?"

"No, sir. She was apprised that someone from Containment wished to speak with her, but not about the details or the individuals. For what it's worth, she's still angry about being incarcerated. And conditions are not to her liking. She has . . . many suggestions."

Of course she did.

"Not a surprise," Gunnar said. "But thank you."

He nodded, and we walked into the narrow hallway, which was dark except for a light on the far right-hand side. A guard stood at the end beneath a pinpoint spotlight.

Gunnar stopped, looked back at me. "You ready?"

I breathed once, nodded, and slipped my hand into Liam's. He squeezed back. "Let's get this over with."

The walls on both sides of the hallway had been replaced with bars, creating small cells that were currently empty of prisoners. The light, I assumed, was hers.

As we moved, lights in the ceiling turned on, casting a soft glow through the hallway.

We reached the end, turned to look into her cell.

It was a square, with a small bed on one side and a desk on another. No sink or toilet, so I assumed they let her take care of necessities elsewhere. She wasn't a physical threat. Just an intellectual one.

She sat at the desk, back straight and feet on the floor as she read the book open in front of her. She was a lovely woman, with pale skin and long hair in the same shade of red as mine. She looked more drawn now; there were hollows in her cheeks, shadows under her eyes, and the dingy gray uniform didn't do her any favors.

She glanced over at us, measuring Gunnar, Darby, then Liam and me in turn. There was no emotion in her gaze, just mild curiosity twined with what I thought was boredom.

"What do you want?" Her words were clipped, efficient.

"Ms. Blackwell," Darby said. "I'm Darby Craig. I'm a research scientist with Containment. You know Gunnar, Liam, and Claire. We need to talk to you."

She rolled her eyes, turned back to the book. "I'm under no obligation to speak with anyone without an attorney."

"We're not here about the charges against you," Gunnar said, "and we're not trying to garner information to be used against you. We're here about one of your Containment projects."

With a sigh, she put a slip of paper in the book, closed it. Then she turned in her seat and crossed her legs and arms, giving us her attention. She looked bored—unless you noticed her eyes. There was a spark there she hadn't quite managed to hide.

"Which project? I was involved in many."

Darby pulled a copy of the Devil's Snare drawing from her folder, held it up against the bars. "This one."

Blackwell's gaze shifted from Darby to Gunnar to Liam to me, and the calculation in her eyes was obvious. I knew what she was going to say before the words fell away.

"You have to pay for information."

I nearly objected, but a look at Gunnar prevented me. There was a glint in his eyes I appreciated. "Ms. Blackwell, considering the charges against you, the accommodations are nicer than you deserve. You should be in Devil's Isle with the Paranormals you worked so hard to destroy. If, however, you'd prefer to stay here, consider these accommodations your prepayment for the information you're about to provide to us."

Blackwell's mouth worked, but she didn't speak. I'm sure she was smart enough to understand the threat. "What do you want?"

Gunnar tapped a finger against the paper Darby still held up. "Tell us about the Devil's Snare."

"A weapon created by Paranormals to fight Paranormals. Cannibalistic, but there you are. It's intended to nullify magic."

"How?" Gunnar asked.

"Magic is energy, and energy can be manipulated. The Snare was very clever. It utilized magic to counteract magic, much in the way an electromagnetic pulse affects electronic devices."

"How did you find out about it?" Darby asked.

"Not all Paras were located when the war was over. During the first several years after the Veil was closed, Containment would occasionally find Paras who'd evaded capture. They were brought in for questioning—to find other Paras in hiding, to get information about the Beyond, about whether the Paras would try to open the Veil again. We had means to obtain the information we needed."

"They were tortured." They were the first words Liam had spoken, and they were powerful. But my mother was a hard woman, and her expression stayed mild.

I had to work to keep my expression blank, to keep from reaching out and throttling that blasé look off her face. Lives were at stake. And she hardly seemed to care.

She slid her gaze to Liam, her expression almost prim, and looked at him for a moment. "You were a bounty hunter. You know how the system works."

"I returned only enemy combatants," Liam said. "And then only to Devil's Isle. Never for intelligence, and never for rendition."

"Beggars can't be choosers, I suppose. These were also, as you say, enemy combatants. Individuals waging a war against us. We took what information we could by whatever means were necessary."

"They *were* combatants," Gunnar said. "You admitted this was after the war was over. And as you're certainly aware, many who fought didn't do so by choice. They were magically conscripted."

"Many humans were drafted into wars that shouldn't have been waged. That doesn't change their culpability." She waved away the concern like she was flicking away an insect.

This wasn't the first time I'd seen proof of her total amorality, her sense that facts were more important than people. But it was still chilling. And it made me worry about how much of that was inside me. How much of her apathy I'd inherited.

"It's irrelevant now. We learned what we learned."

"Which was about the Devil's Snare?" Darby said, driving us back to the point.

"Among other things, yes. Not much of what we learned was useful. Much of it was directed toward their internal political struggle, which wasn't of interest to me."

My irritation ticked up another notch. Never mind it was the reason for the war's beginning, the reason for the death and violence and universal imprisonment, and the reason the war had started up again.

I felt Darby's eyes on me, wondered if she'd noticed my vibrating anger, or just recognized the fury on my face.

"So, you found out about the weapon," Gunnar said. "Then what?"

"We had the information, but we didn't have the components. This particular girl—I believe she was a nymph of some variety—believed at least one of the components had been brought here as some sort of symbolic gesture. A stone, I believe, but we were never able to find it."

She hadn't known my father had it, I thought. I worked very carefully not to smile. Had he put it in the garage specifically to keep it out of her reach, to keep her from using it? I'd never know for sure, but I liked believing that he had. It made me feel a hell of a lot better to imagine him plotting against her. Actively working to keep her from succeeding.

"Since we didn't have the objects, we tried to emulate the design with items we modeled and printed. We were in the process of building simple prototypes when our funding was stripped." And she did not sound happy about that.

"Why was it stripped?" Darby asked.

"Containment became suddenly risk averse about fatalities. We weren't certain how the weapon would affect humans. Containment was afraid humans would be injured because they lacked the protective layer of magic, so to speak."

"Containment thought the weapon would be deadly," Darby said flatly.

"It was only a small risk," Blackwell said impatiently. "There were no humans in the Beyond, so the weapon wouldn't have hurt them. I believed the benefits outweighed the risk."

It was a funny thing, human calculation. The way we weighed costs and benefits, lives against other lives. And how we'd reached the same conclusion, even though we'd done the weighing so very differently.

"What about the mechanism?" Darby asked. "How is the weapon supposed to work, from a technical standpoint?"

"We never got the complete details from Paras. The key element is apparently the rotation of the center stone. That's what spreads the effect of the outer stone."

That explained the prism we'd seen at the garage.

"And how did they address the possibility the weapon's reach would be too broad?" Darby asked.

Blackwell rolled her eyes, shook her head. "They said it was determined by the inclusion in the center stone—its angle relative to the Paras." She leaned forward, hands linked around her knee. "Do you have any idea how powerful it would have been? We wouldn't even need to use it. Just threaten the Paras with it, and we could control their behavior. I offered that as an option—using the prototype as a behavior-modification tool within Devil's Isle. Making an example of someone for some small infraction. It would have been a powerful deterrent." She turned her gaze, full of disapproval, on Gunnar. "But they weren't practical enough to let us finish our work."

"The Commandant tends to frown on harming innocents," Gunnar said dryly, and held up a hand when she started to speak again. "And don't lay the 'look where that got you' bullshit on me. I was at Belle Chasse. I know what you did, and what you started."

"Back to the point," Darby said. "Containment pulled your funding, and the project was scrapped. What happened to the blueprints and prototypes?"

"Containment destroyed them." Every word was said with disgust. "After all the research, the investigation, the work. On to bigger and better things. Or things that were easier for them to justify to the bureaucrats who wrote the checks." Her eyes narrowed, went hungry. "Why are you asking about the Devil's Snare now?"

"Research," Darby said.

"No, I don't think so. Containment is still risk averse. Too risk averse, in my opinion." Her gaze flicked from Darby's face to the paper, then back again. "They've outmatched us, haven't they? Proven they'll do whatever they have to do to win. And we're finally going to play their game."

She sounded gleeful that she'd been right about Paras, about the weapon's need, regardless of the cost paid in the interim. It was all just a game to her. Wins and losses tabulated. Victories paid in lives.

This was what I'd come from. This was half of me.

"But there's more." She narrowed her gaze. "You found the components. The actual pieces. Did the Paras finally bring them in?"

Avarice flashed in her green eyes. "Let me out. Get me out of this prison. Get me a lab and some equipment, and I'll make it work. I *guarantee* it. The weapon will function, it will nullify their power, and you'll win this war. No one else has to die."

I had to bite my tongue to keep from screaming out that we were far past the point where no one else had to die. And those deaths could be laid at her feet, because she'd set the Veil's breach in motion.

I hated her for abandoning us, even if I knew now I was better off without her. But I'd never forgive her for war.

"First of all," Darby said, and there was a haughty edge to her tone that gave me a nice glow, "you have vastly overrated your skills as a scientist and an investigator. You see, lady—can I call you lady?— your mistake is in thinking you're the smartest person in the room. That's arrogance talking. Emotion. That's not science. Smart people— legit smart people—try to surround themselves with the best and the brightest. That's how we learn. That's how we improve. I've already translated your notes, and I'm not impressed with your schematics or your testing protocols. If Containment decides to go forward this time, I can do this better, cleaner, and with less risk."

Blackwell was working hard to look stoic, but she couldn't hide the curl of her lip.

"Second, in case you weren't aware"—Darby leaned forward— "you're an asshole. And I wouldn't work with you if Containment offered me permanent AC and a lifetime supply of Abita."

Blackwell's pale skin mottled crimson. "You know nothing," she said through gritted teeth.

"I know plenty. I was here during the war. I know who lived and who died. I know when force is necessary, and when kindness is a better strategy. And I know selfishness when I see it."

Darby slid the paper back into her folder. And when she looked at Gunnar, her smile was warm and brilliant. "We're done here, if you're ready."

"Fine by me," he said, disgust dripping from the words.

But I wasn't done. "Can I have a minute?"

They all looked at me, and none of them seemed thrilled about leaving me alone with her. Or vice versa.

"Five minutes," Gunnar said, and went to check with the guard.

Liam squeezed my hand. "I'll be right around the corner."

I waited until they were gone, until the guard and I were the only ones left in the hallway. Until I could collect myself.

When I finally raised my gaze to my mother, I saw nothing there but certainty and challenge. There would be no regret or guilt from her. No remorse. Because she couldn't conceive of the possibility that any decision she'd made hadn't been the rational one. And that was the only thing that mattered.

No point in mincing words on my end, then.

"I wish I'd had time to prepare a big speech," I said. "With details, and history, and five-dollar words. But I'll just get to the point. I hope I never have to see you again. Do you have any idea how heartbreaking that is? To have to say that to your own mother? It's the worst. But you're toxic. Plain and simple. You're smart, but you've got no morals. No code of honor. And you've got an agenda, which has nothing to do with New Orleans or war or making lives better. It has to do with you. With your ego and your narcissism."

She started to speak and I held up a hand. "You had most of my life to tell me who you were, and you didn't bother. You didn't give me a single word. You missed your chance, and you won't get another one from me."

With that, I turned on a heel and walked down the hall.

CHAPTER NINE

I found everyone outside. Darby and Gunnar had walked a few feet away, giving Liam and me a bit of space.

"You okay?" he asked, putting an arm around me.

I nodded, let myself be held, until I could feel anger and guilt and grief melt away.

"I am more of my father," I finally said. "I'd wondered, after we met the first time, if there was some of her in me."

"Red hair, good brain," Liam said, kissing my forehead. "And that's it."

I leaned back, looked up at him. "You're so sure."

"Who knows you better?" he asked with a smile. "Except possibly Tadji and Gunnar. You know, the more I learn about your mother, the more I like your father."

I blinked back confusion. "What?"

"Your father and your mother agree she left you, and not the other way around. But that's not the most important part. *He let her walk away.* He knew it was better for both of you if she was gone. Even if it was going to be hard, being a single dad. He let her walk away. And that's a difference between us."

He looked down at me, gold shimmering in the potent blue in his eyes. "I won't ever let you walk."

———

Gunnar drove us back to the store. I was quiet on the ride, trying to process my feelings, and trying to keep them contained enough so I could still function. Because we were quickly reaching that crisis point I'd been dreading.

I needed to sit and think. Lock myself upstairs on the third floor, dump all my complicated feelings about war and Blackwell and magic on the floor, and just look at them. Dive into them, dwell on them, scream and cry about them until they were resolved enough to be locked away again.

But there wasn't time for that. So I'd have to figure out another way.

It was waiting for me outside the store.

"Y'all are fast," Liam said, looking at the pile of plywood, bags, sand, and shovels. Essentials for a good storm-prep party.

"The storm's moving fast," Gunnar explained. "Better to be prepared than not."

I couldn't argue with that.

"I'm going back to the Cabildo," he said. "I'll talk to the Commandant about a trip into the Beyond. Technically, you could walk through right now, assuming you made it past the line. But unless the Commandant allows it, we don't rush to your rescue if shit goes bad."

I held up a hand. "I would like to please be rescued if shit goes bad."

"I figured," he said. "You want Containment's stamp on this. They've got the resources, the authority, the personnel. You're set on going?"

"It looks like the Devil's Snare is our best bet, so yeah. And we can't reach the Citadel without Malachi, so I suspect either he gets his way or the weapon won't happen."

Gunnar nodded. "I'll get back when I can, but probably not until dusk. I'll also check with Darby later, see where she is on Callyth and ideas about the weapon." He gestured to the pile of supplies. "You have plenty to do in the meantime."

We said our good-byes and climbed out of the vehicle. As Gunnar drove off toward the Cabildo, Gavin came outside.

"Perfect timing," Liam said, pointing to the supplies. "Let's get to work."

"Claire's telekinetic," Gavin said with a mild whine. "Can't she just put the sand into the bags?" He looked at me hopefully.

"Then we wouldn't get to enjoy this gorgeous and mild New Orleans weather." He picked up two pairs of heavy-duty gloves, tossed a pair at Gavin. They hit him in the face, dropped to the ground.

Gavin's expression went flat, but he scooped them up and put them on, grumbling all the way.

"I'm going to check in with Tadji," I said, and let my fingers skim along Liam's back. The contact, the connection, made me feel better. But I needed a different kind of comfort right now.

He glanced over, searched my face. "You all right?"

"I'm okay. Need some girl time."

"Okay," he said, and leaned down to brush his lips over mine. "Come back soon."

"You're saying that because you want me to help you shovel."

"Damn right," he said with a wink, and pulled on his own gloves.

I found Tadji inside behind the counter in leggings and a brilliant yellow Royal Mercantile T-shirt she'd turned, with some creative cutting, into a tank top. She wore a contrasting yellow tank beneath, and her hair was a halo of dark waves around her face.

"So, a literal storm is coming," she said, looking up from the pile of papers that sat beside a calculator on the counter. "In addition to the Paranormal nonsense."

"Yeah. Liam and Gavin are working on the supplies Containment dropped off."

"I'm taking inventory of our own supplies. Been a while since the last storm."

"We've been lucky. But I don't think we're going to be lucky this time."

She tilted her head at me, frowning as if she had to figure something out. "How was Delta?"

"I just came back from seeing Laura Blackwell, and we're probably going into the Beyond."

She breathed in once, pushed aside her papers, and linked her hands on the counter. "Tadji's in session. Spill it."

She let the clerk she'd hired run the cash box, and she gave me her undivided attention. Just one of the reasons I loved her.

I told her about Delta, the weapon, the stone. The beams of magic and the trip to see my mother. I told her what Darby had said to her, what I'd said to her, and watched Tadji's eyes light with approval. I told her about the Beyond. And that's when she got quiet and very, very still.

"Only two days," I said. "We'll be back before the storm hits." *If all goes well*, I thought again. "And maybe it will veer off into the Atlantic and bother someone else."

"I want to tell you not to go," Tadji said. "I want to tell you to stay here, where it's safe, because this war is Containment's problem."

She reached out, put her hand on mine, squeezed. "But we both know that's not true. War is war, and this one belongs to all of us. It wasn't won the first time without Sensitives, and it probably won't be won again without you. We've talked before about who we are, about our destinies. I don't have any doubt that you're fulfilling yours. So if that's the direction your destiny goes, you have to follow it. You can't buck destiny."

"Is destiny a euphemism for 'ridiculous plan'?"

"It can be two things," she said with a grin. "Kind of like how you attempted to surprise me with Burke."

"The attempt was successful. You were surprised."

"I was surprised. And initially furious." She narrowed her eyes. "You know that's not my kind of thing."

"I know. But, Tadj, you've been working so hard, and he was so excited to see you, and we just thought you'd enjoy the lift. And if it was a surprise, you wouldn't, like, anticipate it."

Her brows lifted. "I wouldn't 'anticipate' it? What does that mean?"

"You are a rational person."

"Nothing complimentary ever followed a statement like that."

"You think about Burke a lot, and the relationship, and the rules. We just thought—Gunnar mostly thought and I, I guess, moderately supported him—that it might be fun for you, and why are you looking at me like that?"

"You're throwing Gunnar under the bus?"

"I mean, it appears to be a really large bus. So yes."

She sighed. "I'm not mad. And I still don't like shocks. But . . ."

"But?" Hope rose.

"Seeing his face, seeing him just standing there . . . That was pretty phenomenal."

I couldn't have held back the grin if I'd tried. Which I wasn't going to, having been so clearly validated. "Yeah, it was. Same when Liam came back. I was working with the Sensitives and then, boom, there's a Quinn in the park."

"And a Gavin behind him."

"Always," I said. "Hug it out?"

"Hug it out," she said, and we gave each other a squeeze.

"Now," she said when we'd separated, and she'd put a bossy hand on her hip. "Get out there and fill some sandbags."

Gavin and I shoveled, while Liam closed the shutters upstairs and hung plywood above the uncovered windows.

It was hot and humid, and we were drenched and sweaty in minutes. The work was repetitive, but it wasn't as bad when we got into a rhythm, when each strike of shovel into sand was the beat of a song.

I spent the time thinking about storm planning, and not the possibility we'd be walking into the Beyond. In part because we needed to help Tadji get ready, and in part because I knew what a tropical storm looked like, how to prepare for it. How to survive it. The Beyond was a complete mystery.

We'd use up the perishables, move out whatever was left over, barricade the doors with sandbags to keep the rising water at bay. But that would only go so far. If the water rose high enough, the first floor would be inundated. That hadn't happened during Katrina, but who knew what kind of havoc magic could wreak on a storm system? We could try to move some of the smaller antiques upstairs, but many were simply too big to haul up the narrow staircase. They'd have to survive on their own. Or else they'd make good kindling afterward. And that was a damn shame.

And we hadn't done any prep at the gas station. We'd need even more sandbags, more plywood, more time. On the other hand, my father's little museum had survived for seven years without any human intervention. Maybe we'd get lucky.

I wiped my damp forehead, and watched Gavin smile and tip an invisible cap when two female soldiers walked by. They gave him dubious smiles and kept on walking.

"Tough luck," I said.

"They don't know what they're missing."

"Don't they?" I asked with a grin.

"You're cruel," he said. And he was right. I wasn't giving him enough credit. As much as he got on my nerves—mostly because he specifically tried to—he was cute, smart, funny, and a generally stand-up guy. He was the irritating kid brother I'd never had.

"What about Darby?" I asked.

"What about her?"

I just kept looking at him.

"Oh. *Oh*. No."

His tone, at least when he got through the repetition, was firm. But his cheeks had actually gone a little pink, and I didn't think that was just from the sun, so I decided to push a little. For my own amusement.

"She's smart, gorgeous, funny."

"*Man*," he muttered, and rubbed the back of his neck nervously. This was fun.

"You don't find her attractive?"

"Sure." He lifted a shoulder. "She's hot."

"I have never known you to pass up an opportunity for hot."

He groaned, pushed back his hair. "I'm just . . . I don't know if I'm into scientists."

I stared at him. I really hadn't been sure where he was going to land. But I hadn't expected him to land there. Gavin was many things—including vain, cocky, and snarky—but I hadn't expected full-on shallow.

"What?" he asked. "You're putting a lot of pressure on me right now."

"Consider it payback for the possums."

"I didn't put the possums in the truck," he insisted. "And technically it was only one possum. And several of her very wee children. You said they were adorable. I mean after you screamed about rabies." He chewed his lip to keep from smiling.

My lip curled instinctively. "She's single. And so are you. And she's smart. You wouldn't have fun with a girl who's not bright."

His grin was perfectly wicked. "I could have a lot of fun with any girl. It's in my nature. But yes," he said, holding up a hand as if to avoid further argument. "It's not that she's smart. It's that . . . she's so sciencey. It means she has rules and procedures, right? Expectations?"

Understanding dawned. "You don't want to date a hot scientist because you think she wants a commitment."

"Well, I wouldn't have put it so bluntly. But . . . it's a factor."

He was gone a lot, spent even more time in the bayous than Liam, tracking Court units and occasionally running counter-ops. Gavin liked to come and go as he pleased, so I understood the idea of not being tied down. But that assumed a lot about Darby.

"I think presuming you know her mind is a mistake."

He blinked. "You think she's up for some fun?"

"Not if you put it like that." I pointed at his shovel. "Get back to bagging."

Obviously relieved by the dismissal, he got back to work.

Liam came toward us with bottles of water, handed one to each of us. "Are you harassing my brother?"

"I am. He deserved it."

"I'm sure he did."

"I think he got surlier while you were gone."

"I can hear you." Gavin took a drink, then tossed the closed bottle onto a pile of sand.

"I know," I said with a wide smile.

"He's always been surly. He's just more comfortable with you now. Because of the possums."

I pointed a finger at Liam. "You're a traitor."

"Maybe," he said, and pressed a kiss to my neck, just below my ear. "But I'll make it up to you later."

When the sun began to fall, we went inside to refuel, rest, and await Gunnar. And the Commandant's verdict. Moses and Malachi joined us after Malachi deposited the Inclusion Stone in Darby's capable— and scientific—hands.

"She didn't come with you?" I asked them.

"Frigging workaholic," Moses said. "She's in the lab and doesn't want to leave."

"How's the work going?" Liam asked.

"She thinks she's figured out the mechanism for limiting the weapon's spread," Malachi said. "She's at a crucial stage."

"She's doing actual math." Moses snorted. "Can you imagine? Frigging science."

"Frigging science," Liam agreed.

We were obviously trying to be upbeat. Trying to keep our energy and mood up, given what might come next. More destruction. More death. A bigger weapon. A bigger journey. But our nerves were still on edge, frayed and torn. Which was probably part of the Seelies' goal. Not just to destroy what we loved, what was around us, but to grind us down.

When Gunnar came in with Burke just after dusk, when the candles had been lit and bland food served up, he looked exhausted.

"Tell me there's food," Gunnar said, pulling off his messenger bag and dropping it onto the floor as he sat down.

"There's what we're calling food," Liam said, putting a bowl of postwar yaka mein in front of both of them. We'd adapted the New Orleans staple, using ramen noodles, canned broth, green onions, and beef jerky stewed until tender.

Not quite the prewar classic. But close enough to fill the belly.

"What's the latest?" Gavin asked.

"They hit two of the pumping stations," Gunnar said, grimacing as he chewed beef. "Two guards dead, because Seelies are assholes."

"No objection," Moses said.

"I'm sorry," I said.

Gunnar nodded, drank broth. "Everyone is running on empty. Exhausted. And tired of saying good-bye to friends. Which is why you have approval to go into the Beyond to obtain the elements necessary to complete the Devil's Snare. Tomorrow."

I was simultaneously excited and terrified.

He looked up at me. "The team will consist of Gavin, Liam, Claire, Malachi"—he shifted his gaze to Malachi—"and Captain Lewis."

Malachi's answer was immediate. "No. She's military, and they will see her as a threat."

"Then you better figure out a way to finesse that, because this is nonnegotiable. Commandant's orders." He wiped his mouth, met Malachi's gaze. "She's good in the field, and you know that. You've got trackers, humans with magic. You could use someone trained in field operations."

When Malachi didn't respond, Gunnar picked up his spoon again. "And she's outside waiting."

"Ooh, well played," Tadji murmured into her mug of tea, smiling politely at Malachi when he looked her way. "I mean, you have to admit."

"I do not have to admit anything. I am under no obligation to—"

"It's an expression," I intervened, before things got ugly. Eight years in our world, and he was still working on the nuances.

"This party is going to be better than I thought," Moses said, hopping down from his chair. "I'll let her in."

"It's not a party," Tadji said.

"It is now," Moses murmured.

I rolled my eyes, looked apologetically at Malachi. "Are you going to be okay with this?"

"Moses or Rachel?" he asked dryly.

"It looks like both are inevitable."

"And we're all adults," Burke said, pouring pepper sauce into his broth.

"And that," Tadji agreed.

Moses came in, Rachel behind him. No fatigues today, just jeans and a fitted tank top that showed her well-toned arms.

"Hi," she said, and we nodded.

"I don't know most of you as well as you know each other, and it probably feels like I'm an unwanted appendage. But I've got skills, and I can handle myself. And I've got the Commandant's backing." A corner of her mouth lifted. "So if this goes bad, you can blame me."

"Get the girl a seat," Moses said, and Liam pulled out a chair.

"Do you need food?" Gavin asked.

"No, I'm okay. Thanks." She sat down and looked around the table. "But I do think we should review the plan and logistics."

"Agreed," I said. "I'd feel a lot better if I had some idea where we're going."

"Well, Claire, there's this thing called the Veil."

Moses did the honor of punching Gavin in the arm.

"I didn't deserve that," he muttered.

"You did," Gunnar said with a smile that looked a little cheerier. "I'll go with you as far as Belle Chasse. The outpost will help you get through the first obstacle."

"Which is?" Tadji asked.

"Court members guarding the Veil."

I lifted my brows. "Because they don't want us in, or they don't want anyone else out?"

"Both," Gunnar said grimly. "They like to keep the outpost soldiers on their toes, and they only want allies coming through the Veil to assist."

"Have any Consularis members tried to come through?" Gavin asked.

"Not that we're aware of," Gunnar said.

"And how do we cross the no-man's-land?" Gavin asked.

"I'd suggest distraction and slipping through," Rachel said, "but we'll want to see what the field looks like, and where they're positioned, in the morning."

She glanced at Malachi, the question in her eyes obvious: *Can you admit I'm right about this? Because we both know I am.*

Malachi just stared at her, and I realized we were going to have to talk about how they would manage being together on this little journey. Because we couldn't afford distractions.

"So, we make it into the Beyond," Liam said, stretching his arm on the back of my chair so his fingers rested on my shoulder, to warm and reassure.

"Wait," I said, and looked up at Malachi. "What do you call it? The place we're going? I'm assuming 'the Beyond' is our name."

He smiled. "It is called Elysium."

"As in the Elysian Fields?" It was a kind of heaven in Greek mythology—and the avenue that ran right down the middle of the Marigny. Of Devil's Isle.

"I wouldn't presume to tell you the origin of human words," Malachi said, and the smile was knowing.

It wasn't the first time I'd wondered how much of his world had bled over into ours over the course of human history. Maybe someone or something had slipped through the Veil, or the knowledge had gone through by some kind of magical osmosis.

Malachi drew a folded piece of paper from his pocket, spread it on the table. There, he'd drawn a neat map, pale colors washed beneath tidy pen lines.

"Did you make this?" I asked, leaning over.

"I did." His smile was faint, and looked slightly bashful. Not an expression I'd often seen on him.

"It's lovely," I said.

"Quit appraising the art, Claire."

I grinned at Tadji. "I'm head of acquisitions. I'm allowed to look." I smiled up at Malachi. "When we're back, if you wanted to sell this, I'd be interested."

"So, they make it past the Veil," Gunnar prompted. "Tell us what we're going to see in Elysium."

"The boundary between the worlds is located in a rural area," Malachi said, pointing to the line along the bottom of the map. "Rolling hills, some of which is grassland, some forested." With a fingertip, he traced a line to a dotted amoeba-like shape northeast of the original spot. "It is twenty miles to the city where the Citadel is located."

"We walk?" Gavin asked, and Malachi nodded.

"We will walk. It is very navigable terrain. We should reach it within a day."

"It's green and full of bugs," Moses said with an unimpressed sniff.

I looked over at him. "Not a fan?"

"I prefer the city. Technology and magic. Not bird shit and bug noises."

"You do you, Mos."

"Damn right, Red."

Liam crossed his arms. "What about guards, scouts, police? Surely they aren't going to let us tramp through their world?"

"The Beyond is . . . different," Malachi decided. "Movement among districts is not regulated. The world is peaceful, violence rare."

Liam lifted his brows. "But for the Court of Dawn?"

"The rebellion was put down," Malachi said, and there was no bravado in it. "And those who continued their rebellion came here. We may be questioned, but I will be with you."

"Commander of forces."

Malachi shifted his gaze to Rachel. "Yes."

"They'll recognize your position, even after the time that's passed?"

"They will have been made aware that Consularis Paras were conscripted, that we didn't leave or fight voluntarily."

"And yet you made no move to return, even after the Veil was opened again." Rachel's tone was cold.

"I have unfinished business," Malachi said.

"And would that not affect your relationship with the reigning Consularis?"

"They are called the Precepts," he said. "There are three. And I have no reason to believe that it would."

Chill tone or not, the air was beginning to heat as their stares grew fiercer.

"When we get into the city," Liam said, drawing their attention to him. "What happens then? Where do we go? Who do we meet?"

It took five long seconds before Malachi shifted his gaze from Rachel's face. "It's approximately a mile to the city center. That's where we'll find the Citadel. We meet with the Precepts and we ask them for the Abethyl."

"And if they say no?" Rachel asked.

Malachi looked at her. "I will convince them. They owe you that much."

"So we go in optimistic, but prepared." Liam looked at each of them. "That work for everyone?"

Rachel's jaw worked, as if she were chewing the words she wanted to say. "Yes."

"Yes," Malachi said. But it didn't sound like he especially agreed with the notion. "The return trip will be very much the same. We cover the same ground."

"That sounds simple," Gavin said.

"The walk is simple," Malachi said. "There is nothing simple about the Consularis." He looked at me and Liam. "As I said, I'm hopeful that meeting you will help them understand the impact of their refusal to act, and that action has become a necessity."

Liam nodded. "We understand."

"What's the contingency plan?" Gavin asked, and we all groaned.

"You're going to jinx us before we even leave," Liam said.

"It's not a jinx to be prepared." The words were almost prim. He looked at Gunnar. "They say no, and we can't build this weapon, and then what?"

"Tremé" was his simple answer.

Gavin blew out a breath, shook his head. "But no pressure."

"I'd like to offer a prayer," Burke said. "If that would be all right with you?"

"We're not much for church in this assemblage," Liam said. "But we'll take all the help we can get."

"Then let's take hands, and bow our heads."

We all reached out, took the hands of the people beside us, made a circle of anticipation, fear, anger, hope. Of people sick of war, ready for peace and plenty. Tonight, we were a unit. A group, undivided. Tonight, there was possibility. And we had to hope we'd carry that with us tomorrow.

"Heavenly Father," Burke began quietly, an entreaty, and led us through it.

CHAPTER TEN

When the prayer was done, I touched Liam's shoulder. "I'm going to talk to Malachi."

Liam's gaze followed automatically to where the angel stood near the stairs on the other side of the room, looking stern and powerful and trying very hard to ignore Rachel, who was reviewing the map with Burke.

"About the girl?"

"About the girl."

"You think he'll discuss it?"

"I don't know. But I have to ask. This trip is already fraught with damn peril. We don't need to add soap-opera flare-ups to the mix."

"Be careful," he said, and squeezed my hand.

I made my way to Malachi. And stood in front of him for a good three seconds before he lowered his gaze to me.

"Why don't we go for a walk?"

His expression didn't change. "Why would we go for a walk?"

"So we can talk."

"About what?"

This was like arguing with a toddler. "About Rachel."

Malachi's jaw tightened, and seeing it was like watching the curtains being drawn across his emotions.

"We're going into enemy territory," I pointed out, "where we'll have limited resources and no easy way out. I want to know the history, because I don't want whatever that was flashing back on us."

"It wouldn't flash back."

"I know you don't want to tell me—that you prefer to keep your private life private. I don't have to tell Gunnar, Liam, or anyone else the details. But we need to know."

Malachi didn't answer. But he walked toward the door, bell ringing as he stepped onto the sidewalk. He didn't want to talk, but he wanted to talk inside the store even less.

Tadji reached me, watched Malachi move down the sidewalk. "Where is he going?"

"Outside. I'm harassing him about his history with Rachel."

"Good call. That's a powder keg."

Something crashed behind us in the kitchen, then rolled across the floor.

"And speaking of which," she muttered.

"I've got it!" Gavin shouted from the back.

"He is a bull in a damn china shop," Tadji said.

There was more banging, and I shook my head. "Not my drama," I said, and walked to the door.

"Gavin, what the hell are you doing?" Liam asked.

I didn't wait around for an answer.

I found Malachi on the steps of the former Louisiana Supreme Court building, his wings extended. But the look on his face was more sulking teenager than commanding angel.

I climbed up to meet him, crossed my arms, and stared him down.

"I bear no animosity toward her," he said after a very long time.

"You have feelings for her."

"I might have had. If circumstances were different."

"If she wasn't a Containment captain, and you weren't a Consularis commander?"

Malachi's eyes widened. "She told you?"

"No. I used my impeccable powers of deduction."

As if in response to the sarcasm, he closed his wings with a rush of air that blew my hair back.

"You told me you met while closing the Veil," I said. "She was special forces."

He stared at me, as if determining whether I might simply give up and walk away. Then he relented. "Yes. She was sent to New Orleans when Containment agreed to work with Sensitives to close the Veil the first time. We lived in a camp near the breach, worked day and night to come up with a protocol that might work."

"You got to know each other," I guessed. "And then what happened?"

"She jailed two Consularis Paras—trusted friends—because they fought against humans."

I lifted my brows. "So she did what the law required, and what virtually every Containment officer would have done."

"They were Nephilim," he said. Those were fairylike creatures with delicate wings, like more petite versions of Malachi's. "They'd been in hiding for months, waiting for an opportunity to go home again. I told her not to turn them in or to send them to Devil's Isle. She did it anyway."

"She disobeyed your orders and betrayed you."

His chin lifted. "Yes."

"Devil's advocate?"

"The devil doesn't need an advocate."

"Be that as it may, we were at war. Rachel had orders."

"She disobeyed me." He looked absolutely baffled that I didn't understand that was the most important element of the story.

I arched an eyebrow. "Since when are you the king of humans? Why should she have obeyed you?"

"Because I asked her to."

The bafflement on his face was priceless and telling.

"At any rate, they were part of a convoy sent from the breach back to New Orleans. But the convoy was sabotaged, and they escaped."

"It was sabotaged," I said dryly. "The convoy in which your friends were being transported."

"The saboteurs were not found."

"I bet. Total coincidence that they were your friends, and you'd objected to their imprisonment."

"I was right."

"You were both right. And unfortunately, that made you both wrong, and put you in conflict with each other." I watched him for a moment. "Okay. Let's go back to the store."

Malachi's brow furrowed. "That's all you want to know?"

"For now. You're both alpha, and you both did what you thought was right. I can live with that." I glanced at him. "Can you live with it?"

There was a moment of silence. "She was a competent leader."

Coming from him, that was as flattering as praise got.

I gave Liam the details on the way back to the gas station. Once inside, we began assembling gear for the trip.

Backpacks were first, already hanging and ready in the shelter-within-a-shelter my father had built in the basement. We packed water-filtration tablets, thin nylon hammocks that could double as shelters, fire starters, pocketknives, a first-aid kit, and some short pikes of cold iron that made handy weapons.

We carried the backpacks upstairs, testing their weight on the trip to the kitchen, then put them on the counter to add food.

"There's something I want to talk to you about."

"What's that?" I asked absently, and tapped fingers against my lips as I considered what we'd want to bring on the trip. I'd raided the stash for granola bars, nuts, protein bars, and a few MREs. I considered bringing some precooked rice or quinoa, maybe a bag of dried fruit. How did one pack for a trip into a magical land? Because I bet we wouldn't be offered Turkish delight.

"I want to talk about us."

"What about us?" No, it was probably better to travel light, so we could be quick when necessary. The nuts and protein bars would provide calories, and maybe we could supplement by foraging, or finding food in Elysium City.

"Claire."

"What?" I looked back at Liam, found him staring at me. And I couldn't decipher the look in his eyes.

"You aren't taking this seriously," he said.

"Taking what seriously? I'm trying to pack. This isn't a good time to discuss relationships."

His eyes darkened. "We live in a war zone. When would be a good time?"

"Well, not the night before we go into battle." I pulled a box of protein bars from the cabinet, pushed them into his hands. "Get busy packing."

He muttered something in Cajun French that was probably swearing, and gripped the box with white-knuckled hands.

I put a hand on his, looked into his eyes. "Tomorrow could be a mess. I need to get ready for it. Be ready for it. And I don't want to jinx anything."

It was the wrong thing to say, and I knew it as soon as the words were out of my mouth. My regret didn't stop the flash of anger in his eyes.

"You think our relationship would fall apart because of a 'jinx'?"

"No, that's not what I meant. It just—" I had to walk away from him, give myself room to breathe. "It feels like we're so close to the edge, Liam."

"Our relationship?"

"No. I mean, yes. I mean, everything. All of it. This . . . life we've managed to pull out of leftover food and generators and humidity. And that life, everything we've managed to salvage, is so delicate. We're going to be fighting for our lives tomorrow. For New Orleans, because we could lose it. We could lose all of it."

I could lose you, I thought. *And I don't want to risk that.* It felt like tempting fate, like begging the gods—however they existed—to strike us down. *Hey, these two lovebirds made a commitment before going off to war. That tragedy writes itself.* And I couldn't even speak that lame excuse aloud, because even that felt unlucky. It felt dangerous.

He just looked at me, jaw working. "How, in your mind, does that make a commitment with me a problem?"

"Because all those things could be taken away. Because the store is the only thing I have left from my life before. And because people are temporary."

His mouth thinned, jaw clenching. "You think I'm temporary."

"No," I said. "But I don't want to take the chance. I don't want to lose anyone else. I love you, Liam. And I'm afraid."

He rested one hand against the back of my head, his forehead against mine.

And left a lot of space between our bodies.

CHAPTER ELEVEN

I found Liam in the kitchen the next morning, in a pool of light from a battery-powered lantern, eating peanut butter from the jar. He was already dressed, backpack full and waiting on a table in one of the former vehicle bays. He didn't look up when I walked in, which made me simultaneously angry and sad.

I didn't know what to do about it. Liam was entitled to his feelings, to his anger. But so was I. And it was a hell of a time for a fight. The world was falling down around us, and we were about to walk into enemy territory to try to save what was left of it. We had to focus. Didn't we?

I took a bottle of water from the fridge, pulled a canister of dried fruit from a cabinet, and sat down at the island, began to munch. I wished I'd kept the fruit in its original bag so I at least had something to read in the awkward silence.

I chewed strips of dried mango until my stomach stopped growling and my jaw began to ache, then put the lid on the container and looked at him.

Liam was looking at me, and even in the dim lantern light I could tell his face was tight. He was holding his emotions back—holding hurt or anger back. But I wasn't sure which.

I spoke first. "I don't know what to say."

"I don't, either."

Ironic, wasn't it, that by trying to keep us just where we were, I'd managed to push us further apart?

I rose. "I'm going to start loading gear into the truck."

"Okay. I want to check on the dehumidifier, and I'll join you."

"Sure."

He reached out, squeezed my hand, and headed for the stairs.

That moment of kindness made me feel even worse.

The air was hot, thick, and uncomfortable. In other words, typical New Orleans. I put the backpacks in the bed of the truck, not especially thrilled about the idea of fighting to get into the Veil in this heat. It was going to take a toll. But maybe the Beyond would be better. Maybe there'd be cool breezes and low humidity, public pools, and rum drinks with umbrellas in them.

More likely, there'd be hostile magic and Paras who didn't want us around, and certainly didn't want us to take home their prizes. Too bad for them.

I parked Scarlet in front of the store, met Liam's gaze over the bed. "Could we have a truce? Just for now? Just for this?"

He crooked his finger. I'd never been so happy to be beckoned.

"We aren't fighting," he said when I reached him. He looked down at me, stroked a thumb down my jaw. "We're just . . . not entirely aligned."

I wanted to insist that had been exactly my point—that war put up walls, even if you didn't want them. But we didn't have the energy to spare.

"Don't wait to live your life," he said. "Whether for war to be over, or New Orleans to be safe, or anything else. Because you'll miss out on all the good stuff in between."

I rested my forehead against his chest. And I hoped this wasn't the last of the moments we'd have together.

Gunnar, Gavin, and Tadji were at the store when we arrived. Gunnar in pressed fatigues, Tadji in her breezy work wear, and Gavin in a T-shirt and cargos. Gavin flipped through an old magazine; Gunnar and Tadji sat at the table with steaming mugs. The air smelled like sour coffee.

"Good morning, adventurers." Gunnar grinned. "How are Indiana Jones and Lara Croft today?"

"No tomb robbing," Liam said. "Discreet, culturally sensitive inquiries."

"Spoilsport," Gunnar said, and sipped his coffee.

"Did the Seelies do anything overnight?" Liam asked.

"Not that we've found," Gunnar said. "But the sun's barely up and the day is young. Teams are already out searching."

"What about the storm?"

"Tropical Storm Frieda is now Hurricane Frieda," Gunnar said. "Category three and heading northwest toward Miami. Lot of flooding in the Bahamas. It's expected to make landfall over southern Florida tonight, and then move through the Gulf. They've narrowed the target zone for the second landfall—somewhere between Biloxi and Port Arthur."

"That's a big area," Liam said.

"Prediction isn't perfect," Gunnar said. "But New Orleans is right in the middle, so the scope hardly matters."

"Callyth?" I asked.

He blinked. "Didn't I already tell you that?"

"No," I said flatly. "I'd have remembered learning of the reason Paras are gunning for us."

"Sorry," he said. "It has been a very long week, and I'm still half-asleep."

In response, Tadji smiled, pushed his mug closer.

"We found her in the fatality records. She was a Seelie. She was captured about two years after the war."

"About the same time as Aeryth," Liam said.

"Yeah," Gunnar said. "That wasn't a coincidence. They're sisters. We found that out when she was interrogated."

My heartbeat was suddenly a timpani drum, beating in my ears like the climax of a terrible song. "Who—" I had to start again to get the word out. "Who interrogated her?"

Please don't say my mother, I silently pleaded. *Don't say she tortured someone and we're paying the price for it.*

"I don't know. It wasn't in the file. Why?" But he answered his own question, jumping to his feet. "Christ, you look pale as a ghost. Sit down."

I didn't fight when he put me in the chair. Liam moved closer, a panther concerned and prowling.

Gunnar crouched in front of me, put his hands on my knees. "It didn't say your mother, Claire. It didn't. If it did, I'd tell you the truth. Okay?"

I swallowed past the knot of emotion that was strangling my words. "It could have been her. That's what she did—interrogation and rendition." Which would make my mother a cause of all this death. This destruction.

"Was she tortured?" I asked.

"I don't know. Honestly," he added, crossing his heart with a finger. "The document I found only notes her death, that she'd been questioned. It doesn't discuss details. It's just statistics," he said quietly, as if he felt guilty about diminishing even an enemy to a set of numbers. "But she was part of a contingent of Seelies responsible for the deaths of forty-two people that we know of. We'd have wanted to find the others. Tactics would have been used."

"War is ugly," Tadji said quietly.

Gunnar nodded, gently patted my knees, and rose again. "I won't justify what was done to her, because that wasn't my team, and it wasn't my call. But war is ugly. And sometimes that ugly requires more still."

I looked up at him. "I need to know if Blackwell was involved."

"It won't change anything."

"It will for me. And maybe it will for Aeryth."

Liam and Gunnar shared a glance, a nod. "All right," Gunnar said. "I'll find out what I can. But you know, whatever happened, that you aren't responsible for your mother's actions, and your mother isn't responsible for Aeryth's."

"Maybe not responsible," I said. "But we're all connected. All part of the wheel that just keeps on spinning."

"It will continue to spin whether we're in it or not," Tadji said. "We can't control it. We can only react to the best of our abilities." She leaned forward. "If the woman who birthed you—she was *not* your mother, so I won't call her that—killed a Seelie, and Aeryth is punishing all of us because of it, the result is still the same: You stop her. Sympathize with her loss if you must. But we've all lost, Claire. And we aren't committing mass murder."

"I knew I liked you, *cher,*" Liam said, giving Tadji a wink.

"I'm quite likable," she agreed with a nod, sipped her coffee.

I blew out a breath. "You're right. Okay. Okay," I said again, when I was ready to move on to the next thing. Because Tadji was right: We had to move on to the next thing. "What's next?"

"The Beyond," Gavin said, moving a hand in an arc as if marking a horizon.

"You are not helpful," Tadji said.

"But I'm charming," he said with a smile.

"So, we've got field trip, Seelies, hurricane," Tadji said, counting them off on her fingers. "Anything else?"

"Only if Liam gets hangry on this trip," Gavin said, pushing his arms through the straps of a pink backpack. A unicorn glittered across the front, midjump and trailing glittery stars in its wake.

"Working a new style?" Liam asked with a smile.

"What?" Gavin glanced back. "Oh. My other one finally ripped through, and I was out of duct tape. So I grabbed the first one I saw."

From an empty house, he'd meant. Scavenging was one of the great joys of living in a war zone.

Liam flicked a pink pom-pom that hung from one zipper. "From a child's room?"

"Or a raver. Or someone who liked pink and unicorns," Gavin said, utterly unflapped. "Either I wasn't looking and didn't care, or I loved it and picked it specifically." He pointed at us. "You get to decide."

Gavin wiggled to adjust the backpack—which was at least a couple of sizes too small—in the middle of his back.

"He will not be pink-shamed," I said, and watched him stride away. "And I think he's pulling it off."

When everyone had arrived—including a grouchy Moses, who refused to tell us good-bye or good luck and walked right past us into the store—we loaded the gear.

Malachi frowned as he looked down at me. "Magic level?"

I gave it a check. "Fine. Neither too much nor too little."

"Watch the language, kids," Gavin said as he walked by to put a cooler with CONTAINMENT stenciled on the side in the back of the truck. "This show is PG."

"What's in there?" I asked, ignoring him.

"According to Gunnar, supplies for the Belle Chasse outpost. But I didn't ask for details."

Rachel walked up, camouflage backpack over a fitted tank top, cargo pants, hiking boots. She'd pulled her hair into a ponytail and wore a Containment cap to keep the sun from her eyes.

"Good morning," I said.

"Good morning." She shifted her gaze to Malachi. "Commander."

"Captain." His voice was entirely pleasant, and equally uncomfortable. Hopefully they could maintain the peace.

"I think we're ready?" Liam asked, glancing around.

When no one objected, he nodded. "Then let's hit the road."

I tapped on the store window, waved at Tadji and Moses to say good-bye.

She blew me a kiss.

He flipped me off.

"Love," Gavin said beside me, "is a beautiful thing."

I drove Scarlet with Rachel in the front and Liam, Gunnar, and Gavin in the back. Malachi would fly and meet us near the boundary—and ensure from his better vantage point that our position was clear.

Since the drive would take a good hour, I figured I might as well get to know Malachi's nemesis.

"Tell me about yourself," I said, at a slow and steady pace, but keeping my eyes peeled for any sign of Seelies or their crimson calling cards.

"Born in Oregon," Rachel said. "Went to West Point. I graduated two months before the war began, asked for a transfer to Containment."

That put her at around thirty, by my math, which made her about five years older than me.

"Why Containment?"

"I was trained for it. And, frankly, I figured I'd enjoy being part of something otherworldly. It wasn't what I expected."

"It wasn't what we expected, either," I said, thinking of the way Containment had spun the truth about Paranormals, hid the difference between Court and Consularis.

"And Malachi?" I asked. "Was he what you expected?"

She was quiet for a moment. "That was a sneaky little segue."

"I'm pretty proud of it."

Another moment of silence.

"It's not that I don't like him. I respect him as a leader, as a person. But he's . . . egotistical. And always has to have his way."

"I think he's used to being in control. He told me about the Nephilim. That you wanted to incarcerate them."

"They were Paras, and there were procedures. And at the time, Containment didn't know what it does now. Or it knew, and they didn't tell those of us on the ground. Either way, I had a job to do, and I did it. Malachi didn't like that. It was . . . personal for him. I understood that, but I couldn't let it get in the way."

"So you both wanted to do what you thought was right. You just disagreed about the right."

"I suppose." Her gaze narrowed. "Why are you asking me about this?"

I lifted a shoulder. "You two seem to have a connection. So I just wondered why you weren't acting on it."

"With all due respect, I don't like to talk about my personal life. Especially not with people I don't know very well."

"Yeah, that was the point of this talk. Getting to know each other."

Rachel went quiet, and since she seemed genuinely uncomfortable, I figured I'd pushed a little too hard.

"I'm sorry if I'm being nosy. Being in the Zone—I think I've lost my ability to be subtle. And stay out of people's business."

"It's fine," she said, but crossed her arms. "I just don't think there's an easy answer. Or an easy solution."

"But you're cool working together."

"Sure," she said, the word a little too fast, a little too cheerful. But she was right. It was none of my business.

So obviously I'd just try again later.

The Veil, or what remained of it, between our worlds ran on a north–south line, right through the heart of New Orleans.

The Containment outpost was set about a hundred yards back from the gap, a shimmering intersection between our world and theirs. No longer a barrier but an open door.

Containment's modern-day fort was a single building, a low, long box with a wide eave and a short turret on top to provide visibility. The eave kept the exterior of the building shaded, and the large windows provided air circulation, and were designed to keep the building as cool as possible given the frequent power failures.

The squat outpost was surrounded by a palisade of wrought-iron rods of different shapes and sizes. Balcony balusters, fence posts, fireplace pokers. All of them cold iron, salvaged from New Orleans and the surroundings. They'd been placed side by side to form a kind of fence, then installed at an angle so the tops slanted toward attackers and made it as difficult as possible for enemies to break in.

The Containment building looked empty. There was no sign of activity inside or out, and none of the things I'd have expected to see outside a human work space. No obvious front door. No sidewalk. No parking lot or employee vehicles. Just the bread-loaf building and its recycled fence.

"Are you sure someone's actually in there?" I asked. "It looks like it hasn't been used in months."

"It's a bunker," Gavin said with a grin. "That's the point of it."

"They're in there," Gunnar said, walking up behind us. "And yeah, that is the point of it. Gavin starting with a correct observation bodes well for this whole enterprise."

Gavin blinked. "Was I just insulted?"

"You were," Liam said. "You're currently devastated."

"Let's get inside," Gunnar said, walking toward the barricade. When he reached it, he pressed his hand against a plate set into one of the uprights, and a section of the stakes slid open on a metal track.

"Handy," I said, watching it close after we'd walked through. "What do you do when the power's out?"

Gunnar looked back, smiled. "We push."

Guards patrolled the narrow gap between the barricade and the building, and two guards stood outside a heavily fortified door.

They came to attention as Gunnar approached, nodded when he showed them his ID, then scanned his palm for entry into the building.

The door pivoted open, nearly a foot thick, and pushed out a cloud of cold air. The guard on the left sighed lustily as it hit him, eyes closed in pleasure.

"Long day, Pete?" Gunnar asked with a smile.

"Hot out, sir. Happy to serve."

"That's why we love you, Pete. Take your mandatory heat breaks."

"Sir," Pete said with a nod, and we left him to his guarding.

The interior of the building was as staid and solid as the outside, if more technologically advanced. The door opened into a mudroom with hooks and lockers on one side, a hallway that led to offices on the other. And ahead, a glass door that showed the room beyond—and more tech than I'd seen in one place in years. There were monitors along one wall and a handful of sleek comps.

The building seemed to have a gentle background hum, and I wasn't sure if that was related to the tech, the closeness of the Beyond, or the generators stashed somewhere to keep the facility running.

We followed Gunnar through the door, and he approached a woman in fatigues who stood in front of a table topped by a large map.

"Lieutenant Batiste," Gunnar said, offering a hand to the woman.

She was petite and curvy, with brown skin and dark brown hair in a thick braid that crowned her head. Her eyes were big and brown, topped by perfectly arched brows, and her generous lips curled into a smile punctuated by apple cheeks.

"Landreau," she said to Gunnar, then nodded at Rachel. "Captain."

"Lieutenant," Rachel said. "Everyone, this is Lieutenant Shon Batiste. She's in charge of this outpost. Shon, the entry team."

"Welcome to the dead zone," she said. "Everyone hydrated? Hot out there today."

"We're good," Gunnar said, and gestured at the cooler Gavin had brought in. "Ice, as requested."

A popular bribe in New Orleans.

"Appreciate it. AC service is sketchy at best, and we aren't high on the maintenance priority list. Especially now, when they've got pumps to worry about. Understandable, but irritating."

"How's the field looking?" Gunnar asked.

"Cameras are down, because they apparently hate magic. Which is their prerogative. So we'll use the low-tech version." Shon gestured to the middle of the room, where a man sat in a rotating chair, staring into what looked like binoculars as he moved back and forth.

"Periscope," she said, "with visibility through the turret. Gives us a three-hundred-sixty-degree view around the palisade."

She rotated to face the table. "And our plotting map." The map was topographical, with small blocks placed at various positions across the landscape.

"We're green, and they're red." She picked up what looked like a small rake and gestured to a large green box. "Our current location." She gestured to a series of wavy lines. "The boundary between our world and theirs. We call it 'the Veil' for simplicity's sake, although the barrier itself is burned away for more than a mile."

Between the border and the outpost was a field edged on facing sides by the river and the road. That field was the first gauntlet we'd have to cross to get into the Beyond. Our first step of the journey.

Rachel picked up another rake, used the end to point to two small boxes between us and the Veil. "How many Paras?" she asked.

"Presently about twenty," Shon said, mouth setting into a firm line. "All Court and primarily bruisers. Big creatures intended to block progress in or out. Ogres, golems of the automaton variety. A Cyclops or two."

Lot of Cyclopes in southern Louisiana these days, I thought. "Automatons?" I asked.

"Think of them as robots," she said, "but operated by magic instead of hardware, software."

Not a thing I'd run across before. And like much of what came out of the Beyond, a little bit fascinating and a little bit awful.

"They're guarding the barrier from Containment?" Gavin asked.

"We think they're guarding the barrier from the Consularis.

They don't want them going back home, because they don't think the Beyond should belong to the Consularis anymore."

"And they won't want Consularis coming here, because that could affect the war," Gavin said with a nod. "Without magical conscription, they wouldn't fight us."

"That's the operative theory."

"I didn't see any Paras in front of the barrier," I said, drawing Shon's gaze.

"They stay primarily in the trees, in the shade along the sides of the field, closer to the Veil."

"I'm surprised you haven't taken them out," Gavin said.

"When we try offensive maneuvers, they just retreat into the Beyond. And we haven't had clearance to get in there." She glanced at us. "Not until today. I must admit to some jealousy."

"You want to take my place?" Gavin asked. "I could hang out here with the ice."

"I've got my post orders, thanks. But I like the backpack."

His satisfied smile formed slowly.

"What about this?" Rachel asked, pointing to a small box about halfway between the outpost and the Veil.

"Burned-out Humvee," Shon said. "And cover for the approach. We used it on our last offensive. It's a good spot to aim for before you make the final push."

"That makes sense," Rachel said.

"We advance to the vehicle as quickly as possible," Malachi suggested. "Gavin, Liam, and I draw their fire. Claire and Rachel can run to the Veil."

Malachi seemed oblivious to the insult—the suggestion that Rachel and I skip the fight and run for cover.

But Rachel had no qualms about discussing it. "We can 'run to the Veil'? We're a Sensitive and a trained soldier, and your best idea is that we should let you guys take fire while we run for it?"

Malachi glowered. "It would protect you and Claire."

"Since I'm a black belt in tae kwon do, and Claire could probably lift that truck of hers with a flick of her pinkie finger, I'm fairly certain we don't need protecting. And moreover, it would put half the team at risk, and it wouldn't take advantage of Claire's considerable power."

The look on Malachi's face—a glower-plus—could have torched the room. But he managed to stay quiet.

"We're a team," Rachel said. "We act like one." She looked at me. "Thoughts?"

I could feel their gazes on me as I studied the map. "You're the ops expert," I said after my review, "but I'm thinking the truck. We raise it, use it like a shield, push in behind it."

Rachel looked back at the table, brows lifted. "You playing Captain America today?"

"I self-identify as Scarlet Witch," I said. "But that's close enough."

"You could lift it?"

"I could." Or at least I was pretty sure I could. It was probably heavier than the material pile I'd moved in Tremé, if more compact.

I glanced at Liam. "A little help wouldn't be a bad idea."

"My pleasure, *cher.*"

Rachel walked around the table, considering the lie from various angles. "First move to the truck," she said quietly, as if reciting the plan to herself, working it over, looking for weaknesses. "Claire and Liam push forward. Gavin, Malachi, and I watch the flank, the rear."

Gavin managed not to snicker at "rear," which made me very proud.

"Then we arrive at the Veil," she said, then stopped, looked at me. "What do you do with the vehicle to get it out of the way?"

"Toss it back," Liam said, glancing at me for confirmation.

"Yeah. We could do that. We have to put it down at some point. Might as well put it down behind us."

Rachel looked at Malachi. "Does that work for you, Commander?"

There was something about the way she said his title, something that didn't seem quite military. Something that felt intimate. But no one else seemed to notice it, or at least everyone kept their thoughts to themselves, so I did, too.

"It's an acceptable plan," he said. The words were tight, but he wouldn't have agreed if he'd thought it too risky.

"I love a compromise in the morning," Shon said. "We can cover you from here, but it could get messy out there, and we don't want any of you hit by friendly fire. We'll have cleaner shots once you're past the Humvee.

"Bigger problem is, we won't be able to tell when you're coming back on the return trip. We keep eyes on the field through the scope twenty-four/seven, but we won't know you're here until you're here. When we see you, we'll provide what cover we can."

"Do what you can," Liam said. "The rest is on us."

I looked at Malachi. "I'm going to use a lot of magic going in. And it's going to try to refill itself."

"Let it," he said. "Give yourself a minute to refill before you walk in. Better to reach capacity here than in the Veil."

"Fill the bottle with the hose," Gavin translated. "Not in the river."

"A rough metaphor," Malachi agreed.

"Then let's do it," Liam said.

I pulled Scarlet's keys from my pocket, offered them to Gunnar. "You'll be careful with her?"

"I have no interest in provoking your wrath. So yes." He wrapped an arm around me, squeezed. "I love you, Claire-Bear."

"Ahem," Liam said crisply. "Claire-Bear?"

"We've known each other for a long time," I said. "And please never use that again, any of you."

Gavin snorted. "No way. That's going in the permanent file."

I gave Gunnar a narrowed look. "Was that really necessary?"

"It was," he said with a grin. "Be careful."

"I will."

We headed for the door.

"It was a pleasure to meet you," Gavin said, giving the lieutenant a mild salute.

Shon quirked up an eyebrow. "Oh, that's very sweet, but you cannot handle me."

"I wasn't even flirting with her," Gavin murmured as we walked toward the door, and actually sounded sincere.

Maybe he was getting used to the idea of dating a scientist, after all.

CHAPTER TWELVE

We stood between the building and the barrier, facing the latter and the Veil beyond it. Malachi in front, then me and Liam, then Rachel and Gavin behind. The palisade was still closed while gear was checked, clips inserted, knives unsheathed.

My heart was pounding, energy and magic mingling to put a tremble in my fingers. I wouldn't deny I was afraid, but fear was only one part of a complicated mix. I wanted action, to do something after days of feeling helpless. I wanted to see the Beyond. I wanted to stop Aeryth's revenge campaign.

I also wanted Liam safe.

I looked over at him, found his gaze already on me, blue eyes sapphire bright and streaked with gold. It felt like there were still things that needed to be said. But there was no time to say them.

"Claire and Liam," Rachel said. "This would be the time to spin up whatever power you might need."

"On it," I said, and closed my eyes, reached out a hand, began to feel out the magic . . . and almost stumbled back because of the raw power in the air.

"Lot of it," Liam said.

"Yeah. It's raw. Green. Pure."

Without a door to hold it back, magic had drifted through. The feel of it was familiar, but more pronounced now. Stronger, and less diffuse. I began to gather it up.

"Ready," Rachel whispered, and the gate began to *thush* open on its track, just like the one in the back of the building.

In seconds, we had a clear view of the hazy limit of our world and the beginning of the Beyond. There was green on the other side of the haze and, fortunately, no uniformed Paras waiting to attack.

The field in front of us looked clear. Bright and green and oppressively hot, but empty of Paras. Either they hadn't been drawn by our arrival or they were smart enough to keep from showing it.

The Humvee lay almost exactly halfway between us and the Veil, about thirty yards away, and just to the left of our position. The ground was flat, with a few clusters of overgrown grass here and there, but nothing that looked substantial enough to shield us as we ran the gauntlet.

So we'd have to run fast.

"On three," Liam said. "One, two, three."

We ran forward, arms pumping, feet kicking, toward the Humvee. Malachi lifted, took to the sky to scout for movement.

It took only seconds for things to go sideways.

I felt magic before I saw movement, and then it was only a gleaming star of fire. Malachi jerked above us, and began to drop.

"Oh, fuck," Gavin muttered, echoing all our thoughts.

Our direction already set, we skidded behind the vehicle, squeezing into the space between shredded tires.

But Rachel wasn't with us. She'd veered toward Malachi, crossing the field just as he made an awkward touchdown, and wrapped an arm around him.

She'd just helped Malachi to his feet when an ogre emerged from the tree line. Nearly seven feet tall, with a cyclopean build and uglier face with flattened, crooked features and skin the color of a day-old bruise. But his armor was as golden and gleaming as the Seelies' had been. The earth shook with each step, flattening an oval bigger than a basketball in the grass.

She fired and hit him dead in the shoulder. The creature jerked back, grunted, but kept moving.

"Gavin," Liam said, "cover them!"

"*Suppressing fire!*" Gavin yelled, and hit the ground running. He veered toward Malachi and Rachel, firing at the ogres who loped toward the pair.

"Are you supposed to yell out what you're doing?" I asked, trying to concentrate on keeping the magic I'd already spooled ready to use. There was a lot of it, and it wanted release. It wanted to fly.

"No," Liam said. "But he's got his own style. *Merde,*" he swore, and moved around to my right, pulled his own weapon, as a Cyclops—probably with an unpronounceable name—ran toward us from the other side of the field.

I pivoted, hand extended to throw him into the field, but Liam put back an arm. "No," he said. "Keep the magic ready. When everyone is back and mobile, we need to move. This thing is going to take a lot of power."

"I can't just stand here and watch while everybody else fights."

"You aren't. You're keeping the fire stoked and waiting on us to get our shit together." He grabbed me around the waist, pulled me in for a hard and heated kiss.

Then he dropped to a knee, a tire giving him some cover, and fired. He nailed the Cyclops in the knee on the first shot.

Gavin helped Malachi to his feet, and Rachel gave them cover as they hustled back to the vehicle.

Suddenly, a creature darted from the other edge of the tree line to Rachel's left, heading right toward her. It was tall and lean and the color of terra-cotta, its face a smooth, clay approximation of a human's face, its movements stiff and mechanical. A machine trying to mimic a human.

Golem, I realized.

"On your left!" I shouted, and Rachel pivoted, fired.

The shot lodged in his chest, but didn't stop him.

She ran toward the golem, unsheathing a knife as she ran. Then she cartwheeled into the air—knife in hand—to avoid the golem's low swing.

"Damn," I said, impressed, as Gavin helped Malachi behind our mechanical shield.

"You all right?" Liam asked, glancing back between shots at a pair of ogres.

"He nicked a feather." His teeth were gritted, tone sharp. "That disrupted the airfoil. I can walk off the fall. But I can't fly until it's gone."

Rachel ran forward, ducked behind the Humvee. *"Girlfriend,"* I said. "You can move."

She lifted a shoulder. "Part of the job." She turned to Malachi. "Are you okay?"

He grimaced against pain. "You have to pull the feather. I can't fly if it's broken. That's physics."

Rachel considered him for a long moment, gaze narrowed. And I'd have bought a ticket for a peek at what she was thinking as she stared at him.

"The connection points have a lot of nerves, right? So this will hurt you?"

"Yes."

That word, said without fear, put decision in her eyes. "All right," she said, and sheathed her knife. "Stay on the left," she said to Liam, then turned to Gavin, pointed at a shrub fifteen yards from the vehicle. "They don't get closer than that while I do this." Then she looked back at Malachi. "Show me."

Malachi extended a wing, or as much as he could in the shelter of the vehicle. One of the long feathers near the bottom edge was broken and twisted at an awkward angle, and blood was smeared along the feather-covered muscle where it had attached.

Rachel looked without touching, blew out a breath, then looked back at Malachi. "Straight out, or do I need to twist?"

"Straight out," he said, teeth gritted. "Do it now."

She didn't hesitate, but gripped the edge of the feather, her own muscles bunched, and pulled.

His scream was otherworldly, a multilayered sound that rang through my bones like I was standing beneath a bell. Ibises rose and lifted from nearby fields, startled by the sound, and the advancing Paras stopped in their tracks.

His fists were knotted, his chest heaving, his eyes closed as he battled the pain. After a moment, his breathing slowed, and he opened his eyes, turned his gaze to her. The heat in the look could have melted metal. "Thank you."

She just nodded, seemed a little shocked by his reaction.

"I hate to interrupt this rom-com in the making," Gavin said, "but are we ready to move this vehicle? Because we have a lot of company on the way."

We looked back. They were advancing from all sides now, a semi-circle of Paranormals with weapons drawn and ready. If Malachi's scream had given them any pause, they'd worked through it now.

Malachi moved to the edge of the vehicle, extended his wings, stretched them. That halted them for a moment, but they regained their courage quickly enough.

"Malachi, you're on the right," Rachel said. "I've got the left." She looked back at me. "You ready?"

I nodded, blew out a breath, looked at Liam.

"When you're ready," he said, holstering his weapon and taking a position beside me. "You start the song and I'll join in."

I turned to the vehicle, extended my arm, and began to unspool Elysium's wild magic.

It was potent, but thorny. Hard to control. Hard to direct. I clenched my fingers to force the threads of magic into every nook and cranny of the vehicle, filling it until the magic made it buoyant. Or at least that was the theory.

I bore down, and I pushed.

And nothing happened.

It was heavier than I thought it would be. It clung to the earth like a grasping child, refusing to let go. I knew it was only a matter of mass and gravity, but I didn't care about physical laws. I cared about magic—and getting this goddamn vehicle off the ground.

"I saw the turn signal," Gavin said, then fired twice. "So that's great. Just, you know, add in the rest now, Claire."

Liam swore in Cajun, poured more magic into mine, amplifying the power I'd wrapped around it. Our magic danced together, melded, became stronger for the union.

That seemed to be a common theme today.

Metal creaked and groaned, shook, and then hovered, bobbing in the air, lifted by the force of our magic.

"Truck's up," Rachel said. "Gavin, keep an eye on the rear."

"You don't have to tell me twice," Gavin said, and shots fired behind me as we began to move forward.

Each step was a marathon. The ground was uneven, and I had to plant my feet to keep the vehicle aloft, had to use my strength, my magic, and Liam's to keep it in the air. Telekinesis fought against gravity, against friction—and gravity fought back like a living thing.

I bore down, poured all my focus into the truck. Five yards, then ten, then twenty. And then we were close enough to the border that the trees on the other side, the landscape of the Beyond, grew clearer, my head swimming from the open conduit of magic I needed to keep the Humvee in the air and moving forward.

"Ten yards," Rachel called out. "You're almost there, guys. You're doing great."

"Incoming," Gavin said, and something shook the ground a few feet behind us, sparks snapping in the air.

"What the fuck was that?" Liam asked, teeth clenched.

"Peskies now have grenades," Gavin said.

"Peskies," I murmured darkly, "are the bane of my existence."

"Along with that heavy-ass truck?" Gavin asked, metal snicking as he reloaded.

I bit back a smile. I didn't want to lose focus. Not this close. "Along with this heavy-ass truck."

One foot forward, and then another, I was fixated on the underside of the Humvee and the ground beneath my feet.

"All right," Rachel said. "We're five yards out. It's time to dump the truck. Y'all ready?"

"Ready," we said simultaneously.

"One big push," Liam said.

"Just like you're giving birth!"

I heard someone slug Gavin's arm. "Thank you," I said aloud, to whoever deserved the kudos.

"On three," Liam said again. "One, two—"

We were so close to the Beyond, to the magic it contained, that the world was aflame with it. I let it pour in, let it give buoyancy to the truck, so when Liam got to "Three!" tossing it was child's play.

It flew over our heads and behind, and hit the ground twenty feet behind us with a crash and a *squelch* that said we'd probably weaponized it. It bobbled, rolled twice, and came to a rest.

"Go!" Rachel yelled, and ran through the filmy boundary.

Gavin followed, and then Malachi put a hand on my arm, looked at me. "Magic?"

"I'm okay. I had to keep replenishing to keep the car in the air. I can manage."

And I hoped that wasn't just adrenaline talking.

I crossed my fingers and ran through.

"Everybody okay?" Liam asked when we'd made it into the Beyond.

"Fine," Rachel said, holstering her weapon and taking a look around.

Elysium looked . . . a lot like southern Louisiana. The sky was blue, the clouds white and fluffy, a single sun hanging above us. The land was relatively flat and green, with clusters of trees edging wide fields and birds chirping within them.

But it felt like standing inside a power station. The power a steady thrum in my head, a vibration that seemed to reach to the marrow of my bones. Feeling the Veil had been like being washed by a cresting wave of power. This was being set adrift in the ocean with no life preserver, no raft.

The pressure grew until it seemed to fill my head, until the sound of the breeze, the grass, the birds, muted like a light being turned off. My eyes seemed too big for my sockets, my skin too tight to hold my body, my joints uncomfortable as I sank to my knees.

I looked up, saw Liam's mouth was moving, but there was no sound.

My heartbeat was so loud, so slow, I thought it was the march of a coming army. I looked around, trying to find the source, locate the battalion that was obviously moving closer to us. But there was nothing but sunshine and grass. I put my fist against my chest, felt the beats there, and tried to breathe through the haze.

Liam dropped to his knees and placed a hand on my face, and I saw panic in his eyes.

I fought my own rising panic, tried to think what I should be doing about it. And of all the random things, I thought of the last plane ride I'd taken and what had worked when my ears had begun to ache from the pressurization. Without a better idea, I closed my eyes, pinched my nose, and blew.

Sound returned with a sharp *pop* as the pressure equalized in my head.

"Claire? *Claire!*"

"I'm okay," I said, wincing at the sudden volume increase. I was still shaky, and still felt bloated with power. But at least the fog was gone. "It's . . . the magic. I'm adjusting."

"Adjusting well?" Malachi asked, looking me over.

"Adjusting," I said again. "That's all I'm willing to commit to." I looked up at Liam, gave him a quick scan, and found he didn't look any different. "You're okay?"

"I'm fine," he said, but there was an edge to his voice. He looked at Malachi. "It's fighting me."

Malachi moved closer. "How?"

"It wants . . . in. Or out. Or . . . I don't know. Maybe I want it. Want to grab it. Something in my head—the sixth sense, whatever feels the magic. It's . . . aware how much is out there."

"The magic is outside you," Malachi said. "It can't get to you unless you take it in. Unless you pull it in. And you're stronger than that."

His eyes were spinning gold, flashing coins, blinding suns.

"*Ça va,*" Gavin said, squatting in front of us. "Snap out of it, *frère.* Apply some of that big-brother stubbornness and beat it back."

Liam squeezed his eyes closed, shook his head. "It *wants* . . ."

Still dizzy, still full of magic, I put my hands on his face. "Liam. Fight it back."

He shook his head again, sweat glistening across his forehead as he fought the war we couldn't see.

"*Liam*," I said again. "Stop this." I made my tone as sharp as I could manage. As insistent as I could manage. "Ignore the magic and come back. We have things to do and you're wasting time."

"Power," he said quietly. "So much at the ready."

"Not your power," I said. "It's not meant for you, and you don't need it. You've got the self-control. You just have to use it."

He shook his head fiercely, muscles rigid beneath my hands. I dropped them from his face, took his balled fists, brought them to my lips. I kissed each of them in turn.

"I'm here," I whispered. "I know you can do this. You're strong. You're devastatingly handsome, and if you don't shut it down, I'll use my magic to yank the desire right out of you. And I don't think you want that."

His eyes opened. Gold swirled, dissipated . . . and faded to a bare shimmer.

"You in there?" I asked. And I was half-afraid he wouldn't be able to answer.

"I'm here." His eyes narrowed. "Did you threaten to magic me?"

"Only a little. And for your own good."

He closed his eyes, turned his face into my palm, and smiled. "I always wanted a girl I could count on."

I let out the breath I'd been holding. He was back.

"He's all right," I said, and could practically feel the group's collective sigh of relief.

"You're gonna sleep really well tonight," I said. "That was a good workout."

"Not ideal," he said weakly, and I couldn't really argue with that.

We climbed to our feet, stood there a moment until we were both stable.

"Humans don't belong in the Beyond," I said, "is the lesson of this particular experience."

"Cosign," Liam said, running his hands through his hair, then took a swig from the canteen Gavin offered him.

I opened my mouth to suggest we get moving, when an enormous shadow traced the ground. I braced for another fight, another impact, the glint of gold off Seelie armor.

We all looked up—and stared.

Not a Seelie, I realized. Not even a guard or an ironically named welcome committee. And I didn't think it was a Paranormal. Or not really.

It was a *mosquito*. If mosquitoes were more than a foot long.

Its body was a narrow tube striped in brown and white, its legs long, skinny, and segmented, its wings narrow and translucent. And at the end of its disproportionately small face was the tubelike nose that could definitely do some damage.

This thing wasn't just a nuisance. It was a *monster*.

"And speaking of things that shouldn't be in the Beyond," Rachel said.

Liam slid his gaze to Malachi. "You didn't mention this particular part of Elysium."

"It's not native," Malachi said. "It's one of yours."

"It came through the Veil," I realized. "Came through the Veil and was affected by magic."

"So it's a Sensitive," Gavin said with a grin. "Typical. Always with the drama. With the magic. Should we—should we kill it?"

We all looked at Gavin.

"I mean, it's a mosquito, right? It's not here to fix your cable. It's a parasite."

"It is," Liam said. "And it might be carrying viruses."

"Virii," Rachel said with a smile, crouching as the—insect seemed too mild a word—leviathan flew overhead.

"How would you even make a sleeping net for that?" He moved his heads around his head. "They could probably proboscis right through it."

"I don't think you can use 'proboscis' as a verb," I said.

"Contrary to all evidence," Gavin said, giving himself an air check.

"It might be the only one of its kind," I said, feeling suddenly Time Lord–y about it. "An Earth-Beyond hybrid." Not unlike me and Liam and Burke. Affected by two worlds. "Do we really want to kill it?"

Before we could wrestle with the ethics of it, an enormous bird— feathers ink black and gleaming, beak a brilliant vermilion—swooped through the brush and snatched the mosquito midair with clawed feet. Wings beating the air, but making no sound, it lifted and soared into a stand of tall trees and out of sight.

For a moment, we just stared at empty space.

"I think that was our best-case scenario," Liam said quietly.

Rachel nodded. "We were just saved from a moral conundrum."

Gavin looked at Malachi. "If we find more of those, you might as well just burn Elysium to the ground and start over. Malaria isn't worth it."

"Let's get moving," Malachi said, and we began to walk.

CHAPTER THIRTEEN

Malachi had brought his beautiful map, now filled in with additional details about the land we were marching through. He took point, and Rachel held the map, pausing now and again to suggest formations when we crossed something unusual in the landscape.

And as we moved farther from the Veil, the obvious effects of our world began to fade. The terrain dried out, so swamp-edged flats gave way to meadows carpeted with pale purple wildflowers that swayed gently in the breeze.

"This is gorgeous," I said, skimming my hand over the thick fringe of blossoms. The movement put shimmering pollen and the smell of lavender into the air, and left a faint tingle in my fingertips.

It was magic, somehow condensed in the flora. Not magic that deadened soil or scorched trees, but allowed this beautiful landscape to thrive. What would it be like to live in a place like this, where magic was beneficial, not destructive? Where it wasn't a sickness I had to manage, but a gift I could enjoy? A strength, and not a weakness?

We walked through the meadow, following a neatly edged trail of packed grass. The trail curved here and there, but we moved steadily forward. After two hours of walking, most of us silent as we watched the landscape, I realized we'd seen no people, no farms, no roads, no houses, no animals. No sign of wildlife at all but for the distant chirp of some unseen birds. No signs that anyone inhabited this place. Just the rolling expanse of meadows, a breeze that smelled like lavender, and the cheerful call of birds hidden in the deep blanket of grasses.

"Where is everyone?" I asked Malachi.

"The population lives in cities," Malachi said. "Homes and property are communally owned, divided, regulated. And there are fewer beings here than on Earth."

"And fewer still since the invasion," Rachel said.

I expected Malachi to argue, to make some defense of his homeland, but none came.

"And no armed sentries," Gavin said. "No patrols. No cameras, no fences. Are your people so confident?"

"The division was between Court and Consularis," Malachi said. "There had been guards, patrols. Destruction. Apparently they're no longer needed."

But he sounded unsure, as if the pastoral scenery was surprising to him, too. But if he had more to say, he kept it to himself.

We reached a glade of tall and slender trees that looked like willows—the bark almost glossily smooth, the branches delicate and fluid in the breeze. They arced overhead like the dome of a cathedral, sending dappled light. Their branches bore fruit: butter yellow spheres about the size of grapes that hung in clusters of four or five. The skin was bright and gleaming, and they looked like the kind of fruit my father would have warned me was very, very poisonous.

"What are those?" I asked.

Malachi looked, evaluated. "Honoras. They are similar to your, I think, blackberries."

"Can we try one?" I asked.

We might have been on a mission, but this would probably be my first and only trip to the Beyond. I'd need to experience what I could while I could.

With a faintly amused smile, Malachi reached carefully around prickly vines, plucked one out, and offered it to me.

It was heavier than I'd expected. The skin was taut and smooth and, when I took a bite, nearly crisp. The center was softer, like the inside of a mango, and tasted like sunshine.

"It's like a cross between a pineapple and a grape," I said, smiling up at Malachi. "You guys get points for produce."

"While we're snacking . . . ," Gavin began, and pulled a granola bar from his bag. He unwrapped it, began to crunch.

Liam stopped, glared at his brother. "Why are you chewing so loudly? You sound like a damn beaver."

"Do beavers make that much noise?" Gavin asked, crunching again.

"I will take the granola bar away."

"I think you need one. You're irritable and testy."

Liam's lip curled.

"All right, children," I said, and made the risky decision to step between them, putting a hand on each (well-muscled) chest. "We're all tired and hungry. Gavin, stop irritating your brother. Liam, eat a snack, because you're getting hangry."

"This is our Fort Walton Beach road trip all over again," Gavin said.

"Except I have a lot less vomit in my hair."

Malachi's eyes widened. "Why would you put vomit in your hair?"

"I don't think it was put there on purpose," Rachel said with a smile.

I patted Liam's chest. "Have a snack," I repeated, then pointed a warning finger at Gavin. "Chill out," I said quietly, "or I'll place the rest of the granola bar in a very uncomfortable place."

Gavin's eyes narrowed. "You wouldn't."

"You want to test me?"

He watched me for a moment, eyes cool and appraising. It was the same look, I bet, that he'd given the bounties he'd captured. "No," he finally said. "Not because I think you'd do it, but because I don't want to watch you try. And I ate all the granola bar."

If only all conflicts ended so easily. But Malachi's features were still drawn. And I read concern in that tightness.

"Why are you worried?" I asked.

Malachi glanced at me and away again. "I am not worried. But I'd rather keep moving. And quickly."

"Because of winged monkeys, poppies, or twisters?" I figured wicked witches were a given.

He turned back to me, eyes wide. "Earth has monkeys with wings?"

"Not at present. But we aren't in Louisiana anymore."

"Might as well be," Gavin said, slapping the back of his neck. "Bugs are fierce out here."

"Maybe they just like you best," Liam said. "I'm not having any issues."

Then Gavin slapped his arm, his neck again. "What the crap, Beyond?" But then his gaze softened. "Oh," he said, and I looked back.

No mosquito this time, but the tendril of one of the willow branches, long and lithe.

"Oh, wow," Gavin said as the tip of the branch flicked and moved like the zig of a wand or the flick of a whip.

But magic pulsed in the air, and there was nothing friendly about it now. The trees began to rustle and shift, darkness falling over us as the branches overhead moved together, began to braid into a canopy that was no longer lithe and light dappled, but powerful and foreboding.

Magic began to ripple around us, warping the air like heat rising from an asphalt highway. The hair on my arms, the back of my neck, lifted in that magic, and the buzz in my head grew louder.

So much energy. So much power.

"Malachi," Rachel said quietly, moving her weapon. "Are the trees alive? I mean, more than usual?"

"Move closer to me," Malachi said by way of answer, the words low and careful. He dropped his backpack and extended his wings, the sound like the snap of a crisp linen sheet.

"So much magic," Liam said, his voice dusky and low. I looked at him, found gold swimming in his eyes, and feared that his control would slip away in the rising current.

There was a quick whip of sound, and the branch of a willow twined around Gavin's ankle like a shackle, hauled him into the air.

Liam cursed, pulled his knife out.

Another flick, and the knife was gone, too, held tight by the delicate green tip of a willow branch that spiraled around it.

Gavin screamed as another tendril grabbed his other ankle, bound them together, and pulled him higher into the canopy. His head was fifteen feet above the ground now, and he struggled—trying to rise up and loosen the ties at his ankles—but the willow bobbed and weaved so that he couldn't get a grip.

"Stop moving," Malachi told him, as we took shelter in the shadows of his wings.

"You stop moving!" Gavin said, wriggling as the branches moved up his calves, twined around his shins, then his knees.

"Be still," Malachi said. "As long as you move, you are a threat."

Gavin stopped wriggling, let his hands fall past his head, blood rushing to his face as he hung upside down.

The magic shifted, changed direction, a curious breeze now. It moved through and around us, inspecting and investigating us. And as quickly as it had arrived, it seemed to be sucked back into the trees.

"Was that it?" Rachel asked, hand on the nine-millimeter at her side. "Is it gone?"

Malachi didn't even need to say no.

This time, it was the trees themselves that swayed, the slick bark shimmering and moving around the trunks as cells moved and re-arranged.

The bark expanded, thinned, and what looked like fingers began to press through it like it was a curtain. As if a monster was reaching out toward us.

"Okay," Gavin said. "I'm cool that I'm up here now. I'll just hang—*ha ha*—while y'all deal with the anthropomorphizing trees."

As if irritated by the insult, the tree shook him like a rag doll.

"*Blurg*," was his only response.

The fingers pressed farther through the bark, the skin of it so thin it looked like it might snap. An arm followed, then two, then knees and legs, then a torso and the vague outline of a face, hair waving and extending up through the thousand thin branches above us.

The bark's texture lightened and softened, and the shape became that of a woman. She stepped out of the tree, skin pale and pink, as if emerging from a shell. Or, given the quiet sucking sound that accompanied the slide of the creature, from a cocoon.

She was, of course, willowy. She had long limbs and smooth skin, and while the delicacy made me think she was female, she didn't have any of the physical attributes that would have identified any gender. Or humanity.

Her mouth was small. Her nose thin and long. Her eyes enormous pale orbs with irises the color of new leaves, her hair the same color at the tips, but fading to white as it neared her crown.

She stepped closer, her delicate feet making no sound as she moved. Two more of them emerged from trees beside us. One with hair a darker shade of green, the other's red like mine. They formed a triangle, moved together toward us, synchronized like a school of fish, their movements equally fluid.

"Tree nymphs," Rachel quietly said.

Malachi simply nodded.

The one in front, the apex of the triangle, looked us over, final gaze landing on Rachel. Then up at Gavin.

The wind shifted, rustling the leaves. Or I thought it was the wind until I realized her mouth was open, lips and small white teeth moving as she spoke in her particular language.

Whatever she said had the tips of Malachi's wings moving around us, covering our backs.

"No," he said aloud.

The wind blew harder, the willows swaying, branches snapping as they moved back and forth in the air.

"I'm about to pass out," Gavin said above us.

"No," Malachi said again. "You will allow us to continue on our way, or we will fight back. We will take you down."

"Can you stop them?" Rachel asked. "Make them go back into the trees? Tell them we don't mean any harm?"

"They are not critical thinkers," Malachi said. "You are strangers. You are different. They view difference as negative."

"If they don't stop," I said, hoping they'd hear and take the point, "then we'll have to stop them. We'll have to hurt them."

Gavin bobbed to the left. I looked at Malachi. "I can do it without blades."

I got his reluctant nod.

If I could move a Humvee, I figured I could unwrap a vine.

But that was Earth logic talking.

I reached out for magic, was nearly knocked down by the sheer amount of power that answered my call. It was like having an entire power plant at my fingertips. I gathered it up, the filaments of magic fighting back against my grasp, as if it also realized I was different. I was a *stranger*.

I lifted my gaze toward the tree limb, wrapped magic around the tendril, and pulled. When nothing happened, I added more magic, pulled again. The tendril simply jerked in the other direction, like the same poles of two magnets pushing each other away.

Gavin squealed as he rolled through the air, and I stared, trying to figure out what had gone wrong, and how to make it right. Either telekinesis wasn't effective on the tendrils of a Paranormal tree nymph, or it knew what I was doing and was quick enough to avoid it.

The tendril jerked so hard it loosened Gavin's backpack, which glittered to the earth with a heavy *thunk* that made me wonder what he'd packed in there.

And I wasn't the only curious one.

The vine stopped moving, the nymphs going still and glancing down at the backpack, which landed halfway between us.

The backpack was ours, not theirs. It had no magic. This, I figured, I could deal with.

I snatched it up with magic, flung it high into the air, higher than the vines could reach, and I kept it there.

"You can have the backpack," I said, "if you let him go and let us walk away."

The wind rose fiercely, leaves shaking with the nymphs' furious response.

Malachi watched them mildly, then lifted a shoulder. "I cannot control the human. She does as she pleases. If you wish a gift from the Terrans, you must let him go."

I played up the bad-cop element and gave them hard looks.

Something worked—maybe just their covetousness—because the vines began to retract, the trees to straighten and look more like trees than hulking predators.

The tendril wrapped around Gavin's ankle released. He dropped, arms flailing, and fell neatly into Malachi's arms.

"If I wasn't about to vomit," Gavin said, face beet red and sweaty, as he patted Malachi's cheek, "I'd kiss you right on the mouth."

"I do not wish to kiss you," Malachi said, and dropped Gavin to his feet. Liam reached out to give him a steadying hand as he found his footing and the blood began to circulate again.

"Thank you," Malachi said, looking back at the nymphs. "Step back, please."

More wind, more rustling, and the nymphs stepped backward, nearly back to their respective trees. But their gazes didn't waver from the bag.

"Go ahead, Claire," he said, and I nodded.

I swept in more magic, tossed the bag thirty feet away from us, and in the direction opposite from where we needed to go.

The wind screamed as they rushed it, girls and leaves and branches moving like a horde of snakes toward glitter and unicorn and rainbow.

We ran for it.

"I hope you didn't want anything out of that backpack," I said when Malachi had pulled on his backpack, and we'd put a few hundred yards between us and the trees.

Gavin shrugged. "Eh, it was mostly granola bars and UNO cards."

We all looked at him.

"Why did you bring UNO cards on a trip into the Beyond?" Rachel asked.

"To trade with the Paras. They're probably fascinated by earthly artifacts."

"I am intrigued that you consider UNO cards appropriate currency," Rachel said, and held up a hand before he could argue. "But it doesn't matter."

"No, it doesn't. But I told y'all the backpack was baller." He glanced at Malachi. "You might have mentioned the killer trees."

"It seemed better to apologize than seek permission. I believe that's the correct phrase?"

"Who's been teaching him expressions again?" Liam asked, and looked at me.

"Not it," I said.

Gavin patted Malachi collegially on the back. "Next time we go on a mission together, we're going to need to discuss your briefing style."

"I don't have a briefing style."

"Yeah," Gavin said. "That's kind of my point."

"I thought it was invigorating," Liam said, rolling his shoulders. His eyes were nearly solid gold, and gleamed like bright coins.

I felt slow and swollen, as if the magic was taking up space in my body again.

"Are you okay?" Rachel asked, walking toward me, her features pulled into a frown. "You look pale. Well, paler than usual," she added with a smile.

"Magic," I said. "I need to sit." Without waiting for a response, I bent my legs and went to my knees before they could collapse beneath me.

Rachel crouched, gently touched the back of her hand to my forehead. Her hand was chillingly cool, refreshing against the hard and hot pulse of magic, and I nearly leaned into it. And there was worry in her eyes when she glanced at Liam, then Malachi. "She's burning up. Too much magic?"

"Too much pure magic. Her body senses an invasion, an enemy, and it begins to attack."

"She should have stayed in New Orleans," Liam said. "I shouldn't have let her come."

"Not your call," I said. *"My call.* I'll fix this. I'll cast it off."

"But you said she couldn't cast off," Liam said, looking at Malachi. "You told us that before we left."

"Casting off is, relatively speaking, a blunt instrument. It's difficult to calibrate, to expel the right amount, even with experience. But perhaps I can help."

I watched, groggy and with my head spinning, as he reached out a hand toward my chest.

Liam's eyes flashed hot—the sun catching a flipped coin—and he put a halting grip on Malachi's arm. "Watch it."

Malachi's expression barely changed. "You are under the influence as well. You would know that I mean her no harm."

"I don't think it's the harm he's worried about," Rachel said.

"Not the—*oh*," Malachi said, and a flush rose across his cheekbones as he apparently realized exactly what part he'd intended to grab. "Of course not."

"Not flattering," I muttered, and felt like I was watching the conversation happen to someone else.

"Liam, let him help," Rachel said, covering Liam's hand with hers.

It took a moment, but he dropped it, and left red streaks across Malachi's arm—tracks where his fingers had dug in.

"Take a step back," Gavin said, carefully moving Liam aside. "Let him help her." He looked at Malachi. "Maybe when you're done with her, you can take care of the Creature from the Gold Lagoon over here."

Malachi blinked. "There is no lagoon."

"It's a movie reference," Rachel said, stepping into the space between Malachi and Liam, to prevent any further interruptions. "Do what you need to do, and do it quickly. Before any other creatures decide we'd make fun playthings."

Cheeks still pinkened, he nodded, and lifted his hand again. He placed his palm against my breastbone, fingers splayed to just touch my clavicle, and closed his eyes.

"I will take only a little," he said quietly. "Just enough to help you find balance. To relieve the pressure. All right?"

I nodded, not risking myself to speak, and closed my eyes.

My bones began to warm beneath his fingers, the warmth spreading into muscle, into blood, down through my chest and arms, until the heated tingle reached my feet. And with it, the sensation of skin and muscle and bone being adjusted. Being pulled forward, as he drew magic from beneath my skin, from whatever parts of my body had absorbed it, held it tight.

It didn't hurt, exactly, but it was an odd feeling, to be pulled from the inside. To have power drawn out, removed by someone else.

And he'd been right—it was a more careful process than how I usually cast off, which was meant to get rid of as much magic as possible as quickly as possible. To let it spill out, so I could shove it into something else.

This was focused, slow, careful. A trimming away. A tidying up.

When he pulled his hand away, I opened my eyes, blinked at him.

"How do you feel?"

I took an inventory. I no longer felt like too much boudin in too little casing.

"Better," I said, and he stepped aside so Liam could help me to my feet. Hopefully that would help sort out the egos.

"You're good?" he asked quietly, tugging the end of my ponytail.

"For now. You?"

"I'm fine. The need has backed off some. Maybe because I'm getting used to it." He didn't look thrilled at that.

Gavin looked at us. "If everybody's magic is balanced and chi aligned, can we get moving? Because I'd really like to not stand around like prey if we can avoid it."

"Have you had a tough morning?" Rachel asked sympathetically.

"I really have. And I've got a raging headache."

Malachi looked around. "Others will seek us out. They've deemed you enemies because you don't have magic."

"How can they tell that?" Gavin asked.

Malachi lifted an eyebrow. "Can you tell that I do have magic?"

"I mean . . . ," Gavin began, and pointed to his wings. "It's obvious you aren't human. Or that you're really good at cosplay."

"What is—" Malachi began, but Gavin cut him off with a headshake.

"American pop culture lesson later."

"It is obvious to those who have magic that you do not," Malachi said. Then he looked around, surveying the horizon, eyes narrowed as if he was gauging the distance. "We can travel within the sphere of my magic," he decided, and glanced at me, then Liam. "Expand it, to a certain extent, to encompass others."

We'd seen him do it, increasing the range of Burke's abilities when we'd worked to sneak Eleanor and Moses out of Devil's Isle.

"None of us has invisibility magic," Gavin pointed out.

"We don't need it," Malachi said. "You don't need to look like Paranormals. You just need to seem . . . a little less human."

"Is that a compliment or no?" Rachel asked thoughtfully, and with a whisper of a grin curling her mouth.

"It's not an insult," Liam said, and nodded at Malachi. "How do we do it?"

CHAPTER FOURTEEN

We walked in a lump.

You could call it a knot, or a tangle, or a collective. But mostly it was a lump with Malachi in the center, the rest of us jabbing one another with knees and elbows as we tried to move as a unit and stay within the halo of his magic.

It was uncomfortable, and we'd walked nearly ten miles through more glades and over rolling hills, and without another Paranormal in sight. But after the nymphs, it seemed obvious that our not being able to see them didn't mean they weren't there.

It still felt like we were being watched. Evaluated and found unremarkable, and generally left alone, just as we'd wanted. But the feeling was still unnerving, as was the really, really manicured state of our surroundings.

"Too perfect," Gavin muttered.

"Cosign," Liam said. "Like every tree has been arranged just so."

"We're nearly to the city," Malachi said.

"In which case, we'll need to be prepared for what?" Rachel asked.

"Soldiers."

"Of course," Gavin muttered. "You're a commander, right? So you can take care of that?"

"I don't think they'll take up arms against us. At least not at first," he added, just when we'd begun to relax. "The city is just over this rise."

So we paused, adjusted our packs, looked at one another, nodded when we were ready, and began to climb.

My legs ached by the time we reached the top. It had been a long time since I'd made this many miles on foot, and a dull ache had taken residence in my thighs, a sharp pain in my heels where I knew blisters had set in. But we were nearly there. And adrenaline kept me walking past my stopping point.

I wasn't sure what I'd see over the crest. An emerald city, a world of skyscrapers and flying cars, or Greek-style temples and columns.

It was none of those. But it was magnificent all the same.

The buildings—tall and slender cylinders of pale stone—gleamed beneath the deeply blue sky. The roof of each building was covered in greenery, in trees that reached toward the sky and flowering vines that trailed down the sides like icing. A lake smooth as a mirror was nestled between them, the shore crowned with more flowering shrubs and trees.

"It's beautiful," Rachel said, with awe in her voice.

"It's lush," Liam agreed, but his tone said he wasn't sure if what he was seeing was good or bad.

What appeared to be a park spread out before us. A lake on one side, a square of stone in the middle with a fountain, and stands of flowering shrubs and trees at pretty intervals. Green lawns were intersected with narrow channels of sparkling water; children with tiny wings floated small paper boats on the water while their parents lounged nearby on golden blankets.

There were Paras on the sidewalk, on the shores. Some obviously different; others I couldn't distinguish from humans. They wore gowns and capes of thin and fluid fabric that gathered and twisted in the cooling breeze.

It was impossible to deny that the scene looked perfect. The weather was perfect. The landscaping was perfect. The buildings were perfect. The people—clean and healthy and diverse and beautifully dressed—were perfect.

Where was the trash? The dead stalks of grass? The messy hair?

Not here. And that increased the vague sense of discomfort I'd had since stepping foot in this place.

"Paradise?" Gavin asked quietly.

"Something," Rachel said, gaze appraising, and not a little suspicious.

"Elysium is not paradise," Malachi said. "Unless you define it very, very narrowly."

On the other side of the square was an enormous building, several rectangles of pale pink granite that gleamed in the sunlight around a taller central cube. Recesses in the structure formed balconies edged with tall gray columns, and the first level on the front of the central building was open through to the other side, so the green sweep of a soft hill was visible even from the front.

Trumpets sounded, the sound ringing like crystal through the air, while beings with enormous ivory wings descended from the sky.

"The hell did they come from?" Gavin muttered, and Liam shook his head.

There were three angels—two men and a woman. They were all trim and handsome. The woman had pale, freckled skin and a mop of dark curls; the man on the left, dark skin and shorn hair; the man in the center, tan skin and long dark hair gathered in a topknot.

The woman wore a dress with a snug and sleeveless bodice, a column of linen, above a skirt made of strips of earth-toned fabric. They all wore brown leather boots or sandals.

"Commander!" said the man in the center, and he held out his arms. He stepped forward, and he and Malachi exchanged forearm-to-forearm handshakes; then the others repeated the gesture.

"It has been a long time," the man said, then glanced behind Malachi to look at us. "And you have brought guests."

His English was perfect and unaccented, like that of someone manning a customer service line. And there was no anger in his tone, no apparent concern that strangers had entered his land. No surprise that humans had made it through the Veil, or that Malachi had brought us here.

Was he confident, or dissembling?

"I have," Malachi said. "I thought they should have an opportunity to meet the men and women who irreparably changed their world."

Well, that wasn't the diplomatic opening I'd anticipated.

The man in front lifted his brows. "We have irreparably changed their world?"

"They are from the nonmagic land," Malachi said. "You'll have heard that war has begun again. That the Court have renewed their attacks."

"Only rumors," the man said, and looked at us appraisingly. "If you'd introduce the Terrans?"

"Claire, Liam, Gavin, Rachel," Malachi said. "Camael, Uriel, Eae. They are the Precepts, the leaders of Elysium City."

Camael was the man in the center, Eae the woman, and Uriel the second man.

"We are pleased to have Terran visitors," Eae said. She smiled, but it didn't quite reach her eyes, which made her seem more mannequin than living creature.

"You all speak English?" I asked.

"We speak in any tongue necessary," Uriel said. "It is part of our gift."

"We are glad to see you again," Camael said. "It has been too long. Why have you come?"

"For the Abethyl."

Camael looked at each of us. "You wish to see it? To learn of its past?"

"We seek to create the Devil's Snare," Malachi said.

Camael watched Malachi carefully for a moment, the way a male wolf might watch another newly arrived in its territory. With care, with consideration, and with no little suspicion.

"You are tired from your travels," Camael said, his voice lower now. I guessed this wasn't a conversation he wanted to have publicly. "We will retire to the Citadel. There we can speak freely."

Without waiting for another response, they took flight and disappeared.

"Friendly," Rachel said. "No concern that we're strangers or invaders?"

"They are politicians," Malachi said. "Ambassadors of the culture they have created. They have greeted us without violence, and expect we will follow them."

"And will we?" Rachel asked.

"We will," he said. "For now."

The Citadel was the large building on the other side of the square. We walked across the park, feeling the curious gazes of everyone we passed, and then into the shade of the Citadel.

The columns of the open first floor were perfectly situated to frame the view on the other side of the square—soft, green hills beneath a brilliant sky, the grass interrupted here and there by low buildings of glass and marble that shone like diamonds. Water gurgled in narrow channels that cut through the marble floor, and two wide staircases stood sentinel along the sides. The ceiling was high, leading to an open balcony, where Paras with all-business expressions walked to and fro.

"Uncanny supernatural valley," Rachel murmured.

I felt the tension leave my shoulders, relieved that I wasn't the only one who found the perfection entirely creepy. "Thank you. It's Stepford."

"Concur," she said with a nod. "The place, the perfection, the sameness. It feels very . . . unnatural."

"It is unnatural," Malachi said, but didn't have time to elaborate. A small deer with immense eyes walked toward us on dainty hooves that clicked on the stone, then turned its wide eyes to each of us.

"You have been summoned," it said.

Malachi looked unruffled by the sudden appearance of a talking deer. The rest of us, not so much.

"Follow me," it said, and turned a circle, walked toward the staircase on the left.

"I have . . . many thoughts and feelings," Liam murmured.

"Same page," Rachel said, but Malachi fell in line behind the deer, so we fell in line behind Malachi.

The second floor ringed around the atrium of the first, then spilled into a long open space with a low marble bench on a dais in the middle of the room.

The angels were already seated on the bench, waiting for us to arrive. They were perfectly positioned so they looked like characters in a painting of classical Rome, angled so the light of a golden sunset hit them perfectly.

"They just . . . present themselves," Gavin whispered. "Like a painting they only want us to see at a particular angle."

"That's exactly what they've done," Malachi muttered.

We approached, but let Malachi take the lead, and formed a line of humans behind him. Humans who, it seemed, were to make their case to this particular jury—and then wait for the verdict.

"You speak of the Devil's Snare," Camael said, accepting a gleaming silver chalice offered by another winged creature.

"Eight years ago," Malachi began, then told the Precepts of the first war. I watched their faces, wondering how much they'd known about the rebellion, and how much it had cost our world. None of them looked surprised, but then none of them looked guilty, either. Whatever they knew, they were careful to keep off their faces.

"Our magic has impacted their world irreparably," Malachi said. "Magic poisons their soil, affects their bodies. Some, those called Sensitives, can feel and wield the magic from our world."

"Impossible," Camael said with a smile. "Human bodies cannot hold magic."

"A certainty," Malachi said. "I have brought Sensitives with me."

The Precepts looked us over. Camael put down his chalice, sat up straight to look us over.

"You have proof?" he asked.

Malachi looked back at me, the question obvious in his eyes.

The thought of working magic in front of them made my hands sweat, and I could all but feel Liam's radiating concern. But I trusted Malachi, even if I didn't entirely understand the game he was playing. He wouldn't have made the unspoken request if he didn't think it was necessary.

So proof they'd get.

There was too much magic in the air to open myself to it completely, so I accessed that plane only slightly. The threads of magic—green and vibrant and shimmering with power—were so abundant here it took only a second to gather enough of them.

I extended my hand, caught guards flinching from the corner of my eye, and lifted Camael's chalice in the air with a fingertip.

There were gasps around us as I swung it toward Malachi, who snatched it out of the air, took a long sip of the contents.

"Claire should get the wine," Gavin murmured, and I appreciated the support, and the sentiment.

"Proof," Malachi said, giving me a sly smile.

Camael's mouth was an unimpressed line, and the other Precepts bore similar expressions. But in their eyes was something new. Something that replaced the smug forbearance, the tolerance of Malachi's appearance and antics.

"Party tricks do not transform humans into something else," Camael said.

Malachi put back a hand to stop me just before I jumped forward to tell Camael exactly what I thought of the "party trick" their magic had bestowed on Sensitives.

"The magic requires balancing," Malachi said. "If they are incautious, the magic consumes them and they become monsters. Pitiable degradations. You have wrought this.

"And that is not all," he added, before they could interject. "War has come again to Earth. The Veil was opened, and the Court have come through again, begun their reign of terror against humans. They are led by the Seelies."

Uriel looked surprised. "There has been only peace here."

He didn't seem to realize the irony of that statement—that it was quiet in Elysium because the Seelies were in our world trying to kill us.

"Aeryth had been captured in the first war," Malachi said, ignoring the comment. "Seelies came through the Veil and freed her from the prison where she was being held. And now, as in the first war, they have begun a campaign to destroy the Terran cities. They have destroyed property, burned land, killed humans. For the goal, as I suspect you already know, of conquering the Terran lands and claiming them for their own. And in the meantime, they plan to make the land uninhabitable for humans."

"So they may raise it again in their own image?" Camael asked.

Malachi nodded. "The humans learned of the Devil's Snare by interrogating a member of the Court who was captured."

"The Court knew not of the weapon," Uriel said, leaning forward with a hand on his knee.

"Incorrect," Malachi said flatly. "They knew of the weapon, understood the plan. A sketch was prepared for the humans by the Court citizen. And that sketch was accurate. In a final effort to save their land, the humans wish to build the Devil's Snare," Malachi said. "They have the Inclusion Stone."

Camael's brows lifted. "The Inclusion Stone was stolen from us. Where is it?"

"In a safe location," Malachi said, and his gaze went sly. "Would you like to leave the city to take it?"

Camael didn't look thrilled about the question. "You refuse to return the stone to us, and you ask to also take the Abethyl. You must know that cannot be. It is part of our history—our shared history—and it is too precious to leave this place."

"I don't know that," Malachi said. "It is, at best, a relic." He looked at each of the Precepts, met their gazes frankly. "I suspect there are none here who need the reminder of the Abethyl's power. Those who doubted your plan, your authority, have already exited this world, have they not? They are in the Terran lands, destroying what they will"

"Do the humans not have weapons to use against the Court?" Uriel asked, brow furrowed in what looked to me like fake confusion. Like he knew very well the dangers of magic.

"The Court is powerful" was all Malachi said.

It took me a moment to realize that he didn't want to confess our weaknesses to the Consularis, and that he didn't trust them any more than we did.

"We have no authority in the Terran lands," Eae said. "How could we affect their behavior there?"

She looked like she *mostly* believed that was true. But there was something sly in her eyes that I didn't like. Something that said they knew about our troubles, and either didn't care or were relieved the trouble had migrated somewhere else. Maybe both.

"The Terran lands cannot concern us," Eae said, "any more than our concerns should worry Terrans. We choose not to fight, not to have conflict. We've reached a higher form of existence here."

"Have you?" Liam asked, not bothering to hide his disgust.

"We have," Camael said. "We are a unified people. We have no crime, no poverty, no illness. Our magic has cured those ills. And as for decisions that affect the community, we reach agreement on a chosen course of action before we act, and we share the benefits according to our rank."

"What about dissent?" Gavin asked.

"There isn't any."

"Maybe not in deed," Gavin said. "But you can't control a person's mind."

"You misunderstand," Camael said, and his patient smile had a condescending edge. "There is no dissent; it has been eradicated. Magic is not just a power. It is a *biological force*. It creates us, determines us. By application of magic, even the mind and heart can be changed."

"You're talking about genetics?" Gavin asked. "About manipulating who you are with magic?"

"Genetics is . . . elementary," Camael said. "It ignores the role of choice, the impact of community."

"The force of coercion?" Malachi asked, his tone dark.

"Do you see coercion?" Camael asked, patience wearing thin in his voice. "Our doors and windows are open because there is no foul weather, no risk of theft. Unification is our accomplishment, the great victory of an epoch of struggle and effort. And to return to your quest, the Abethyl stone is symbolic of the struggle. Come," he said, and turned to the left, gestured for us to follow him.

A dozen yards away, atop a granite plinth, sat the Abethyl. A wheel of variegated stone about eight inches across and three inches deep. The edges were rough, but the front was smooth except for carvings that seemed to run in a spiral to the empty center. It was mounted at two opposite points on its circumference to a thin crescent of gold that rose from a golden stand.

We were ten feet away, and I could still feel the faint pulse of it. Not power, but the absence of it. A void in the warp and weft of magic that seemed to cover this place.

"What are the symbols?" Gavin asked.

"An incantation," Uriel said. "In simple terms, it guides the power of the object."

"And what is that power, exactly?" Rachel asked.

"It is the power of oppression," Uriel said. "Those who came before were ignorant. We do not blame them for their actions; they knew no better. Magic came to this land slowly, over time. Those who were given the gift first were believed to be infected. Dangerous. Deadly."

"They believed their world was under threat from magic," continued Eae. "That it was a punishment, a way to control and terrorize. Beings with magic, beings of magic, were locked away, until they became too numerous to ignore."

Camael picked up the story. "Then they were punished. Tortured. Reeducated, although there was no education in what they did. Eventually the populace believed the danger large enough that a new solution had to be found."

"A permanent solution," Uriel said. "One that required magic. Many opposed its use even in this scenario. But others believed it was the only way to stem the tide."

"The Abethyl," I said, and he nodded.

"The rock was pulled from the Undine Mountains, the carvings intended to perform the most sacred of rituals. To absorb the magic they believed was so evil."

It was, like Malachi had suggested, not unlike casting off. But instead of my placing magic into the object, the object pulled out the magic on its own. Absorbed it, like rice absorbing moisture in a saltshaker.

"It was used on nearly one hundred citizens before the practice was stopped," Camael said.

"And why was it stopped?" Liam asked.

"Because they came to their senses." Eae slipped her hands into the folds of her gown. "Not immediately, mind. And not without debate, discussion. It was tragedy that turned the tide—an illness that mutated, began to kill children. Magic, they finally acknowledged, was a tool that could be wielded for evil, or for good. They decided to try the good."

"And it was that simple?" Rachel asked, shifting her gaze from the architecture to the angels. "Suddenly, they decide everything is good?"

"There is nothing simple about that," Uriel said. "But our community determined the conversion was necessary, and so the conversion was carried out."

The *conversion*. I guessed that was a more polite term for "coercion."

"And the Devil's Snare?" she asked.

"It was intended as a punitive measure," Uriel said. "To remove the magic of those who refused to accept the will, the consensus. Fortunately, it proved unnecessary. Magic, as it turns out, is its own reward."

That might have been the party line, but wasn't the answer simpler? That the beings they'd wanted to punish just brought their bad behavior into our world? They certainly weren't going to admit that here and now, but I'd have bet a month's supply of ice that I was right.

"We host the Abethyl in the Citadel as a reminder of what came before, and what we have accomplished." Camael gestured to it. "To remind us that magic is a gift, and should be wielded as such. But certainly should be wielded."

"If you had the Abethyl," Liam asked, "which could do that already, why did you need the Devil's Snare?"

"Because the Abethyl was not strong enough," Malachi said grimly, eyes on Camael, "its effects too slow, too narrow. The absorption takes time—hours for any one individual. Together with the Inclusion Stone, they could target hundreds at a time."

"And the effect would be nearly instantaneous," Uriel said. "It was an efficient idea." He linked his hands in front of him. "If ultimately unnecessary." His gaze shifted to Malachi. "And now you wish to use it again. On people of the Beyond."

"On invaders of Earth," Gavin said.

"Without it," Malachi said, "there is little hope to save their lands from the Seelie threat."

"Are their lands worth so much trouble?"

"Was Elysium worth so much trouble? When the rebellion came, did you simply abandon it to the Court of Dawn?"

Camael's gaze went cold. "Are you implying something, Commander?"

"There is nothing to imply," Malachi said. "It is the humans' home—their place of memory—and they do not wish to lose it. We can help them."

There was silence for a moment as Camael regarded Malachi. "We are, of course, sympathetic to the cause and understand the havoc the Court can wreak. But surely you know we cannot release the Abethyl. It is a touchstone, a symbol."

"We've come a long way," Rachel said. "We need your help, and it's help you can offer."

"Our hands are tied," Camael said.

"Then come with us," she said. "Come back with us to Earth—to Terra—and help us defeat the Court."

"We cannot interfere," Camael said.

"*Now*," Rachel said. "You mean you can't interfere now. Because choosing not to help for the last eight years has been its own kind of interference, hasn't it?"

Her tone was chilly, and the ice in her eyes was decidedly unfriendly. But there was approval in Malachi's eyes. Maybe the gap between them could be bridged.

"Again, we understand your frustration. It is simply that you do not understand our ways." Eae's voice was equally pleasant and condescending, the voice of a parent explaining something to a recalcitrant child.

"You have traveled far," Camael said. "You will stay here tonight as honored guests. Rooms shall be prepared for you."

We looked at Malachi. While I, for one, could certainly use a rest, he'd know better than the rest of us whether that was wise.

"That is kind and appreciated," Malachi said, nodding as Camael rose and walked away, presumably to make arrangements.

Malachi warned us with a look not to talk, so we waited in awkward silence, looking around, smiling occasionally at the lovely Paras who glanced our way, and generally being uncomfortable.

We were escorted up another staircase that curved gracefully to the third floor. The banisters—marble—were carved with happily writhing bodies that curved beneath our fingers.

"For you," the guide said, gesturing at me and Liam, then opened two massive carved wooden doors. She extended a hand, clearly intended us to walk inside, but we looked back at the others.

"Where will we be?" Gavin asked. "We're all pretty close. Family, really."

"Of course," the woman said magnanimously. "You'll all be staying in this complex." She looked at me. "I understand yours is the only room . . . for a couple?"

"Correct," Rachel answered. "The rest of us would appreciate separate rooms."

"In that case," the woman said, "the chimes will sound when dinner is prepared." She gestured to a hanging display of delicate bells. "You will be escorted."

We walked into our room and she closed the doors behind us, leaving us alone.

I pulled off my backpack, dropped it onto the floor, and looked around.

Calling it a "room" hardly did it justice. It was a palace, with stone floors and arched ceilings with gold stenciling.

The room was at least thirty feet long. A platform poster bed took up one side of the room, all made of pink granite, natch. And on the other side, fragrant water steamed in an enormous pool built into the granite floor.

The wall opposite the door was open to the city and covered by gauzy white linen. Each time the curtains swayed, they revealed a bit of the city beyond. The breeze was deliciously cool, and the air smelled of wisteria.

I pushed aside the curtain and walked to the heavy balustrade, the stone cold beneath my fingers, and looked down at the city sparkling below.

Liam moved behind me, the heat of his body and his solidity a comfort, even in the midst of apparent luxury.

"It would be easy to live here," I said. "Constant electricity. Hot water on demand. Plenty of food and drink. Cool air, mild climate. And unlike humans, they didn't incarcerate us the second we walked through."

I wouldn't deny the idea of settling into this drowsy kind of life had some appeal. Assuming I could find some way to balance my magic, and Liam could find some way to deal with his magically created desire.

"In fairness, we didn't come through solely to attack and destroy them."

"Acknowledged," I said. "Still . . ."

"Still," he agreed.

"I know New Orleans isn't perfect," I said. "It's old and decayed and gritty and occasionally stinky. And it's hot. But it's also, I guess, rich. Layered. Complex."

"It's real," he said, slipping an arm around my waist as he stood beside me. "From the Ursuline Convent to Storyville, Bourbon Street to Devil's Isle. New Orleans has always been New Orleans. And usually without apology."

We stood in silence for a moment, looking over the undeniably beautiful, but alien, land.

"It's handcrafted and artisanal," I said quietly.

Liam looked at me, a confused smile at one corner of his mouth. "What did you say?"

"Handcrafted and artisanal. I hate those words, the way they're used. Hate when they're applied to modern crafts, like we're the only ones—the first—to come up with the idea of actually making things. They ignore everything that came before them. They're . . . plastic words. They're fake labels. And this place feels the same. Like a pretty shell that's been laid over all the pain that came before."

"Like there's no past," Liam said quietly. "Just an inoffensive future."

"Yeah." I turned away from the view, looked back into the room. "And that pool of a bath looks pretty inoffensive right now. I'm exhausted, and I don't think there's a single part of my body that doesn't ache."

"Well, we did cross a foreign land on foot today, so it's understandable. We'll do dinner and then we'll take a break. Get some rest." He began to knead my shoulder, digging into a knot, which sent delicious shivers down my back.

"Can you just do that for six or twelve hours?"

"I don't think I have six or twelve hours of activity in me."

I looked at him. "Are you okay? Magic-wise?"

"I'm exhausted," he said, and now I could see it in his eyes. Not because he looked physically tired, but because he looked more defeated than I'd seen him in a long time.

"You're still fighting it."

He nodded. "Every second. Whatever is inside me, it's needy. It can feel the magic, and it wants more."

"It's hungry."

"It's voracious," he said, and sounded relieved that I understood. "I'm trying to keep it at a low murmur in the back of my mind. Not a screaming banshee."

"Maybe I can help," I said, and clutched his T-shirt to pull him closer, lifted my mouth to his. When he groaned, the sound rich and harsh and full of desire, I deepened the kiss, drawing him closer, drawing him in, trying to take his mind away from the struggle.

My struggle was different from his, but only in form. At base, it was the same. Human versus magic. And he was the one who'd seen my particular demon, who'd pushed me to find another way.

I knew a kiss wasn't a permanent solution. But when he melted against me, his lips soft and seductive, his hand at my waist, pulling me closer, I knew I'd done what little I could.

And then the chimes sounded.

He growled, nipped my lip. "We will finish this later."

"We absolutely will," I said, and opened my eyes, was relieved to find mostly blue ones staring back at me. "And I'm planning some strategic escalations."

"I'm intrigued, Claire-Bear."

Damn Gunnar. "Can we forget about that, maybe?"

"Never. 'Cause you're my Claire-Bear now." He sighed, wrapped his arms around me. "This time tomorrow, we'll be home again. I'm going to hold to that."

"But without the Abethyl?" I wondered. "After we traveled all this way."

"I imagine Malachi has a plan. And it won't be long before we see it in action."

CHAPTER FIFTEEN

We cleaned up as best we could, but I still felt grubby in a T-shirt and cargo pants, and wondered if I should have thought to pack something more formal for the dinner.

Frankly, while I hadn't thought the Paras of the Beyond would attack—if they were that violent, wouldn't they have handled the Court long ago?—I also hadn't expected the apparent hospitality. Hiking shoes were going to look weird beside gauzy tunics and sandals. But I managed to wash my face, brush my hair, tidy up a little.

We were met outside our doors by the wee deer and taken back downstairs and onto the lawn on the other side of the Citadel.

The courtyard was, as all other places we'd seen in Elysium so far, enormous. There didn't seem to be a shortage of real estate here. A vast flat lawn with a view of the hills in the distance, dotted here and there with statuary, carefully pruned shrubs, and covered stone colonnades for lounging. Birdsong was a pretty background melody, although I didn't actually see any birds.

Maybe they'd been magically corrected, too.

I looked down at the deer and its innocent eyes, wondered if it felt odd about escorting us. But I couldn't read its expression. Because it was a deer.

We followed it to the patio, large slabs of marble in the dappled shade of the fabric woven between stone beams above the colonnade. There were tables in the shade, and the scent of roasting meats was in the air.

"You may sit," the deer said, then trotted on its tiny hooves to the lawn, where it began to gnaw the manicured grass.

"It's so cute," Rachel said. "And so unsettling."

"Do they eat deer here?" Gavin asked quietly as we took seats at a table near the edge of the colonnade. And we'd brought our backpacks. Both in case we needed to make a quick exit.

"Deer, yes," Malachi said with a smile. "But not magi—creatures who can shift forms. His name is Terrence."

Of course it was.

Other Paranormals began to mill through the space, take their own seats. Less variety, I thought, than the Paras in Devil's Isle, but that was probably because there were both Court and Consularis there. I guessed only the winners made it to the table at the Citadel.

They looked at us as they passed, some with interest, some with lusty gazes aimed specifically at Malachi. We were curiosities; he was a hot dish. Rachel seemed to make a point of ignoring the glances, and that said enough.

"We have prepared a feast to tempt the senses," said a Para with pale green skin and short horns, possibly a relative of Moses's, "and share the bounty of our world." He gestured as four men bore a very large roast beast on an enormous wooden tray.

They placed the tray on a table, and another man stepped toward it, began to carve the beast. Another cadre of people came out with plates laden with food. They stopped at the platter, waited for the carver to load meat onto their plates, and then surrounded our table. With the synchronized movement of dancers, they lowered the plates to the table in front of us.

There was so much food piled up I couldn't see the ceramic beneath.

The beast was . . . a beast, and that's about as much as I could identify it. Some of the smells of the other dishes were familiar—roasted meat and spices and herbs—but the colors were strange. There were blue strips, flowers in some sort of jelly, smears of bright green and dark fuchsia pastes, and more of the honora berries we'd seen earlier today.

Glasses and goblets were placed around the plate and filled with what smelled like wine, and more platters of food were put on the table until it was as full as the individual plates.

"*Charlie and the Chocolate Factory,*" Gavin said. "If someone tries to take you down a chocolate tunnel, *decline.*"

We just looked at him.

"Am I wrong?"

"Eat," Liam said, and picked up the two-tined fork mounted to a holder at the edge of his plate. "This is probably your only chance to take a meal in the Beyond."

"And it's very good deer," Malachi said, chewing a bit of the meat.

We stared hard at the platter, and I imagined big eyes staring back at me.

"That's a joke," he said. "I'm developing my sense of humor."

"Not fast enough," Gavin said, pushing back his plate. "Not fast enough."

Wave after wave of Paras brought in a seemingly endless supply of trays and food. We ate and watched and were surrounded by the din of conversation as Paras chatted, laughed, moved from table to table to see and be seen. None of them talked to us.

It was uncomfortable to be different. To be vulnerable. And to be surrounded by so much excess when the Zone was filled with so much want. A single tray of food would have fed a Devil's Isle family for a week.

"Is it because we're foreign, or because we lack acceptable magic?" Liam wondered, sipping spiced wine from a golden goblet.

"Both," Malachi said. "I think you are an affront to their unity. To their conception of their own magic."

His tone wasn't unpleasant, but matter-of-fact.

"Is that why we're here?" I asked. He shifted his gaze to me, and while he didn't smile, there was a kind of approval in his eyes.

"In part," he admitted.

He hadn't eaten more than a few bites; he'd spent most of dinner staring at the dancers, their apparent contentedness.

"How are you doing?" Rachel asked, concern obvious in her eyes.

"It is strange to be here, in surroundings that should be so familiar to me, and still feel so out of place."

"You haven't been home in a long time," I said. "I imagine everything starts to feel unfamiliar after so much time has passed."

"Perhaps," Malachi said. "Or maybe I've changed. I'm too Paranormal for the human world, and not quite Paranormal enough for this one."

Rachel sipped from her goblet, then placed it on the table again, played with the stem. "There's a saying on Earth: 'You can never go home again.' I think that's what you're saying." She looked up. "I'm from Portland. The war hasn't touched it, and I'm not sure—after being here for so long—if I could ever go home again. If I could ever figure out how to fit in."

"That's one of the bummers of growing up," Gavin said. "And growing old. Places change. People change. But memories don't. It's hard to let memories go.

"Speaking of which," he said, leaning closer, "what do we do about the Abethyl? Is there a plan? Something including stealing it and returning triumphantly to our home world?"

I raised a hand. "No B and E for me, please. I've only just stopped being a fugitive, and I'm really enjoying not being on the run."

"If you run, I'll bring you back," Liam said. While his grin was wide and his tone was teasing, there was something very serious in his expression. And I liked it.

"We sleep," Malachi said. "And tomorrow I will speak with the Precepts again."

Gavin lifted his brows. "That's it? We sleep on it, and you give them a stern lecture. Do you think the Precepts will really change their minds?"

It took a moment for Malachi to answer. "I think they'll find a conversation with me enlightening."

I considered Malachi not just an ally but a friend. And given the chill in his eyes and the threat woven into those words, I was really glad he was on our side.

No one attacked us at dinner, and when the crowd began to disperse, and the weariness of travel sank into our bones, we rose to head back to our rooms.

We'd made it inside the Citadel's first floor when we heard the commotion, the noise from the public square beyond.

We walked to the threshold and looked out, saw a crowd of people watching a woman who'd climbed onto the wide base of a statue of a roaring lion.

Malachi kept walking closer. Liam and I exchanged a glance, followed him toward the square and toward the group who'd assembled there.

The woman looked young, with golden skin and lavender eyes,

and long hair so pale and fine it billowed behind her in the light breeze. Her nose was small, her ears narrow and pointed, her fingers long and slender.

"We propose to name the square after the Minotaurean Battalion," she was saying, "in honor of their sacrifice to Elysium during the Rebellion. It would be such a small token, but an important one for our community."

The sound of marching footsteps rose as several men and women wearing long tunics and boots, and holding golden staffs, began to move across the square, trying to break up the crowd.

"Security?" Liam asked, and Malachi nodded.

We moved closer, watching the groups meet each other.

"Representatives from the Citadel have joined us," the woman said, smiling, and gesturing toward the guards. "We are glad to have you here, to discuss these matters with you."

"Disperse," one of them said, using a golden horn to send the word across the area. "You are violating the Law for Peaceable Assembly."

The speaker's face went hard. "The Law for Peaceable Assembly forbids us from assembling."

Ironic, I thought.

"The Precepts assemble," the guard said. "Those who violate the laws are dissenters. They seek to injure the peace, the citizens."

"I'm suggesting only that we honor someone who sacrificed," she said, looking up at the crowd to try to plead her case. "How could that possibly be wrong? How could that be anything other than good? Than right?"

But the people just watched as guards took her by the arms, pried her from the pedestal.

"We honor all," one of the guards said. "So we mention none."

The woman tried to keep a smile on her face, and worked to

wrench away from the guards who held her. "We should mention them. It's our history. It's part of who we are."

"We are Elysium," said the guard with the horn. "Disperse."

The crowd looked uncertain for a moment, not sure if they should stay and watch, or help the girl, or just keep moving. Keep the peace and enjoy the evening.

The woman stepped on a guard's foot, then pivoted to try to break free of their hold. But another guard slapped her, as the crowd began to drop away, scattering at the edges, a droplet dissolving into the sea. They'd listen if there were no consequences. But they wouldn't intervene.

Rachel moved to step forward, but Malachi gripped her arm.

She looked up at him, her eyes wide. "We have to do something. That woman wasn't doing anything wrong."

"She violated the law. Whether we agree with the law or not, it is the law of this place. It is their law."

"It's wrong," she said, looking at us for support. "And it's unfair."

"It may be," Malachi said. "But we cannot help that now. Even if we wanted to, we're vastly outnumbered, and don't have the strength to face down all of Elysium. And more, you have no rights here. We'd be lucky if they merely sent you back to Earth. If that happens, we ruin our chance to obtain the Abethyl and save your world."

"So we let her be the sacrifice?" Rachel shook her head, jaw working as she bit back her argument. "That's a shitty choice."

"It is," Malachi agreed.

"What will happen to her?" Liam asked.

"Magic," Malachi said, and disgust tinged his voice. "Her failure will be treated with magic, the dissent dissolved with magic, so that she fits neatly into the structure once again. So their peace is not interrupted. Because they have learned nothing."

He turned and stalked away, moving to the edge of the square, where grass and stone were checkered into a border. Putting distance between himself and the crowd.

We followed him, put a semicircle of humans between him and the others.

"Time to vent," Gavin said, giving Malachi a friendly pat on the back. "God knows you listen to us bitch about Paras and Containment and—" He stopped short when Rachel nailed him with a look.

"Not that Containment isn't doing a great job and everything in our awesome little postapocalyptic paradise. 'Cause they are."

"He talks too much," Liam said, giving Gavin a dour look, "but he's right about the venting. You might as well get it out."

Malachi looked at us, brow furrowed as if he was puzzled by the offer. "You want me . . . to complain to you."

"Yup," Gavin said. "It's healthy. Puts hair on your chest."

Malachi glanced down.

"Idiom," Liam and I said together. "He doesn't mean it literally."

"Go ahead," Rachel said. Malachi looked at her, then back at the crowd.

"I did not ask to be conscripted, to be taken into your world," he began. "But Elysium had been shattered. The war had been violent; land and buildings destroyed, just as on Earth. Citizens dead." His gaze went hazy, as if he was remembering the sights and sounds of war. They were hard memories. Powerful memories. And they popped up at inconvenient times.

"There was so much death and destruction. The rebellion, the hatred, the violence. Now there are manicured parks. Gleaming buildings. Laughing children. They have stripped away the image of violence, but they seem to have learned nothing from it. The world is more . . . sterile than it was before I left. Difference treated even more harshly. They haven't solved their problems. They've only deferred them."

"Is there no opportunity for change?" Rachel asked. "For elections or some other way of putting a new person, a new group, in power?"

"The Precepts hold their thrones by what they deem the dictate of the citizens. They are convinced they've made Elysium a better place, a utopia. And look around," he said. "Many tiers of citizens live well. They enjoy the weather, the stability, and they have what they need. They have the correct type of lives. The correct type of magic. They believe, or want to believe, the violence is behind them, so they have no incentive to change. Even if they see dissent, because it's rare they believe it shows only that the system is working."

"And since they don't allow dissent, nothing will change," Liam said.

Malachi nodded.

"There could still be change," I said, and he shifted his gaze to me. "That woman was rebelling in some small way. She was showing the current order is wrong, or at least partly wrong. Maybe there are underground groups? Rebels working quietly on the sidelines?"

"I know of none," Malachi said.

"But you do," Liam said. "Most of them are in our world. Moses and Lizzie and the other Consularis who'd probably come back if they could. Even the Seelies, Aeryth. The Court knew the system is wrong. But instead of fighting the good fight, they abandoned Elysium to the Consularis and invaded our world."

"They wanted power," Malachi said, "to be the oppressors, more than they wanted to free the oppressed. And so here we are. Let's get you back to the Citadel."

He didn't wait for our response, but turned and walked back toward the building.

"What time shall we assemble tomorrow?" Gavin asked when we reached our rooms.

"However the conversation with the Precepts goes, I'd like to be walking again by dawn," Malachi said. "I don't think we want to reach the Veil in the dark."

"Agree," Rachel said. "I could deal with twilight—harder for us to see, but same for them. But full dark would be dangerous. We need some visibility."

"Dawn," Liam said with a nod. "We'll meet you right here."

"And until then," Gavin said, looking around, "I wonder if there's fun to be had in Creepyland."

Liam turned Gavin to face his room. "Have fun in there with the door locked. Maybe you'll get lucky and there's a minibar with more of that spiced wine."

"Okay," Gavin said after a moment. "That could be fun."

"Are you in for the night?" Liam asked Malachi.

"I believe I would like to walk."

"Would you like some company?"

Malachi's eyes widened at Rachel's question, and the look he gave her was part curiosity, part naked need. "I . . . wouldn't mind."

She nodded. "I'm ready when you are."

Malachi gestured toward the stairs, and they walked together toward them. They made for an interesting contrast. Rachel, petite and dark haired. Malachi, tall and blond. And of course the wings and biological differences.

"Because we haven't already walked enough today?" Gavin murmured when they walked away. "How could they possibly want to walk more? There's a pool in my room." He looked at us. "Does yours have one?"

"It does," Liam said. "And they're walking because he's coming to terms with what's happened in his homeland. And because they're in love with each other."

"What?" Gavin said, jerking his head to look in the direction they'd walked. "No way."

"You are not that oblivious," Liam said dryly. "Haven't you noticed how they look at each other?"

"Yeah, like they're pissed off. Which is my point."

I patted his cheek. "Oh, you sweet summer child. They're pissed off because they're in love and don't feel like they can do anything about it."

Gavin just stared at us. "That's . . . really stupid."

"That's love, *mon frère.*"

We left him in the hallway contemplating relationships, and escaped into the breezy glow of our palatial bedroom.

"Bath," I said, and began peeling off clothing on my way to the steaming pool. But I'd managed to get only my shirt off, and begun to toe off a hiking boot, when pain flashed through my foot.

"Ow," I said, and sat down on the marble surround.

"What's wrong?"

"Blisters on blisters on blisters."

He came over, went down to one knee. "May I assist?"

He was so damn sexy with those wicked blue eyes, the glint of humor in the lifted corner of his mouth.

"Be gentle," I agreed.

Carefully, while I gnawed my bottom lip to take my mind off the pain, he slid the boot from my foot, then the sock.

My foot was a mess. Blisters had already formed and disintegrated, leaving raw red spots where the boot had rubbed.

"Oh, *cher*."

"New boots," I said. "Well, not *new* new, but I haven't worn them in years. Haven't run distance in years. Only when being chased."

Liam smiled, repeated the process with foot number two, then removed the rest of my clothing. Then he picked me up, carried me gingerly to the pool. My feet objected to the first sting of heat, but as the rest of my body slipped into deliciously hot water, they retracted their objections.

"Sometimes a world that's a little too perfect is actually just right."

Liam smiled at me and pulled his shirt over his head. Then the pants, the boxers, until he was tall and honed and utterly naked.

"You're a hell of a thing to look at," I said, then blinked back surprise at the husky drowsiness in my tone.

Liam's chuckle was low and satisfied. "While I probably ought to object to being objectified, hard to complain when a beautiful woman says she likes the look of you." He slid into the water, graceful as a seal. He stayed under for a moment before popping up again, slicking his hair back off his eyes. They shone with amusement and mirrored the heat of the water. But when I tried to reach out to him, I found I didn't even have the energy to trickle fingers down his chest.

"I can tell you're exhausted," he said, and moved around to sit behind me, then pulled my body against his. I dropped my head back to his shoulders, closed my eyes, and let my body relax.

"There's my girl," he said, and pressed a kiss to my neck. "For now, relax. Let me do the worrying. You just take a breath."

I took one, and then another, until my mind was blank as I floated in the warm and scented water.

I remember being lifted, the brush of chill air against my skin. Being swaddled in a thick towel and carried again. Being placed atop a soft bed that seemed to undulate beneath me, and cool sheets that seemed to wick away any lingering pain.

And then his fingers trailed across my limbs, the tingle of his teasing touch delicious. He grinned at me, slid away the towel, and pressed a kiss to my stomach.

His lips were warm and soft, and I closed my eyes to savor the sensation, the feel of him.

Gold spun in his eyes, catching the light of the candles, then fading again as he shifted. A moment of shimmering brilliance.

He maneuvered over me, held himself up by strong arms, that gorgeously muscled body, before pressing a kiss to my lips.

I reached up, fingers toward his abdomen, and he lifted an arm to swivel and maneuver just out of reach.

"You're a tease."

"I'm a man with a plan."

"Do I get to know the plan ahead of time?"

"No," he said, and dipped down to kiss me again.

I grabbed his waist before he could get away, tugged him closer. "Then I'll have to spoil your plan. Because I have a plan, too."

"Do you, now?" he asked, sliding a hand along my ribs, his palm warm against my skin.

"I do," I said, arching beneath his touch. He found my breast and mouth simultaneously, fingers and tongue equally nimble, equally seeking. Wanting something good. Something clean. Holding to a different kind of hunger.

This was about solidarity, about warmth and honesty. It was a bringing together, a reminder that we were facing the obstacles together, after so many years of facing them alone.

He deepened the kiss and pressed his body, heavy with muscle and magic and love, to mine, blocking out the fear, the darkness. For now, we were here, and we were alive, and we had each other.

I tunneled fingers through his hair and pulled him closer, wanting love and desire to replace hopelessness and fear. Wanting connection, instead of fear and dread.

I used hands to touch the stacked muscles of his abdomen, to feel the thudding heartbeat beneath his strong chest. Hands and mouths explored as desire rose, as movements became more hurried, as skin became more feverish.

And I rose over him, hair streaming around my shoulders, the fierce possession in his eyes pushing me on, forward, further. Hands grasped, found, clenched as desire rose, lifted higher toward that beautiful crest, until love became magic. Became stars and sensation.

We lay together in each other's arms—together and, for now, at peace.

CHAPTER SIXTEEN

I woke to the smell of coffee. Or something at least coffee-esque.

I opened my eyes . . . and found a woman in a gauzy gown staring down at me.

"Oh, my God!" I screamed, and jolted fully awake. Liam sat up like he'd been propelled out of bed.

"What is it?"

"Her," I said, and gestured to the woman, who was staring at us with wide brown eyes. Her long and pointed ears extended through straight dark hair, and there were pale stripes across her face.

"I have brought you beverages." She gestured to two small ceramic cups that sat on the edge around the bed. "Would also you care for food to break your fast?"

I pulled the sheet up over my chest, opened my mouth to tell her to get out.

"We'd like some food," Liam said before I could offend. "But if you could just leave it outside the door, that would be fine."

She blinked. "You do not wish to be serviced?"

"We do not," I said, clapping a hand over Liam's mouth. I wasn't entirely sure what service she was offering, but it seemed best to sidestep whatever it might have been. They were awfully accommodating, and didn't entirely seem to understand human etiquette. "Just leave the food outside the door, thank you, and that will be all."

She gave a precise nod, turned with a rustle of her white skirts, and walked silently to the door.

"Stepford city," Liam said, when I moved my hand from his face. "And add 'no privacy' to the list of things I don't like about this place."

Then he scratched his jaw as he looked contemplatively at the door, the night's stubble making a rasping sound. "What services do you think she'd provide, exactly?"

I hit him with a pillow. And that just started things again.

An hour later, Liam hopped down from the platform, began to pull on jeans, walked toward the door.

"I'm hungry," I said, looking for my own clothes, "but slightly concerned that whatever we find outside the door will be drugged or just—I don't know—a jar of mayonnaise."

He glanced back. "Mayonnaise?"

"Poster condiment for bland sameness."

He nodded his general agreement, kept walking to the door. Opened it, came back a moment later with a gold tray. On it were two hamburgers atop piles of spaghetti.

He put the tray on a side table, looked down at it with hands on his hips. "This appears to be a guess about what humans eat."

"How rude would it be to not eat it?"

He glanced back at me, gaze sardonic. "Do we really care what these people think about us? Given what they've done?"

I considered that for a beat. "Excellent point."

He picked up what looked like a cinnamon stick—a bit of dusky brown bark rolled in the middle—and sniffed it. "Ah," he said.

"Is it cinnamon?"

"I'm not sure." He held it out to me.

I took a whiff—and got a noseful of fish-soaked dirty tennis shoes. "Good God," I said, pushing his hand away. "That is disgusting."

Liam burst into laughter, then tossed the stick back on the tray. I punched him in the arm.

"That's not funny."

"The look . . . on your face . . . is very funny," he said between snorting laughs. He lifted a hand to wipe away a tear, then jolted, stared down at his fingers. Then he took a cautious sniff, turned his face away in disgust.

"And now I need to bleach my hand."

"Serves you right," I said as he strode off toward the bath.

I looked down at the bark, and considered. I bet I knew someone who would absolutely adore it. So I used the napkin to pick it up, then folded it carefully into a tight packet that I stuffed into a zip pocket on my backpack.

At least Moses couldn't complain that we hadn't brought him a souvenir.

The sun had just breached the horizon when we met outside the rooms. Liam and I, Gavin and Rachel. Everyone slightly bleary-eyed, but looking eager to get home again.

"Where's Malachi?" Liam asked.

Gavin shrugged, bit into a granola bar, this one chewy. "Haven't seen him yet."

With perfect timing, his door opened, and he emerged in his usual white T-shirt and jeans, golden curls a soft cloud around his beautiful face.

"Good morning," I said, and noticed the flush on Rachel's cheeks when he looked her way, smiled. I guess the threat of war breaking out between them was officially nil.

"We can go home now."

"Can we?" Liam asked.

"We can. Our mission is complete." He adjusted his backpack, which looked heavier than it had on the trip here—and was marked by that magical blankness we'd experienced in the Citadel the night before. It was easy to guess it held the Abethyl. Harder was figuring out exactly how he'd managed that.

"You got the Abethyl?" Rachel asked.

"I did."

"And how was that accomplished?"

"Persuasion," Malachi said. "I convinced them it was in their interest to let us borrow the stone, rather than have their citizens learn about the many ways in which they've refused to solve the problems they've created. Including the fact that humans can wield magic."

"They think humans are less," I said. "So the truth would be insulting."

"Just so," Malachi said with a smile. "They do not know you as I do."

"So you blackmailed them," Gavin said.

"I did."

"I mean, whatever works."

"I actually have a request," Malachi said to Gavin. "Would you mind carrying it back? I admit to some discomfort carrying an object that nullifies magic all the way back to the Veil."

I thought I saw discomfort in Gavin's eyes, too, but he lifted his shoulder. "Sure," he said, and, since he'd lost his backpack, accepted Malachi's, slid his arms between the straps. "Now can we get the hell out of here before they change their minds?"

"An excellent plan," Rachel said, and we headed for the stairs.

The Consularis were apparently late risers, as the city was nearly empty as we left the Citadel, headed across the square and into the hills again.

Having learned our lesson, we began the trip by walking within the umbrella of Malachi's magic, and passed most of the time talking about the general weirdness of the Beyond.

But that was hardly the only thing bothering me.

"What's wrong?" Liam asked, walking beside me at the back of the pack.

"I just . . . I still can't believe they let him walk away with the stone."

"He didn't walk away with it. He threatened to expose the facade. The lies. Oppressing people becomes a whole lot harder when they're able to tell truth from lies. To see the real nature of the corruption."

"Yeah, but do you think they'd really care about that? The population has to know about the war, about the Veil. If they haven't done anything about it before, why are they going to care now?"

He stopped, looked down at me. "You think it's more likely an angel would steal an artifact and then lie to us about it?"

"He's not a religious angel," I pointed out. "And, yeah, I think most people would lie under the right circumstances."

Liam ran a hand through his hair. "I think it's better not to ask, and to assume he handled it appropriately. It's his world, after all."

"That's putting a pretty spin on it."

"It's war," Liam said. "I don't think we need to put a pretty spin on anything. I'd be okay with him stealing it after punching out a guard. Given what this place has done to us—and apparently its own citizens—I don't really care how he got it. As long as he got it, and there's a chance for peace."

He had a point. Did I care?

I guess I was less concerned about the way he might have stolen it—about the moral issues—than about the possibility they'd come after us when they found out it was gone. But after we'd walked for four hours and seen no sign of chase, of magical fury, of fire in the sky or apocalyptic horsemen intent on finding and destroying us, I stopped thinking about it.

I had blisters to consider. And hurricanes. And a magical weapon still tied too close to my mother for my own comfort.

We moved quickly, efficiently, purposefully. We didn't pass through the same glen of willows, so I assumed Malachi had wisely steered us around them. And I had to assume that we were hurrying back. But I didn't know if that was because of the Seelies, the hurricane, or the Abethyl.

The border was a waving blur ahead of us when I felt a faraway rumble, like a storm far past the horizon. And there was a hot energy in the air. I reached down, put a hand against the earth, and could feel a vibration beneath my fingers.

"Malachi, are we standing on a fault line?"

"No. Why?"

I looked up at him. "Because the earth is literally moving beneath our feet."

His expression didn't change. But there was a momentary flicker of alarm in his eyes.

"Malachi," Liam said, stepping toward us. "What is it?"

The rumbling grew louder, and it began to resolve as it grew closer. Not thunder, but the beating of air.

Wings.

I looked back at Malachi, and suspicions began to resolve into certainty. "They didn't let you have it. They didn't offer it up in apology or to help us. You took it."

"What?" Rachel said, head snapping toward Malachi.

"He stole the Abethyl," I said.

"Of course he did," Gavin said, looking around. "We all knew that, right?"

Liam thumped him on the ear.

"I took the Abethyl," Malachi said, "because it is our best option. Because they are selfish. Because they owe it to you. Because *we* owe it to you."

"Why weren't there any alarms?" Liam asked.

"Only at the edges of the city," Malachi said.

"Because no one ever steals in Elysium," I said, thinking of what the angels had said the night before. "You don't need alarms in the land of the perfect."

"Except, apparently, to get outside city limits." Liam looked at Malachi. "I assume that's why Gavin was carrying it? Because the alarm is triggered somehow by Paras, not humans. We're, what, voids? Like the Abethyl."

"Something like that," Malachi said, and the golden-eyed look Liam leveled at Malachi was hot even by New Orleans standards.

"You used us."

"We used each other," Malachi said, and Gavin snorted.

"How are you not pissed?" Liam asked him, incredulous.

"How am I the only one who realized what was happening?" Gavin asked, amusement in his voice. "Obviously he stole the Abethyl, and obviously I carried it out because he couldn't. Y'all are not nearly shifty enough for covert missions."

Rachel frowned in the direction of the tsunami of sound that was rolling closer. "What's done is done," she said. "Now it's time to get the hell out of here." She clipped the front strap on her backpack tight across her chest.

"We can't outrun them," Gavin said. "They're flying."

"Not all of them," Malachi said. "Some will be mounted."

"Whatever we're doing, we need to decide now," I said.

"We stay together," Malachi said. "Splitting up—dividing our skills—doesn't help us. It helps them."

"Agreed," Liam said.

"I want to talk to them first," Malachi said. "But let's be ready."

"Ready" meant standing by with weapons unholstered and magic spooled, Malachi in front of us. We had a plan, or as much of one as we could muster given our position and the limited amount of time we had to prepare.

Now we'd wait.

Two dozen Consularis Paras astride stocky horses with golden leather saddles and bells woven into their hair, their hooves wide as summer melons, thundered toward us. No wonder the ground shook. They rode in a battle line, golden weapons raised. And in front of them, flying low and steady, with their gleaming tunics and brilliant wings, the Precepts.

They touched down in a run, wings extended behind them until they folded and disappeared in the way that angels had. And they looked royally pissed.

My heart beat fast. Not just because of the anticipation, but from the magic that seemed to vibrate through my bones. Elysium magic, so much stronger than Earth magic, seemed to permeate deeper. I didn't care for that.

I glanced at Liam, got his nod, and felt him reach out with his magic, touch mine, even though we stood ten feet apart.

"Camael," Malachi said coolly as the angel strode forward, his eyes swirling gold.

"Return what you have stolen," he said.

"I have stolen nothing," Malachi said. "I have taken possession of a tool you used as a decorative object. A tool the humans need in order to repair the mess you've made of their world."

"As you are aware, we have no part in that war."

"Yes," Malachi said. "That's exactly the problem." He seemed taller as he stared at them across the swaying grasses, the wildflowers. "You created a problem that you refuse to resolve. A problem that has brought death and destruction to their world. If you refuse to act, I must. I cannot in good conscience stand by while you allow this destruction to continue."

"You choose them over us."

"I choose life over death. I choose attention over ignorance. I choose to act."

It was probably inappropriate, but I stole a look at Rachel, saw the approval in her eyes. I approved of her approval.

Uriel stepped forward. "You understand our society, its conditions, the rules by which we live. The reasons we do not intervene in another culture's disagreements."

"Your reasons are wrong. You will have the Abethyl back when the Court has been neutralized. When peace has returned. When their community has been restored."

Eae stepped forward, and the gold in her eyes turned to icy shards, the magic in the air hot and sharp as lightning. "You wouldn't dare."

"I have the Abethyl," Malachi said. "So obviously I would. And I don't believe you'll attack. Because at heart, I think you are afraid of war. I think you are afraid to fight."

Horses whinnied and shifted, ready to surge forward, to fight. The Paras on their backs looked equally eager. Anger danced in their eyes, and a good dose of haughtiness.

The longer I was around them, the more I was convinced the best Consularis Paras lived on Earth, not in the Beyond.

"You want it?" Malachi said, eyes blazing gold. "Come and get it. Walk through the Veil and face down the Court. Walk through the Veil and stare down the result of the war you could have stopped years ago. Walk through the Veil and see the destruction. See what you have wrought. Find me, and take it back."

That was our cue.

"Now," Rachel said, and Liam and I gripped hands, and joined our magic, and began to move the ground itself. We'd learned with the nymph that using our magic to move magical things in the Beyond was nearly impossible. But we could move nonmagical things. And soil qualified.

If nothing else, New Orleanians knew how to build a levee.

I'd spooled so much magic I felt like I might float up on the cloud of it, but moving tons of dirt—pulling grass and soil from beneath the army and shaping it into a long and narrow hill in front of them—took a lot of power.

It took only seconds to make them invisible, to create the nearly vertical wall that horses couldn't climb over, and to have them screaming instructions on the other side.

"Go!" Malachi shouted. And with the barrier in place, we began to run toward the filmy air that marked the boundary of Earth.

Wings began to beat the air as the Precepts lifted up. They landed between us and the Veil, even as the sound of hooves began to beat the ground behind us, the Consularis army driving their steeds around the wall we'd made.

"You will not take it from us," Camael said, landing in front of us.

"Try me," Rachel said, unsheathing her knife and jumping forward. Gavin pulled his gun, began to fire at Uriel, who lifted into the air to join the fight. Malachi ran toward Eae, and their wings beat fiercely against air as they rose in combat, fists swinging.

"Our turn," Liam said, and we ran toward the border as the sounds of hooves and huffing horses and angry Consularis Paras grew louder behind us.

Dashing toward it, our feet pounding soil, the hazy view of our world cleared as we moved closer, until we could see the hulking form of the tossed Humvee.

And then there was whistling overhead.

"Above you!" Gavin shouted, and we looked up as a flight of golden spears flew toward us. Liam pulled me close, wrapped his arms around me as they punctured the earth with a *thwack*, forming a golden cage around us.

Or so they hoped. We squeezed between the spears and ran through the boundary, the magic like hot rain against my skin, and we stepped into the magical desert of our own world.

The field was empty. Birds and crickets chirped as the sun began to head for the horizon.

We ran to the Humvee, climbed on top of it, and waved our arms, signaling the outpost. The turret turned our way, and after a moment, we heard the sound of one of the outpost's gates sliding along its rail—and then the roar of an engine. Seconds later, Scarlet rounded the building, Gunnar at the wheel. He roared across the field.

At the same time, chaos erupted behind and around us. Seeing another chance to take us down, ogres burst into the meadow from the tree line. As the outpost's siren began to wail, Malachi and Camael flew in, arms linked as they fought for control.

"Incoming!" The word was garbled, but I recognized Gavin's voice through the Veil. He ran through, Rachel almost immediately behind him, followed by Uriel and Fae. And they came up short when they realized where they were, and saw the ogres charging toward them. Wings made them a very big—and obvious—target.

A dozen Containment soldiers took the field, and began firing at the ogres. A shot hit Uriel's left wing and he screamed in agony. As if in answer to his cry, a whistling came through from the other side of the Veil.

"Incoming!" I screamed, and Liam and I jumped into Scarlet's bed, hit our stomachs. Brilliant points of light broke through from the Beyond. It had to be luck, since the Paras on the other side couldn't actually see clearly to Earth, but they took down two ogres and impaled the truck's gate.

"Assholes!" I said, and crawled back. "They speared my truck!" I worked to wrench away the spear, the metal warm and vibrating with magic.

An ogre pounded toward us.

"Claire!" Liam called out.

"I see him!"

But Gunnar was already out of the truck, leaving the door open and slipping around its side.

I wrenched the spear loose just as Gunnar reached the back of the truck. He pulled his weapon, a shocker used to incapacitate Paranormals, and pressed it into the ogre's leg.

The ogre barely flinched, but struck out, massive arm swinging like a wooden club. He caught Gunnar in the chest, and I heard the crack of ribs as the momentum sent Gunnar flying through the air like a rag doll. He hit the ground hard nearly twenty feet away.

Later, Liam would tell me I screamed like a banshee. But I didn't hear it. I swung the spear at the ogre like a hitter with the bases loaded. It connected with his temple, and he fell straight down.

"Shit," I said, and handed the spear back to Liam, jumped out of the truck bed, using the ogre as a springboard, and ran toward my fallen friend.

"Gunnar!" I screamed as Containment officers fired around me and downy feathers fluttered through the air like rain. "Gunnar, hold on!"

I reached him, fell to my knees. He was unconscious, his arms and legs twisted. There was blood on his head, blood on one of his legs, blood on his side.

And scattered around him, chunks of metal and shrapnel from previous battles, including one chunk beneath his hip, large enough to put his body at a cant. He'd fallen right on top of it. A fulcrum of past fights.

"Gunnar!" I screamed, and the world became a blur.

CHAPTER SEVENTEEN

It was Malachi who lifted him, flew him back to the outpost, and Liam who drove the rest of us back in Scarlet as Containment cleared the field.

"What have we got?" the med tech asked, pulling on gloves as we met him at the gate, and Malachi placed Gunnar on a gurney gently as he would a child.

"Hit by an ogre in the chest," Shon said. "Flew twenty feet and landed hard in a shrapnel field."

"Mm-hmm," the medic said calmly, cutting away clothes and inspecting the patient.

"He waited for you," Shon said as the medic looked him over. "Spent the night in the outpost, because he wanted to be here when you came through again. Just in case."

Of course he had. And because of that, because of his loyalty, he was bleeding out on a cot.

"Fuck," I muttered, and had to work against the rising panic. "Fuck."

"Scalp laceration, and he's going to need surgery on the hip," the medic said, looking up. "I can only triage him, and I will, but he's going to need more than we can give him. He needs a doctor and a good facility."

"He needs Lizzie," I said, thinking of the Para nurse who practically ran the clinic in Devil's Isle. I looked at Malachi. "You could fly him back faster than we can drive."

"I can't keep him stable." Malachi's voice was kind, but sad. "I can't treat and fly him at the same time."

"Fuck," I said again, letting anger rise up, because anger felt better than cold and bone-deep fear. And God knew I had plenty of that.

"You drive," I told Liam. "I'll ride in the back with Gunnar, try to keep him stable."

"It's pouring rain," Liam said.

"There's not enough room to stretch him out in the cab." I looked at Shon. "You've got a tarp?"

"Finicki," she called out, and a soldier jumped up from his seat. "Grab the tarp and figure out a way to secure it on the back of that truck."

"On it, sir," he said, and ran for the door.

"Gavin and I can ride in the back, too," Rachel said. "Keep the tarp in place, help keep him stable, keep an eye out for unfriendlies from the rear." She looked at Malachi. "You can fly ahead? Keep an eye on the road, and let Lizzie know we're coming when we get close, so she can get set up?"

"Can and will," Malachi said.

Five minutes later, we were on our way.

Liam drove fast, faster than Scarlet had probably ever been driven. I was in the back with Gunnar, huddled beneath the tarp and cushioning his head from the cracks and potholes we hit along the way. We made it in forty minutes, and I'd need to spend weeks to get Scarlet back into fighting mode.

But it was worth it for Gunnar.

Malachi had done good work; we were waved through the gates

of Devil's Isle, where an aggressive four-wheeler with lights flashing and sirens blaring escorted us to the clinic.

Gunnar still hadn't regained consciousness by the time we pulled up in front, where Rachel and Gavin ripped off the tarp, and Lizzie and her staff jumped into action, loaded Gunnar on a stretcher, and moved him inside.

"I'll go find Tadji and Gunnar's parents," Gavin said, hopping out of the truck.

Every member of Gunnar's family had left New Orleans, most after Belle Chasse. But his parents had come back; they hadn't been able to stay away from their son—or their city.

"Thanks," Liam said, and I heard the sounds of guy hugging and backslapping. They drove each other crazy, but they knew when to come together, when to be family. This was one of those times.

I was still on my knees in the truck bed, jeans and shirt soaked through with rain, one of my best friends bleeding and unconscious. And now that he was inside, safe in the hands of a woman I trusted, I began to shake.

"Shit," Liam said, and climbed into the bed. "Come on, *cher*. Let's get you inside and out of those clothes."

He got me to my feet, handed me over to Malachi, who got me on the ground and under the balcony of the first building that made up the clinic, which was spread among several interconnected town houses, guest homes, and cottages.

"You are very wet," Malachi said.

"And how are you?" I asked, raising my gaze to his.

"I'll be fine." There was concern in his eyes. "I'm stronger than most humans."

"Not the time to rub it in," I said.

"I am sorry for his injuries," Malachi said. "For whatever part my theft played in them."

"I don't need an apology for that," I said. "We need the Abethyl, and you figured out a way to get it. I can't blame you for that. But I will blame you for not just telling us the truth in the first place. We'd have been better prepared. You could have trusted us."

"I should have," he said. "And that is my failing, not yours."

Liam was quiet during the exchange, but I knew he'd want his own words with Malachi later. For now, Gunnar was our focus.

This waiting room, the second I'd visited in the cluster of buildings that made up the clinic, was small and still very New Orleans. Mismatched chairs were placed here and there in a former living room, hardwood floors squeaked with every step, and there was a small table in the corner that held a water dispenser and a coffeepot.

Rachel made coffee, while I changed into a pair of dry scrubs.

"I'm going to the Cabildo," she said, when we were all together again. "I want to update the Commandant, let him know about Gunnar. And change clothes myself."

She looked at me. "I know this won't make you feel better now," Rachel said, squeezing my arm, "but you're good in a crisis. He's going to come through because you moved quickly, knew what to do, how to treat him."

She was right. It didn't make me feel better, but I managed a nod. "Thanks."

"I'm going to get the package to Darby," Malachi said. "I'll be back."

Because the show had to go on, even if Gunnar was unconscious and bleeding.

When Liam and I were the only ones left in the room, he touched my arm. "Are you all right?"

I didn't hesitate. I turned into the sanctuary of his arms, and let the tears fall.

"It's all right, Claire. Let it go."

"I'm tired of war. I'm tired of prisons. I'm tired of fighting."

"I know."

He let me get it out, then pulled back, brushed away the tears beneath my eyes. "We could stop fighting. We could leave all of this behind."

Emotion swamped me, so many feelings that I had to look away. "I can't leave New Orleans. It's all I have left of him. If I leave, that all disappears."

"*Ahh,*" Liam said, apparently realizing I'd meant my father. "He'll always be with you. Whether you're here or somewhere else. He's in your mind, in your heart. In the minds and hearts of everyone he met, everyone he helped."

That didn't feel like enough. Not now.

"But I'm not going anywhere." He held me tighter. "I'm not leaving you, and neither is Gunnar."

Hospital waiting was a board game. In and out of chairs, shifting from one room to the next as you were made to stop, were allowed to move forward, waited for the next move.

Time passed in arrivals and departures, the movement of people in and out of the waiting room—nurses getting coffee, Containment soldiers wanting an update on Gunnar.

Gavin, with Burke and Tadji in tow, was the first of our crew to return.

"Gunnar's family?" Liam asked, rising to shake Burke's hand, give Tadji a hug.

"They weren't at home. Containment's sending a soldier to the house to wait. I thought I'd be more use here."

"Thank you," Liam said, and squeezed his shoulder.

Tadji's eyes were huge, swollen, when she came to me.

"It's going to be fine," I said, embracing her, and hoping against hope that was true. Because I wouldn't accept anything else.

"What happened?" she asked, when we were seated in two remarkably uncomfortable ladder-back chairs and she leaned into me, my arm around her shoulder. I told her about the Beyond, about what we'd seen, about Malachi's injury and Rachel's skills, about Elysium City and pools and talking deer. About the Abethyl and the battle at the Veil, and the hit Gunnar had taken.

About the drive back to New Orleans, holding my best friend's head in my hands, praying that we made it in time.

"I wish the Veil had never opened," she said. "I wish none of this had ever happened."

I understood the wish, the heartache it would have spared. But I looked around the room, at Liam and Gavin sitting across from us, at the Paras who'd come to check on Gunnar, at Moses, who'd dropped by to say hello and promise he'd be back after he finished watching *Adventures in Babysitting* on VHS. Because they'd reached a "crucial moment."

I probably wouldn't have met her, Liam, or Gunnar. Certainly not Malachi or Moses or Rachel. Tadji wouldn't have started working at the store, and I wouldn't have started teaching.

The Veil shouldn't have been breached, and the Court shouldn't have come here looking for war. We hadn't made the tragedy. But we'd tried to make something *of* the tragedy. To adapt and evolve, and find our fit in the sometimes uncomfortable new world. In that way, at least, we'd won.

Rachel came in, having changed into Containment fatigues and pulled her hair into a ponytail

"How is he?" she asked, taking a seat beside me.

"Nothing new," Liam said. "We're still waiting. What's the latest on the storm?"

"The hurricane crossed over southern Florida yesterday. Right now it's a category four over the Gulf, and it's only going to get stronger. It's expected to make landfall late tomorrow. Rain's already started, as you can see."

"Evacuations?" Liam asked.

"Devil's Isle is the designated shelter for Paras," she said. "The president doesn't want them to scatter outside the Zone. There are caravans out of the Zone for humans tonight and tomorrow morning."

"Anybody still here is probably hard-boiled enough to want to stay," Liam said.

"Maybe," Rachel said. "But New Orleans is already hard. I'd bet there won't be many who want to stay to see it get harder. On the plus side, the Seelies didn't attack anything today."

Before she could elaborate, Lizzie appeared in the doorway.

We all stood up, Tadji and Liam and I holding hands.

Lizzie looked us over, her expression perfectly neutral even as flames spun beneath her skin. "His family?"

"We haven't found them yet," Gavin said. "We're working on it."

Lizzie glanced around. "Technically, we're supposed to report to the family of non-Paras, not friends. But given you're his family, too, I'll just tell you—he took a hard knock. Some internal bleeding, but we think we have that handled. Concussion when he hit his head, and he's got some minor swelling in the brain. We're monitoring that, and so far, it's stable, but we'll have to see."

Fear began to rise, to tighten my throat and put burning tears at the backs of my eyes. But I knew there was no better place for him to be right now. And no one I trusted him with more, so I made myself breathe, in and out.

"Three broken ribs. Wrenched shoulder, but nothing broken there. His hip is a mess, but we've set the bones as best we can. He'll need physical therapy. But he's young and he's strong, and there's every reason to be optimistic."

"Is he awake?" Tadji asked. "Can we talk to him?"

Pity crossed Lizzie's face, was gone in a flash. "He's still unconscious." When Tadji sucked in a breath, Liam put an arm around her shoulder, and Lizzie held up her hands as if to stem the tide of panic.

"That's not unexpected or unusual," she said. "It's a response to stress. He's healing, and it will take time."

"How long until he wakes up?" Liam asked.

"There's no way to tell."

"Can we stay until he does?"

Lizzie shifted her gaze to me, tried for a smile. "Of course. If you're willing to risk uncomfortable chairs, rooms that never go quite dark, and the constant movement of nurses in and out."

I didn't see that we had much choice.

Tadji leaned against me, and we waited together.

It was two more hours before Gunnar was moved into a room, and another twenty minutes before they let us see him. They'd be situating him, I knew. Hooking up monitors and machines powered by Devil's Isle's impressive generators.

When we finally went in, I didn't like seeing him there, face pale, eyes closed, wired like a machine. A stripe of his thick, dark hair had been shaved for a neat line of stitches.

"He's going to be really mad about his hair," Tadji said with a half laugh. "It was his pride and joy."

"Yeah, but in fairness he has a lot of pride and joy." I squeezed her hand. "Gunnar is not humble."

She laughed, swiped at a tear. "No, that's not a word I'd use."

"And you know a lot of words," Gavin said. He came in with steaming cups, offered one to Tadji. Liam was behind him, offered one to me.

"I'm okay," I said. But in truth I was exhausted, riding on fear and adrenaline.

The door opened, and a man looked in. He was tall and broad shouldered, with tousled auburn hair, and blue eyes staring from a face with a strong jaw. His gaze went to the bed, and there was something in his eyes that wasn't just friendship.

Tadji glanced at me, her brows lifted. I shrugged, glanced back at the man.

"Hi," I said. "I'm Claire. You're a friend of Gunnar's?"

His brow knit. "I'm not entirely sure." He ran a hand through his hair, biceps bunching with the move. "I mean, we were friends before. We hadn't really talked about—I guess I'm not sure . . ." He held up his hands, closed his eyes as if to compose himself. "Sorry, I'm a mess today. Let me just get myself together."

There'd been longing in his eyes. Gunnar hadn't mentioned a romance, so maybe they were still in the friends-and-dancing-around-the-possibility-of-something-more stage.

"We've all been in the same boat," Tadji said. "Take your time."

When he opened his eyes again, they seemed clearer. "I'm Cam. Cameron."

"Tadji," she said, then introduced everyone else. Handshakes were exchanged, people evaluated.

He stepped to the end of the bed, looked defeated as he stared down at Gunnar. So I scooched over, made some room.

"Come on over, Cameron," I said. "Looks like you're having a shit day like the rest of us."

"Not the greatest," he said, moving beside me.

"Shit day all around," Gavin agreed.

There was a knock at the door. We looked back, and found Cantrell and Stella Landreau in the doorway.

They might have come back for New Orleans and Gunnar, but they'd refused to give up their home, their lifestyle, their pretensions, their fantasy that life would just go on as it always had. And everything touched by magic, everything that made the world dangerous for Gunnar, was an enemy.

Including me.

I hadn't seen them since they'd come back. They both looked older, more worn—and very unhappy. I braced for impact.

"Mr. and Mrs. Landreau."

"Claire. Tadji."

"You may not know Gavin Quinn," I said, and introduced him, then gestured to Cameron. "This is Cameron, one of Gunnar's friends."

They exchanged greetings, and we rose so the Landreaus could move closer to the bed. Stella stood at the bedside, wept as she touched Gunnar's arm. Cantrell moved beside her, taking her hand in his and putting his other one on the rail.

Tears threatened again, and I looked at the ceiling, blinking them back. No more tears today. We'd gotten Gunnar where he needed to go, and I had to trust him, trust Lizzie, to come out of it.

Liam moved in behind me, put a hand on my back, leaned his head against mine. I felt better just for the contact. For having him there.

Lizzie stepped into the doorway, and we shifted positions to let her through.

"You're the parents?" she asked, and gave them a moment to look over the woman who was caring for their son, and the fire that moved beneath her skin.

"We are," Cantrell said. "I'm a surgeon. Was a surgeon—I'm retired."

She nodded briskly, glanced back at the rest of us. "Excellent. I'm Lizzie. I've been coordinating your son's care. Let's discuss his treatment."

We left them to talk.

Lizzie came into the waiting room a few minutes later, chewing on the end of an energy bar.

"They'd like to talk to you," she said, looking at me.

Shit, I thought, and knew they were going to relieve their stress and fear by dumping it on me. Blaming me and Paranormals everywhere for more harm befalling their family.

I'd have liked to send them directly to Camael to give that feedback.

"Okay," I said, and rose.

"I can go with you." Liam's voice was firm and tinged with anger. He didn't want them blaming me any more than I did. But I shook my head.

"He's my friend. I have to handle it."

He looked at me for a moment, then nodded. "Okay."

"If you need some ass kicking," Gavin said, not looking up from the ancient copy of *Highlights* he'd taken from the rack by the door, "I'm here for you. Soon as I finish this article."

I found the Landreaus in chairs they'd pulled beside the bed. They stood up when I came in.

"Claire," Cantrell said, "we wanted to talk with you. If we could have a moment?"

"Sure," I said as the door closed behind me with a click that echoed off the walls.

"It's been several months," Stella said.

"Yes, it has. How is the family?"

"Good. Zach is in Atlanta, where we stayed for several months. Emme is in New York now. After the . . . incident, she needed a new start."

The incident had been the wraith attack that had seemed to turn them against me in the first place.

"And that's what we wanted to talk to you about," Cantrell said. They looked at each other, clasped hands. "We wanted to apologize."

I stared at them, and it took a good minute before I could process what they'd said. "Excuse me?"

"I'm sorry," Cantrell said. "The last time we saw you and your friends, we were harsh. We spread around a lot of blame for Emme's attack. That was before we understood you were a Sensitive, but even after we knew . . . even then, it took time for me to admit I'd been unfair. Longer than it should have," he added. "So I'm sorry."

"You're forgiven," I said, and he looked at me for a long moment. "So easily."

"The Zone is hard enough with the enemies we've got. We don't need to make more." I put a hand atop his, squeezed. "And Gunnar doesn't need fighting right now."

He put his other hand atop mine, squeezed again. "I think you're right about that."

The hours passed in a haze of nurses, beeps, friends coming and going, passing along their best wishes. And the rain growing steadier, the wind louder. We sent Tadji back to the store with Gavin so they could get some sleep.

The Containment chaplain, the only remaining priest in New Orleans as far as I was aware, prayed with the family, words aloud and whispered, requests to keep him safe, to heal him, to bring him back, to bring him peace.

Sobs nearly choked me at that, and I had to walk out of the room to keep from breaking down. I moved through the clinic, ignoring everyone I passed, until I reached the front door and the long porch that wrapped the front of the building.

There was a worn wooden swing, white paint peeling, chain rusting, just close enough to the wall to keep the rain from reaching it.

I sat down . . . and just breathed. Air in, air out, until the worry subsided, until my hands stopped shaking. Until I stopped imagining life without my best friend.

"He'll be fine," I murmured, as if the words alone were enough to push health back into him. "He'll be fine."

Because I couldn't lose anything else.

The swing wobbled, and I opened my eyes, found Lizzie beside me. Her legs were stretched out, ankles crossed above those thick-soled shoes nurses seemed to prefer, arms folded over her chest. Her eyes were closed, giving me a moment to watch the flames that danced beneath her skin as if to music I couldn't hear.

"It's fine to look," she said, and I nearly jumped from the sound. She opened one eye, looked at me. "Barely holding it together?"

"That's pretty much it."

She nodded. "Gets that way for everyone, whether you work here or not. Sometimes you have to take a minute." She used the tips of her toes to push the swing back, then forth, then back again. "They painted."

"What?"

She pointed at the porch, which was a shade of unnaturally bright green I hadn't even noticed when we'd come in, or when I'd sat down.

"Oh. Yeah."

"Green is supposed to be calming." She pushed the swing again, the chains creaking. "Although I'm not sure that applies to this particular shade. Anyway, they painted it because they wanted the clinic to feel cheerier after it was consolidated with Memorial." She glanced at me. "Do you feel cheerier?"

"Not even a little bit. My whole mood about New Orleans right now is—" I held out my hand, thumb down, in the international symbol for dislike.

I didn't want to live in Elysium. The visit had made that clear. But in the twenty-four hours I'd spent there, I'd been ruined for power outages, stale food, heat, dirt. We lived in a place where everything was hard. Aeryth had made it her mission to make things harder.

Lizzie nodded. "Sometimes I wonder why I stayed here. In Devil's Isle, I mean."

I looked at her. "Why did you?"

She was quiet for a moment, and she scratched a particularly bright flicker of flame on her forearm. "Because I'm already here. Because there's work to be done. Because I'm not sure where else I'd belong after all this time."

"The Devil's Isle you know versus the devil you don't?"

She frowned. "Your language is very strange. But I suppose, yes, that's part of it. There was war in the Beyond, too. But I understand it's over now?"

She wanted confirmation, although I wasn't sure of what.

"We didn't see any fighting. Everything we saw was—well, beautiful. It was, I guess, manicured. To the nth degree. Uniform. Similar. And kind of plastic. We didn't like it."

"We?"

"Everyone who went. Malachi included."

She nodded, sighed deeply, as if letting go of something she'd been holding in for a long time. "I think that's part of what happens after fighting, after chaos. When the Consularis initially worked to unify us, I mean. But they went too far. And apparently they didn't learn a thing from the Court's rebellion."

I tried to nod, but instead yawned hugely.

"You should get some sleep."

"The chairs in the waiting room aren't exactly comfortable."

"No, they aren't. Keeps people from staying too long." She smiled. "We've got a sleeping room for visitors. We've had more humans in since the fighting started, and their loved ones—who don't live here—want to stay close. Couple of old patient beds in there. I'm not saying it will be comfortable, but it will be dark and quiet."

That sounded like absolute heaven.

CHAPTER EIGHTEEN

Dawn broke to a slate gray sky and hard rain. I left Liam sleeping and walked to the porch to get some air.

It wasn't entirely fresh; the city smelled wet in the way New Orleans always did during rainstorms. And the water had already started to puddle, collecting in the street and outside the sandbags that ringed the building.

"*Attention,*" called a voice on a loudspeaker that echoed across the neighborhood. "The final caravan will leave New Orleans in two hours. If you intend to remain, please make your way to your designated shelter. *Attention . . .*" The message began again, and repeated three times before the world went silent again.

I went back in, washed my face in the small guest bathroom, then finger-combed and braided my hair to hide the fact it had been through a battle and a rainstorm since I'd washed it last. There were dark circles under my eyes, which made me look even paler than usual. But I couldn't do anything about that. And I was procrastinating by thinking about it. Trying not to think about Gunnar.

I gave myself one last deep breath, made myself step into the corridor and walk down the hall again. And found it eerily quiet. The same nurse who'd been here last night, this time with bags beneath her eyes, tabbed through color-coded files on a tall shelf behind the counter. She glanced up at the sound of my footsteps, nodded with recognition.

The rest of the rooms were empty; either everyone had been healed or they'd sought shelter elsewhere.

I opened the door, and found Cameron and Cantrell in chairs on either side of the bed, legs stretched and arms folded over their chests as they slept.

The door squeaked as it closed, and Gunnar's father batted his eyes open, squinted to focus on me. Then slipped his gaze to Gunnar, whose chest rose and fell as he slept.

"Nothing yet," Cantrell whispered, and sat up, scrubbed his hands over his face. Then he yawned, shifted his gaze to Cameron, to the window.

"What time is it?"

"About five thirty. I'm sorry I woke you."

"It's fine. I just dropped off. Felt like I needed to be here."

"Did Stella go home?"

"I sent her home yesterday. Back to Atlanta."

Out of the Zone, he meant. Away from New Orleans and Seelies and the storm.

I didn't know how I felt about that. Was I angry that he'd given up? That someone else was running away? Or jealous that they'd finally managed to break the bonds that kept us here? The memories that tied us to this dying place.

Maybe a bit of both.

The misery in his eyes said enough. "She didn't want to go. She didn't want to leave Gunnar or me or the house. The city. But I had to keep her safe. We shouldn't have come back."

I nodded, reached out, and squeezed his hand. "Life here gets harder every day. Some of us can stay. Some of us can't. And that's okay. That's why the rest of us are here. Because we know that not everyone can stay."

His eyes filled, and my heart broke a little. "Thank you for that." His voice was rough as he worked to hold back the emotion.

"You're welcome."

Cameron stirred, blinked, pushed himself upright. "I didn't know I was out," he said, looking from me to Cantrell to Gunnar.

"Nothing?" he quietly asked.

"Not yet," Cantrell said. He stood up, stretched side to side from the waist.

"Why don't you guys go grab some coffee?" I offered. "I'll stay here with him."

"I could use a stretch," Cantrell said. "Maybe a walk around the block." He glanced out the window. "Or I could have, if it wasn't pouring." He looked back at me. "Frieda?"

I nodded. "Landfall tonight. Here."

"Oh, good," he said dryly. "Another gift from the heavens."

I curled up in the chair still warm from the vigil. Rain beat hard against the window, like every drop was trying to find its way in.

"You look like crap."

I froze at the hoarse voice, thought for a moment a Peskie had come through the door to insult me. Because that seemed like the kind of thing a Peskie would do.

And then I looked at Gunnar, and saw the smile lifting the corner of his mouth.

Tears began to fall. "You look like crap." I leaned over, pressed a kiss to his forehead. "About time you woke up. It's not like a hurricane isn't bearing down on us."

"That hurricane is presently in my head." He looked around the room. "No flowers? No balloons?"

"No florists," I said dryly. "But there is a gorgeous redhead—other than me—who sat by your bed all night."

Both eyes popped wide, just like his smile. "Cameron was here?"

"Is here. He's with your dad. Getting coffee." I leaned forward. "And Cantrell apologized to me for being a jerk after Emme was hurt."

Gunnar opened his mouth, closed it again. "Did hell actually freeze over? Because that's the typical threshold for Cantrell to apologize for anything."

"You're in a very wet New Orleans." I took his hand, squeezed gently. "And I'm really, really, really glad to see you awake."

"I'm glad to be awake." He tried to sit up, to look down, and winced. "Everybody else okay?"

"Everybody else is fine. Except possibly Scarlet. Liam drove like a bat out of hell, and she will never be the same."

"Add it to my tab," he said, and lay back again.

"Bet your ass."

"Well, it's not good coffee," Cantrell said, stepping into the doorway, "but it is—" He stopped short when he saw Gunnar, realized his son was awake, then swallowed hard.

"Gun," he said, then moved to the bed, set the coffee on the side table. "You're awake."

"I am, Pop. Sorry for scaring you."

"Probably just hanging out in bed for the fun of it. Lazy," Cantrell said, wiping with the back of his hand at the tear he hadn't managed to control. "Always said that about you."

He curled around his son, kissed his forehead.

Gunnar smiled weakly. "Yeah, you did. But you didn't see my heroic acts." He glanced at me. "They were heroic, right?"

"Oh, utterly. Incredibly. Stories will be written. Odes and poems and ballads, even. You were always too brave for your own good."

Gunnar gestured to his body with his unbandaged arm. "Case in point."

"I'm going to go get Lizzie," Cantrell said, and passed Cameron on the way out.

He stepped into the doorway, was obviously working to keep the smile off his face. Working to stay calm. I knew that face, because I'd made the same one when I'd realized Liam was back.

"I'll help your father get Lizzie," I said, and stood up. "Because that's totally a thing that's not made-up." I kissed his cheek, then went for the door, gave Cameron a thumbs-up Gunnar couldn't see.

"Hey," I heard Cameron say.

"Hey," Gunnar said back, and I closed the door.

Even though I really didn't want to.

There was a literal hurricane outside, but our spirits were up. Rachel had gone back to the Cabildo, and we still hadn't seen Malachi.

"I hope he's okay," I said, and pushed back the ancient blinds to look outside. Not that there was anything to see. Gray sky and water.

"He may have stayed with Darby," Liam said. "He knows Gunnar is in good hands with Lizzie—and you—and he's got the Devil's Snare to think about."

"There's a lot to do," I said. "I need to update Tadji, check on the store, find out where Darby is with the weapon. And I guess we should talk about the last caravan. Whether we're going to try to get a spot."

Liam's brow arched, his jaw twitched, and I could all but see him itching for a fight. "We've already decided whether to stay or go. We're still here."

I looked up at him.

"You aren't leaving," he said. "Even if you wanted to leave New Orleans, you couldn't leave him, because that's not the kind of person you are. And I'm not leaving without you."

I just stared at him, trying to process what he'd said. To understand it. And realized that on some level I'd been expecting him to leave again. Waiting for him to say good-bye and join Eleanor outside the Zone, to send a note back explaining how happy he was outside the Zone.

I couldn't imagine myself with anyone else. But I hadn't believed he felt the same way about me.

I hadn't believed in us.

Liam *had*, so much that he was willing to accept living here, with magic, in order to be with me. He loved me enough to sacrifice. And that was everything.

Since I didn't have the words, I moved into his arms. It surprised him, enough that it took a moment for him to embrace me, to pull me closer. I gave myself that moment, the chance to be loved, to be wanted before the world interrupted us again.

"Thank you," I said quietly. I wasn't sure if I'd said it loudly enough for him to hear—or if I wanted him to hear—but he stroked my hair.

"You don't have to thank me for love. It's mine to give, Claire. Without strings or conditions."

Now I leaned back, narrowed my eyes. "Are you trying to win a Boyfriend of the Year award?"

"Depends. What's the prize?"

I leaned up and kissed him. "I love you. And that's mine to give."

"Good," he said.

"Now that we've cleared that up, I want to tell Gunnar good-bye."

"Okay. I'll wait in the lobby."

We parted ways, and I went back to Gunnar's room, found him alone, staring out the window at the falling rain.

"Where is everyone?" I asked.

He looked at me. "Cameron went to check on his dog. Cantrell went back to the house. We're getting reports about flooding, so I made them go."

"You're getting reports?"

"Plenty of work to do. Especially now." He patted the bed. "Come here."

I sat on the edge of the bed, tried to find somewhere to put my hands in this awkward position, and settled on my lap. "Is this when you declare your undying love for me?"

"It's when I ask about you and Liam."

"Me and Liam? You were nearly killed by Paranormals, and you want to know about my love life?"

"I want to know if you're okay. You seem . . . strained. Or you did."

I didn't think it had been that obvious. I guess I'd been wrong. "Growing pains."

"Because you're commitment-phobic."

I narrowed my gaze. "Excuse me?"

"I mean, aren't we all a little commitment-phobic? Consider where we live, what we do. Things change quickly. Hard to commit when you don't know what's coming next."

"Yeah," I said, and felt better that I wasn't the only who felt that way. "That's about it. He said he'd stay in New Orleans because of me."

"Of course he will."

"What do you mean, 'of course'? We just talked about it."

Gunnar just looked at me. "You really should have dated more in high school."

"I would have gone to homecoming, but there was suddenly this paranormal war, so I had to change my plans."

"Ha ha." He put a hand on mine, squeezed. "He loves you, Claire. And he's already decided to stay. He sent Eleanor away, probably would have sent Gavin, too, if he could have. But he stayed. And, sadly, I don't think he stayed for me."

I pointed at him. "Hands off."

"You know, if you weren't dating him, I'd probably take a stab."

"I am dating him, and he's straight."

"I like to think of sexuality as"—Gunnar drew his hands apart—"a spectrum."

"How come you only say that when we're talking about my boyfriends? And how come I didn't know about Cameron?"

His cheeks actually turned pink.

"So you do have a thing," I said.

"It's the beginning of a thing. We've only been talking. And I didn't want to jinx it."

God, we were too much alike.

"I like him, Claire."

I smiled. "I like him, too. He stayed all night. Your father in one chair, him in the other."

"No constant vigil from Claire-Bear?"

"There were no more vigiling chairs," I said. "When we have time, I want details about how you met, his IQ, how he treats waiters, what he looks like under those clothes."

"Work, high, no idea, hopefully great."

"That's just the table of contents," I said, rising.

"Claire, do me a favor."

I looked back at him.

"Like I told Cantrell and Cameron, don't come back today; it's too risky. Stay inside. If anything happens, Lizzie will get word to you."

I didn't want to agree with him, but knew he was right. "I will if you'll get some rest, because we're going to need you. And I need to see a girl about a war machine."

But first, I needed to see a girl with a store.

Liam and I left the clinic in Scarlet and drove through driving rain toward the Devil's Isle gate. By the time we made it across the neighborhood, I was pretty sure she'd cracked a shock on the trip from Belle Chasse.

When all was said and done, she was going to deserve a good pampering.

I slowed down when we reached the gate to give the guards time to open it, but it was already open, as a dozen people in ponchos and rain jackets or just holding blankets over their heads waited in line to get into Devil's Isle. Most looked older. One was in a wheelchair. Another woman had two small children, who splashed in the water in bright yellow rain boots.

I cranked down the window, squinted into the rain at the guard. "Everything okay?" I asked, nearly yelling over the roar of wind and water.

He wore a plastic poncho over his fatigues, and looked generally miserable in the blowing rain. "The community gardens are washed out and food's running low." He had to raise his voice over the rain. "And there's already flooding in Lakeview and Gentilly, and there's a shuttle running humans down here. They should have taken the damn caravan."

I made a noncommittal noise and rolled up the window, waited for a gap in the traffic, moved through the gate, and waved at the people who waited in line.

"New soldiers," Liam said ruefully, rubbing his forehead as he gazed out the side window. "They were sent here because we needed personnel, and they don't get New Orleans. They don't get the people, or why they'd want to stay even in a crisis. Or that some people simply have nowhere else to go, and the idea of leaving is incomprehensible."

It became more comprehensible as we moved through the Quarter. The edges of the streets had begun to fill, but water hadn't yet reached the sidewalk. The curb was sloped away from the middle of the street to keep water moving toward the collection basins. But if the pump system wasn't working, that would be the sticking point. Literally. And this wasn't even storm surge, not yet. Just rainwater that hadn't yet made it into the broken pump system. We'd see how far it rose.

The store was open, but looked empty from the outside. We found a note taped to the door.

ATTENTION RESIDENTS:
Due to hurricane warning, 8:00 p.m. curfew is now in effect.
Due to limited fuel supplies, mandatory blackout
will begin at 9:00 p.m.

It was going to be a long night.

We walked inside, found Tadji behind the counter. She was the only person in the store, and she looked up when the door opened. "What's happened?"

"Curfew and mandatory blackout," I said, handing her the note. "And Gunnar is awake and says hello and he loves you." I actually couldn't remember if he'd said either of those things. I was exhausted.

She looked at the ceiling, blew out a breath. "Thank God."

"His parents apologized to me."

"Has hell officially frozen over?"

"Ha! That's what Gunnar said."

"And the official answer is 'no,'" Liam said. "But it's still raining."

"Thank you for that insightful weather report, Burt." Tadji pretended to tap documents on the countertop.

"You're welcome, Jenny."

I smiled at the byplay. "How's it going here?"

"I'm worried about the storm, and the power's definitely going to go out, and we're just about out of MREs. So, you know, par for the course.

"I rounded up every candle and jug I could find." She pointed toward the community table, which was now stacked with candles and bottles of water. Larger jugs were stacked on the floor. "There are blankets on the third floor and a few more candles. Who knows if anyone will actually show up, other than the core group, but we'll be ready if they do."

"The core group," I repeated with a smile. Our strange little human and Para family. If we were going to have to wait out a hurricane, I didn't mind waiting it out with them.

But I was going to need some energy if I was going to wait anything out. I grabbed a protein bar from the kitchen. I barely had the plastic wrapper off before I began to chew.

"When was the last time you guys ate a meal?" she asked. "You look worn-out."

I blinked. "I have no idea."

"I could heat something up," she said. "We might as well use the food while we can."

"This is fine for now," I said. "Have you heard from Malachi? Or Darby?"

"Malachi, no, but Darby, yes. I forgot—she asked you to come by when you can. You know, because the Seelies are intent on destroying us."

"Because of that," I agreed. "Did she say whether she'd made progress?"

"She did not."

I looked at the door, not especially eager to go back out in the storm. But I didn't really have a choice.

"Hell of a thing," Tadji said quietly. "If this is about Aeryth losing her sister, I sympathize, but she could have gone the Taj Mahal route."

"No kidding," I said, and ignored the twinge of regret. I hadn't done anything to Callyth. And for all we knew, my mother hadn't, either.

But how many interrogators did Containment have?

No, I told myself. I'd wasted enough mental energy on Laura Blackwell for one lifetime. Her crimes, whatever they might be, couldn't be my burden.

"I'll go see her," I said, then stuffed the last of the protein bar into my mouth.

"While she's gone," Tadji said to Liam, "could you move a couple of sandbags to the back? It's getting a little soggy back there."

"I can." Liam glanced at me. "You okay talking to Darby alone?"

"He's asking if you can swim if necessary," Tadji said.

"I can." I put a hand on his chest, stretched up to kiss him. "I'll be fine. Thank you for helping with the store."

"I'm trying to woo the owner," he said. "It's a bribe."

"Oh, speaking of bribes, I nearly forgot." I pulled the wrapped bark I'd brought from Elysium from my backpack. "Can you give this to Moses?"

"What is it?" she asked, lifting her head to keep the bark out of nose reach. Which was a good move.

"Disgusting," I said. "He'll love it."

I pulled on rubber boots and a plastic Saints poncho—musts for every hurricane kit—for the walk to the museum, and probably would have enjoyed the splashing if it hadn't been for the torrential, horizontal rain and punishing winds. The rain slapped so hard I half expected to find bruises when I pulled the poncho off again.

Palm trees bent in the wind, and unsecured shutters knocked against walls. A gust pulled one away as I watched, sent it spinning through the air like an awkward Frisbee.

Chartres Street was a little higher than Royal, since it was closer to the river and the city dipped in the middle. I passed Napoleon House, which sat on the corner, in order to get to the museum. The antique building was more than two hundred years old, and had definitely seen its share of New Orleans history. It was looking worse for wear today—shutters hanging from their brackets, windows shattered, and rain-exfoliated stucco peeling away from the walls. It probably wasn't going to get any better over the next few hours.

I found the museum's door locked, pounded on it. "Darby! It's Claire!"

I peeked through the window, straining to hear anything in the whistling wind. Finally, after a good minute, there was a scrape, and the door opened.

"Sorry," she said, waving me inside. "Wind kept blowing the door open, so I had to block it."

With a grunt, she pushed to close it again, then scooted a low metal cart in front of it, locked it.

Darby had paired cutoff denim shorts today with a snug T-shirt that showed off her curves, and red rubber boots. Her face was bare, her dark hair pulled back in a kerchief. Like the rest of us, she looked tired.

She blew out a breath. "Freaking miserable out there."

"Yeah, and it's only going to get worse. Landfall later tonight." I pulled off the poncho, hung it over the cart. Not that it had done much good. I was soaked through.

"I know," she said. "Current path shows it moving quickly with landfall over Bay St. Louis, but who knows how the Seelies will screw with that? How's Gunnar?"

"Awake and doing better. How are you?"

"I'm ready for a break," she said.

"Where's Lowes?" I asked as I followed her to the soda fountain.

"Back in Devil's Isle. Apparently has a bit of hydrophobia."

"Well, that is inconvenient in New Orleans. On a related note, have you seen Malachi? I haven't talked to him since we got back from the Beyond."

"He came by this morning with Rachel to see how we were doing."

My eyes widened, matched by my smile. "With Rachel? Like, on purpose?"

Darby grinned, which lit her pale face. "Yup. They weren't holding hands or anything, but they weren't fighting, and they did seem to be more in sync, if that makes sense."

"It does. She was really good on the trip. Can definitely handle herself."

"Yeah, she seems like the type. And here we go."

Without segue, and skipping the preliminaries, she waved her hand at an—"amalgamation" seemed the best word—of metal and stone that sat on the counter. A cast-iron skillet had been wedged into an antique silver toast holder. The Abethyl had been wedged into the skillet, and the Inclusion Stone wedged into the nook in the Abethyl.

"This is . . . an interesting setup," I said.

"You've brought me two rocks, but not the stand. I had to improvise."

I hadn't even thought about the stand. "Sorry about that."

"A good scientist makes do."

As I got closer, I realized there was a little bit of green liquid in the skillet. "And what's the liquid?"

"Electrolytic solution intended to stabilize the effect."

"You made an electrolytic solution, too?" I asked, impressed.

She smiled. "It's Gatorade."

"Wow."

"If I was Cajun, I'd call it Cajun ingenuity. I'm not, so let's just say I'm resourceful."

"So how does it work?" I asked, and tried not to hide my disappointment at how accidental it looked. It didn't look like The Thing That Would Save Us.

Darby pointed to the Abethyl. "This bad boy pulls out the magic, nullifies it." Then she pointed to the Inclusion Stone. "Blackwell told us the truth. This one rotates within the Abethyl, and in doing so, it spreads the Abethyl's effect. That's the tricky part."

"Because?"

"Because getting the right spread is what determines whether you're sucking the magic out of just the bad guys—or out of every Para in the vicinity. And it's testy." She pointed to the Inclusion Stone's interior crack. "It comes down to how the inclusion is aligned within the Abethyl. And a millimeter difference creates a really big difference."

"How are you testing the effects?"

"Moses's old socks."

I just looked at her. "What?"

She lifted a shoulder. "They're magically imbued—and also disgusting, but they served their purpose. Basically, I made a grid out of them, tested the Snare at different alignments. Moses was my gauge—telling me how much magic I'd actually managed to pull out." She frowned. "Or he just liked sniffing his socks."

Another vote of nonconfidence for this janky weapon.

"It sounds like you're making progress." There was a metallic scream outside, and we looked out to see a strip of metal rippling down the sidewalk. "We're going to need to nail this down," I said. "And real soon. By tonight."

"Yeah, that's actually where you come in." She looked at me. "Testing on objects only goes so far. In order to see that I've gotten the alignment correct, I need to test on a person. I need to aim it at you and see what happens."

"To see if I suddenly lose my abilities?"

"Pretty much."

"Oh."

I looked at the Devil's Snare, then down at my fingers, not sure how I felt about the idea of losing my magic in the flash of a Consularis weapon. I hadn't been "just" human in a long time.

On the other hand, what other choice did we have? Malachi, Moses, Lizzie—they were all inherently magical. It was part of who they were, part of their DNA. My magic was a castaway. An interloper. A freak trick of nature. What right did I have to make them test the weapon instead of me?

"I guess I'm the best person for the job."

She just looked at me for a moment. "Do you want to try to say that with conviction? 'Cause the first try wasn't convincing at all." Her smile was kind. "It's okay to be glad you have magic. And to worry about losing it."

I nodded. "I've gotten used to having it," I admitted. "To being a Sensitive with a capital 'S.' I don't want to give it up." I looked at the windows, at the building storm. "Especially not now."

"When they're waiting for us."

Frowning, I turned back to her. "What did you say?"

"When they're waiting for us." She gestured toward the storm. "Basically weather Paras, right?"

"When they're waiting for us," I said quietly, and walked to the window. "When was their last attack?"

Darby followed me, frowned. "I don't know. I don't think they've hit anything since before you left. Since the pumps."

"Since the pumps," I murmured.

"Are you going to keep mysteriously repeating what I'm saying, or tell me what you're thinking?"

"They're waiting," I said, looking back at her. "They destroyed a lot of houses, then Seabrook, then the pumps. And then nothing, for nearly two days."

"While the hurricane gets closer," Darby said. "Maybe they don't like the wind or rain."

"They're air spirits," I said. "We've seen them manipulate air and water to create magical tornadoes, waterspouts, fog. Could they control an entire hurricane?"

"No," Darby said, shaking her head. "There's no way. Do you know how much energy is wrapped up in a hurricane? A nuclear bomb has nothing on it. So even if, what, all forty of them were involved, there's no way they'd have the power to create an entire storm."

"Seelies don't create," I said. "They manipulate. And what if they only needed to do a little manipulation to a storm that was already moving toward us?"

I saw understanding dawn on her face. "They're not avoiding the rain," she said. "They're resting up for something big."

"What's the worst-case scenario with a hurricane?"

She pursed her lips as she considered. "A slow moving category five? So you get all the wind, all the rain, all the storm surge, and it just camps out in place. It stalls, to use the terminology. It would be catastrophic." Eyes wide, she looked back toward the Devil's Snare. "We have to test this weapon."

"Yeah, we do." I gave myself another moment—potentially a last moment—with my magic, then nodded. "Let's do this."

Because we were running out of time.

CHAPTER NINETEEN

A few minutes later we stood in the courtyard, the wind and rain roaring around us.

The Devil's Snare was on a table facing a former crab trap that held a pair of Moses's torn and stained socks.

"I don't want to do this inside," she yelled, buttoned up in a bright yellow slicker. "Not when I'm not certain how it will react."

"That's very comforting!" I yelled. "Where do I go?"

Back to the store was the first idea that came to mind, but I kept that to myself. I didn't want to puncture her confidence right before she experimented on me.

"Behind the socks, and to the right!"

I went where she directed me, which put me in the back corner of the courtyard, the wooden fence rattling behind me.

"That's good! Don't move!" She gave me a thumbs-up.

I did the same. Mine was much less heartfelt.

She fiddled with the Devil's Snare, then looked up. "I just have to push the Inclusion Stone all the way in, and we'll be good to go. It'll make some noise, vibrate some, and, when it's done, go still again." She chuckled. "And that's not a euphemism!"

I couldn't even fake a laugh.

"Here we go," she said, and completed the connection.

I squeezed my eyes closed.

And nothing happened.

"Huh," she said. "That worked earlier. Maybe the battery's dead, right?" She peered at it, then gave the side of the skillet a good knock with the palm of her hand.

It began to vibrate.

"Is this what it's supposed to do?" I asked as the Inclusion Stone began to spin in the middle, sending a spray of light and—from what I could feel behind it—magic.

"Standard!" she yelled out.

To the right, Moses's socks began to shake and bounce inside the trap like angry crabs.

I could feel a tingle in my hands, the pins-and-needles feeling of a limb waking up, and was momentarily afraid I was actually feeling the magic leaving my body. But two seconds later, the Inclusion Stone stopped spinning, and the socks stopped shaking.

Something cracked and crashed outside the courtyard wall, and I instinctively reached for magic, was relieved when I was still able to access it. But no squadron of Seelies peered over the wall at us, and there wasn't a tingle in the air.

"What the hell was that?" Darby asked after we'd waited in silence for a long, tense moment.

"Just wind damage, right?"

Darby looked back at the Devil's Snare, clearly not convinced by my explanation. I wasn't entirely convinced, either.

"Check the socks," she said, and began to adjust the stones.

I'd been prepared for disappointment. Shaking socks and tingling fingers weren't exactly the effects of the intimidating weapon I hoped we'd created. But when I opened the trap and lifted them out . . . it was instantly obvious there wasn't a single drop of magic in them. They were just . . . mundane.

The Devil's Snare had actually worked.

"It worked!" I said, holding them up. "The socks are empty! They're still disgusting, but no magic!"

"Perfect! How are you?"

I was done with rain and screaming over it, so I walked her way, signaled her back into the museum.

"I'm fine," I said when we were inside, and dropped the damp socks onto a side table. "Still magical." Which relieved me more than I'd have thought possible a year ago.

"So we can absolutely aim that thing," she said. "Malachi is going to be very relieved."

"Yeah, but socks are pretty minor. You really think it will work against a few dozen Seelies?"

"Sure," she said. "As long as they're within range."

"Then we still have a problem. We have to get the Seelies in front of the weapon. We have to get them in range."

"That is the downside of a narrow spread," she agreed. "No accidental magic taking, but you really need to stick the landing. Maybe we could use the Devil's Snare as bait? Aeryth may want the Inclusion Stone or the Abethyl, or the entire thing, especially if she thinks she could use it against the Consularis."

"Yeah," I said. "Or, we could use Callyth. Maybe we could promise Aeryth information. That might be a lure."

Darby tapped fingers against her forehead. "In my scientific haze, I nearly forgot to tell you: Laura Blackwell didn't kill Callyth. Or interrogate her."

I snapped my gaze back to her. "What?"

"Gunnar asked me to look. He knew you were worried about it, so I did it fast. Blackwell kept really good records. There was no mention of a Seelie, and that seems like the kind of thing she'd have noted, recorded. So I started looking at other Containment records. With a little help from a friend."

"Moses?"

"Of course."

"So who did question her?" *And kill her,* I thought, but didn't say it aloud.

"I've narrowed it down to two agents. Guy named Lawrence Pelletier. And Jack Broussard."

My brows lifted. We knew Broussard. Or had known him. He'd been a Containment agent with a bad attitude and an eye toward magical conspiracies. He'd been murdered.

"Who's Pelletier?"

"Very nasty character," she said. "He's got a long and complicated file, several complaints about aggression, use of force. But he seemed to be effective, because they kept him around and in play. Supposedly, he's one of the officers who realized cold iron was effective against Paras."

"No kidding."

"None." Her gaze went flat. "Learned it by bashing someone over the head with a bit of balcony railing."

"Is he still alive?"

"Killed three years ago. Driving at night, flipped his jeep into a canal. Couldn't swim."

"So they're both dead. I don't know if Aeryth will buy that, or care." That Seelies thought of us as fungible kept coming up. "It's humans who are at fault, collectively. How did she die?"

Darby nodded. "Medical incident."

"She went to the clinic?" I asked.

"No. Had a seizure while in custody, and didn't survive treatment. They cremated her, buried her remains in St. Louis Number One. The plot is marked."

That was specific information, at least. Ethically questionable not to tell Aeryth where her sister was buried until we got what we wanted, but so was their destruction of our city.

But first we had to get the Seelies here. "We can discuss our options at the store. You're coming over, right?"

"Instead of staying here alone in a hurricane? Yes. I like my privacy, but I'm not interested in floating alone down Chartres tomorrow."

"Let's take the Devil's Snare," I said. Just in case we needed it . . .

I'd barely finished the thought when the door slammed open. I shoved Darby behind me, held out a hand to the dark shadow in the doorway.

And my heart didn't start beating again until Liam and Malachi stepped inside.

Liam strode toward me, took my arms, and hauled me up to my toes as he looked me over. "You're all right?"

"I'm fine. Why?"

"We heard the explosion. And saw Napoleon House."

"What about Napoleon House?" I asked.

They looked at each other. Liam went back to the door, beckoned us outside. I was already sick of rain, but darted out in it and checked the corner . . . and could see the interior walls of Napoleon House through a gaping hole in an exterior wall. The wall closest to the museum and our little magic trick.

"Not our fault," we said together. Which just made us look guilty.

Liam's gaze narrowed. "Why would it be your fault?" he asked when we'd hustled inside again.

"We're just nervous because of the proximity," Darby said. "It was nice of you to come check on us."

"Mm-hmm. How's the Devil's Snare?"

"Pretty damn good," I said. "Darby did good work."

And that work couldn't have brought down half of one of the most historic buildings in the French Quarter. That was just a really unlucky coincidence.

"We just have to use it on the Seelies," Darby began, "before they use the power they've been saving up to manipulate the hurricane into, probably, stalling over New Orleans and destroying us completely."

Liam and Malachi stared at her.

"I mean, it's a theory," she said.

"Shit," Liam murmured. "They're going to try to freeze the hurricane in place. It fits. And it's the most complete way to wipe us out."

"They take us out with pure magic," I said, "and they ruin the soil, the water. Nothing will grow, so the ground isn't useful to them."

"Instead," Malachi said, "they use a cleansing rain."

"Yeah," I said. "And since we aren't going to let that happen, we better do some serious brainstorming tonight. Pun intended."

Liam and I walked arm in arm back to the store. Not just because of our connection, but because the punishing wind and horizontal rain meant we needed the help to make it two blocks.

A flag flew past, followed by a palm frond ripped from some poor and unsuspecting tree. And it wasn't a comforting sign that a canoe was tied to one of the balcony supports outside the door.

"In case we have to help someone," Liam said, and I squeezed his hand, glad he'd had the thought.

And all that goodwill was wiped away when we walked inside to find a fight in progress.

Moses and his cousin Solomon stood in front of each other, both of them under four feet tall, fingers pointed in each other's faces. Once the biggest kingpin in Devil's Isle, Solomon was now a constant pain in Moses's ass. I assumed he was sheltering here tonight. That was fine, but I was not in the mood for shenanigans.

"Break it up," I said, stepping to them. "Hurricanes aren't the time for squabbling."

"We aren't squabbling," Moses said, and I belatedly realized he and Solomon weren't pointing at each other, but at the chandelier that hung above them—and the small buzzing creature that was swinging from it, laughing hysterically as she pretended to hump one of the crystals. She had pale skin and blondish dreadlocks, iridescent wings at her back, and not a scrap of clothing.

I narrowed my gaze. "*No.* No Peskies in my store. I won't allow it."

"We can't send her out in the storm," Tadji said.

I swore between my teeth as the Peskie flew down, middle fingers raised, before turning around and sticking out her butt.

"You can blame Solomon," Malachi said dourly. "He's the one who told her she could stay."

"They don't even like me," I said as she buzzed around my head and yanked my hair. I swatted at her, missed, and she landed on the chandelier again, stuck out her tongue. "So why would she want to come here?"

"Because it's magically sheltered."

I stopped, looked at Solomon. "What did you say?"

"It's shielded, right?" He pointed to the brick wall. "Seelies can't use their magic on it."

I knew the building was shielded, but I thought that meant only that the monitors couldn't detect magic through the walls. I didn't know it also meant it would provide shelter from a magical attack.

"Seelies can't use their magic on it," I said, and a plan began to form. But while I worked out the details, I pointed a finger at Solomon.

"Handle her," I said, "or I'll lock her in an armoire and she won't get out until Christmas."

She was still screaming when I walked away.

The power failed before the sun went down. This time, not because of magic, but because of the storm.

We'd all gathered at the store, lit candles, gathered up food, and helped in a couple of soldiers who'd gotten stuck in the flooding, as well as a couple of residents who'd decided they were too nervous to stick it out in their own French Quarter homes. We installed them on the second floor with their own pile of water bottles, blankets, and lanterns.

Burke came in with a poncho and a damp messenger bag. "Have y'all looked outside? Half of Napoleon House came down. Wouldn't have thought a hurricane would take it, considering how many it's already seen."

"Strange," Liam said, and managed not to look at me. I guess there was no point in owning up to it now.

Tadji helped him with his poncho, his messenger bag.

He looked at me. "I've just come from the hospital, and Gunnar says hello."

"How's he doing?" Darby asked.

"Better, and he's made everyone promise again they'll stay inside until this is over. They think he's going to be released in a couple of days, depending on how it goes."

"Devil's Isle locked down?" Liam asked.

"Sandbagged and boarded," Burke said with a nod. "Generators are still running, but only for security of the remaining Court Paras. They've closed the big door. They'll wait out the storm now. And speaking of which . . ."

He pulled color printouts, slightly damp at the edges, from the bag, spread them on the table.

The danger they showed was obvious, but beautiful. The crisp white spiral atop the deep blue of the Gulf. A nautilus of destruction.

"Everybody say hi to Frieda, the category five hurricane. What we're seeing outside right now is the northern edge. It's moving fast, which is something, at least. The eye will probably pass very late tonight, very early tomorrow. Depends."

"How long until it moves off completely?" Gavin asked.

"Sixteen, eighteen hours? The storm begins to weaken the moment it crosses land, but it's a big storm, and that's going to take time."

"And that's without Seelie manipulation."

They all looked at me. "Seelies can't affect a hurricane," Burke said. "It's too big."

"They don't have to create it," Liam reminded us. "They only have to help it along. Make it stall over New Orleans, dump wind and water for a few dozen hours, and they're set."

"Well, shit," Burke said. "There's already flooding in Metairie, Algiers. Storm surge is coming in, and the pumps can't handle it. Two feet of standing water in Mid-City. And the Seelies got in one final hit."

"What?" Liam asked.

"They hit the Lake Borgne Surge Barrier yesterday, and it took us nearly ten hours to realize it. They killed the guards on duty, and the change of shift."

Where Seabrook kept Lake Pontchartrain out of northern New Orleans, the surge barrier kept Lake Borgne—and the rest of the

Gulf of Mexico—out of eastern New Orleans. It was largely that storm surge that had buried the city during Katrina.

"*Merde,*" Liam murmured, rising from his chair and walking to the door, then placing one hand on the jamb as he stared into the gray.

"We're done for," Gavin said, linking his hands atop his head. "There's no point in taking the risk with the weapon, with fighting back. There's going to be nothing left to save."

I understood the discouragement, because I felt it, too. But we weren't the only ones in trouble. And we weren't going to give up.

I stood up, chair squeaking as I rose. That put the gazes in the room back on me.

"We aren't going to do this," I said. "We aren't going to just hand them a victory. And we aren't going to insult everyone who made it through Katrina, who made it through flooding and heat and death and misery. We have each other, we have resources"—I looked at Liam—"and we have magic."

"But what's the point?" Gavin said.

"The point is *what's left,*" I said. "Maybe we'll lose part of the city. Maybe New Orleans won't be inhabitable in the way it was before. But we don't stop fighting because we lose ground. That's what this is—it's losing ground. There are still people in this city trying to eke out an existence on what's left. They aren't going to walk away, and we aren't, either."

"Yeah," Moses said, pounding a fist on the table. "What she said."

"Thanks for that ringing endorsement, Mos."

He pounded his fist again. "You're welcome."

Gavin unlinked his hands, sat up. "You think the Devil's Snare is going to work?"

"Yes," I said. "We tested it, and I survived with magic intact. We just have to get the Seelies in its path."

Solomon perked up. "The Devil's Snare?" he asked, looking around. "That's what you've been working on?"

"Yeah," Mos said, eyes narrowed. "Why? What do you know about it?"

"Nullification," Solomon said. "Some stones, some magic, and it knocks the power right out of you."

"How did you hear that?" I wondered, and felt Liam's curious gaze on me.

"Heard talk."

"Did Aeryth know about it?"

He shrugged. "I don't know. Court knows about it. Heard about it in Elysium. That's one of the reasons the fighting started."

I looked up at Liam and Gavin, caught their nods. The Precepts had been so sure the Court hadn't known about their secret weapon. But they absolutely had. Little wonder Aeryth and the others had decided to take their chances in our world when the other option was having their magic stripped away completely.

Something hard struck the plywood that covered the third-floor window, and then the wrench of metal screamed through the darkness.

Gavin and Liam went to the front of the store, looked through the gap we'd left in the plywood so we could keep an eye on things outside.

"Balcony railing," Liam said.

There was another screech of metal, a shearing away that shook the store's foundations, and then another crash.

"And balcony," Gavin added.

And canoe, I thought. I decided I wasn't going to worry about the ornaments as long as the walls stayed up. I hoped to God the walls would stay up.

"Would they have pulled off bricks?" I wondered.

"Shouldn't have," Liam said, "but Gavin will go look."

"Are you volunteering me?"

"Cost of room and board during the storm, *frère*."

Gavin grumbled, but tramped up the stairs.

"Back to the other drama," Tadji said. "What do we do about the Seelies?"

"We get them in front of the weapon," I said.

"How?" Tadji asked. "We send them a pigeon?"

"Not exactly," I said, and looked at Liam. "We use a bat signal."

"A bat—*ahh*," he said, nodding. "The beam from the Inclusion Stone," he said, and explained to the room what it had done in the garage.

"If it works across a room," I said, "why not try shooting it into the sky?" I looked at Malachi. "That would work, right?"

He blinked in surprise, then considered. "The magic should refract off the water in the air, create additional brilliance. So, theoretically, yes."

"So the Seelies see that, and they're going to wonder what's happening."

"You think they'll see it, investigate."

"Or know what it is and come to claim what's theirs."

"And when Aeryth arrives?"

"I'll offer her a deal. We give her the Devil's Snare, and she goes back to the Beyond and leaves us alone."

"No," Malachi said. "We cannot risk it falling into her hands."

"We won't let it. We won't even let her get close to it, and you'll all be there, out of sight. Along with some Containment agents. You and Burke have made people invisible before."

They'd used a similar trick when we'd gotten Eleanor out of Devil's Isle. Burke manifested the invisibility; Malachi helped him extend it. Now they had Liam to add to the mix.

"That's not a bad idea," Liam said, crossing his arms over his chest. "But they may assume it's a trap and stay away."

"You only need them to take a look," Moses said. "Aeryth's not going to resist the chance to get her hands on the weapon."

"She'll think she can take out humans with the storm," Malachi said, "and Paras with the Devil's Snare."

Gavin came down again. "Walls are fine. Third floor is leaking like a sieve, but the water is hitting the pots you left out. We'll need to dump them eventually."

"Storms are a pain in the ass," Moses said.

"How are you going to do all this luring in the middle of a hurricane?" Tadji asked.

"I also prefer a less drenchy option," Gavin said.

"It won't be easy," Liam said. "But we can't very well sit here while they flood us out."

"Is this weapon safe?" Moses asked. "It won't screw us in the process?"

"It won't," Darby promised.

"But you can stand behind me just in case," I told him.

"Okay," he said with a nod. "That's better."

"The Devil's Snare isn't going to completely disable them," Burke said. "It will take their magic, but not their physical strength. And they're going to fight."

"We've got Containment, Consularis Paras, and ourselves," Liam said. "And if we're going to fight them, it's better to do it on our turf. There's almost no one left in the Quarter but Containment, so injuries and fatalities can be controlled. And if there's flooding, it will likely be less here than in other parts of the city. Ground's higher."

"And if we do this right," I said, "Devil's Isle is right down the road for their ultimate incarceration."

"It's a simple plan," Gavin said. "But simple plans can go wrong just like complex ones."

"Ah, but it's not a simple plan," Tadji said with a smile. "It's just that you've finally made it to the last step. Think about it—Darby finds the notes. Claire's dad finds the Inclusion Stone. You go into the freaking Beyond to get the other thing—" She glanced at me.

"The Abethyl," I said with a smile.

"That," Tadji said, nodding. "You make it back alive, you figure out how to put this weapon together, and you come up with a way to use the weapon against the bad guys. Very complex," she said. "And you've nearly reached the end."

"It's a good plan," Burke said. "But Containment won't go for it during the storm."

We all looked at him—and the grim expression on his face.

"What do you mean?" Gavin asked.

He pointed to the window. "Category five hurricane. One-hundred-and-fifty-mile-per-hour winds, and that's not including the rain, debris, flooding, storm surge. Containment has done some crazy shit, but even they won't run an op in a hurricane."

"So we just let them destroy us?"

"I don't think that's our only option." I looked at Darby. "They can't stop the hurricane completely, right?"

She shook her head. "There's no way they have the magic for that. Slow it down, sure, enough to do some real damage. But not stop it completely. There's too much energy."

"How does that help us?" Burke asked.

"Because the hurricane will continue moving north or north-northeast," I said. "And it will give us a respite."

"The eye," Darby said.

"Exactly. That's our window. The rain breaks; we use the Inclusion

Stone; we lure them in. We take their magic, and Containment rides to the rescue. But that's hours away. What do we do in the meantime?"

"We get a message to Containment," Burke said, pulling out a satellite phone. "And we try our best to survive."

CHAPTER TWENTY

As the eye drew closer, the storm got worse. The noise was incredible. The wind screamed like a freight train bearing down on us, and the rain was percussive, each drop striking the window like a hammer.

It was obvious this wasn't an ordinary storm. Red lightning crackled as the magic built up, discharged. And there was a vibration in the building, in the air, that didn't have anything to do with temperature or pressure. It was the residue of the Seelies' magic, of the power they piled on top of the storm to keep it fueled, to keep it stationary. To keep it dumping inch after inch of water on New Orleans.

When water began to seep beneath the front door, we took the stairs to the third floor, sat or stretched out on spare mattresses, blankets, and pillows around a dozen candles and the bowls and coolers that sat on the floor to catch drips from the ceiling.

Moses claimed the only bed, because "Dibs still works in hurricanes." Tadji sat in front of it, her back against the foot, a book in one hand and a mini-flashlight in the other, reading a book as Burke stared at the ceiling, his head on her legs. Liam's back was against the interior wall, and I sat in his arms, staring up at the glowing stars that dotted the ceiling. I'd nearly forgotten about them, and finding them shimmering in the dark made me feel better.

Even the Peskie was quiet; she'd fallen asleep after getting into the bottle of wine we'd opened. She'd found a thimble and convinced Solomon to fill it up. Half a dozen times.

It was comforting to have everyone here together, to know they were relatively safe despite the noise and shuddering. And as I looked around at them, it finally occurred to me: Maybe home wasn't just a latitude or a bit of brick and stone. Maybe it wasn't just heat or humidity or purple and gold.

Maybe it was safety. Maybe it was familiarity. Maybe it was about feeling at home wherever you were. Maybe it was not about the place, but about the people. And hadn't I found mine? Tadji, Burke, and Gunnar. Liam and Gavin. Moses and Malachi. We'd laughed and cried and fought together, loved and hated and won together. Hidden and run together.

Those things would exist outside New Orleans, outside the Zone. Whether they'd exist outside war would depend on us—on whether we stayed together or drifted apart, and whether we were bound together by something more than survival.

I thought we were. I thought we were a kind of family, and the ties between us weren't just because of location or circumstance, but because we were right for each other, all of us. Tadji's seriousness, Burke's sense of duty, Gavin's snark, Gunnar's loyalty, Liam's sense of honor.

If we wanted a chance to grow, to become more, we might need that to happen outside the boundaries of New Orleans. Without the boundaries of New Orleans—and the limitations placed on us by war and wants.

We were survivors. We had grit. And we'd have those things outside New Orleans, too. And we'd have one another.

My heart was so full. So as the world fell apart outside, I was finally ready to accept the gift I'd been offered.

I looked back at Liam, candlelight flickering across his beautiful face.

"Yes," I said.

He'd been looking toward the window, and it took a moment for him to turn back at me. "Yes, what?"

"Yes—to us."

It took another moment for understanding to dawn in his eyes. And when it did, it was glorious. The haze of shimmering gold spread light across the room. Enough that a few of the others looked over.

"You were right," I told him. "You don't say no to love because you're afraid the world will fall apart around you. You say yes because you're afraid the world will fall apart around you. Because that's what keeps you together. Because love is the reason you keep trying."

His smile blossomed, and he leaned in, pressed his lips to mine. "I love you, Claire."

"I love you, too."

"But I need you to stay here." And he wiggled out of our warm little embrace and headed for the stairs. He was gone before I could ask what he was doing.

"Not the reaction I was hoping for," I murmured.

"It's because you're too tall," Moses said. "I've always said that about you."

I rolled my eyes.

There was thumping on the stairs, and Liam appeared again, then rounded the banister.

"What's it look like down there?" Burke asked.

"Wet," Liam said with a cheeky grin, and went to his knees on the floor. And opened his palm to reveal a navy velvet ring box.

Tadji sucked in a breath just as something big hit the roof, caught, and with a scream peeled away wood and tar paper in the corner of the bedroom.

Water began to pour in.

"Grab that tarp!" Gavin said, and he and Malachi used the bright blue plastic we'd brought upstairs to create a make-do patch.

I was torn between watching them repair my beloved store and staring down at the box in Liam's hand. My heart was thudding, and that had nothing to do with Frieda.

"Is this actually happening?" Darby asked. "Right now? In the middle of a mother-loving hurricane?"

"Holy shit," I said, a whisper the only thing I could manage.

A corner of Liam's mouth lifted. "I think that's the appropriate response." He flipped the box open, revealing beauty. A princess-cut diamond surrounded by a delicate silver filigree that arced around the edges of the ring like lace.

"Oh," I said, leaning forward. "Belle époque, probably three-quarters of a carat. A really gorgeous vintage setting."

There were groans across the room.

"Will you please quit appraising the jewelry?"

"I can't." I looked back at him, grinned. "Have you seen this thing?"

"I have, yes."

"Where did you get it?"

"Eleanor," he said, with his dimpled smile. "It was hers. She sent it in the box with the chocolate."

"Sneaky," I said approvingly. And then I simply ran out of words. I looked at it again, tried to take in the fact that Liam Quinn was proposing to me, and with his grandmother's diamond ring. And I only had to say yes. I only had to reach out, to accept the happiness, the happy ending, that was being offered to me.

"I haven't yet heard your answer."

"We're all waiting," said a member of the audience.

I put my hand over the box, fingers hovering inches above it, and looked back at Liam. "Gavin's okay with you giving me your grandmother's ring?"

"It was my idea," Gavin said, and my heart melted a little.

"Y'all talked about this. About me. About us."

"Of course we did. I love you." His tone darkened. "And, for better or worse, he's family."

Gavin sat up from his pallet across the room. "What do you mean, better or worse?"

"I mean what I said." Liam kept his gaze on me. "Claire, you frustrate me. You challenge me. You inspire me. I love you, and I want you to be my wife. Will you have me?"

As it turned out, the answer was easy. "Yes."

Cheers erupted as Liam pressed his lips to mine and slipped the ring onto my finger.

"I can't promise forever," he said, lips against my cheek, "because that's not mine to offer. But as long as I'm alive, as long as my heart beats, it's yours."

We sent Gavin downstairs for the single bottle of champagne we'd been hiding for months, waiting for good news to crack it open. He came back up with a corkscrew, a sleeve of red plastic cups, and a grimace.

"Very, very wet," he said. "Inch of water on the first floor, but the building seems to be holding."

"She'll hold," I said, and hoped I was right. If a magically protected building couldn't deflect a Seelie-inflicted hurricane, what was the point of the protection?

"Big brother's getting married," he said, pouring champagne

into the cups. "Let's lift a glass to him and his future bride, Claire-Bear."

"To Liam and Claire-Bear!" they shouted, and given the occasion, I let it go.

The night passed in darkness, vibrations, and noise. The rain was constant, and wind roared like a freight train, punctuated by concussions as debris slammed into the building or those nearby.

And the ferocity only grew as the eye grew closer, and the eye wall—the ring of destruction that surrounded it—spun closer.

As we waited and prayed and flicked errant water from our faces, I kept looking down at the diamond on my finger; I hadn't worn jewelry in a long time, and I wasn't used to the sensation. Or what it meant. Represented. I was still coming to terms with the possibility of commitment and forever, but I knew I'd get used to that, too.

But even with the weight of love on my finger, it was hard not to worry about the store, the Quarter, the city.

I sat beside Liam, my arms around my knees, ears pricked for some drop in the volume that would signal the eye was nearly here. "Where would we go?"

He leaned back against the wall, looked at me. "Go?"

"If we lose New Orleans. Where will we go?"

"We aren't going to lose New Orleans."

"Maybe not," I said. "But maybe we will. And we'll be a family regardless. So where will we go?"

"Somewhere with reliable electricity," Gavin said, cooling himself with a paper fan advertising a Bourbon Street strip club.

"Where the hell did you get that thing?" Liam asked.

"What?" Gavin asked, and fanned faster. "Found it in a box on one of my walkabouts."

"Your breaking-and-entering trips around the city?" Liam translated.

"Like we don't all do it" was Gavin's retort. He had a point.

"Paris?" Darby offered, steering the subject back again. "Montreal? If you want the French feel."

"Charleston," I said. "Eleanor and Foster are there."

"I like Chicago," Tadji said. "Or maybe we skip it all and go to the beach. Bermuda."

"Or north," Gavin said. "Iceland."

"What the hell would you do in Iceland?" Liam asked.

"I don't know. The things you do in Iceland."

"I think they mostly involve sheep," I said. "And glaciers. And probably fish."

"I'm cool with all those things."

"You certainly would be in Iceland," Burke said with a grin.

"And what are we going to do in this fantasyland?" Gavin asked, then snapped the fan closed and pointed it at Tadji. "Linguistics professor." Then Burke. "Special ops." Liam. "Cop." Then me, and that's where he paused. "Do you prefer flea market or hipster antiques?"

"Neither?"

"Correct answer. Future Nobel Prize winner," he said, pointing at Darby, whose cheeks pinkened.

Liam stretched out. "And what about you? Layabout? Slacker?"

"Sure, if I can find a sugar mama to finance my lifestyle."

"Nope," Tadji said, shaking her head and pushing curls behind her ear. "There's no way. You're going to be a volunteer coordinator or a kindergarten teacher or something."

"That's insane," Gavin said. "Why would I ever be that . . . responsible?"

"Because you've got a squishy little heart behind the layers of sarcasm, my friend." She narrowed her gaze appraisingly, nodded. "You're a pushover."

"Objection," he said, shaking his head. "I'm a hard-ass."

"With a gooey center," she said, and gave him a wink. "Don't worry, Gavin. We won't tell anyone."

Gavin snorted, but there was a happy little gleam in his eyes. Snarky or not, he was glad Tadji had seen his expanded Grinch heart.

"I might also write some postapocalyptic fantasy. Because," she said, and twirled a finger in the air, gesturing at the world around us.

"Honestly, it would be nice to read about it instead of living it for once," Gavin said.

Truer words.

CHAPTER TWENTY-ONE

We didn't sleep. We watched as hazy dawn light began to filter across the room, and waited for the rattling wind to slow, to signal that we'd reached the eye.

When the howl began to lessen, Liam and I walked downstairs to check the store, found three inches of dirty water that had pooled on hardwood. I had to fight back tears as it lapped at the bottoms of antiques, soaked rugs and knickknacks. Because they weren't the point. They were just the details.

We sat on the stairs above the waterline, others stirring to join us on stairs above.

"How long will we have?" Liam asked when Darby sat on a creaking tread. She'd fallen asleep beside Gavin, her head on his shoulder. They looked good together.

She rubbed her temples. "For the eye? Given how slow the storm is moving, I'd say a couple of hours at the outside if Seelies manage to keep their control. When they lose it, things are going to speed up. And then we've got the eye wall again."

"We're only going to get one chance," Liam said.

We nearly jumped at the knock on the door, pulled back the plywood to find Rachel. She wore fatigues and rubber boots, and carried a large paper bag.

Behind her, Royal was drenched in several inches of water, and the sky was cloudy. The air was eerily still compared with the hurricane, but the hum of magic was still noticeable. And the remains of the store's balconies were a block down the street, twisted around a metal fire escape like a lover.

"Nourishment," Rachel said, passing out apples, water, and granola bars. "Commandant got Burke's message," she said as we sat on the staircase to talk. "And I raided the Cabildo." She peeled open a granola bar. "I haven't eaten yet. It's been a long night."

"You didn't sleep?" Tadji asked, from her perch a few steps up beside Burke.

"Ran ops all night," Rachel said. "Two house rescues in the Lower Ninth. Helped with a generator blowout at Devil's Isle."

"How's the city?" Liam asked.

"Most of northeastern New Orleans is under six to eight feet of water. New Orleans East, the Lower Ninth, Gentilly, Algiers, Chalmette."

"Storm surge?" Gavin asked.

"Storm surge, unmanned and broken pumps, floodwater, Lake Pontchartrain." She looked up at us, and there were shadows beneath her eyes, and not much hope there. "It sat on top of us for nearly twelve hours, thanks to the Seelies."

"Have you seen them?" Malachi asked, stepping onto the landing.

"I haven't. But there have been a dozen reports, mostly from rescue workers. A 'circle of witches,' they're calling them."

"What about Devil's Isle?" I asked. "Gunnar?"

"Devil's Isle has flooding in a few low-lying areas, but that's it. Damage to some buildings, and they're rationing power, because there's only one running generator. A few dozen minor injuries, mostly from debris. No fatalities. And I haven't talked to Gunnar specifically, but I'm in touch with the man on post. He got some sleep overnight, but not much. Word is," she said with a growing smile, "he was ordering Cam around this morning. Trying to get information, get resources moved, that kind of thing."

I blew out a breath I didn't know I'd been holding. I knew he was in good hands, but this wasn't the time to get complacent.

"Speaking of resources," Burke said, rising, "I need to get to the Cabildo to coordinate. If ops can make it here, materiel can make it down the road. I'll be back."

"Be careful," Rachel said. "And watch out for gators."

"Job hazard." He turned to Tadji. "I'll see you."

"Yes, you will."

He smiled, cupped her head, and pressed a kiss to her forehead, then turned to me. "Thanks for the slumber party, and congratulations."

I nodded at him, waved as he splashed to the door.

"Congratulations indeed," Rachel said, taking my hand to peer down at the diamond. "That is lovely."

"It was Eleanor's," I said. "Liam's grandmother."

"I didn't have the pleasure of meeting her while she was here, but understand she is quite a lady." She checked her watch. "You've got no more than a two-hour window, and troops are on the way. So if we're going to hit them, we need to hit them now."

"Okay," I said, and stood, looked up at Darby, who was looking more awake now that we were on the precipice of an operation. "You ready to go?"

"Sure thing."

"You get it ready, and I'll be waiting."

"Why you?" Liam asked, tone dark.

"Because if something goes wrong, I can live without my magic."

"How close does she have to be?" he asked.

"The effect can go far," Darby said, "but the spread is narrow. Twenty or thirty feet. We need to be sure all the good guys are behind the weapon."

I looked at Rachel. "You might put out an alert, if you can keep it quiet. Get word to any Paras outside Devil's Isle that they need to stay downriver of the Quarter. Just in case."

Liam looked at Rachel. "Your soldiers ready to draw down?"

"Is this a Wild West show or an op?" she asked with a smile.

"Whatever gets the job done," he said. "If they don't have magic, you should be able to round them up easily, reimprison them in Devil's Isle. And that should be the end of the Seelie threat."

"Until the next round of assholes comes through," Moses said grimly. Then gnawed on the end of the bark I'd brought back from the Beyond.

"Eat your bark, you grumpus," Tadji said. "We deal with the crisis in front of us. Because that's the best we can do." She looked up at me. "Right?"

"Right."

"There are still contingencies," Rachel said. "The Seelies actually showing up, the weapon working, and our beating them in combat." She held up her hands at our dour looks. "Containment is on board with the plan. But there are a lot of civilians in here, and they want you to be aware of the risks."

"It's worth the risks," Liam said, and looked at me. "Saving New Orleans, saving ourselves, saving our community, makes it worthwhile."

Happiness bloomed and warmed from the inside. Not because our circumstances had suddenly gotten better, but because I had a partner who loved me. Who believed in me.

That was a very good start.

It began with a kiss. And dirty underwear.

Tadji was in the store, piling things onto tables to get them out of the water. Gavin pointed out there wasn't much point in that if the battle went bad.

"Are you gonna wear dirty underwear if you know you're getting into a car wreck?" she'd asked.

He didn't have a response to that.

Liam pulled me aside as Darby and Malachi set up the pieces of the Devil's Snare outside, and Rachel organized Containment's troops around the perimeter. Before I could say anything, my back was pressed against the wall, his lips on mine.

"Is this a good luck kiss?"

"Call it whatever you want, *cher*," he said, lips near my ear. "Just be careful out there."

I wrapped my arms around his neck. "I have every intention of coming back for more of this later."

"Damn right," he said, and then his face brightened. "Well, well. What do we have here?"

I looked back, found Gunnar on the sidewalk in a nonmotorized wheelchair, water three inches up the spokes.

"Holy crap," I said, and ran to the door, then outside, looked him over. He was bruised and thoroughly bandaged, and still wearing hospital-style pajamas. But there was a grim determination in his eyes.

Lizzie was at his side. I nodded at her, turned my gaze to Gunnar. "What the hell are you doing out here? You should be in bed."

"I'm stable, just a little banged up. And I'm not going to sit in Devil's Isle while you go toe-to-toe with Aeryth and the Seelies."

"Little-known follow-up to Josie and the Pussycats," Gavin put in.

"I'm not going toe-to-toe. I'm just here for the bluffing." And I pointed toward the Cabildo. "You'll go back there while this is happening."

"I'll just hang out in the store," Gunnar said with a smile. "It's magically insulated after all, right?" Before I could answer, he shifted his gaze to Liam. "Burke tells me you've swept our girl off her feet. Congratulations." Gunnar held out a hand, and they shook.

"Thank you," Liam said.

"Let's get you inside," Lizzie said, and Gunnar looked up at me.

"Give 'em hell," he said. "If we survive this, I have a date next week."

"Always good to have priorities, Gun," I said, and kissed his cheek. "I'm glad you're here." At least this way I could keep an eye on him. And he'd probably thought the same thing about me.

Fifteen minutes later, I stood in the middle of Royal Street, rubber boots over my jeans.

The Inclusion Stone sat on a table to keep it out of the floodwater. Malachi held the rest of the Devil's Snare inside the store behind me—the Abethyl now in an improved stand Darby had created last night from borrowed antiques. No cast iron or Gatorade required.

Now it was time to call a Seelie.

Pulling in the magic was easy now. I'd done it in a hurricane, in the Beyond, in a fierce battle. Peace and quiet and gentle rain was nothing.

I took more than I had before when we'd tested the stone in the gas station. I wasn't sure how much it would take to send the beam into the sky, to actually get Aeryth's attention, but I figured there was no point in being stingy. I'd refuel soon enough.

I funneled the magic into the stone, and I was relieved when it began to glow red, that I'd managed the first part of the task. That the rain hadn't quelled the power.

"Three, two, one," I murmured, and watched the golden beam of light rise into the gray sky. Malachi was right—it was visible in the humid air, as light and water and magic mixed together, so that the beam appeared to be glitter.

It was beautiful. And it would work.

So I watched, and I waited.

It took eighteen minutes.

They descended through the break in the clouds. Aeryth had added a fluttering white cape to her ensemble, which gathered around her like a cloud when she touched down nearby. The others touched down in an arc behind her, as if she were the designated spokesmodel.

I was worth only a flick of a glance. Then Aeryth's gaze went to the Inclusion Stone. She blanked her face quickly, but not fast enough to hide the interest. And greed.

I thought I'd be afraid. Fearful or nervous when she touched down, when the inevitable threats would begin.

But I wasn't. So much of war was waiting and anticipation and fear. And I was sick of all of it. Today, we'd move the needle. And then we'd figure out where our futures lay.

"For once," she said, "a human does something interesting." But her face went hard. "Where did you get this? It does not belong to you."

"It does now. 'Finders keepers' is something we humans take very seriously."

"It is a relic from our world."

"It is a relic you stole and brought to our world," I countered. "And we have it now. And because of that, I'm able to offer you a onetime deal."

"What deal?" she asked flatly, and I was half-surprised she didn't roll her eyes. She certainly didn't think there was much to the notion of negotiating with me.

"A deal with humans," I said. "We'll give it to you as a gift, in exchange for leaving our world forever."

She laughed. "What would I want with old stones?"

So she'd play it off as a relic, just in case we didn't know its value.

"The Inclusion Stone?" I lifted a shoulder. "That's up to you. But you might want its companion. You might want the Abethyl. And you might want the Devil's Snare."

Aeryth went absolutely still. "You do not have the Abethyl."

"I do. We went to Elysium. We took it, and we brought it back. And you know what you could do with the Devil's Snare, Aeryth. You know the trouble you could cause at the Citadel?"

She looked momentarily confused, as if baffled that I'd somehow learned to speak her language. "You lie. You do not have the Abethyl. I would sense it."

Bingo, I thought. The Abethyl was currently in Malachi's hands inside the store, where she literally couldn't sense it. Yet.

"Do we have a deal?"

"I could tell you whatever I wanted," she said, taking a step forward. "I could tell you that we'll leave your home and never return. And I might stay and crown myself queen. Because you are weak. So it hardly matters what I say, or what I do. The peace won't last for long, and neither will the center of the storm. And when the wind comes back, there will be nothing left of you. Not a single mark upon the land to show that you were here." Her eyes were hard, her smile thin and cold as a gator's. "You will be forgotten."

"Like Callyth?"

Heat flashed in her eyes now, and I felt the thrum of magic like a bass throb in my chest.

"You are not worthy to speak her name."

"So I shouldn't tell you about her death?" A story that would take a little time to impart. Time for Containment soldiers to surround the Seelies, for the snipers on the nearby roofs to get into position, in case the Seelies attempt to take flight.

Aeryth went very still, her eyes narrowing to slits. "You know her murderer?"

"She wasn't murdered. She was captured, interrogated as an enemy combatant. She wasn't tortured, at least as far as we can tell."

"Lies," Aeryth said, but she didn't look entirely certain.

"Truth," I said. "She wasn't harmed during the interrogation. She became ill, had a seizure, and died before the morning was done."

"Seelies do not *sicken*," Aeryth spat out.

"This one did. And if you're so keen on justice, on judgment, the two men who interrogated her are dead." I softened my voice. "Her remains are in the cemetery north of here. You could take her home again."

The Seelies in her battalion looked north, wondering about the final resting place of their comrade. Aeryth took a menacing step forward, but she looked shaken. "Lies," she said again, with less conviction.

"Believe what you will. I wanted to give you the chance. I know how it feels to lose someone you love. To lose someone you depend on. How it eats at you, makes you sad and guilty. But this isn't about Callyth. It's about you, and it's about destruction. Doesn't matter whether it's Earth or Elysium. You just like to break other people's things."

I looked behind me. "Might as well come out and play," I said to the seemingly empty street. "She's not interested in negotiating."

The air shimmered, and the illusion dissolved. Burke and Liam stood side by side, let their magic drop as Malachi joined them.

And that power had been enough to hide the three of them, plus Rachel and a battalion of Containment officers.

"You are very much surrounded," I said with a smile.

Seeing her window for escape closing, Aeryth lunged forward toward the Inclusion Stone.

But I'd already planned for that. I powered up, lifted the stone into the air, sent it careening back toward Rachel. She caught it neatly, set it partially into the Devil's Snare, which Malachi held like the monstrance in which the stone had once lived. We didn't want the magic flaring too early.

I moved behind him, and out of its range.

"I will give you one chance," he said, gaze on Aeryth. "One chance to leave this place, before we use on you the weapon that should never have been created."

"You are a traitor," Aeryth said as another unit of Containment troops moved in behind her. "To all of our kind."

"We are not of a kind," Malachi said smoothly. "I have killed because I must. You kill because you wish, and you cover it with demagoguery. But having a cause doesn't make what you do any better."

He tapped the Abethyl. "You may recognize this, Aeryth. It's the Devil's Snare, the weapon conceived by the Consularis to fight you. We've managed to reassemble it. And it's very effective. This is your final chance—lay down your arms and agree to return to Elysium, and we will not use it against you."

Malachi pushed in the stone, held the Devil's Snare out toward the Seelies.

The stone and the Abethyl began to spin, putting a low rumble into the earth, like an engine moving beneath our feet, and the air in front of it began to wave with the vibrations.

But not fast enough.

The blast of wind they sent down Royal knocked us over like bowling pins.

I hit the ground on my back, splashing in floodwater, and it took a moment to reorient and make it to my feet again. I looked around for the Devil's Snare, found the contraption still in Malachi's hands. He was airborne now, wings extended and fury in his face.

"If you are not content to allow the storm to destroy you, then we shall take you one by one!" Aeryth screamed. "Forward!"

Chaos erupted.

Containment charged, weapons drawn, and began firing. Soldiers clashed, metal clanging against metal, knives against breastplates.

Some of the Seelies took to the air; others met the humans with golden weapons of their own. Malachi initiated the Devil's Snare again, aimed it at one of the Seelies in the air. She screamed. No longer able to fly, she fell, splashing down in dirty water.

"So we'll do this one Seelie at a time," I said, and set my sights on Aeryth.

She watched her colleague go down and her eyes widened in horror. "Into the air!" she screamed, and began to rise.

"Wild West show," I said, thinking of Rachel's comment, and reached out for the magic, pulled the filaments of it into rope, and sent it streaming through the air toward Aeryth.

Like a lasso, it caught her around the waist.

She jerked in midair and looked down with unshielded surprise, then fury as she realized that I was the one who'd managed to trap her.

She lifted farther, stretching the tendrils of magic I'd wrapped around her, and swore at me in a language I didn't understand. I was too busy sweating and trying to control the magic, to keep her tethered to the land.

But she was having none of it.

I saw the intention in her eyes, the decision she'd reached, and buckled down my fear.

A second later, we were airborne.

I heard Liam's voice calling my name as she dragged me through the sky.

It wasn't a view I'd expected to get of New Orleans—twenty feet in the air, attached by a magical connection to a flying Paranormal. And if I wasn't careful, it was the last view I was going to have. Aeryth was powerful, but she'd separated from the rest of her crew, and that diminished her abilities.

We made it four blocks before she began to stutter, to drop, and I began to prepare myself to hit the ground.

And then the tether snapped, or she snapped it, and we were both falling.

I hit the ground, rolled, heard her fall a few yards away.

Stunned, I sucked in air, trying to catch my breath as magic rushed in, and realized I was lying on grass. Behind that, overgrown shrubs, and the familiar fence.

Jackson Square. We'd landed in Jackson Square. At least that was familiar territory.

I climbed to my knees, looked around, and found her in front of the Jackson statue, dress snagged and stained and the now-familiar hatred in her eyes.

She took a step forward, and my heart began to hammer again. Since my hands were still shaking from the magic, I pulled the knife I'd stowed in my boot.

"Do you think that will help you?"

"I don't think I'm the one that needs help. You're facing the end of the road, Aeryth. A couple of minutes, and Malachi will be here with the Devil's Snare. And you can say good-bye to your magic."

"Even without magic, you will not defeat us. We are stronger than you, better skilled. And we will see this city destroyed. Every last building, stone, flower, human, crushed into the soil."

Hatred burned in her eyes, echoing the apocalypse she was trying to ignite.

"Why bother? You could go anywhere else. Be anywhere else."

"Because no other place, no other people, killed my sister."

"Your sister was a murderer."

"She was a *soldier*," Aeryth spat. "She was young. She was beautiful. She fought beside me in Elysium, here. When we claimed victory, she would have stood at my right hand. But she is gone."

"You came into our world to fight. To wage war. What did you think would happen? Did you think we'd roll over and let you have our world because you couldn't win in yours?"

"She wasn't killed in battle," Aeryth said, her eyes flashing with anger. "Not with honor. Not so she would be received beyond the High Mountain as a hero. She was captured, tortured by humans. They tortured her because she gave them nothing. Because she was strong. And because she was not useful to them, they killed her."

"Wrong," I said. "A convenient story to justify your killing, but wrong. She was sick," I said, "and she died. And that's the end of her story. This is your story. And killing us won't bring her back. Destroying New Orleans won't change what happened to her."

There was darkness in her gaze, in the curl of her lips. Bare and obvious loathing that she didn't bother to hide. "That doesn't make you deserve it any less."

She held out a hand and magic flashed—the same red lightning we'd seen in the storm. And magic flashed toward me, hit me with the force of a thousand needles burrowing into skin. The pain was so hot, so vibrant, that I couldn't remember how to breathe, that my heart seemed to forget how to pump.

I hit the ground on my knees, tears stinging my eyes at pain so sharp I could see the red haze of it, could hear the chalkboard-scratch sound of her magic striking each nerve. And could feel the slowing of my blood as she pushed the power deeper.

I'd ridden with a Seelie, flown through the air through Devil's Isle, survived half of a hurricane. And I would die because a Seelie wanted to inflict pain. My vision dimmed at the edges, my head bobbing as my eyes began to close.

Until that red haze shifted, crackled, and something in her eyes changed, went vacant. She froze, then hit the ground.

And pain simply fell away, the relief of its absence bringing tears to my eyes. I sucked in a breath, looked over to see that Malachi stood a few yards away, Devil's Snare in his hands, pointed directly at her.

And on the ground, Aeryth sat with arms and legs akimbo, like a broken doll, dress disheveled, and shock was in her eyes.

She looked at me, and that look of blank devastation flashed into loathing again.

"He told you to stop," I said. "He gave you fair warning."

"I will kill you all," she said, rising on unsteady feet and pulling a dagger from her belt. "And I'll start with you, little Sensitive. Human thief."

Malachi stepped forward, but I held out a hand, held him off.

She was mine, and I'd take her down. Except that she was a soldier, and I wasn't. I'd learned a lot in the last year, but I knew I wasn't strong enough to fight her hand to hand. I didn't have those skills.

But I had others. I'd use some of that magic she was so fond of. I rose to my knees, as unsteady as she had been. I kept my gaze on hers, and began to feel out the magic in the air, gather the threads.

She came at me with the knife, and I dodged, circled. Still, pain shattered my concentration as she traced a line down the edge of my arm.

"You will fail," she said, and rotated to strike again, barely missing my throat with the blade's lethal tip.

I wasn't a fighter. I was a Sensitive. But I kept my gaze on her, kept gathering magic, and knew I was going to pay later for the treachery I was doing to my body, the work I kept asking of it. And I thought of the tree nymph we'd met in the Beyond, and what she'd done with a little greenery.

Focus, I demanded, and reached out with the magic I'd gathered—the latent magic that saturated New Orleans and the pricklier magic she'd put into the air—and I reached toward the tangled vines behind us. I pulled with every ounce of power I could muster, every drop of hatred and bile she'd spilled, and watched as the vines began to snake forward, rustling toward her.

She lifted her knife again, blade down as she prepared to strike, as the vines reached her feet. She looked down, jerked back as they snaked up her arms and around her neck.

She angled the knife, slashed at the vines, and managed to cut through some before I gathered more.

"You could have walked away," I said, tightening the vines. The knife dropped, blade perfectly vertical in the soft ground, as she began to claw at the vines.

"Never," she said hoarsely, and I drew them tighter.

The memory of the pain she'd inflicted on me was still powerful. If I didn't take her out, she'd hurt all of us. Kill all of us. She'd destroy everything. So it was up to me. And I'd use that magic—the magic from her world—to take her out. She'd no longer be a threat.

And then I heard my name. "Claire."

It was Liam. Not in my head, but beside me. Standing beside me, clothes wet and disheveled and smelling of blood and dirty water.

"Claire," he said again. "Let her go. It's time."

"She'd have destroyed us all."

"Yes, she would have. But you stopped her. She's on her knees, Claire, and Containment is here to bring her in."

"I will stop her." I swallowed hard, ignored the trembling in my fingers. "I'll stop her. She'll never do this again. She won't take New Orleans away from me. She won't take my father away."

"Nobody will take them away, Claire. Because however long you live, and wherever you live out the remaining days of your life, they will always be with you. Always. Killing her won't bring them back, any more than killing us would bring back her sister. Let Containment have her."

For a long moment, I watched her, hatred burning in her eyes even as she stared death in the face. And I knew he was right. That killing her wouldn't bring them back. It wouldn't change the past. It would only shadow my future.

My fingers tightened, clenched. And let go.

Aeryth hit the ground on her hands and knees, sucked in air.

Burke ran to her, cuffed her hands with cold iron, dragged her to her feet. "Come on, sister. Back to Devil's Isle for you."

She kicked and screamed, voice hoarse, and was unceremoniously hauled away.

"Good girl," Liam said, and wrapped me in his arms. "Good girl."

I couldn't help the tears now, and knew I was crying for all of us, for everyone, for this city and its people, those who'd been forced to leave, and those who didn't have the heart to stay.

I heard Containment moving around us, Seelies screaming as they were transported to Devil's Isle. And I waited until the world was quiet again. Until we were alone.

He leaned back, wiped tears from my cheeks. "Are you okay?"

"No," I said. "But I will be." Exhaustion had settled in, and was suddenly bone-deep. "Can we go sleep for a week?"

"Yes. And then we'll decide what we want to do next. And where we want to do it."

I smiled at Liam, then grabbed his face and took him for a hard and hot kiss. "As long as we're together," I said, leaning my forehead against his, my hands still on his cheeks, "anywhere."

I had time only to smile once more before the earth trembled beneath us, and a roar of sound echoed through the canyon of buildings in the Quarter.

Liam cursed in Cajun French, and we ran toward the sound . . .

And found the Consularis army barreling down Royal, three angels at the helm.

CHAPTER TWENTY-TWO

Camael at the head of the army, Uriel and Eae behind him. And behind them, a force even larger than we'd seen in the Beyond. Scores of Consularis Paras, golden armor gleaming in the sun that managed to filter through the clouds.

Around us, the wind began to pick up again. We'd had more than an hour of peace, and the eye wall was nearly here.

Malachi walked forward, put himself between us and the angels, and waited for them to speak. "Your timing is impeccable. As usual, you've waited until the fighting is done to come forward."

"A fortunate coincidence," Camael said haughtily, and he didn't sound nearly as convinced as he should have to work that particular line. He looked at the Seelies, the Containment army. All activity had stopped at their arrival, everyone watching . . . and waiting . . . to see if the battle would start again.

Part of me wanted it to begin. Part of me wanted to finish the fight, to show our fury with magic and action and bullets. That they'd dared come here, marched their army down our streets, was infuriating.

Apparently feeling I was ready to move, Liam put a hand on my arm. "Hold on, tiger," he whispered.

"You have made use of the stone, the Abethyl," Camael said. "Return them to us now."

"Or what?" Malachi asked, head tilted. "You'll take them from us? You'll engage in a war between magic and bullets? Between gold and steel?" He smiled, but there was no happiness in it. Only hot derision and anger. "I think not."

Malachi paused, looked back. The crowd parted, and Gunnar wheeled himself forward, the Commandant at his side. Gunnar looked up at the Commandant, who nodded.

"Go ahead," he said. "This bargain is yours to make."

Gunnar nodded in answer, then turned his gaze back to the angels, who looked at him and his chair curiously. "We will return one component of the weapon to you. In exchange, you will take them back to the Beyond—the Seelies and the other Court of Dawn members." He looked at Malachi, got Malachi's nod.

They'd split up the stone, the Abethyl. One in our world, one in theirs. To reduce the odds the Devil's Snare could fall into the wrong hands.

Camael's chin lifted. "Both objects are owned by us."

"The idea was created by you," Malachi said. "Humans made the weapon function and they now have possession of it. Perhaps you'd like a test of its strength?"

Camael's eyes were murderously gold, like angry weapons glinting. "You wouldn't dare take magic from us."

"I absolutely would."

Camael's eyes flashed. "While we may be in your world now, Commander, I am still your superior. I would suggest you watch your tone."

"In no way are you my superior," Malachi said. "Nor can you assert a claim on me eight years after you washed your hands of the

Court's behavior and the conflict. Make no mistake—I am no longer Consularis. The Court should not have brought death to this land, but they were not wrong to fight back against you. Against the oppression of your supposed community."

The wind picked up, strong enough to rustle armor, while Camael stared at Malachi. Then lifted his chin and put that haughty expression back in place. "We will take the Seelies. We will take the Court. We will take the Abethyl and seal the door behind us."

The crowd went silent. Gunnar went very still, but for the muscle that twitched in his jaw. "You can do that? Repair the Veil? Close it?"

"We can."

Gunnar's body went rigid, and the look in his eyes absolutely murderous. "Then why didn't you do that before?"

Camael arched a single eyebrow. "It didn't require closing before. You closed it yourselves." His tone was that of a condescending expert to a childish amateur. And Gunnar's rage looked barely banked in response.

"After a year of war," Gunnar said. "And that was eight years ago. It's been open again for seven months, and we haven't been able to close it."

Camael lifted a shoulder as nonchalantly as if Gunnar had asked about the weather. "As I have told your colleagues, this is not our world. It is not my place to make decisions here."

"You could have ended the first war, prevented the second. People died. Children. Families. Murdered in their beds because you let the Court come through the Veil."

"If we'd sought to intervene here, then what? If I'd come through the Veil, I'd have been imprisoned as a terrorist, and even if I hadn't been, I can't imagine you'd have willingly accepted a challenge to your own autonomy. What good would it have done then, to my world or yours?"

"You are lying," Malachi said calmly. "You chose not to close it."

"Because he wanted them to leave," I said, understanding dawning. "He hoped the Court would simply pack up and walk through the open door, and he'd have no more trouble from the rabble-rousers. No more complaints against his regime."

"Yes," Malachi said simply.

"The Precepts rule Elysium," Camael said. "Not the Terran lands. And we will rule it in a manner most beneficial to our citizens as they consent to be governed."

"No," Malachi said. "You rule in a manner most beneficial to your own convenience. Ruling is hard. Leadership is hard. Balancing the interests of a people is hard. You don't lead. You condone a society in which dissent is simply wiped away with the wave of a hand."

"Our community has chosen peace."

"Perhaps you should engage with your community about the cost of that peace to our world. About the death and destruction your peace has wrought. Because it's hardly peace if it stands on the backs of those you've trampled to get it."

Camael's eyes went dark.

"There will be a reckoning," Malachi said. "The Court and Consularis who have been in this world know the truth just as you now do, and there is no room for denial. But more importantly, the seeds of knowledge have already been planted in Elysium. I saw to that when I was there."

Camael's jaw worked. "We will not be extorted."

"There is no need for extortion," Malachi said. "There is simply no more room to hide who and what you really are."

Camael looked at him for a moment, fuming and frustrated. "We will take the Court," he bit out. "We will take the Abethyl. And in one week's time, we will return to close the Veil, and take any

Consularis who wish to return to their homeland. And then we will have no more of Earth."

He turned on his heel and walked back to his army, Uriel and Eae following behind him.

Right on cue, it began to rain.

We went to the Cabildo while the Precepts discussed with the Commandant preparations to move the Court back to the Beyond.

Without the Seelies' boost, entropy found Hurricane Frieda. The spiraling storm began to dissipate to a hard rain that waiting soldiers didn't seem to mind.

I watched Malachi, and finally understood why he'd stolen the Abethyl. He might have been able to convince the Precepts to give it to him. But that wasn't the point. That wasn't the goal.

"You wanted them to follow us here."

He looked back at me, all emotion hidden. "What?"

"The Precepts. You stole the Abethyl, made them chase us, because you wanted them to come here. You wanted them to see first-hand what their arrogance had caused. You wanted them to consider the Veil. You wanted them to fix it."

He looked at me for a long moment. "They are not entirely heartless," he finally said. "The Consularis genuinely believe life is better lived in the way they have arranged it. That rules and order and similarity are the antitheses of chaos and violence and pain."

I had a hard time faulting them for trying that approach, given how many times humans had tried to forcibly assimilate those who weren't like us—and failed miserably. Caused only more pain and death and violence.

"But they are also self-centered, and care little for worlds beyond theirs. I thought, perhaps, if I showed them what effects their behavior had, they might change. And, frankly, the possibility of humans with powerful magic who might challenge theirs adds incentive to closing the Veil."

"Why not ask them about closing the Veil when we were in Elysium?"

His mouth moved into the lightest smile. "I did. They refused. I thought it best to give them another chance to see the truth—and answer for their crimes."

Malachi walked to Rachel. Liam joined me, put an arm around my waist. "What was that all about?"

"Our very conniving—and very kind—friend." And I told him what Malachi had done. "Do you think he'll stay?"

"I don't know. I suspect he doesn't feel like he can go back now." Malachi looked down at Rachel with obvious love, desire, need. "Or that he has much to go back to."

I smiled. "I wonder if they'll be bored by peace."

Liam was silent for a moment. "We might all be bored by peace. But I imagine new struggles and drama will filter in soon enough. That's the nature of humans."

"And Paras," I said, resting my head against his arm. "We all like drama."

Burke came over. "You guys have to see this."

"What is it?"

He gestured us forward, and we followed him to the street. And grinned.

It was goats.

Dozens of them—white and black and calico—walking down Royal Street even in the diminishing rain of the floundering storm, bells on their collars chiming musically as the group moved downtown, bleating and lapping up the standing rainwater.

Two quick dogs, black-and-white and low to the ground, ran along the sidewalks beside the herd, keeping them in line.

It was surreal. And it was wonderful.

When they'd nibbled up the shrubs and grass that poked through the water, they disappeared down the street, leaving behind the tinkle of bells.

We stood there for a moment in the afterglow.

"That was good luck, right?" Gavin asked.

"One hundred percent," Burke said.

Gavin looked at me and Liam. "I thought the engagement was pretty good, but this tops it."

Liam lifted his brows. "A random flock of goats tops our engagement?"

"I mean, they're goats. And I'm pretty sure it's a herd, not a flock."

"Hardly the point," Liam said, putting an arm around my waist. "Apparently a proposal during a hurricane doesn't beat out random and smelly goats. I'll try better next time, *cher*."

I had no doubt he would.

One week later

The crowd was boisterous, but the mood was bittersweet. The floodwaters had receded from the Quarter, and there was a party going on in Jackson Square. A good-bye to the Consularis Paranormals who'd lived in Devil's Isle for nearly eight years and had decided to go home.

Containment had supplied cheap red punch and chocolate chip cookies the size of silver dollars, and nearly as dry. We'd made streamers of old holiday decorations, and the Paras had brought their suitcases to the square, where they'd be loaded onto the buses that would take them to Belle Chasse and the army that awaited them.

Some had waited eight years for an opportunity to go home, never quite assimilating into the community in Devil's Isle, and not interested in assimilating into the human world outside it. Others—some members of the same families—had grown into their new lives, in the internment camp that had become their home, with the neighbors who'd become their friends. I'd never had to live in a prison. But after seeing the sameness of Elysium, I understood why they'd want something different.

Liam talked with Lizzie and Malachi, who'd decided to stay. Moses talked with Solomon, who'd decided to go home now that he was no longer the local big shot. And around the park there were hugs and tears and trepidation, as they all prepared for their lives to change.

I sat on a metal bench in the shade, sipping punch from a paper cup and thinking about the connections that had been made over the last eight years. And how much they'd be changing.

Moses came toward me.

"Hey," I said. "How's Solomon doing?"

"Here or at home, he's a scammer. And I think he's ready for a new set of tricks."

"I bet."

He cleared his throat. "I wanted to talk to you about something."

His tone was grim, had me frowning at him. "About what?"

"I'm leaving, too."

It's not that I thought he was joking. I just didn't think *anything*. Couldn't wrap my mind around what the words meant. "What?"

"I'm leaving. I'm going home."

"You're . . . what?" I asked again.

He jumped up to sit beside me. "I wasn't ready to tell you yet, Red. You're . . . not as much of an asshole as the others."

It began to hit me then, and warm dread settled into my chest. "You want to go back? After everything?"

"It's my home. Don't get me wrong. I like this place. I like the electronics and the canned goods and those birds with the really big mouths—"

"Pelicans."

He pointed at me. "Yeah, those. But this isn't my home. It's not my place. Living in Devil's Isle—it wasn't great in a lot of ways. But in other ways it wasn't too bad. I was there with my people. We had our own community, even if it was infested by Peskies, the little shits. But most humans don't even see me here." He looked at me. "Not because I'm small, mind. Because they don't want to notice me, because I'm weird. Because I don't look like they think I should look." He pointed to his short horns.

"I notice you. Liam and Gavin notice you. Tadji and Gunnar notice you."

"I know you do. You're all pains in my butt, but I've learned to deal with you. But I want to be seen." He looked up at me, and there was pain in his eyes. "I don't want to feel . . . invisible."

I reached out and squeezed his hand, and for a moment we just looked at each other. Then he pulled his hand away and rubbed it on his pants.

"Human hands are all damp and sweaty," he said, and surreptitiously wiped away a tear.

I had to look away to keep myself from watering up. "Humans are generally damp and sweaty. It's one of our grosser qualities."

"You said it." He cleared his throat. "And there's no reason to get all emotional. 'Cause I made you something." He reached into the bottom pocket of his rolled-up cargo pants, pulled out a small plastic box, handed it to me.

It was a child's radio in red and white plastic, with a small antenna on one end. The white hadn't actually been white in many years, and there was several years of grime in the plastic grooves. On-off switch, tuner, volume wheel. And for some reason, a cartoon image of a yellow duck pulling a wagon.

"I don't know why a pelican needs a wagon," he said.

"Duck," I corrected, and I was pretty sure he knew exactly what the bird was. "Does it work?"

"Of course it freaking works. You think I'm a novice? An amateur? I know what I'm doing. But it's not a radio."

I looked at him, then at the box. "You lost me."

"It's kind of a way to say hello." He wiggled his hand, and when I passed it back, he flicked the on-off switch with a thumbnail. A soft thump pulsed from the speaker, staticky around the edges, but audible. A quick-step throb. *Beat-beat. Beat-beat. Beat-beat.*

"What is that?"

"It's me," he said, and I looked at him. "My heartbeat," he said. "I know that's kind of a big deal for humans. You like the connection."

Tears welled when I looked at him. "It will work even when the Veil's closed?"

"Long as I'm alive, it will work. And I'll probably be alive forever, so . . ." He lifted a shoulder, cleared his throat. "I'm going to miss you, Red."

"I'm going to miss you, too, Mos." I leaned over and hugged him, and his arms on mine were fierce and strong.

"Why do you smell like pickles?" I asked when I pulled back.

"The juice is good for the skin."

"I doubt that's true."

His eyes narrowed. "You're just trying to make me angry so you don't get all human and teary eyed."

"You caught me," I said, and let him go. And we sat on the bench together in silence and watched the world go by.

Thirty minutes later, when the buses were waiting and the Paras began to climb aboard, Liam found me still on the bench, still gutted.

"You okay?"

I shrugged a shoulder. "He's a jerk. And he likes the grossest foods. But he's part of the family."

"He is. But I'm glad he can go home."

"Yeah."

Moses took the first step, looked back across the crowd, searching for us. And, when he found us, gave us a smile.

And then flipped us off.

He'd be okay.

We all would.

Keep reading for an excerpt from the first
Heirs of Chicagoland Novel,

WILD HUNGER

Available now from Berkley

Vampires were made, not born.

All except one.

All except me.

I was the daughter of vampires, born because magic and fate twisted together. I'd spent nineteen years in Chicago. Tonight, I stood nearly four hundred feet above Paris, several thousand miles away from the Windy City and the Houses in which most of its vampires lived.

Around me, visitors on the second level of the Eiffel Tower sipped champagne and snapped shots of the city. I closed my eyes against the warm, balmy breeze that carried the faint scent of flowers.

"Elisa, you cannot tell Paris good-bye with your eyes closed."

"I'm not saying good-bye," I said. "Because I'm coming back."

I opened my eyes, smiled at the vampire who appeared at my side with two plastic cones of champagne. Seraphine had golden skin and dark hair, and her hazel eyes shone with amusement.

"To Paris," I said, and tapped my cone against hers.

It had been four years since I'd last stepped foot in Chicago. To-morrow, I'd go home again and visit the city and spend time with family and friends.

For twenty years, there'd been peace in Chicago among humans and sups, largely because of efforts by my parents—Ethan Sullivan and Merit, the Master and Sentinel, respectively, of Cadogan House. They'd worked to find a lasting peace, and had been so successful that Chicago had become a model for other communities around the world.

That's why Seri and I were going back. The city's four vampire Houses were hosting peace talks for vampires from Western Europe, where Houses had been warring since the governing council—the Greenwich Presidium—dissolved before I was born. And vampires' relations with the other supernaturals in Europe weren't any better. Chicago would serve as neutral territory where the Houses' issues could be discussed and a new system of government could be hammered out.

"You look . . . What is the word? Wistful?" Seri smiled. "And you haven't even left yet."

"I'm building up my immunity," I said, and sipped the champagne.

"You love Chicago."

"It's a great city. But I was . . . a different person in Chicago. I like who I am here."

Paris wasn't always peaceful. But it had given me the time and distance to develop the control I'd needed over the monster that lived inside me. Because I wasn't just a vampire . . .

Seri bumped her shoulder against mine supportively. "You will be the same person there as you are here. Miles change only location. They do not change a person's heart. A person's character."

I hoped that was true. But Seri didn't know the whole of it. She didn't know about the half-formed power that lurked beneath my skin, reveled in its anger. She didn't know about the magic that had grown stronger as I'd grown older, until it beat like a second heartbeat inside me.

Sunlight and aspen could kill me—but the monster could bury me in its rage.

I'd spent the past four years attending École Dumas, Europe's only university for supernaturals. I was one of a handful of vampires in residence. Most humans weren't changed into vampires until they were older; the change would give them immortality, but they'd be stuck at the age at which they'd been changed. No one wanted to be thirteen for eternity.

I hadn't been changed at all, but born a vampire—the one and only vampire created that way. Immortal, or so we assumed, but still for the moment aging.

The university was affiliated with Paris's Maison Dumas, one of Europe's most prestigious vampire Houses, where I'd lived for the past four years. I'd had a little culture shock at first, but I'd come to love the House and appreciate its logical approach to problem solving. If Cadogan was Gryffindor, all bravery and guts, Dumas was Ravenclaw, all intellect and cleverness. I liked being clever, and I liked clever people, so we were a good fit.

I'd had four years of training to develop the three components of vampire strength: physical, psychic, and strategic. I graduated a few months ago with a sociology degree—emphasis in sup-human relations—and now I was repaying my training the same way French vampires did, with a year of mandatory armed service for the House. It was a chance to see what I was made of, and to spend another year in the city I'd come to love.

I was three months into my service. Escorting delegates from Maison Dumas to Chicago for the peace talks was part of my work.

"How many suitcases are you bringing?"

I glanced at Seri with amusement. "Why? How many are you bringing?"

"Four." Seri did not travel lightly.

"We'll only be in Chicago for four days."

"I have diplomatic responsibilities, Elisa."

I sipped my champagne. "That's what French vampires say when they pack too much. I have a capsule wardrobe."

"And that is what American vampires say when they do not pack enough. You also have diplomatic responsibilities."

"I have responsibilities to the House. That's different."

"Ah," she said, smiling at me over the rim of her drink. "But which one?"

"*Maison Dumas,*" I said, in an accent that was pretty close to perfect. "I'm not going to Chicago on behalf of Cadogan House. It's just a bonus."

"I look forward to meeting your parents. And I'm sure they'll be glad to see you."

"I'll be glad to see them, too. It's just—I've changed a lot in the last few years. Since the last time I went home."

They'd visited Paris twice since I'd been gone, and we'd had fun walking through the city, seeing the sights. But I still felt like I'd been holding myself back from them. Maybe I always had.

"It's not about you or Cadogan or Chicago," I'd told my father, when we'd stood outside the private terminal at O'Hare, in front of the jet that would take me across the world. I'd been struggling to make him understand. "It's about figuring out who I am."

In Chicago, I was the child of Ethan and Merit. And it had been hard to feel like anything more than a reflection of my parents and my birth, which made me a curiosity for plenty of sups outside Cadogan House who treated me like a prize. And the possibility I might be able to bear children made me, at least for some, a prize to be captured.

I'd wanted to be something more, something different . . . Something that was just me.

"You couldn't fail us by living your life the way you want," my father had said. "It's your life to live, and you will make your own choices. You always have."

He'd tipped my chin up with the crook of his finger, forcing me to meet his gaze.

"There are some decisions that we make, and some that are made for us. Sometimes you accept the path that's offered to you, and you live that path—that life—with grace. And sometimes you push forward, and you chart your own path. That decision is yours. It's always been yours.

"I don't want you to go, because I'm selfish. Because you are my child." His eyes had burned fiercely, emeralds on fire. "But if this is your path, you must take it. Whatever happens out there, you always have a home here."

He'd kissed my forehead, then embraced me hard. *"Test your wings,"* he'd quietly said. A suggestion. A request. A hope. *"And fly."*

I had flown. And I'd read and walked and learned and trained, just like everyone else.

In Paris, I'd been just another vampire. And the anonymity, the freedom, had been exhilarating.

"We all carry expectations," Seri said quietly, her eyes suddenly clouded. "Sometimes our own, sometimes others'. Both can be heavy."

Seri came from what the European Houses called "good blood." She'd been made by a Master vampire with power, with money, with an old name, and with plenty of cachet—and that mattered to French vampires. Seri had been the last vampire he'd made before his death, and those of his name were expected to be aristocrats and socialites. Unlike in the U.S., French vampires selected their own Houses. She'd picked Maison Dumas instead of Maison Bourdillon, the House of her Master. That hadn't made her many friends among Bourdillon's progeny, who decided she was wasting her legacy.

"Are you excited to see Chicago?" I asked her.

"I am excited to see the city," she said, "if not optimistic about what will come of the talks. Consider Calais."

The most recent attack had taken place in Calais a week ago. Vampires from Paris's Maison Solignac had attacked Maison Saint-Germaine because they believed they weren't getting a big enough cut of the city port's profits. In the process, four vampires and two humans had been killed.

The European Houses had lived together peacefully, at least by human standards, for hundreds of years. But after the GP's dissolution, all bets were off. There was power to be had, and vampires found that irresistible.

More than a dozen delegates from France, including Seri and Marion, the Master of Maison Dumas, would participate in the talks. Marion and Seri would be accompanied by nearly a dozen staff, including Marion's bodyguard, Seri's assistant, Odette, and me.

"Yeah," I said. "I don't know how successful it will be, either. But refusing to talk certainly isn't doing much good."

Seri nodded and drank the last of her champagne as two guards passed us—one human, one vampire—and silenced the chatter. They wore black fatigues and berets, and looked suspiciously at everyone they passed. Part of the joint task force created by the Paris Police Prefecture to keep the city safe.

The vampire's eyes shifted to me, then Seri. He acknowledged us, scanned the rest of the crowd, and kept walking, katana belted at his waist.

Vampires in the U.S. and Western Europe used the long and slightly curved Japanese swords, which were sharp and deadly as fangs, but with a much longer reach.

Sorcerers had magic. Shifters had their animal forms. Vampires had katanas.

"There's Javí," Seraphine whispered, and watched as they kept moving, then disappeared around the corner. Javí was a Dumas vampire doing his year of service.

These weren't the only guards at the Eiffel Tower. Humans and vampires alike stood at the edge of the crowd below, wearing body armor and weapons and trying to keep safe the tourists and residents enjoying a warm night in the Champ de Mars.

We turned back to the rail, looked over the city. So much white stone, so many slate roofs, so many people enjoying the warm night. But the specter of violence, of fear, hung over it. And that was hard to shake. No city was perfect, not when people lived in it.

"Let us take a photo," Seri said, clearly trying to lift the mood. She put an arm around me, then pulled out her screen and angled the narrow strip of glass and silicon for a perfect shot.

"To Paris!" she said, and we smiled.

The moment recorded, she checked the time before putting the device away again. "We should get back. The Auto will arrive in a few hours." She slipped an arm through mine. "This will be an adventure, and we will be optimists. And I look forward to pizza and Chicago dogs and . . . *Comment dites-on 'milk shake de gâteau'?*"

"Cake shake," I said with a smile. "You and my mother are going to get along just fine."

We'd only just turned to head toward the elevator when screams sliced through the air, followed by a wave of nervous, fearful magic that rolled up from the ground.

We looked back and over the rail.

Even from this height, they were visible. Five vampires in gleaming red leather running through the green space with katanas in one hand and small weapons in the other.

Not knives; there was no gleam from the flashing lights on the Tower.

What was shaped like a knife, but held no metal, and would turn a vampire to dust?

Humans had been wrong about vampires and crosses, but they'd been absolutely right about stakes. An aspen stake through the heart was a guaranteed way to put the "mortal" in "immortal."

I didn't know which House the vampires were from. I was too high up to see their faces, and the gleaming red leather didn't give anything away. Leather was a vampire favorite, and French vampire Houses appreciated fashion as much as the French fashion houses did.

But their intent was clear enough. They ran through the crowd, weapons drawn, and took aim at everyone in their path. Screams, sharp and terrified, filled the air. I watched one person fall, another dive to the ground to avoid the strike, a third try unsuccessfully to fight back against the vampire's increased strength.

Paris was under attack. My stomach clenched with nerves and anger.

I wanted to help. I was stronger and faster than most humans, and trained as well as any vampire from Maison Dumas would have been. But there were rules. There were roles and responsibilities. The Paris police, the task force members, were supposed to respond to events. I was just a civilian, and only a temporary one at that. I worked for Dumas, and should have been focused on getting Seri safely back to Maison Dumas.

But the screams . . .

The guards who'd walked past minutes before ran back to the rail beside us and stared at the scene below in horror. And neither of them made a move toward the ground. It took only a second to guess why.

"Can you jump?" I asked Javí, the vampire.

He looked at me, eyes wide. *"Quoi?"*

I had to remember where I was, shook my head, tried again.

"*Pouvez-vous sauter?*"

"*Non.*" Javí looked down. "*Non. Trop haut.*"

Too high. Most vampires could jump higher and farther than humans, and we could jump down from heights that would easily kill humans. But the trick required training, which I'd learned the hard way—believing I could fly from the widow's walk atop Cadogan House. I'd broken my arm, but vampires healed quickly, so that hadn't been much of a deterrent. My mother had taught me the rest.

Javí couldn't jump, so he'd have to wait for the elevator or take the hundreds of stairs down to ground level.

But I didn't have to wait.

I squeezed Seri's hand, told Javí to take care of her, and hoped he'd obey.

Before anyone could argue, or I could think better of it, I slid the katana from his scabbard, climbed onto the railing, and walked into space.

I descended through rushing darkness. A human might have had a few seconds of free fall before the deadly landing. But for a vampire, it was less a fall than a long and lazy step. Maybe we compressed space; maybe we elongated time. I didn't understand the physics, but I loved the sensation. It was as close to flying as I was likely to get.

The first level of the Eiffel Tower was wider than the second, so I had to jump down to the first level—causing more than a few humans to scream—before making it to the soft grass below. I landed in a crouch, katana firmly in hand.

My fangs descended, the predator preparing to battle. While I couldn't see it, I knew my eyes had silvered, as they did when vampires experienced strong emotions. It was a reminder—to humans, to prey, to enemies—that the vampire wasn't human, but something altogether different. Something altogether more dangerous.

Two humans were dead a few feet away, their eyes open and staring, blood spilling onto the grass from the lacerations at their necks. The vampires who'd murdered them hadn't even bothered to bite, to drink. This attack wasn't about need. It was about hatred.

I was allowed only a moment of shocked horror—of seeing how quickly two lives had been snuffed out—before the scent of blood blossomed in the air again, unfurling like the petals of a crimson poppy.

I looked back.

A vampire knelt over a human woman. She was in her early twenties, with pale skin, blond hair, and terror in her eyes. The vampire was even paler, blood pumping through indigo veins just below the surface. His hair was short and ice blond, his eyes silver. And the knife he held above the woman's chest was covered with someone else's blood.

Anger rose, hot and intense, and I could feel the monster stir inside, awakened by the sheer power of the emotion. But I was still in Paris. And here, I was in control. I shoved it back down, refused to let it surface.

"Arrêtez!" I yelled out, and to emphasize the order, held my borrowed katana in front of me, the silver blade reflecting the lights from the Eiffel Tower.

The vampire growled, lip curled to reveal a pair of needle-sharp fangs, hatred burning in his eyes. I didn't recognize him, and I doubted he recognized me beyond the fact that I was a vampire not from his House—and that made me an enemy.

He rose, stepping away from the human as if she were nothing more than a bit of trash he'd left behind. His knuckles around the stake were bone white, tensed and ready.

Released from his clutches, the human took one look at my silvered eyes and screamed, then began to scramble away from us. She'd survive—if I could lure him away from her.

The vampire slapped my katana away with one hand, drove the stake toward me with the other.

I might have been young for a vampire, but I was well trained. I moved back, putting us both clear of the human, and kicked. I made contact with his hand, sent the stake spinning through the air. He found his footing and picked up the stake. Undeterred, he moved toward me. This time, he kicked. I blocked it, but the force of the blow sent pain rippling through my arm.

He thrust the stake toward me like a fencer with a foil.

The movement sent light glimmering against the gold on his right hand. A signet ring, crowned by a star ruby—and the symbol of Maison Saint-Germaine.

I doubted it was a coincidence Saint-Germaine vampires were attacking the ultimate symbol of Paris only a few nights after they'd been attacked by a Paris House. While I understood why they'd want revenge, terrorizing and murdering humans wasn't the way to do it. It wasn't fair to make our issues their problems.

I darted back to avoid the stake, then sliced down with the katana when he advanced again.

"You should have stayed in Calais," I said in French, and got no response but a gleam in his eyes. He spun to avoid that move, but I managed to nick his arm. Blood scented the air, and my stomach clenched with sudden hunger and need. But ignoring that hunger was one of the first lessons my parents had taught me. There was a time and a place to drink, and this wasn't it.

I swept out a leg, which had him hopping backward, then rotated into a kick that sent him to his knees. He grabbed my legs, shifting his weight so we both fell forward onto the grass. The katana rolled from my grasp.

My head rapped against the ground, and it took a moment to realize that he'd climbed over me and grabbed the stake. He raised it, his eyes flashing in the brilliantly colored lights that reflected across the grass from the shining monument behind us.

I looked at that stake—thought of what it could do and was almost certainly about to do to me—and my mind went absolutely blank. I could see him, hear the blood rushing in my ears, and didn't have the foggiest idea what I was supposed to do, like the adrenaline had forced a hiccup in my brain.

Fortunately, beyond fear, and beneath it, was instinct. And I didn't need to think of what would bring a man down. He may have been immortal, and he may have been a vampire. Didn't matter. This move didn't discriminate.

I kicked him in the groin.

He groaned, hunched over, and fell over on the grass, body curled over his manhood.

"Asshole," I muttered, chest heaving as I climbed to my feet and kicked him over, then added a kick to the back of his ribs to encourage him, politely, to stay there.

Two guards ran over, looked at me, then him.

"Elisa Sullivan," I said. "Maison Dumas." Most vampires who weren't Masters used only their first name. I'd gotten an exception since it wasn't practical for a kid to have just one name.

They nodded, confiscated the stake, and went about the business of handcuffing the vampire. I picked up the katana, wiped the blade against my pant leg, and dared a look at the field around me.

Two of the other Saint-Germaine vampires were alive, both on their knees, hands behind their heads. I didn't see the others, and unless they'd run away, which seemed unlikely, they'd probably been taken down by the Paris police or Eiffel Tower guards. Fallen into cones of ash due to a deadly encounter with aspen.

Humans swarmed at the periphery of the park, where Paris police worked to set up a barrier.

Some of the humans who'd survived the attack were helping the wounded. Others stood with wide eyes, shaking with shock and fear. And more yet had pulled out their screens to capture video of the fight. The entire world was probably watching, whether they wanted to see or not.

I found Seri standing at the edge of the park, her eyes silver, her expression fierce and angry. She wasn't a fighter, but she knew injustice when she saw it.

I walked toward her, my right hip aching a bit from hitting the ground, and figured I'd passed my first field test.

I suddenly wasn't so sad to be leaving Paris.

Photo by Dana Damewood Photography

Chloe Neill—*New York Times* bestselling author of the Chicagoland Vampires Novels, the Heirs of Chicagoland Novels, the Dark Elite novels, and the Devil's Isle Novels—was born and raised in the South but now makes her home in the Midwest, just close enough to Cadogan House, St. Sophia's, and Devil's Isle to keep an eye on things. When not transcribing her heroines' adventures, she bakes, works, and scours the Internet for good recipes and great graphic design. Chloe also maintains her sanity by spending time with her boys—her favorite landscape photographer (her husband), and their dogs, Baxter and Scout. (Both she and the photographer understand the dogs are in charge.)

CONNECT ONLINE

chloeneill.com
facebook.com/authorchloeneill
twitter.com/chloeneill